ALSO BY STEVE BERRY

The Amber Room
The Romanov Prophecy

THE THIRD SECRET

THE
THIRD
SECRET

A Novel

STEVE BERRY

BALLANTINE BOOKS

NEW YORK

The Third Secret is a work of fiction. Though some characters, incidents, and dialogues are based on the historical record, the work as a whole is a product of the author's imagination.

Copyright © 2005 by Steve Berry
Map copyright © 2005 by David Lindroth

Published in the United States by Ballantine Books, an imprint of The Random House Publishing Group, a division of Random House, Inc., New York.

BALLANTINE and colophon are registered trademarks of Random House, Inc.

Library of Congress Cataloging-in-Publication Data is available from the publisher upon request.

ISBN 0-345-47613-1

Printed in the United States of America

Ballantine Books website address: www.ballantinebooks.com

987654321

FIRST EDITION

Book design by Carole Lowenstein

For Dolores Murad Parrish
Who left this world far too soon
1930—1992

ACKNOWLEDGMENTS

As always, lots of thanks. First, Pam Ahearn, my agent, for her ever wise counsel. Next, to all the folks at Random House: Gina Centrello, a terrific publisher who went an extra mile for this one; Mark Tavani, whose editorial advice transformed my rough manuscript into a book; Cindy Murray, who patiently endures my idiosyncracies and handles publicity; Kim Hovey, who markets with expert precision; Beck Stvan, the artist responsible for the gorgeous cover image; Laura Jorstad, an eagle-eyed copyeditor who keeps us all straight; Carole Lowenstein, who once again made the pages shine; and finally to those in Promotions and Sales—nothing could be achieved without their superior efforts. Also, I cannot forget Fran Downing, Nancy Pridgen, and Daiva Woodworth. This was the last manuscript we did together as a writers group, and I truly miss those times.

As always my wife, Amy, and daughter, Elizabeth, were there every step of the way providing needed doses of loving encouragement.

This book is dedicated to my aunt, a wonderful woman who did not live to see this day. I know she would have been proud. But she's watching and, I'm sure, smiling.

The Church needs nothing but the truth.
—Pope Leo XIII (1881)

*There is nothing greater than this fascinating and sweet mystery
of Fatima, which accompanies the Church and all of humanity
throughout this long century of apostasy, and without a doubt will
accompany them up to their final fall and to their rising up again.*
—Abbé Georges de Nantes (1982),
on the occasion of Pope John Paul II's
first pilgrimage to Fatima

Faith is a precious ally in the search for truth.
—Pope John Paul II (1998)

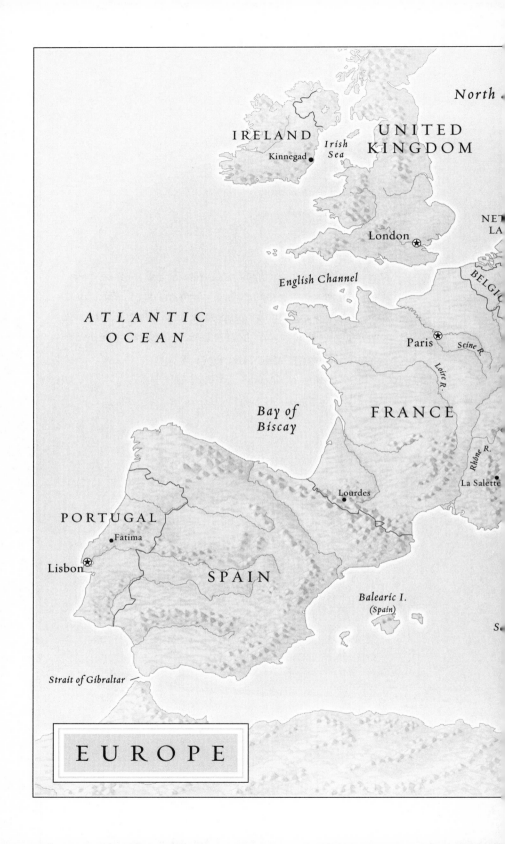

THE THIRD SECRET

PROLOGUE

FATIMA, PORTUGAL
JULY 13, 1917

LUCIA STARED TOWARD HEAVEN AND WATCHED THE LADY DE-
scend. The apparition came from the east, as it had twice before,
emerging as a sparkling dot from deep within the cloudy sky. Her
glide never wavered as She quickly approached, Her form brightening as it settled above the holm oak, eight feet off the ground.

The Lady stood upright, Her crystallized image clothed in a
glow that seemed more brilliant than the sun. Lucia lowered her
eyes in response to the dazzling beauty.

A crowd surrounded Lucia, unlike the first time the Lady appeared, two months before. Then it had been only Lucia, Jacinta,
and Francisco in the fields, tending the family sheep. Her cousins
were seven and nine. She was the oldest, and felt it, at ten. On her
right, Francisco knelt in his long trousers and stocking cap. To her
left Jacinta was on her knees in a black skirt, a kerchief over her dark
hair.

Lucia looked up and noticed the crowd again. The people had
started amassing yesterday, many coming from neighboring villages,
some accompanied by crippled children they hoped the Lady would
cure. The prior of Fatima had proclaimed the apparition a fraud and

urged all to stay away. *The devil at work,* he'd said. But the people had not listened, one parishioner even labeling the prior a fool since the devil would never incite people to pray.

A woman in the throng was shouting, calling Lucia and her cousins impostors, swearing God would avenge their sacrilege. Manuel Marto, Lucia's uncle, Jacinta and Francisco's father, stood behind them and Lucia heard him admonish the woman to be silent. He commanded respect in the valley as a man who'd seen more of the world than the surrounding Serra da Aire. Lucia derived comfort from his keen brown eyes and quiet manner. It was good he was nearby, there among the strangers.

She tried not to concentrate on any of the words being screamed her way, and blocked from her mind the scent of mint, the aroma of pine, and the pungent fragrance of wild rosemary. Her thoughts, and now her eyes, were on the Lady floating before her.

Only she, Jacinta, and Francisco could see the Lady, but only she and Jacinta could hear the words. Lucia thought that strange—why Francisco should be denied—but, during Her first visit, the Lady had made it clear that Francisco would go to heaven only after saying many rosaries.

A breeze drifted across the checkered landscape of the great hollow basin known as Cova da Iria. The land belonged to Lucia's parents and was littered with olive trees and patches of evergreens. The grass grew tall and made excellent hay, and the soil yielded potatoes, cabbage, and corn.

Rows of simple stone walls delineated the fields. Most had crumbled, for which Lucia was grateful, as it allowed the sheep to graze at will. Her task was to tend the family flock. Jacinta and Francisco were likewise charged by their parents, and they'd spent many days over the past few years in the fields, sometimes playing, sometimes praying, sometimes listening to Francisco work his fife.

But all that had changed two months ago, when the apparition first appeared.

Ever since, they'd been pounded with unceasing questions and scoffed at by nonbelievers. Lucia's mother had even taken her to the parish priest, commanding her to say it was all a lie. The priest had listened to what she'd said and stated it was not possible that Our Lady had descended from heaven simply to say that the rosary should be recited every day. Lucia's only solace came when she was alone, able then to weep freely for both herself and the world.

The sky dimmed, and umbrellas used by the crowd for shade started to close. Lucia stood and yelled, "Take off your hats, for I see Our Lady."

The men immediately obeyed, some crossing themselves as if to be forgiven for their rude behavior.

She turned back to the vision and knelt. *"Vocemecê que me quere?"* she asked. What do you want of me?

"Do not offend the Lord our God anymore because He is already much offended. I want you to come here on the thirteenth day of the coming month, and to continue to say five decades of the rosary every day in honor of Our Lady of the rosary to obtain the peace of the world and the end of the war. For She alone will be able to help."

Lucia stared hard at the Lady. The form was transparent, in varied hues of yellow, white, and blue. The face was beautiful, but strangely shaded in sorrow. A dress fell to Her ankles. A veil covered Her head. A rosary resembling pearls intertwined folded hands. The voice was gentle and pleasant, never rising or lowering, a soothing constant, like the breeze that continued to sweep over the crowd.

Lucia mustered her courage and said, "I wish to ask you to tell us who you are, and to perform a miracle so that everyone will believe that you have appeared to us."

"Continue to come here every month on this day. In October I will tell you who I am and what I wish, and I will perform a miracle that everyone will have to believe."

Over the past month, Lucia had thought about what to say. Many had petitioned her with requests concerning loved ones and

STEVE BERRY / 6

those too sick to speak for themselves. One in particular came to mind. "Can you cure Maria Carreira's crippled son?"

"I will not cure him. But I shall provide him a means of livelihood, provided he says the rosary every day."

She thought it strange that a lady of heaven would attach conditions to mercy, but she understood the need for devotion. The parish priest always proclaimed such worship as the only means to gain God's grace.

"Sacrifice yourselves for sinners," the Lady said, "and say many times, especially when you make some sacrifice: 'O Jesus, it is for your love, for the conversion of sinners and in reparation for the sins committed against the Immaculate Heart of Mary.'"

The Lady opened Her clasped hands and spread Her arms. A penetrating radiance poured forth and bathed Lucia in a warmth much like that of a winter sun on a cool day. She embraced the feeling, then saw that the radiance did not stop at her and her two cousins. Instead, it passed through the earth and the ground opened.

This was new and different, and it frightened her.

A sea of fire spread before her in a magnificent vision. Within the flames blackened forms appeared, like chunks of beef swirling in a boiling soup. They were human in shape, though no features or faces were distinguishable. They popped from the fire then quickly descended, their bobbing accompanied by shrieks and groans so sorrowful that a shudder of fear crept down Lucia's spine. The poor souls seemed to possess no weight or equilibrium, and were utterly at the mercy of the conflagration that consumed them. Animal forms appeared, some she recognized, but all were frightful and she knew them for what they were. Demons. Tenders of the flames. She was terrified and saw that Jacinta and Francisco were equally scared. Tears were welling in their eyes and she wanted to comfort them. If not for the Lady floating before them, she too would have lost control.

"Look at Her," she whispered to her cousins.

They obeyed, and all three turned away from the horrible vision, their hands folded before them, fingers pointing skyward.

"You see Hell, where the souls of poor sinners go," the Lady said. "To save them, God wishes to establish in the world the devotion to my Immaculate Heart. If they do what I will tell you, many souls will be saved, and there will be peace. The war is going to end. But if they do not stop offending God, another and worse one will begin in the reign of Pius XI."

The vision of hell disappeared and the warm light retreated back into the Lady's folded hands.

"When you shall see a night illuminated by an unknown light, know that it is the great sign that God gives you that He is going to punish the world for its crimes by means of war, hunger, and persecution of the Church and the Holy Father."

Lucia was disturbed by the Lady's words. She knew that a war had raged across Europe for the past several years. Men from villages had gone off to fight, many never returning. She'd heard the sorrow of the families in church. Now she was being told a way to end that suffering.

"To prevent this," the Lady said, "I come to ask the consecration of Russia to my Immaculate Heart and the Communion of Reparation on the first Saturdays. If they listen to my requests, Russia will be converted and there will be peace. If not, she will scatter her errors through the world, provoking wars and persecutions of the church. The good will be martyred, the Holy Father will have much to suffer, various nations will be annihilated. In the end my Immaculate Heart will triumph. The Holy Father will consecrate Russia to me, and it will be converted, and a certain period of peace will be granted to the world."

Lucia wondered what *Russia* was. Perhaps a person? A wicked woman in need of salvation? Maybe a place? Outside of the Galicians and Spain, she did not know the name of any other nation. Her world was the village of Fatima where her family lived, the nearby hamlet of Aljustrel where Francisco and Jacinta lived, the Cova da Iria where the sheep grazed and vegetables grew, and the Cabeco grotto where the angel had come last year and the year before, announcing the Lady's arrival. This *Russia* was apparently quite important to capture the Lady's attention. But Lucia wanted to know, "What of Portugal?"

"In Portugal, the dogma of the faith will always be kept."

She smiled. It was comforting to know that her homeland was well considered in heaven.

"When you say the rosary," the Lady said, "say after each mystery, 'O my Jesus, pardon us and deliver us from the fires of hell. Draw all souls to salvation, especially those in need.' "

She nodded.

"I have more to tell you." When the third message was completed, the Lady said, "Tell this to no one, as yet."

"Not even Francisco?" Lucia asked.

"You may tell him."

A long moment of silence followed. No sound leaked from the crowd. All of the men, women, and children were standing or kneeling, in rapture, enthralled by what the three seers—as Lucia had heard them labeled—were doing. Many clutched at rosaries and muttered prayers. She knew no one could see or hear the Lady—their experience would be one of faith.

She took a moment to savor the silence. The entire Cova was locked in a deep solemnity. Even the wind had gone silent. Her flesh grew cold, and for the first time the weight of responsibility settled onto her. She sucked in a deep breath and asked, "Do you want nothing more of me?"

"Today I want nothing more of you."

The Lady began to rise into the eastern sky. Something that sounded like thunder rumbled past overhead. Lucia stood. She was shaking. "There She goes," she cried, pointing to the sky.

The crowd sensed that the vision was over and started to press inward.

"What did she look like?"

"What did she say?"

"Why do you look so sad?"

"Will she come again?"

The push of people toward the holm oak became intense and a sudden fear swept through Lucia. She blurted out, "It's a secret. It's a secret."

"Good or bad?" a woman screamed.

"Good for some. For others, bad."

"And you won't tell us?"

"It's a secret and the Lady told us not to tell."

Manuel Marto picked Jacinta up and started to elbow his way through the crowd. Lucia followed with Francisco in hand. The stragglers pursued, pelting them with more questions. She could only think of one answer to their pleas.

"It's a secret. It's a secret."

PART ONE

ONE

MONSIGNOR COLIN MICHENER HEARD THE SOUND AGAIN AND closed the book. Somebody was there. He knew it.

Like before.

He stood from the reading desk and stared around at the array of baroque shelves. The ancient bookcases towered above him and more stood at attention down narrow halls that spanned in both directions. The cavernous room carried an aura, a mystique bred in part by its label. *L'Archivio Segreto Vaticano.* The Secret Archives of the Vatican.

He'd always thought that name strange since little contained within the volumes was secret. Most were merely the meticulous record of two millennia of church organization, the accounts from a time when popes were kings, warriors, politicians, and lovers. All told there were twenty-five miles of shelves, which offered much if a searcher knew where to look.

And Michener certainly did.

Refocusing on the sound, his gaze drifted across the room, past frescoes of Constantine, Pepin, and Frederick II, before settling on an iron grille at the far side. The space beyond the grille was dark and quiet. The Riserva was accessed only by direct papal authority, the key to the grille held by the church's archivist. Michener had never entered that chamber, though he'd stood dutifully outside while his boss, Pope Clement XV, ventured inside. Even so, he was aware of some of the precious documents that the windowless space contained. The last letter of Mary, Queen of Scots, before she was beheaded by Elizabeth I. The petitions of seventy-five English lords asking the pope to annul Henry VIII's first marriage. Galileo's signed confession. Napoleon's Treaty of Tolentino.

He studied the cresting and buttresses of the iron grille, and the gilded frieze of foliage and animals hammered into the metal above. The gate itself had stood since the fourteenth century. Nothing in Vatican City was ordinary. Everything carried the distinctive mark of a renowned artist or a legendary craftsman, someone who'd labored for years trying to please both his God and his pope.

He strode across the room, his footfalls echoing through the tepid air, and stopped at the iron gate. A warm breeze swept past him from beyond the grille. The right side of the portal was dominated by a huge hasp. He tested the bolt. Locked and secure.

He turned back, wondering if one of the staff had entered the archives. The duty scriptor had departed when he'd arrived earlier and no one else would be allowed inside while he was there, since the papal secretary needed no babysitter. But there were a multitude of doors that led in and out, and he wondered if the noise he'd heard moments ago was that of ancient hinges being worked open, then gently closed. It was hard to tell. Sound within the great expanse was as confused as the writings.

He stepped to his right, toward one of the long corridors—the Hall of Parchments. Beyond was the Room of Inventories and Indexes. As he walked, overhead bulbs flashed on and off, casting a succession of light pools, and he felt as if he were underground, though he was two stories up.

He ventured only a little way, heard nothing, then turned around.

It was early in the day and midweek. He'd chosen this time for his research deliberately—less chance of impeding others who'd gained access to the archives, and less chance of attracting the attention of curial employees. He was on a mission for the Holy Father, his inquiries private, but he was not alone. The last time, a week ago, he'd sensed the same thing.

He reentered the main hall and stepped back to the reading desk, his attention still on the room. The floor was a zodiacal diagram oriented to the sun, its rays able to penetrate thanks to carefully positioned slits high in the walls. He knew that centuries ago the Gregorian calendar had been calculated at this precise spot. Yet no sunlight leaked in today. Outside was cold and wet, a midautumn rainstorm pelting Rome.

The volumes that had held his attention for the past two hours were neatly arranged on the lectern. Many had been composed within the past two decades. Four were much older. Two of the oldest were written in Italian, one was in Spanish, the other in Portuguese. He could read all of them with ease—another reason Clement XV coveted his employment.

The Spanish and Italian accounts were of little value, both rehashes of the Portuguese work: *A Comprehensive and Detailed Study of the Reported Apparitions of the Holy Virgin Mary at Fatima—May 13, 1917, to October 13, 1917.*

Pope Benedict XV had ordered the investigation in 1922 as part of the Church's investigation into what supposedly had occurred in a remote Portuguese valley. The entire manuscript was handwritten, the ink faded to a warm yellow so the words appeared as if they were scripted in gold. The bishop of Leira had performed a thorough inquiry, spending eight years in all, and the information later became critical in the 1930 acknowledgment by the Vatican that the Virgin's six earthly appearances at Fatima were *worthy of assent.* Three appendices, now attached to the original, had been generated in the 1950s, '60s, and '90s.

Michener had studied them all with the thoroughness of the

lawyer he'd been trained by the Church to be. Seven years at the University of Munich had earned him his degrees, yet he'd never practiced law conventionally. His was a world of ecclesiastical pronouncements and canonical decrees. Precedent spanned two millennia and relied more on an understanding of the times than on any notion of *stare decisis*. His arduous legal training had become invaluable to his Church service, as the logic of the law had many times become an ally in the confusing mire of divine politics. More important, it had just helped him find in this labyrinth of forgotten information what Clement XV wanted.

The sound came again.

A soft squeak, like two limbs rubbing together in a breeze, or a mouse announcing its presence.

He rushed toward the source and glanced both ways.

Nothing.

Fifty feet off to the left, a door led out of the archive. He approached the portal and tested the lock. It yielded. He strained to open the heavy slab of carved oak and the iron hinges squealed ever so slightly.

A sound he recognized.

The hallway beyond was empty, but a gleam on the marble floor caught his attention.

He knelt.

The transparent clumps of moisture came with regularity, the droplets leading off into the corridor, then back through the doorway into the archive. Suspended within some were remnants of mud, leaves, and grass.

He followed the trail with his gaze which stopped at the end of a row of shelves. Rain continued to pound the roof.

He knew the puddles for what they were.

Footprints.

TWO

THE MEDIA CIRCUS STARTED EARLY, AS MICHENER KNEW IT would. He stood before the window and watched as television vans and trailers eased into St. Peter's Square and claimed their assigned positions. The Vatican press office had reported to him yesterday that seventy-one press applications had been approved for the tribunal from North American, English, and French journalists, though there were also a dozen Italians and three Germans in the group. Most were print media, but several news outlets had asked for and were granted on-site broadcast permission. The BBC had even lobbied for camera access inside the tribunal itself, part of a documentary it was preparing, but that request was denied. The whole thing should be quite a show—but that was the price to be paid for going after a celebrity.

The Apostolic Penitentiary was the senior of three Vatican tribunals and dealt exclusively with excommunications. Canon law proclaimed five reasons a person could be excommunicated: Breaking the confidentiality of the confessional. Physically attacking the pope. Consecrating a bishop without Holy See approval. Desecrating the Eucharist. And the one at issue today—a priest absolving his accomplice in a sexual sin.

Father Thomas Kealy of St. Peter and Paul Church in Richmond, Virginia had done the unthinkable. Three years ago he'd engaged in an open relationship with a woman, then in front of his congregation he'd absolved them both of sin. The stunt, and Kealy's scathing comments on the Church's unbending position regarding celibacy, had garnered a great deal of attention. Individual priests and theologians had long challenged Rome on celibacy, and the usual response was to wait the advocate out, since most either quit or fell into line. Father Kealy, though, took his challenge to new levels by publishing three books, one an international best seller, that directly contradicted established Catholic doctrine. Michener well knew the institutional fear that surrounded him. It was one thing when a priest challenged Rome, quite another when people started listening.

And people listened to Thomas Kealy.

He was handsome and smart and possessed the enviable gift of being able to succinctly convey his thoughts. He'd appeared across the globe and had attracted a strong following. Every movement needed a leader, and church reform advocates had apparently found theirs in this bold priest. His website, which Michener knew the Apostolic Penitentiary monitored on a daily basis, scored more than twenty thousand hits a day. A year ago Kealy had founded a global movement, Catholics Rallying for Equality Against Theological Eccentricities—CREATE—which now boasted over a million members, most from North America and Europe.

Kealy's bold leadership had even spawned courage among American bishops, and last year a sizable bloc came close to openly endorsing his ideas and questioning Rome's continued reliance on archaic medieval philosophy. As Kealy had many times pronounced, the American church was in crisis thanks to old ideas, disgraced priests, and arrogant leaders. His argument that *the Vatican loves American money, but not American influence* resonated. He offered the kind of populist common sense that Michener knew Western minds craved. He had become a celebrity. Now the challenger had come to meet the champion, and their joust would be recorded by the world press.

But first, Michener had a joust of his own.

He turned from the window and stared at Clement XV, flushing from his mind the thought that his old friend might soon die.

"How are you today, Holy Father?" he asked in German. When alone, they always used Clement's native language. Almost none of the palace staff spoke German.

The pope reached for a china cup and savored a sip of espresso. "It is amazing how being surrounded by such majesty can be so unsatisfying."

The cynicism was nothing new, but of late its tone had intensified.

Clement tabled the cup. "Did you find the information in the archive?"

Michener stepped from the window and nodded.

"Was the original Fatima report helpful?"

"Not a bit. I discovered other documents that yielded more." He wondered again why any of this was important, but said nothing.

The pope seemed to sense what he was thinking. "You never ask, do you?"

"You'd tell, if you wanted me to know."

A lot had changed about this man over the past three years— the pope growing more distant, pale, and fragile by the day. While Clement had always been a short, thin man, it seemed of late that his body was retreating within itself. His scalp, once covered by a thatch of brown hair, was now dusted with short gray fuzz. The bright face that had adorned newspapers and magazines, smiling from the balcony of St. Peter's as his election was announced, loomed gaunt to the point of caricature, his flush cheeks gone, the once hardly noticeable port wine stain now a prominent splotch that the Vatican press office routinely airbrushed from photos. The pressures of occupying the chair of St. Peter had taken a toll, severely aging a man who, not so long ago, scaled the Bavarian Alps with regularity.

STEVE BERRY / 20

Michener motioned to the tray of coffee. He remembered when wurst, yogurt, and black bread constituted breakfast. "Why don't you eat? The steward told me you didn't have any dinner last night."

"Such a worrier."

"Why are you not hungry?"

"Persistent, too."

"Evading my questions does nothing to calm my fears."

"And what are your fears, Colin?"

He wanted to mention the lines bracketing Clement's brow, the alarming pallor of his skin, the veins that marked the old man's hands and wrists. But he simply said, "Only your health, Holy Father."

Clement smiled. "You are good at avoiding my taunts."

"Arguing with the Holy Father is a fruitless endeavor."

"Ah, that infallibility stuff. I forgot. I'm always right."

He decided to take that challenge. "Not always."

Clement chuckled. "Do you have the name found in the archives?"

He reached into his cassock and removed what he'd written just before he'd heard the sound. He handed it to Clement and said, "Somebody was there again."

"Which should not surprise you. Nothing is private here." The pope read, then repeated what was written. "Father Andrej Tibor."

He knew what was expected of him. "He's a retired priest living in Romania. I checked our records. His retirement check is still sent to an address there."

"I want you to go see him."

"Are you going to tell me why?"

"Not yet."

For the past three months Clement had been deeply bothered. The old man had tried to conceal it, but after twenty-four years of friendship little escaped Michener's notice. He remembered precisely when the apprehension started. Just after a visit to the archives—to the Riserva—and the ancient safe waiting behind the locked iron grille. "Do I get to know when you will tell me why?"

The pope rose from his chair. "After prayers."

They left the study and walked in silence across the fourth floor, stopping at an open doorway. The chapel beyond was sheathed in white marble, the windows a dazzling glass mosaic fashioned to represent the Stations of the Cross. Clement came every morning for a few minutes of meditation. No one was allowed to interrupt him. Everything could wait until he finished talking with God.

Michener had served Clement since the early days when the wiry German was first an archbishop, then a cardinal, then Vatican secretary of state. He'd risen with his mentor—from seminarian, to priest, to monsignor—the climb culminating thirty-four months back when the Sacred College of Cardinals elected Jakob Cardinal Volkner the 267th successor to St. Peter. Volkner immediately chose Michener as his personal secretary.

Michener knew Clement for who he was—a man educated in a postwar German society that had swirled in turmoil—learning his diplomatic craft in such volatile postings as Dublin, Cairo, Cape Town, and Warsaw. Jakob Volkner was a man of immense patience and fanatical attention. Never once in their years together had Michener ever doubted his mentor's faith or character, and he'd long ago resolved that if he could simply be half the man Volkner had been, he would consider his life a success.

Clement finished his prayers, crossed himself, then kissed the pectoral cross that graced the front of his white simar. His quiet time had been short today. The pope eased himself up from the prie-dieu, but lingered at the altar. Michener stood quiet in the corner until the pontiff stepped over to him.

"I intend to explain myself in a letter to Father Tibor. It will be papal authority for him to provide you with certain information."

Still not an explanation as to why the Romanian trip was neces-sary. "When would you like me to go?"

"Tomorrow. The next day at the latest."

"I'm not sure that's a good idea. Can't one of the legates handle the task?"

"I assure you, Colin. I won't die while you are gone. I may look bad, but I feel fine."

Which had been confirmed by Clement's doctors not less than a week ago. After a battery of tests, the pope had been proclaimed free of any debilitating disease. But privately the papal physician had cautioned that stress was Clement's deadliest enemy, and his rapid decline over the past few months seemed evidence that something was tearing at his soul.

"I never said you looked bad, Holiness."

"You didn't have to." The old man pointed to his eyes. "It's in there. I've learned to read them."

Michener held up the slip of paper. "Why do you need to make contact with this priest?"

"I should have done it after I first went into the Riserva. But I resisted." Clement paused. "I can't resist any longer. I have no choice."

"Why is the supreme pontiff of the Roman Catholic Church without choices?"

The pope stepped away and faced a crucifix on the wall. Two stout candles burned bright on either side of the marble altar.

"Are you going to the tribunal this morning?" Clement asked, his back to him.

"That's not an answer to my question."

"The supreme pontiff of the Roman Catholic Church can pick and choose what he wants to answer."

"I believe you instructed me to attend the tribunal. So, yes, I'll be there. Along with a roomful of reporters."

"Will she be there?"

He knew exactly who the old man was referring to. "I'm told she applied for press credentials to cover the event."

"Do you know her interest in the tribunal?"

He shook his head. "As I told you before, I only learned of her presence by accident."

Clement turned to face him. "But what a fortunate accident."

He wondered why the pope was interested.

"It's all right to care, Colin. She's a part of your past. A part you should not forget."

Clement only knew the whole story because Michener had needed a confessor, and the archbishop of Cologne had then been his closest companion. It was the only breach of his clerical vows during his quarter century as a priest. He'd thought about quitting, but Clement talked him out of it, explaining that only through weakness could a soul gain strength. Nothing would be gained from walking away. Now, after more than a dozen years, he knew Jakob Volkner had been right. He was the papal secretary. For nearly three years he'd helped Clement XV govern a derisive combination of Catholic personality and culture. The fact that his entire participation was based on a violation of his oath to his God and his Church never seemed to bother him. And that realization had, of late, become quite troubling.

"I haven't forgotten any of it," he whispered.

The pope stepped close to him and laid a hand on his shoulder. "Do not lament for that which was lost. It is unhealthy and counterproductive."

"Lying doesn't come easy to me."

"Your God has forgiven you. That is all you need."

"How can you be sure?"

"I am. And if you can't believe the infallible head of the Catholic Church, who can you believe?" A smile accompanied the facetious comment, one that told Michener not to take things quite so seriously.

He smiled, too. "You're impossible."

Clement removed his hand. "True, but I'm lovable."

"I'll try and remember that."

"You do that. I'll have my letter for Father Tibor ready shortly. It will call for a written response, but if he desires to speak, listen to him, ask what you will, and tell me everything. Understand?"

He wondered how he would know what to ask since he had no idea why he was even going, but he simply said, "I understand, Holiness. As always."

Clement grinned. "That's right, Colin. As always."

THREE

MICHENER ENTERED THE TRIBUNAL CHAMBER. THE GATHERING hall was a lofty expanse of white and gray marble, enriched by a geometric pattern of colorful mosaics that had borne witness to four hundred years of Church history.

Two plain-clothed Swiss guards manned the bronze doors and bowed as they recognized the papal secretary. Michener had purposely waited an hour before walking over. He knew his presence would be cause for discussion—rarely did someone so close to the pope attend the proceedings.

At Clement's insistence, Michener had read all three of Kealy's books and privately briefed the pontiff on their provocative content. Clement himself had not read them since that act would have generated too much speculation. Yet the pope had been intently interested in what Father Kealy had written and, as Michener slipped into a seat at the back of the chamber, he saw, for the first time, Thomas Kealy.

The accused sat alone at a table. Kealy appeared to be in his midthirties, with bushy auburn hair and a pleasant, youthful face. The grin that flashed periodically seemed calculated—the look and manner almost intentionally whimsical. Michener had read all of the background reports the tribunal had generated, and each one painted Kealy as smug and nonconformist. *Clearly an opportunist,* one of the investigators had written. Nonetheless, he could not help but think that Kealy's arguments were, in many ways, persuasive.

Kealy was being questioned by Alberto Cardinal Valendrea, the Vatican secretary of state, and Michener did not envy the man's position. Kealy had drawn a tough panel. All of the cardinals and bishops were what Michener regarded as intensely conservative. None embraced the teachings of Vatican II, and not one was a supporter of Clement XV. Valendrea particularly was noted for a radical adherence to dogma. The tribunal members were each garbed in full vestments, the cardinals in scarlet silk, the bishops in black wool, perched behind a curved marble table beneath one of Raphael's paintings.

"There is no one so far removed from God as a heretic," Cardinal Valendrea said. His deep voice echoed without need of amplification.

"It seems to me, Eminence," Kealy said, "the less open a heretic is, the more dangerous he would become. I don't hide my disagreements. Instead, open debate is, I believe, healthy for the Church."

Valendrea held up three books and Michener recognized the front covers of Kealy's works. "These are heresy. There is no other way to view them."

"Because I advocate priests should marry? That women could be priests? That a priest can love a wife, a child, and his God like others of faith? That perhaps the pope is not infallible? He's human, capable of error. That's heresy?"

"I don't think one person on this tribunal would say otherwise."

And none of them did.

Michener watched Valendrea as the Italian shifted in his chair. The cardinal was short and stumpy like a fire hydrant. A tangled fringe of white hair looped across his brow, drawing attention to itself simply by the contrast with his olive skin. At sixty, Valendrea enjoyed a luxury of relative youth within a Curia dominated by much older men. He also possessed none of the solemnity that outsiders associated with a prince of the Church. He smoked nearly two packs of cigarettes a day, owned a wine cellar that was the envy of many, and regularly moved within the right European social circles. His family was blessed with money, much of which was bestowed on him as the senior male in the paternal line.

The press had long labeled Valendrea *papabile,* a title that meant him eligible by age, rank, and influence for the papacy. Michener had heard rumors of how the secretary of state was positioning himself for the next conclave, bargaining with fence straddlers, strong-arming potential opposition. Clement had been forced to appoint him secretary of state, the most powerful office below pope, because a sizable bloc of cardinals had urged that Valendrea be given the job and Clement was astute enough to placate those who'd placed him in power. Plus, as the pope explained at the time, *let your friends stay near and your enemies nearer.*

Valendrea rested his arms on the table. No papers were spread before him. He was known as a man who rarely needed reference material. "Father Kealy, there are many within the Church who feel the experiment of Vatican II cannot be judged a success, and you are a shining example of our failure. Clerics do not have freedom of expression. There are too many opinions in this world to allow discourse. This Church must speak with one voice, that being the Holy Father's."

"And there are many today who feel celibacy and papal infallibility are flawed doctrine. Something from a time when the world was illiterate and the Church corrupt."

"I differ with your conclusions. But even if those prelates exist, they keep their opinions to themselves."

"Fear has a way of silencing tongues, Eminence."

"There is nothing to fear."

"From this chair, I beg to differ."

"The Church does not punish its clerics for thoughts, Father, only actions. Such as yours. Your organization is an insult to the Church you serve."

"If I had no regard for the Church, Eminence, then I would have simply quit and said nothing. Instead, I love my Church enough to challenge its policies."

"Did you think the Church would do nothing while you breached your vows, carried on with a woman openly, and absolved yourself of sin?" Valendrea held the books up again. "Then wrote about it? You literally invited this challenge."

"Do you honestly believe that all priests are celibate?" Kealy asked.

The question caught Michener's attention. He noticed the reporters perk up as well.

"It matters not what I believe," Valendrea said. "That issue is with the individual cleric. Each one took an oath to his Lord and his Church. I expect that oath to be honored. Anyone who fails in this should leave or be forced out."

"Have you kept your oath, Eminence?"

Michener was startled by Kealy's boldness. Perhaps he already realized his fate, so what did it matter.

Valendrea shook his head. "Do you find a personal challenge to me beneficial to your defense?"

"It's a simple question."

"Yes, Father. I have kept my oath."

Kealy seemed unfazed. "What other answer would you offer?"

"Are you saying that I am a liar?"

"No, Eminence. Only that no priest, cardinal, or bishop would dare admit what he feels in his heart. We are each bound to say what the Church requires us to say. I have no idea what you truly feel, and that is sad."

"What I feel is irrelevant to your heresy."

"It seems, Eminence, that you have already judged me."

"No more so than your God. Who *is* infallible. Or perhaps you take issue with that doctrine as well?"

"When did God decree that priests cannot know the love of a companion?"

"Companion? Why not simply a woman?"

"Because love knows no bounds, Eminence."

"So you are advocating homosexuality, too?"

"I advocate only that each individual must follow his heart."

Valendrea shook his head. "Have you forgotten, Father, that your ordination was a union with Christ? The truth of your identity—which is the same for everyone on this tribunal—comes from a full participation in that union. You are to be a living, transparent image of Christ."

"But how are we to know what that image is? None of us was around when Christ lived."

"It is as the Church says."

"But is that not merely man molding the divine to suit his need?"

Valendrea's lifted his right eyebrow in apparent disbelief. "Your arrogance is amazing. Do you argue that Christ Himself was not celibate? That He did not place His Church above everything? That He was not in union with His Church?"

"I have no earthly idea what Christ's sexual preference was, and neither do you."

Valendrea hesitated a moment, then said, "Your celibacy, Father, is a gift of yourself. An expression of your devoted service. That is Church doctrine. One you seem unable, or unwilling, to understand."

Kealy responded, quoting more dogma, and Michener let his attention drift from their debate. He'd avoided looking, telling himself that it was not the reason he'd come, but his gaze quickly raked the hundred or so present, finally settling on a woman seated two rows behind Kealy.

Her hair was the color of midnight and possessed a noticeable depth and shine. He recalled how the strands once formed a thick mane and smelled of fresh lemon. Now they were short, layered, and finger-combed. He could only glimpse an angled profile, but the dainty nose and thin lips were still there. The skin remained the tint of heavily creamed coffee, evidence of a Romanian Gypsy mother and a Hungarian German father. Her name, Katerina Lew, meant "pure lion," a description he'd always thought appropriate given her volatile temper and fanatical convictions.

They'd met in Munich. He was thirty-three, finishing his law degree. She was twenty-five, deciding between journalism and a career writing novels. She'd known he was a priest, and they spent nearly two years together before the showdown came. *Your God or me,* she declared.

He chose God.

"Father Kealy," Valendrea was saying, "the nature of our faith is that nothing can be added or taken away. You must embrace the teachings of the mother Church in their entirety, or reject them totally. There is no such thing as a partial Catholic. Our principles, as expounded by the Holy Father, are not impious and cannot be diluted. They are as pure as God."

"I believe those are the words of Pope Benedict XV," Kealy said.

"You are well versed. Which increases my sadness at your heresy. A man as intelligent as you appear to be should understand that this Church cannot, and will not tolerate open dissent. Especially of the degree you have offered."

"What you're saying is that the Church is afraid of debate."

"I am saying that the Church sets rules. If you don't like the rules, then muster enough votes to elect a pope who will change them. Short of that, you must do as told."

"Oh, I forgot. The Holy Father is infallible. Whatever is said by him concerning the faith is, without question, correct. Am I now stating correct dogma?"

Michener noticed that none of the other men on the tribunal had even attempted to utter a word. Apparently the secretary of state was the inquisitor for the day. He knew that all of the panelists were Valendrea loyalists, and little chance existed that any of them would challenge their benefactor. But Thomas Kealy was making it easy, doing more damage to himself than any of their questions might ever inflict.

"That is correct," Valendrea said. "Papal infallibility is essential to the Church."

"Another doctrine created by man."

"Another dogma *this* Church adheres to."

"I'm a priest who loves his God and his Church," Kealy said. "I don't see why disagreeing with either would subject me to excommunication. Debate and discussion do nothing but foster wise policies. Why does the Church fear that?"

"Father, this hearing is not about freedom of speech. We have no American constitution that guarantees such a right. This hearing is about your brazen relationship with a woman, your public forgiveness of both your sins, and your open dissension. All of which is in direct contradiction to the rules of the Church you joined."

Michener's gaze drifted back to Kate. It was the name he'd given her as a way of imposing some of his Irish heritage on her Eastern European personality. She sat straight, a notebook in her lap, her full attention on the unfolding debate.

He thought of their final Bavarian summer together when he took three weeks off between semesters. They'd traveled to an Alpine village and stayed at an inn surrounded by snowcapped summits. He knew it was wrong, but by then she'd touched a part of him he thought did not exist. What Cardinal Valendrea had just said about Christ and a priest's union with the Church was indeed the basis of clerical celibacy. A priest should devote himself solely to God and the Church. But ever since that summer he'd wondered why he couldn't love a woman, his Church, and God simultaneously. What had Kealy said? *Like others of faith.*

He sensed the stare of eyes. As his mind refocused, he realized Katerina had turned her head and was now looking directly at him.

The face still carried the toughness he'd found so attractive. The slight hint of Asian eyes remained, the mouth tugged down, the jaw

STEVE BERRY / 32

gentle and feminine. There were simply no sharp edges anywhere. Those, he knew, hid in her personality. He examined her expression and tried to gauge its temperature. Not anger. Not resentment. Not affection. A look that seemed to say nothing. Not even hello. He found it uncomfortable to be this close to a memory. Perhaps she'd expected his appearance and didn't want to give him the satisfaction of thinking she cared. After all, their parting all those years ago had not been amicable.

She turned back to the tribunal and his anxiety subsided.

"Father Kealy," Valendrea said, "I ask you simply. Do you renounce your heresy? Do you recognize that what you have done is against the laws of this Church and your God?"

The priest pulled himself close to the table. "I do not believe that loving a woman is contrary to the laws of God. So the forgiving of that sin was therefore inconsequential. I have a right to speak my mind, so I make no apologies for the movement that I head. I have done nothing wrong, Eminence."

"You are a foolish man, Father. I have given you every opportunity to beg forgiveness. The Church can, and should, be forgiving. But contrition works in both directions. The penitent must be willing."

"I do not seek your forgiveness."

Valendrea shook his head. "My heart aches for you and your followers, Father. Clearly, all of you are with the devil."

FOUR

ALBERTO CARDINAL VALENDREA STOOD SILENT, HOPING THE euphoria from earlier at the tribunal would temper his rising irritation. Amazing how quickly a bad experience could utterly ruin a good one.

"What do you think, Alberto?" Clement XV said. "Is there time for me to view the crowd?" The pope motioned to the alcove and the open window.

It galled Valendrea that the pope would waste time standing before an open window and waving to people in St. Peter's Square. Vatican Security had cautioned against the gesture, but the silly old man ignored the warnings. The press wrote about it all the time, comparing the German to John XXIII. And, in truth, there were similarities. Both ascended the papal throne near the age of eighty. Both were deemed caretaker popes. Both surprised everyone.

Valendrea hated the way Vatican observers also analogized the pope's open window with *his animated spirit, his unassuming openness, his charismatic warmth.* The papacy was not about popularity. It was about consistency, and he resented how easily Clement had dispensed with so many time-honored customs. No longer did aides genuflect in the pope's presence. Few kissed the papal ring. And rarely did Clement speak in the first person plural, as popes had done for centuries. *This is the twenty-first century,* Clement liked to say, while decreeing an end to another long-standing custom.

Valendrea remembered, not all that long ago, when popes would never stand in an open window. Security concerns aside, limited exposure bred an aura, it encouraged an air of mystery, and nothing promulgated faith and obedience more than a sense of wonder.

He'd served popes for nearly four decades, rising in the Curia quickly, earning his cardinal's hat before fifty, one of the youngest in modern times. He now held the second most powerful position in the Catholic Church—the secretary of state—a job that interjected him into every aspect of the Holy See. But he wanted more. He wanted the most powerful position. The one where no one challenged his decisions. Where he spoke infallibly and without question.

He wanted to be pope.

"It is such a lovely day," the pope was saying. "The rain seems gone. The air is like back home, in the German mountains. An Alpine freshness. Such a shame to be inside."

Clement stepped into the alcove, but not far enough for him to be seen from outside. The pope wore a white linen cassock, caped across the shoulders, with the traditional white vest. Scarlet shoes encased his feet and a white skullcap topped his balding head. He was the only prelate among one billion Catholics allowed to dress in that manner.

"Perhaps His Holiness could engage in that rather delightful activity after we have completed the briefing. I have other appointments, and the tribunal took up the entire morning."

"It would only take a few moments," Clement said.

He knew the German enjoyed taunting him. From beyond the open window came the hum of Rome, that unique sound of three million souls and their machines moving across porous volcanic ash.

Clement seemed to notice the rumble, too. "It has a strange sound, this city."

"It is *our* sound."

"Ah, I almost forgot. You are Italian, and all of us are not."

Valendrea was standing beside a poster bed fashioned of heavy oak, the knicks and scrapes so numerous they seemed a part of its craftsmanship. A worn crocheted blanket draped one end, two over-sized pillows the other. The remaining furniture was also German— the armoire, dresser, and tables all painted gaily in a Bavarian style. There hadn't been a German pope since the middle of the eleventh century. Clement II had been a source of inspiration for the current Clement XV—a fact that the pontiff made no secret about. But that earlier Clement was most likely poisoned to death. A lesson, Valendrea many times thought, this German should not forget.

"Perhaps you are right," Clement said. "Visiting can wait. We do have business, now don't we?"

A breeze eased past the sill and rustled papers on the desk. Valendrea reached down and halted their rise before they reached the computer terminal. Clement had not, as yet, switched on the machine. He was the first pope to be fully computer literate—another point the press loved—but Valendrea had not minded that change. Computer and fax lines were far easier to monitor than telephones.

"I am told you were quite spirited this morning," Clement said. "What will be the outcome of the tribunal?"

He assumed Michener had reported back. He'd seen the papal secretary in the audience. "I was unaware that His Holiness was so interested in the subject matter of the tribunal."

"Hard to not to be curious. The square below is littered with television vans. So, please, answer my question."

"Father Kealy presented us with few options. He will be excommunicated."

The pope clasped his hands behind his back. "He offered no apology?"

"He was arrogant to the point of insult, and dared us to challenge him."

"Perhaps we should."

The suggestion caught Valendrea off guard, but decades of diplomatic service had taught him how to conceal surprise with questions. "And the purpose of such an unorthodox action?"

"Why does everything need a purpose? Perhaps we should simply listen to an opposing point of view."

He kept his body still. "There is no way you could openly debate the question of celibacy. That has been doctrine for five hundred years. What's next? Women in the priesthood? Marriage for clerics? An approval of birth control? Will there be a complete reversal of all dogma?"

Clement stepped toward the bed and stared up at a medieval rendition of Clement II hanging on the wall. Valendrea knew that it had been brought from one of the cavernous cellars, where it had rested for centuries. "He was bishop of Bamberg. A simple man who possessed no desire to be pope."

"He was the king's confidant," Valendrea said. "Politically connected. In the right place at the right time."

Clement turned to face him. "Like myself, I presume?"

"Your election was by an overwhelming majority of cardinals, each one inspired by the Holy Spirit."

Clement's mouth formed an irritating smile. "Or perhaps it was affected by the fact that none of the other candidates, yourself included, could amass enough votes for election?"

They were apparently going to start feuding early today.

"You are an ambitious man, Alberto. You think wearing this white cassock will somehow make you happy. I can assure you, it won't."

They'd had similar conversations before, but the intensity of their exchanges had risen of late. Both knew how the other felt. They were not friends, and never would be. Valendrea found it amusing how people thought just because he was a cardinal and Clement pope, theirs would be a sacred relationship of two pious souls, placing the needs of the Church first. Instead, they were vastly different men, their union born purely of conflicting politics. To their credit, neither had ever openly feuded with the other. Valendrea was smarter than that—the pope was required to argue with no one—and Clement apparently realized that a great many cardinals supported his secretary of state. "I wish nothing, Holy Father, except for you to live a long and prosperous life."

"You don't lie well."

He was tiring of the old man's prodding. "Why does it matter? You won't be here when the conclave occurs. Don't concern yourself with the prospects."

Clement shrugged. "It matters not. I'll be enshrined beneath St. Peter's, with the rest of the men who have occupied this chair. I couldn't care less about my successor. But that man? Yes, that man should care greatly."

What was it the old prelate knew? It seemed a habit lately to drop odd hints. "Is there something that displeases the Holy Father?"

Clement's eyes flashed hot. "You are an opportunist, Alberto. A scheming politico. I might just disappoint you and live another ten years."

He decided to drop the pretense. "I doubt it."

"I actually hope you do inherit this job. You'll find it far different than you might imagine. Maybe you should be the one."

Now he wanted to know, "The one for what?"

For a few moments the pope went silent. Then he said, "The one to be pope, of course. What else?"

"What is it that bites your soul?"

"We are fools, Alberto. All of us, in our majesty, are nothing but fools. God is far wiser than any of us could even begin to imagine."

"I don't think any believer would question that."

"We expound our dogma and, in the process, ruin the lives of men like Father Kealy. He's just a priest trying to follow his conscience."

"He seemed more like an opportunist—to use your description. A man who enjoys the spotlight. Surely, though, he understood Church policy when he took his oath to abide by our teachings."

"But whose teachings? It is men like you and me pronouncing

the so-called Word of God. It's men like you and me, punishing other men for violating those teachings. I often wonder, is our precious dogma the thoughts of the Almighty or just those of ordinary clerics?"

Valendrea considered this inquiry just more of the strange behavior this pope had shown as of late. He debated whether to probe, but decided he was being tested, so he answered in the only way he could. "I consider the Word of God and the dogma of this Church one and the same."

"Good answer. Textbook in its diction and syntax. Unfortunately, Alberto, that belief will eventually be your undoing."

And the pope turned and stepped toward the window.

FIVE

MICHENER STROLLED INTO THE MIDDAY SUN. THE MORNING
rain had dissipated, the sky now littered with mottled clouds, the
patches of blue striped by the contrail of an airplane on its way east.
Before him, the cobbles of St. Peter's Square bore the remnants of
the earlier storm, puddles littered about like a multitude of lakes
strewn across a vast landscape. The television crews were still there,
many now broadcasting reports back home.

He'd left the tribunal before it adjourned. One of his aides later
informed him that the confrontation between Father Kealy and
Cardinal Valendrea had continued for the better part of two hours.
He wondered about the point of the hearing. The decision to ex-
communicate Kealy had surely been made long before the priest had
been commanded to Rome. Few accused clerics ever attended a tribunal, so Kealy had most likely come to draw more attention to his
movement. Within a matter of weeks Kealy would be declared *not in
communion with the Holy See,* just another expatriate proclaiming the
Church a dinosaur heading toward extinction.

And sometimes Michener believed critics, like Kealy, might be
right.

STEVE BERRY / 40

Nearly half of the world's Catholics now lived in Latin America. Add Africa and Asia and the fraction rose to three-quarters. Placating this emerging international majority, while not alienating the Europeans and Italians, was a daily challenge. No head of state dealt with something so intricate. But the Roman Catholic Church had done just that for two thousand years—a claim no other of man's institutions could make—and spread out before him was one of the Church's grandest manifestations.

The key-shaped square, enclosed within Bernini's two magnificent semicircular colonnades, was breathtaking. Michener had always been impressed with Vatican City. He'd first come a dozen years ago as the adjunct priest to the archbishop of Cologne—his virtue having been tested by Katerina Lew, but his resolve solidified. He recalled exploring all 108 acres of the walled enclave, marveling at the majesty that two millennia of constant building could achieve.

The tiny nation did not occupy one of the hills upon which Rome was first built, but instead crowned Mons Vaticanus, the only one of the seven ancient designations people still remembered. Fewer than two hundred were actual citizens, and even fewer held a passport. Not one soul had ever been born there, few besides popes died there, and even fewer were buried there. Its government was one of the world's last remaining absolute monarchies and, in a twist Michener had always thought ironic, the Holy See's United Nations representative could not sign the worldwide declaration of human rights because, inside the Vatican, there was no religious freedom.

He gazed out into the sunny square, past the television trucks with their array of antennas, and noticed people looking off to the right and up. A few were crying *"Santissimo Padre."* Holy Father. He followed their upturned heads to the fourth floor of the Apostolic Palace. Between the wooden shutters of a corner window the face of Clement XV appeared.

Many started waving. Clement waved back.

"Still fascinates you, doesn't it?" a female voice said.

He turned. Katerina Lew stood a few feet away. Somehow he'd known she would find him. She came close to where he stood, just inside the shadow of one of Bernini's pillars. "You haven't changed a bit. Still in love with your God. I could see it in your eyes in the tribunal."

He tried to smile, but cautioned himself to focus on the challenge before him. "How have you been, Kate?" The features on her face softened. "Life everything you thought it would be?"

"I can't complain. No, I won't complain. Unproductive. That's how you once described complaining."

"That's good to hear."

"How did you know I'd be there this morning?"

"I saw your credentials application a few weeks back. May I ask what's your interest in Father Kealy?"

"We haven't spoken in fifteen years and that's what you want to talk about?"

"The last time we spoke you told me never to speak of *us* again. You said there was no *us*. Only me and God. So I didn't think that was a good subject."

"But I said that only after you told me you were returning to the archbishop and devoting yourself to the service of others. A priest in the Catholic Church."

They were standing a bit close, so he took a few steps back, deeper into the shadow of the colonnade. He caught a glimpse of Michelangelo's dome atop St. Peter's Basilica being dried by a brightening midautumn sun.

"I see you still have a talent for evading questions," he pointed out.

"I'm here because Tom Kealy asked me to come. He's no fool. He knows what that tribunal is going to do."

"Who are you writing for?"

"Freelance. A book he and I are putting together."

She was a good writer, especially of poetry. He'd always envied her ability, and he actually wanted to know more about what happened to her after Munich. He was aware of bits and pieces. Her stints at a few European newspapers, never long, even a job in America. He occasionally saw her byline—nothing heavy or weighty, mainly religious essays. Several times he'd almost tracked her down, longing to share a coffee, but he knew that was impossible. He'd made his choice and there was no going back.

"I wasn't surprised when I read of your papal appointment," she said. "I figured when Volkner was elected pope, he wouldn't let you go."

He caught the look in her emerald eyes and saw she was struggling with her emotions, just as she had fifteen years ago. Then, he was a priest working on a law degree, anxious and ambitious, tied to the fortunes of a German bishop whom many were saying could one day be a cardinal. Now there was talk of his own elevation to the Sacred College. It was not unheard of that papal secretaries moved directly from the Apostolic Palace into a scarlet hat. He wanted to be a prince of the Church, to be part of the next conclave in the Sistine Chapel, beneath the frescoes of Michelangelo and Botticelli, with a voice and a vote.

"Clement is a good man," he said.

"He's a fool," she quietly stated. "Just somebody the good cardinals put on the throne until one of them can muster enough support."

"What makes you such an authority?"

"Am I wrong?"

He turned from her, allowing his temper to cool, and watched a group of souvenir peddlers at the square's perimeter. Her surly attitude was still there, her words as biting and bitter as he remembered. She was pushing forty, but maturity had done little to abate her consuming passions. It was one of the things he'd never liked about her, and one of the things he missed. In his world, frankness was unknown. He was surrounded by people who could say with conviction what they never meant, so there was something to be said for truth. At least you knew exactly where you stood. Solid ground. Not the perpetual quicksand he'd grown accustomed to dealing with.

"Clement is a good man charged with a nearly impossible task," he said.

"Of course if the dear mother Church would bend a little, things might not be so difficult. Pretty hard to govern a billion when everyone has to accept that the pope is the only man on earth who can't make a mistake."

He didn't want to debate dogma with her, especially in the middle of St. Peter's Square. Two Swiss guards, plumed and helmeted, their halberds held high, marched past a few feet away. He watched them advance toward the basilica's main entrance. The six massive bells high in the dome were silent, but he realized the time was not that far off when they would toll at Clement XV's death. Which made Katerina's insolence all the more infuriating. Going to the tribunal earlier and talking with her now were mistakes. He knew what he had to do. "It's been nice seeing you again, Kate." He turned to leave.

"Bastard."

She spit out the insult just loud enough for him to hear.

He turned back, wondering if she truly meant it. Conflict clouded her face. He stepped close and kept his voice down. "We haven't spoken in years and all you want to do is tell me how evil the Church is. If you despise it so much, why waste your time writing about it? Go write that novel you always said you would. I thought maybe, just maybe, you might have mellowed. But I see that hasn't occurred."

"How wonderful to know you might actually care. You never considered my feelings when you told me it was over."

"Do we have to go through all that again?"

"No, Colin. There's no need." She retreated. "No need at all. Like you said, it's been good seeing you again."

For an instant he registered hurt, but she seemed to quickly conquer whatever weakness may have swelled inside her.

He stared back toward the palace. Many more were now calling out and waving. Clement was still waving back. Several of the television crews were filming the moment.

"It's *him*, Colin," Katerina said. "*He's* your problem. You just don't know it."

And before he could reply, she was gone.

SIX

VALENDREA CLAMPED THE HEADPHONES OVER HIS EARS, pushed PLAY on the reel-to-reel recorder, and listened to the conversation between Colin Michener and Clement XV. The eavesdropping devices installed in the papal apartments had again performed flawlessly. There were many such receivers throughout the Apostolic Palace. He'd seen to that just after Clement's election, which had been easy since, as secretary of state, he was charged with ensuring the security of the Vatican.

Clement had been right earlier. Valendrea wanted the current pontificate to run a little longer, time enough for him to secure the few remaining stragglers he'd need in the conclave. The current Sacred College was holding at 160, only 47 members over the age of eighty and ineligible to vote if a conclave happened within the next thirty days. At last count he felt reasonably confident of forty-five votes. A good start, but a long way from election. Last time he'd ignored the adage, *He who goes into the conclave as pope comes out a cardinal.* No chances would be taken this time. The listening devices were just one aspect of his strategy to assure that the Italian cardinals did not repeat their prior defection. Amazing the indiscretions princes of the Church engaged in on a daily basis. Sin was no stranger to them, their souls in need of cleansing like everyone else. But Valendrea well knew that, sometimes, penance had to be forced upon the penitent.

It's all right to care, Colin. She's a part of your past. A part you should not forget.

Valendrea removed the earphones and glanced up at the man sitting beside him. Father Paolo Ambrosi had stood at his side for over a decade. He was a short, slender man with straw-thin gray hair. The crook of his nose and the cut of his jaw reminded Valendrea of a hawk, an analogy that also amply described the priest's personality. A smile was rare, a laugh even more so. A grave air constantly sheathed him, but that never bothered Valendrea because this priest was a man possessed of passion and ambition, two traits Valendrea greatly admired.

"It's amusing, Paolo, how they speak German as if they're the only ones who might understand." Valendrea switched off the recorder. "Our pope seems concerned about this woman Father Michener is apparently familiar with. Tell me about her."

They were sitting in a windowless salon on the third floor of the Apostolic Palace, part of the enormous square footage allocated to the Secretariat of State. The tape recorders and radio receiver were stored there inside a locked cabinet. Valendrea was not concerned about anyone finding the hardware. With more than ten thousand chambers, audience halls, and passages, most of which were secured behind locked doors, little danger existed of this hundred or so square feet being disturbed.

"Her name is Katerina Lew. Born to Romanian parents who fled the country when she was a teenager. Her father was a professor of law. She's highly educated with a degree from the University of Munich, and another from the Belgian National College. She returned to Romania in the late 1980s and was there when Ceauşescu was deposed. She's a proud revolutionary." He caught the touch of amusement that laced Ambrosi's voice. "She met Michener in Munich when they were both students. They had a love affair that lasted a couple of years."

"How do you know all this?"

"Michener and the pope have had other conversations."

Valendrea knew that while he perused only the most important tapes, Ambrosi savored everything. "You've never mentioned this before?"

"It seemed unimportant until the Holy Father showed interest in the tribunal."

"I might have underestimated Father Michener. He appears human, after all. A man with a past. Faults, too. I actually like this side of him. Tell me more."

"Katerina Lew has worked for a variety of European publications. She calls herself a journalist, but she's more of a freelance writer. She's had stints with *Der Spiegel, Herald Tribune,* and London *Times.* Doesn't stay long. Her slant is leftist politics and radical religion. Her articles are not flattering to organized worship. She's co-authored three books, two on the German Green party, one on the Catholic Church in France. None was a big seller. She's highly intelligent, but undisciplined."

Valendrea sensed what he really wanted to know. "Ambitious, too, I'd guess."

"She was married twice, after she and Michener split. Both brief. Her connection to Father Kealy was more her idea than his. She's been in America the past couple of years working. She appeared at his office one day and they've been together ever since."

Valendrea's interest was piqued. "Are they lovers?"

Ambrosi shrugged. "Hard to say. But she seems to like priests, so I would assume so."

Valendrea snapped the headphones back over his ears and switched on the recorder. Clement XV's voice filled his ears. *I'll have my letter to Father Tibor ready shortly. It will call for a written response, but if he desires to speak, listen to him, ask what you will, and tell me.* He slipped off the earphones. "What is that old fool up to? Sending Michener to find an eighty-year-old priest. What could possibly be served by that?"

"He's the only other person left alive, besides Clement, who has actually seen what is contained within the Riserva regarding the Fatima secrets. Father Tibor was given Sister Lucia's original text by John XXIII himself."

His stomach went hollow at the mention of Fatima. "Have you located Tibor?"

"I have an address in Romania."

"This requires close monitoring."

"I can see that. I'm wondering why."

He wasn't about to explain. Not until there was no choice. "I think some assistance in monitoring Michener could prove valuable."

Ambrosi grinned. "You believe Katerina Lew will help?"

He rolled the question over again in his mind, gauging his response to what he knew about Colin Michener, and what he now suspected about Katerina Lew. "We shall see, Paolo."

SEVEN

8:30 P.M.

MICHENER STOOD BEFORE THE HIGH ALTAR IN ST. PETER'S Basilica. The church was closed for the day, the silence disturbed only by maintenance crews polishing the acres of mosaic floor. He leaned against a thick balustrade and watched while workmen ran mops up and down marble stairs, whisking away the day's debris. The theological and artistic focal point of all Christendom lay just beneath him in St. Peter's grave. He turned and cocked his head upward toward Bernini's curlicued *baldacchino,* then stared skyward into Michelangelo's dome, which sheltered the altar, as one observer had noted, *like the cupped hands of God.*

He thought of the Vatican II council, imagining the nave surrounding him lined with tiered benches holding three thousand cardinals, priests, bishops, and theologians from nearly every religious denomination. In 1962 he was between his first Holy Communion and confirmation, a young boy attending Catholic school on the banks of the Savannah River in southeast Georgia. What was happening three thousand miles away in Rome meant nothing to him. Over the years he'd watched films of the council's opening session as John XXIII, hunched in the papal throne, pleaded with traditionalists and progressives to work in unison so *the earthly city may be brought to the resemblance of that heavenly city where truth reigns.* It had been an unprecedented move. A absolute monarch calling together subordinates to recommend how to change everything. For three years the delegates debated religious liberty, Judaism, the laity, marriage, culture, and the priesthood. In the end the Church was fundamentally altered. Some argued not enough, others thought too much.

A lot like his own life.

Though born in Ireland, he was raised in Georgia. His education started in America and finished in Europe. Despite his bicontinental upbringing, he was considered an American by the Italian-dominated Curia. Luckily, he fully understood the volatile atmosphere surrounding him. Within thirty days of arriving in the papal palace, he'd mastered the four basic rules of Vatican survival. *Rule one—never contemplate an original thought. Rule two—if for some reason an idea occurs, don't voice it. Rule three—absolutely never set a thought to paper. And rule four—under no circumstance sign anything you foolishly decided to write.*

He stared back out into the church, marveling at harmonious proportions that declared a near-perfect architectural balance. A hundred and thirty popes lay buried around him, and he'd hoped tonight to find some serenity among their tombs.

Yet his concerns about Clement continued to trouble him.

He reached into his cassock and removed two folded sheets of paper. All of his research on Fatima had centered on the Virgin's three messages, and those words seemed central to whatever was upsetting the pope. He unfolded and read Sister Lucia's account of the first secret:

> *Our Lady showed us a great sea of fire which seemed to be under the earth. Plunged into this fire were demons and souls in human form, like transparent burning embers, all blackened or burnished bronze. This vision lasted but an instant.*

The second secret was a direct result of the first:

You see Hell, where the souls of poor sinners go the Lady told us. To save them, God wishes to establish in the world the devotion to my Immaculate Heart. If they do what I will tell you, many souls will be saved, and there will be peace. The war is going to end. But if they do not stop offending God, another and worse one will begin in the reign of Pius XI. I come to ask for the consecration of Russia to my Immaculate Heart and the Communion of reparations on the First Saturdays. If my requests are heeded Russia will be converted and there will be peace, if not she will spread her errors throughout the world causing wars and persecutions of the Church. The good will be martyred, the Holy Father will have much to suffer, various nations will be annihilated. In the end my Immaculate Heart will triumph. The Holy Father will consecrate Russia to me and she shall be converted and a period of peace will be granted the world.

The third message was the most cryptic of all:

After the two parts which I have already explained, at the left of Our Lady and a little above, we saw an Angel with a flaming sword in his left hand, flashing. It gave out flames that looked as though they would set the world on fire, but they died out in contact with the splendor that Our Lady radiated towards him from her right hand. Pointing to the earth with his right hand, the Angel cried out in a loud voice: 'Penance, Penance, Penance!,' and we saw in an immense light that is God. Something similar to how people appear in a mirror when they pass in front of it. A bishop dressed in white, 'we had the impression that it was the Holy Father,' other bishops, priests, men and women Religious going up a steep mountain, at the top of which there was a big Cross of rough-hewn trunks as of a cork-tree with the bark. Before reaching there the Holy Father passed through a big city half in ruins and half trembling with halting step, afflicted with pain and sorrow. He prayed for the souls of the corpses he met on his way. Having reached the top of the mountain, on his knees at the foot of the big Cross he was killed by a group of soldiers who fired bullets and arrows at him, and in the same way there died one after another the other bishops, priests, men and women religious, and various lay people of different ranks and positions. Beneath the two arms of the Cross there were two Angels each with

a crystal aspersorium in his hand, in which they gathered up the blood of
the Martyrs and with it sprinkled the souls that were making their way
to God.

The sentences bore the cryptic mystery of a poem, the meanings
subtle and open to interpretation. Theologians, historians, and conspiratorialists had for decades postulated their own varied analyses.
So who knew anything for sure? Yet something was deeply troubling
Clement XV.

"Father Michener."

He turned.

One of the nuns who'd prepared his dinner was hustling toward
him. "Forgive me, but the Holy Father would like to see you."

Usually Michener dined with Clement, but tonight the pope
had eaten with a group of visiting Mexican bishops at the North
American College. He glanced at his watch. Clement was back early.
"Thank you, Sister. I'll head to the apartment."

"The pope is not there."

That was strange.

"He's in the L' Archivio Segreto Vaticano. The Riserva. He asked
that you join him there."

He concealed his surprise as he said, "All right. I'll head there
now."

He walked the empty corridors toward the archives. Clement's
presence again in the Riserva was a problem. He knew exactly what
the pope was doing. What he couldn't figure out was why. So he allowed his mind to wander, reviewing once more the phenomenon of
Fatima.

In 1917 the Virgin Mary revealed herself to three peasant children in a great hollow basin known as Cova da Iria, near the Portuguese village of Fatima. Jacinta and Francisco Marto were brother
and sister. She was seven and he was nine. Lucia dos Santos, their
first cousin, was ten. The mother of God appeared six times from

May to October, always on the thirteenth of the month, at the same place, at the same time. By the final apparition, thousands were present to witness the sun dancing across the sky, a sign from heaven that the visions were real.

It was more than a decade later that the Church sanctioned the apparitions as *worthy of assent*. But two of the young seers never lived to see that recognition. Jacinta and Francisco both died of influenza within thirty months of the Virgin's final appearance. Lucia, though, lived to be an old woman, having died only recently, after devoting her life to God as a cloistered nun. The Virgin even foretold those occurrences when She said, *I will take Jacinta and Francisco soon, but you, Lucia, shall remain here for a certain time. Jesus wishes to use you to make Me known and loved.*

It was during Her July visit that the Virgin told three secrets to the young seers. Lucia herself revealed the first two secrets in the years after the apparitions, even including them in her memoirs, published in the early 1940s. Only Jacinta and Lucia actually heard the Virgin convey the third secret. For some reason Francisco was excluded from a direct rendition, but Lucia was given permission to tell him. Though pressed hard by the local bishop to reveal the third secret, all of the children refused. Jacinta and Francisco took the information with them to their graves, though Francisco told an interviewer in October 1917 that the third secret "was for the good of souls and that many would be sad if they knew."

It remained for Lucia to be the keeper of the final message.

Though she was blessed with good health, in 1943 a recurring pleurisy seemed to spell the end. Her local bishop, a man named da Silva, asked her to write the third secret down and seal it in an envelope. She initially resisted, but in January 1944 the Virgin appeared to her at the convent in Tuy and told her that it was God's will that she now memorialize the final message.

Lucia wrote the secret and sealed it in an envelope. On being asked when the communication should be publicly divulged, she would only say, *in 1960*. The envelope was delivered to Bishop da Silva and placed inside a larger envelope, sealed with wax, and deposited in the diocese safe, where it remained for thirteen years.

In 1957 the Vatican requested all of Sister Lucia's writings be sent to Rome, including the third secret. On its arrival, Pope Pius XII placed the envelope containing the third secret inside a wooden box bearing the inscription SECRETUM SANCTI OFFICIO, Secret of the Holy Office. The box stayed on the pope's desk for two years and Pius XII never read its contents.

In August 1959 the box was finally opened and the double envelope, still sealed with wax, was delivered to Pope John XXIII. In February 1960 the Vatican issued a curt statement pronouncing that the third secret of Fatima would remain under seal. No other explanation was offered. By papal order, Sister Lucia's handwritten text was replaced in the wooden box and deposited in the Riserva. Each pope since John XXIII had ventured into the archives and opened the box, yet no pontiff ever publicly divulged the information.

Until John Paul II.

When an assassin's bullet nearly killed him in 1981, he concluded that a motherly hand had guided the bullet's path. Nineteen years later, in gratitude to the Virgin, he ordered the third secret revealed. To quell any debate, a forty-page dissertation accompanying the release interpreted the Virgin's complex metaphors. Also, photographs of Sister Lucia's actual writing were published. The press was fascinated for a while, then the matter faded.

Speculation ended.

Few even mentioned the subject any longer.

Only Clement XV remained obsessed.

Michener entered the archives and passed the night prefect, who gave him only a cursory nod. The cavernous reading room beyond was cast in shadows. A yellowish glow shone from the far side, where the Riserva's iron grille was swung open.

Maurice Cardinal Ngovi stood outside, his arms crossed beneath a scarlet cassock. He was a slim-hipped man with a face that carried the weather-beaten patina of a hard-fought life. His wiry hair was sparse and gray, and a pair of wire-framed glasses outlined eyes that offered a perpetual look of intense concern. Though only sixty-two, he was the archbishop of Nairobi, senior of the African cardinals. He was not a titular bishop, bestowed with an honorary diocese, but a working prelate who'd actively managed the largest Catholic population in the sub-Sahara region.

His day-to-day involvement with that diocese changed when Clement XV summoned him to Rome to oversee the Congregation for Catholic Education. Ngovi then became involved with every aspect of Catholic education, thrust to the forefront with bishops and priests, working closely to ensure that Catholic schools, universities, and seminaries conformed to the Holy See. In decades past his had been a confrontational post, one resented outside Italy, but Vatican II's spirit of renewal altered that hostility—as had men like Maurice Ngovi, who managed to soothe tension while ensuring conformity.

A spirited work ethic and an accommodating personality were two reasons Clement had appointed Ngovi. Another was a desire for more people to come to know this brilliant cardinal. Six months back, Clement had added another title—camerlengo. This meant Ngovi would administer the Holy See after Clement's death, during the two weeks until a canonical election. It was a caretaker function, mainly ceremonial, but nonetheless important since it assured Ngovi would be a key player in the next conclave.

Michener and Clement had several times discussed the next pope. The ideal man, if history was any teacher, would be a noncontroversial figure, multilingual, with curial experience—preferably the archbishop of a nation that was not a world power. After three fruitful years in Rome, Maurice Ngovi now possessed all of those traits, and the same question was being posed over and over by Third World cardinals. *Was it time for a pope of color?*

Michener approached the entrance of the Riserva. Inside,

Clement XV stood before an ancient safe that once bore witness to Napoleon's plunder. Its double iron doors were swung back, exposing bronze drawers and shelves. Clement had opened one of the drawers. A wooden box was visible. The pope clutched a piece of paper in his trembling hands. Michener knew Sister Lucia's original Fatima writing was still stored in that wooden box, but he also knew there was another sheet of paper there, too. An Italian translation of the original Portuguese message, created when John XXIII had first read the words in 1959. The priest who'd performed that task was a young recruit in the Secretariat of State.

Father Andrej Tibor.

Michener had read diaries from curial officials, on file in the archives, which revealed how Father Tibor had personally handed his translation to Pope John XXIII, who read the message, then ordered the wooden box sealed, along with the translation.

Now Clement XV wanted to find Father Andrej Tibor.

"This is disturbing," Michener whispered, his eyes still on the scene in the Riserva.

Cardinal Ngovi stood close but said nothing. Instead the African grasped him by the arm and led him away, toward a row of shelves. Ngovi was one of the few in the Vatican he and Clement trusted without question.

"What are you doing here?" he asked Ngovi.

"I was summoned."

"I thought Clement was at the North American College for the evening." He kept his voice hushed.

"He was, but he left abruptly. He called me half an hour ago and told me to meet him here."

"This is the third time in two weeks he's been in there. Surely people are noticing."

Ngovi nodded. "Thankfully, that safe contains a multitude of items. Hard to know for sure what he's doing."

"I'm worried about this, Maurice. He's acting strange." Only in private would he breach protocol and use first names.

"I agree. He dismisses all my inquiries with riddles."

"I've spent the last month researching every Marian apparition ever investigated. I've read account after account taken from witnesses and seers. I never realized there were so many earthly visits from heaven. He wants to know the details on each one, along with every word the Virgin uttered. But he will not tell me why. All he does is keep returning here." He shook his head. "It won't be long before Valendrea learns of this."

"He and Ambrosi are outside the Vatican tonight."

"Doesn't matter. He'll find out. I wonder sometimes if everybody here doesn't report to him."

The snap of a lid closing echoed from inside the Riserva, followed by the clank of a metal door. A moment later Clement appeared. "Father Tibor must be found."

Michener stepped forward. "I learned from the registry office of his exact location in Romania."

"When do you leave?"

"Tomorrow evening or the following morning, depending on the flights."

"I want this trip kept among the three of us. Take a holiday. Understand?"

He nodded. Clement's voice had never risen above a whisper. He was curious. "Why are we talking so low?"

"I was unaware that we were."

Michener detected irritation. As if he wasn't supposed to point that out.

"Colin, you and Maurice are the only men I trust implicitly. My dear friend the cardinal here cannot travel abroad without drawing attention—he's too famous now—too important. So you are the only one who can perform this task."

Michener motioned into the Riserva. "Why do you keep going in there?"

"The words draw me."

"His Holiness John Paul II revealed the third Fatima message to the world at the start of the new millennium," Ngovi said. "Beforehand, it was analyzed by a committee of priests and scholars. I served on that committee. The text was photographed and published worldwide."

Clement did not respond.

"Perhaps a counsel with the cardinals could help with whatever the problem may be?" Ngovi said.

"It is the cardinals I fear the most."

Michener asked, "And what could you hope to learn from an old man in Romania?"

"He sent me something that demands my attention."

"I don't recall anything coming from him," Michener said.

"It was in the diplomatic pouch. A sealed envelope from the nuncio in Bucharest. The sender said he'd translated the Virgin's message for Pope John."

"When?" Michener asked.

"Three months ago."

Michener noted that was just about the time Clement began visiting the Riserva.

"Now I know he spoke the truth, so I no longer desire for the nuncio to be involved. I need you to go to Romania and judge Father Tibor for yourself. Your opinion is important to me."

"Holy Father—"

Clement held up his hand. "I do not intend to be questioned on this matter any further." Anger laced the declaration, an unusual emotion for Clement.

"All right," Michener said. "I'll find Father Tibor, Holiness. Rest assured."

Clement glanced back into the Riserva. "My predecessors were so wrong."

"In what way, Jakob?" Ngovi asked.

Clement turned back, his eyes distant and sad. "In every way, Maurice."

EIGHT

9:45 P.M.

VALENDREA WAS ENJOYING HIS EVENING. HE AND FATHER AM-
brosi had left the Vatican two hours ago and rode in an official car to
La Marcello, one of his favorite bistros. Its veal heart with artichokes
was, without question, the best in Rome. The *ribollíta,* a Tuscan soup
made from beans, vegetables, and bread, reminded him of childhood. And the dessert of lemon sorbet in a decadent mandarin
sauce was enough to ensure that any first-timer would return. He'd
suppered there for years at his usual table toward the rear of the
building, the owner fully aware of his wine preference and his re-
quirement of absolute privacy.

"It is a lovely night," Ambrosi said.

The younger priest faced Valendrea in the rear of a stretched
Mercedes coupe that had ushered many diplomats around the Eternal City—even the president of the United States, who'd visited last
autumn. The rear passenger compartment was separated from the
driver by frosted glass. All of the exterior windows were tinted and
bulletproof, the sidewalls and undercarriage lined with steel.

"Yes, it is." He was puffing away on a cigarette, enjoying the
soothing feel of nicotine entering his bloodstream after a satisfying
meal. "What have we learned of Father Tibor?"

He'd taken to speaking in the first person plural, practice that he hoped would come in handy during the years ahead. Popes had spoken that way for centuries. John Paul II was the first to abandon the habit and Clement XV had officially decreed it dead. But if the present pope was determined to discard all the time-honored traditions, Valendrea would be equally determined to resurrect them.

During dinner he hadn't asked Ambrosi anything on the subject that weighed heavily on his mind, adhering to his rule of never discussing Vatican business anywhere but in the Vatican. He'd seen too many men brought down by careless tongues, several of whom he'd personally helped fall. But his car qualified as an extension of the Vatican, and Ambrosi daily ensured it was free of any listening devices.

A soft melody of Chopin spilled from the CD player. The music relaxed him, but also masked the conversation from any mobile eavesdropping devices.

"His name is Andrej Tibor," Ambrosi said. "He worked in the Vatican from 1959 to 1967. After, he was an unremarkable priest who served many congregations before retiring two decades ago. He lives now in Romania and receives a monthly pension check that's regularly cashed with his endorsement."

Valendrea savored a deep drag on his cigarette. "So the inquiry of this day is, what does Clement want with that aging priest?"

"Surely it concerns Fatima."

They'd just rounded Via Milazzo and were now speeding down Via Dei Fori Imperiali toward the Colosseum. He loved the way Rome clung to its past. He could easily envision emperors and popes enjoying the satisfaction of knowing that they could dominate something so spectacularly beautiful. One day he would savor that feeling as well. He was never going to be content with the scarlet biretta of a cardinal. He wanted to wear the *camauro*, reserved only for popes. Clement had rejected that old-style hat as anachronistic. But the red velvet cap trimmed in white fur would serve as one of many signs that the imperial papacy had returned. Western and Third World Catholics no longer would be allowed to dilute Latin dogma.

The Church had become far more concerned with accommodating the world than with defending its faith. Islam, Hinduism, Buddhism, and too many Protestant sects to count were cutting deeply into Catholic membership. And it was all the devil's work. The one true apostolic church was in trouble, but he knew what its corpus needed—a firm hand. One that ensured priests obeyed, members stayed, and income rebounded. One he was more than willing to provide.

He felt a touch to his knee and looked away from the window. "Eminence, it's just ahead," Ambrosi said, pointing.

He glanced back out the window as the car turned and a progression of cafés, bistros, and flashy discos streamed by. They were on one of the lesser streets, Via Frattina, the sidewalks packed with night revelers.

"She's staying in the hotel just ahead," Ambrosi said. "I located the information on her credentials application filed in the security office."

Ambrosi had been thorough, as usual. Valendrea was taking a chance visiting Katerina Lew unannounced, but he hoped the hectic night and the late hour would minimize any curious eyes. How to make actual contact was something he'd been considering. He didn't particularly want to parade up to her room. Nor did he want Ambrosi doing that. But then he saw none of that would be necessary.

"Perhaps God is watching over our mission," he said, gesturing to a woman strolling down the sidewalk toward an ivy-encased entrance for the hotel.

Ambrosi smiled. "Timing is everything."

The driver was instructed to speed past the hotel and ease alongside the woman. Valendrea pressed a button and the rear window descended.

"Ms. Lew. I am Cardinal Alberto Valendrea. Perhaps you recall me from the tribunal this morning?"

She ceased her casual stride and stood facing the window. Her body was supple and petite. But the way she carried herself, how she planted her feet and considered his inquiry, the way her shoulders squared and her neck arched, signaled something more substantial in her character than her size might indicate. There was a languorous trait about her, as if a prince of the Catholic Church—the secretary of state, no less—approached her every day. But Valendrea also sensed something else. Ambition. And that perception instantly relaxed him. This might be far easier than he'd first imagined.

"Do you think we might have a conversation? Here in the car?"

She threw him a smile. "How could I refuse such a gracious request from the Vatican secretary of state?"

He opened the door and slid across the leather seat to give her room. She climbed inside, unbuttoning her fleece-lined jacket. Ambrosi closed the door behind her. Valendrea noticed a hike in her skirt as she settled into the seat.

The Mercedes inched forward, stopping a little way down a narrow alley. The crowds had been left behind. The driver exited and walked back to the end of the street, where Valendrea knew he would make certain no cars entered.

"This is Father Paolo Ambrosi, my chief assistant in the Secretariat of State."

Katerina shook Ambrosi's offered hand. Valendrea noticed Ambrosi's eyes soften, enough to signal calm to their guest. Paolo knew exactly how to handle a situation.

Valendrea said, "We need to speak with you about an important matter we were hoping you might assist us on."

"I fail to see how I could possibly help someone of your stature, Eminence."

"You attended the tribunal hearing this morning. I assume Father Kealy requested your presence?"

"Is that what this is about? You concerned about bad press on what happened?"

He offered a self-deprecating expression. "With all the reporters that were present, I assure you bad press is not what this is about. Father Kealy's fate is sealed, as I'm sure you, he, and all the press realized. This is about something much more important than one heretic."

"Is what you're about to say for the record?"

He allowed himself a smile. "Always the journalist. No, Ms. Lew, none of this is for the record. Still interested?"

He waited as she silently weighed her options. This was the moment when ambition must defeat good judgment.

"Okay," she said. "Off the record. Go ahead."

He was pleased. So far, so good. "This is about Colin Michener."

Her eyes showed surprise.

"Yes, I'm aware of your relationship with the papal secretary. Quite a serious matter for a priest, especially one of his importance."

"That was a long time ago."

Her words carried the tone of denial. Perhaps now, he thought, she realized why he was so willing to trust her *off-the-record* assertion— this was about her, not him.

"Paolo witnessed your encounter with Michener this afternoon in the piazza. It was anything but cordial. *Bastard,* I believe, is what you called him."

She cast a glance at his acolyte. "I don't recall seeing him there."

"St. Peter's Square is a large place," Ambrosi said in a low voice.

Valendrea said, "You are perhaps thinking, how could he have heard that? You barely whispered. Paolo is an excellent lip-reader. A talent that comes in handy, wouldn't you say?" She seemed not to know how to respond, so he allowed her to linger a moment before saying, "Ms. Lew, I'm not trying to be threatening. Actually, Father Michener is about to embark on a journey for the pope. I need some assistance from you regarding that journey."

"What could I possibly do?"

"Someone must monitor where he goes and what he does. You would be the ideal person for that."

"And why would I do that?"

"Because there was a time when you cared for him. Perhaps even loved him. You might even still. Many priests like Father Michener have known women. It's the shame of our times. Men who care nothing about a vow to their God." He paused. "Or for the feelings of the women they might hurt. I sense that you would not want anything to harm Father Michener." He let the words take hold of her. "We believe there's a problem developing, one that could indeed harm him. Not physically, you understand, but it could hurt his standing within the Church. Perhaps jeopardize his career. I'm trying to keep that from happening. If I were to charge someone from the Vatican with this task, that fact would be known within a matter of hours and the mission would fail. I like Father Michener. I would not want to see his career hurt. I need the secrecy you can provide to protect him."

She motioned at Ambrosi. "Why not send the padre here?"

He was impressed with her spunk. "Father Ambrosi is too well known to accomplish the task. By a stroke of luck, the mission Father Michener has undertaken will take him to Romania, a place you know well. So you could appear without him asking too many questions. Assuming he even learned of your presence."

"And the purpose of this visit to my homeland?"

He waved off the question. "That would only taint your report. Instead, just observe. That way, we don't risk slanting your observations."

"In another words, you're not going to tell me."

"Precisely."

"And what would be the benefit of my doing this favor for you?"

He allowed a chuckle as he slid a cigar from a side pocket on the door. "Sadly, Clement XV will not last much longer. A conclave is approaching. When that happens, I can assure you that you will have a friend who will provide more than enough information to make your reports an important commodity in journalistic circles. Maybe enough to get you back to work with all those publishers who let you go."

"Am I supposed to be impressed that you know things about me?"

"I'm not trying to impress you, Ms. Lew, only secure your assistance in return for something any journalist would die for." He lit the cigar and savored a draw. He made no effort to crack the window before he exhaled a thick fog.

"This must be important to you," she said.

He noticed how she phrased the statement. Not *important to the Church*—*important to you*. He decided to add a dash of truth to their discussion. "Enough that I've come to the streets of Rome. I assure you, I will keep my end of the arrangement. The next conclave will be a monumental one, and you will have a reliable source of first-hand information."

She seemed to still be debating with herself. Maybe she'd thought Colin Michener was going to become the unnamed Vatican source she could quote to validate the stories she'd peddle. Here, though, was another opportunity. A lucrative offer. And all for such a simple task. He wasn't asking her to steal or lie or cheat. Just take a trip back home and watch an old boyfriend for a few days.

"Let me think about it," she finally said.

He sucked another lungful from the cigar. "I wouldn't take too long. This is going to happen fast. I'll phone at your hotel tomorrow, say two o'clock, for an answer."

"Assuming I say yes, how do I report what I find?"

He motioned to Ambrosi. "My assistant will contact you. Never attempt to call me. Understand? He'll find you."

Ambrosi folded his hands across the front of his black cassock and Valendrea allowed him the pleasure of the moment. He wanted Katerina Lew to know that this priest was not someone she wanted to defy, and Ambrosi's rigid pose communicated the message. He'd always liked that quality in Paolo. So reserved in public, so intense in private.

Valendrea reached beneath the seat and produced an envelope, which he handed across to his guest. "Ten thousand euros to help with airline tickets, hotel, whatever. If you decide to assist me, I would not expect you to fund the venture yourself. If you say no, keep the money for your trouble."

He stretched an arm across her and opened the door. "I have enjoyed our conversation, Ms. Lew."

She slipped out of the car, envelope in hand. He stared out into the night and said, "Your hotel is just back to the left on the main *via*. Have a nice evening."

She said nothing and walked away. He pulled the door shut and whispered, "So predictable. She wants us to wait. But there's no question what she'll do."

"It was almost too easy," Ambrosi said.

"Precisely why I want you in Romania. This woman bears watching, and she'll be easier to monitor than Michener. I've arranged with one of our corporate benefactors to have a private jet available. You leave in the morning. Since we already know where Michener is headed, get there first and wait. He should arrive by tomorrow evening, or the next day at the latest. Stay out of sight, but keep an eye on her and make sure she understands we want a return on our investment."

Ambrosi nodded.

The driver returned and climbed behind the wheel. Ambrosi tapped on the glass and the car backed toward the *via*.

Valendrea shifted his mood away from work.

"With all this intrigue over, perhaps a cognac and some Tchaikovsky before bed? Would you like that, Paolo?"

NINE

KATERINA ROLLED OFF FATHER TOM KEALY AND RELAXED. HE'D been waiting for her when she'd come upstairs and listened as she'd told him about her unexpected meeting with Cardinal Valendrea.

"That was nice, Katerina," Kealy said. "As usual."

She studied the outline of his face, illuminated by an amber glow spilling in through partially drawn drapes.

"I'm stripped of my collar in the morning, then laid that night. And by a most beautiful woman, no less."

"Kind of takes the edge off."

He chuckled. "You could say that."

Kealy knew all about her relationship with Colin Michener. It had actually felt good to empty her soul to someone she thought might understand. She'd made the first contact, prancing into Kealy's Virginia parish, wanting an interview. She was in the States working freelance for some periodicals interested in radical religious slants. She'd made a little money, enough to cover expenses, but she thought Kealy's story might be the ticket to something big.

Here was a priest at war with Rome on an issue that tugged at the hearts of Western Catholics. The North American Church was trying desperately to cling to members. Scandals concerning pedophile priests and child molestation had devastated the Church's reputation, and Rome's lackadaisical response had done nothing but complicate an already difficult situation. The bans on celibacy, homosexuality, and contraception only added to the popular disillusionment.

Kealy had asked her to dinner the first day, and it wasn't long before she was in his bed. He was a pleasure to spar with, both physically and mentally. His relationship with the woman that caused all the commotion had ended a year before. She'd tired of the attention and did not want to be the focus of a supposed religious revolution. Katerina had not taken her place, preferring to stay in the background, but she had recorded hours of interviews that, she hoped, would provide an excellent basis for a book. *The Case Against Priestly Celibacy* was her working title, and she envisioned a populist attack on a concept that Kealy said was as useful to the Church "as teats on a boar hog." The Church's final assault, Kealy's excommunication, would form the basis of the promotional scheme. *A priest defrocked for disagreeing with Rome lays out a case for the modern clergy.* Clearly, the concept had played before, but Kealy offered a new, daring, folksy voice. CNN was even talking about hiring him as a commentator for the next conclave, an insider who could provide a counter to the usual conservative opinions traditionally heard at papal election time. All in all, their relationship had been mutually beneficial. But that was before the Vatican secretary of state approached her.

"What about Valendrea? What do you think of his offer?" she asked.

"He's a pompous ass who could well be the next pope."

She'd heard the same prediction from others, which made Valendrea's offer all the more interesting. "He's interested in whatever it is Colin is doing."

Kealy rolled over and faced her. "I must admit I am, too. What could possibly concern the papal secretary in Romania?"

"As if nothing of interest lay there?"

"Touchy, aren't we?"

Though she never really considered herself a patriot, she was nonetheless Romanian and proud of the fact. Her parents had fled the country when she was a teenager, but later she had returned to help overthrow the despot Ceauşescu. She was in Bucharest when the dictator made his final speech in front of the central committee building. It was supposed to be a staged event, one to demonstrate workers' support for the communist government, but it turned into a riot. She could still hear the screams when pandemonium broke out and the police moved in with guns, as prerecorded applause and cheers boomed from loudspeakers.

"I know you may find this hard to believe," she said, "but actual revolt isn't donning makeup for a camera, or posting provocative words on the Internet, or even bedding a woman. Revolution means bloodshed."

"Times have changed, Katerina."

"You won't change the Church so easily."

"Did you see all that media there today? That hearing will be reported around the world. People will take issue with what happens to me."

"What if no one cares?"

"We receive more than twenty thousand hits a day on the website. That's a lot of attention. Words can have a powerful effect."

"So can bullets. I was there, those few days before Christmas, when Romanians died so that a dictator and his bitch of a wife could be shot dead."

"You would have pulled the trigger, if asked to, wouldn't you?"

"In a heartbeat. They ruined my homeland. Passion, Tom. That's what moves revolt. Deep, unabiding passion."

"So what do you plan to do with Valendrea?"

She sighed. "I have no choice. I have to do it."

He chuckled. "There are always choices. Let me guess, this opportunity might allow you another chance with Colin Michener?"

She'd come to realize that she'd told Tom Kealy far too much about herself. He'd assured her that he would never reveal anything, but she was concerned. Granted, Michener's lapse occurred long ago, but any revelation, whether true or false, would cost him his career. She'd never publicly acknowledge anything, no matter how much she hated the choice Michener had made.

She sat still for a few moments and stared up at the ceiling. Valendrea had said that a problem was developing that could harm Michener's career. So if she could help Michener, while at the same time helping herself, then why not?

"I'm going."

"You're entangling yourself with serpents," Kealy said in his good-humored tone. "But I think you're well qualified to wrestle with this devil. And Valendrea is that, let me tell you. He is one ambitious bastard."

"Which you are well qualified to identify." She couldn't resist.

His hand eased over to her bare leg. "Perhaps. Along with my abilities for other things."

His arrogance was amazing. Nothing seemed to faze him. Not the hearing this morning before solemn-faced prelates, and not the prospect of losing his collar. Perhaps it was his boldness that had initially attracted her? Regardless, Kealy was growing tiresome. She wondered if he'd ever cared about being a priest. One thing about Michener—his religious devotion was admirable. Tom Kealy's loyalty was only to the moment. Yet who was she to judge? She'd latched onto him for selfish reasons, ones he surely recognized and exploited. But all that could now change. She'd just talked with the Holy See's secretary of state. A man who'd sought her out for a task that could lead to so much more. And, yes, just as Valendrea said, it might just be enough to get her back to work with all those publishers who'd let her go.

A strange tingle surged through her.

The evening's unexpected events were working on her like an aphrodisiac. Delicious possibilities about her future swirled through her mind. And those possibilities made the sex she'd just enjoyed seem far more satisfying than the act warranted—and the attention she wanted now that much more enticing.

TEN

MICHENER PEERED DOWN THROUGH THE HELICOPTER'S WINdow at the city below. Turin lay wrapped in a wispy blanket as a bright morning sun fought to rid the air of fog. Beyond was the Piedmont, that region of Italy snuggled close to France and Switzerland, an abundant lowland plain walled in by Alpine summits, glaciers, and the sea.

Clement sat next to him, two security men opposite them. The pope had come north to bless the Holy Shroud of Turin before the relic was once again sealed away. This particular viewing had begun just after Easter and Clement should have been present for the unveiling. But a previously scheduled state visit to Spain had taken precedence. So it was decided he would come for the close of the exhibition, adding his veneration as popes had done for centuries.

The helicopter banked left and started a slow descent. Below, the Via Roma was packed with morning traffic, the Piazza San Carlo likewise congested. Turin was a manufacturing center, cars mainly, a company town in the European tradition, not unlike many Michener had known from childhood in the south of Georgia where the paper industry dominated.

The Duomo San Giovanni, its tall spires cloaked in mist, slipped into view. The cathedral, dedicated to St. John the Baptist, had stood since the fifteenth century. But it was not until the seventeenth century that the Holy Shroud was ensconced there for storage.

The helicopter's skids gently touched the damp pavement.

Michener unbuckled his seat belt as the rotors whined down. Not until the blades were perfectly still did the two security men slide open the cabin door.

"Shall we?" Clement asked.

The pope had said little on the journey from Rome. Clement could be like that when he traveled, and Michener was sensitive to the older man's quirks.

Michener stepped out into the piazza, followed by Clement. A huge crowd lined the perimeter. The air was brisk, but Clement had insisted on not wearing a jacket. He cast an impressive sight in his white simar, a pectoral cross dangling before his chest. And the papal photographer began snapping pictures that would be available to the press before the end of the day. The pope waved and the crowd returned his attention.

"We should not linger," Michener whispered to Clement.

Vatican security had been emphatic that the piazza was not secure. This was to be an in-and-out affair, as the security teams tagged it, the cathedral and chapel the only locations swept for explosives and manned since yesterday. Because this particular visit had been highly publicized and arranged long in advance, the less time in the open, the better.

"In a moment," Clement said, as he continued to acknowledge the people. "They've come to see their pontiff. Let them."

Popes had always freely traveled throughout the peninsula. It was a perk Italians enjoyed in return for their two-thousand-year parentage of the mother Church, so Clement took a moment and acknowledged the crowd.

Finally the pope made his way into the cathedral's alcove. Michener followed, intentionally dropping back to allow the local clergy an opportunity to be photographed with the Holy Father.

Gustavo Cardinal Bartolo waited inside. He wore a scarlet silk cassock with a matching sash that signified his senior status in the College of Cardinals. He was an impish man with white, lusterless hair and a heavy beard. Michener had often wondered if the appearance of a biblical prophet was intentional, since Bartolo's reputation was not one of intellectual brilliance or spiritual enlightenment, but more of a loyal errand boy. He had been appointed bishop of Turin by Clement's predecessor and elevated to the Sacred College, which made him prefect of the Holy Shroud.

Clement had allowed the appointment to stand even though Bartolo was also one of Alberto Valendrea's closest associates. Bartolo's vote in the next conclave was not in doubt, so Michener was amused when the pope walked straight to the cardinal and extended his right hand palm-down. Bartolo seemed to instantly realize what protocol entailed, and with priests and nuns watching, the cardinal had no choice but to accept the hand, kneel, and kiss the papal ring. Clement had, by and large, dispensed with the gesture. Usually in situations like this, inside closed doors and confined to Church officials, a handshake sufficed. The pope's insistence on strict protocol was a message the cardinal apparently understood, as Michener read a momentary glare of annoyance that the elder cleric was trying hard to suppress.

Clement seemed unconcerned with Bartolo's discomfort and immediately started to exchange pleasantries with the others present. After a few minutes of light conversation, Clement blessed the two dozen standing around, then led the entourage into the cathedral.

Michener lagged back and allowed the ceremony to proceed without him. His job was to be nearby, ready to assist, not to become part of the proceedings. He noticed that one of the local priests waited, too. He knew the short, balding cleric was Bartolo's assistant.

"Will the Holy Father still be staying for lunch?" the priest asked in Italian.

He did not like the brisk tone. It was respectful but carried a hint of irritation. Clearly, this priest's loyalties were not with an aging pope. Nor did the man feel the need to hide his animosity from an American monsignor who would surely be unemployed once the current Vicar of Christ died. This man carried visions of what *his* prelate could do for him, much like Michener two decades ago when a German bishop took a liking to a shy seminarian.

"The pope will be staying for lunch, assuming the schedule is maintained. We're actually a little ahead of time. Did you receive the menu preference?"

A slight nod of the head. "It is as requested."

Clement did not care for Italian cuisine, a fact the Vatican went to great lengths to keep quiet. The official line was that the pope's eating habits were a private matter, unrelated to his duties.

"Shall we go inside?" Michener asked.

Lately he'd found himself less inclined to banter on Church politics since he realized that his influence was waning in direct proportion to Clement's health.

He made his way into the cathedral and the irritating priest followed. Apparently this was his guardian angel for the day.

Clement stood at the intersection of the cathedral's nave, where a rectangular glass case hung suspended from the ceiling. Inside, illuminated by indirect light, was a pale, biscuit-colored linen about fourteen feet long. Upon it was the faint image of a man, lying flat, his front and back halves joined at the head, as if a corpse had been laid on top then covered from above. He was bearded with shaggy hair past the shoulders, his hands crossed modestly across his loins. Wounds were evident to the head and wrist. The chest was slashed, the back littered with scourge marks.

Whether the image was that of Christ remained solely a matter of faith. Personally, Michener found it difficult to accept that a piece of herringbone cloth could stay intact for two thousand years, and he thought the relic akin to what he'd been reading with great intensity over the past couple of months concerning Marian apparitions.

He'd studied the accounts of each supposed seer claiming a visit from heaven. Papal investigators found most to be a mistake, or a hallucination, or the manifestation of psychological problems. Some were simply hoaxes. But there were about two dozen incidents that, try as they might, investigators had been unable to discredit. In the end, no other rationalization was found except an earthly appearance by the Mother of God. Those were the apparitions deemed *worthy of assent.*

Like Fatima.

But similar to the shroud hanging before him, that *assent* came down to a matter of faith.

Clement prayed a full ten minutes before the shroud. Michener noted that they were falling behind schedule, but no one dared interrupt. The assembly stood in silence until the pope rose, crossed himself, and followed Cardinal Bartolo into a black marble chapel. The cardinal-prefect seemed anxious to show off the impressive space.

The tour took nearly half an hour, prolonged by Clement's questions and his insistence upon personally greeting all of the cathedral attendants. The timetable was now being strained, and Michener was relieved when Clement finally led the entourage into an adjacent building for lunch.

The pope stopped short of the dining room and turned to Bartolo. "Is there a place where I might have a moment with my secretary?"

The cardinal quickly located a windowless alcove that apparently served as a dressing chamber. After the door was closed, Clement reached into his cassock and withdrew a powder-blue envelope. Michener recognized the stationery the pope used for private communications. He'd bought the set in a Rome store and presented it to Clement last Christmas.

"This is the letter I wish you to take to Romania. If Father Tibor is incapable or unwilling to do as I have asked, destroy this and return to Rome."

He accepted the envelope. "I understand, Holy Father."

"The good Cardinal Bartolo is quite accommodating, isn't he?" A smile accompanied the pope's question.

"I doubt he accrued the three hundred indulgences granted for kissing the papal ring."

It had long been tradition that all who *devoutly* kissed the pope's ring would receive a gift of indulgences. Michener often wondered if the medieval popes who created the reward were concerned about forgiving sin or just making sure they were venerated with the appropriate zeal.

Clement chuckled. "I imagine the cardinal needs more than three hundred sins forgiven. He's one of Valendrea's closest allies. Bartolo might even replace Valendrea in the Secretariat of State, once the Tuscan secures the papacy. But the thought of that is frightening. Bartolo is barely qualified to be bishop of this cathedral."

This was apparently going to be a frank conversation, so Michener felt at ease to say, "You'll need all the friends you can get in the next conclave to ensure that doesn't happen."

Clement seemed to instantly understand. "You want that scarlet biretta, don't you?"

"You know I do."

The pope motioned to the envelope. "Handle this for me."

He wondered if his errand to Romania was somehow tied to a cardinal appointment, but quickly dismissed the thought. That was not Jakob Volkner's way. Nonetheless, the pope had been evasive, and it wasn't the first time. "You still won't tell me what troubles you?"

Clement moved toward the vestments. "Believe me, Colin, you don't want to know."

"Perhaps I can help."

"You never did tell me about your conversation with Katerina Lew. How was she after all those years?"

Another change of subject. "We spoke little. And what we did say was strained."

Clement's brow curled in curiosity. "Why did you allow that to happen?"

"She's headstrong. Her opinions of the Church are uncompromising."

"But who could blame her, Colin. She probably loved you, yet could do nothing about it. Losing to another woman is one thing, but to God . . . that can be hard to accept. Restrained love is not a pleasant matter."

He again wondered about Clement's interest in his personal life. "It doesn't make any difference anymore. She has her life and I have mine."

"But that doesn't mean you can't be friends. Share your lives in words and feelings. Experience the closeness that someone who genuinely cares can provide. Surely the Church doesn't forbid us that pleasure."

Loneliness was an occupational hazard for any priest. Michener had been lucky—when he'd faltered with Katerina, he'd had Volkner, who'd listened and granted him absolution. Ironically, that was the same thing Tom Kealy had done, for which he was to be excommunicated. Perhaps that was what drew Clement to Kealy?

The pope stepped to one of the racks and fingered the colorful vestments. "As a child in Bamberg, I served as altar boy. I remember that time fondly. It was after the war and we were rebuilding. Luckily, the cathedral survived. No bombs. I always thought that an appropriate metaphor. Even in the face of all that man can work, our town church survived."

Michener said nothing. Surely there was a point to all this. Why else would Clement delay everyone for this conversation, which could have waited?

"I loved that cathedral," Clement said. "It was a part of my youth. I can still hear the choir singing. Truly inspiring. I wish I could be buried there. But that's not possible, is it? Popes have to lie in St. Peter's. I wonder who fashioned that rule?"

Clement's voice was distant. Michener wondered who he was really talking to. He stepped close. "Jakob, tell me what's wrong."

Clement released his grip on the cloth and clenched his trembling hands before him. "You're very naïve, Colin. You simply do not understand. Nor can you." He talked through his teeth, hardly moving his mouth. The voice stayed flat, stripped of emotion. "Do you think for one moment we enjoy any measure of privacy? Don't you understand the depth of Valendrea's ambition? The Tuscan knows everything we do, everything we say. You want to be a cardinal? To achieve that you must grasp the measure of that responsibility. How can you expect me to elevate you when you fail to see what is so clear?"

Rarely in their association had they spoken cross words, but the pope was chastising him. And for what?

"We are merely men, Colin. Nothing more. I'm no more infallible than you. Yet we proclaim ourselves princes of the Church. Devout clerics concerned only with pleasing God, while we simply please ourselves. That fool, Bartolo, waiting outside, is a good example. His only concern is when I am going to die. His fortunes will surely shift then. As will yours."

"I hope you don't speak like this with anyone else."

Clement gently clasped the pectoral cross that hung before his chest. The gesture seemed to calm his tremors. "I worry about you, Colin. You're like a dolphin confined to an aquarium. All your life keepers made sure the water was clean, the food plentiful. Now they're about to return you to the ocean. Will you be able to survive?"

He resented Clement's talking down to him. "I know more than you might think."

"You have no idea the depth of a person like Alberto Valendrea. He is no man of God. There have been many popes like him— greedy and conceited, foolish men who think power is the answer to everything. I thought them part of our past. But I was wrong. You think you can do battle with Valendrea?" Clement shook his head. "No, Colin. You're no match for him. You're too decent. Too trusting."

"Why are you telling me this?"

"It needs to be said." Clement stepped close. They were now only inches apart, toe-to-toe. "Alberto Valendrea will be the ruin of this Church—if I and my predecessors have not already been. You ask me constantly what is wrong. You should not be as concerned with what troubles me as with doing what I ask. Is that clear?"

He was taken aback by Clement's bluntness. He was a forty-seven-year-old monsignor. The papal secretary. A devoted servant. Why was his old friend questioning both his loyalty and his ability? But he decided to argue no further. "It is perfectly clear, Holy Father."

"Maurice Ngovi is the closest thing to me you will ever have. Remember that in the days ahead." Clement stepped back and his mood seemed to shift. "When do you leave for Romania?"

"In the morning."

Clement nodded, then reached back into his cassock and withdrew another powder-blue envelope. "Excellent. Now, would you mail this for me, please?"

He accepted the packet and noticed it was addressed to Irma Rahn. She and Clement were childhood friends. She still lived in Bamberg, and they'd maintained a steady correspondence for years. "I'll take care of it."

"From here."

"Excuse me?"

"Mail the letter from here. In Turin. You personally, please. No delegation to others."

He always mailed the pope's letters personally, and had never needed a reminder before. But again he decided not to question.

"Of course, Holy Father. I'll mail it from here. Personally."

ELEVEN

VALENDREA STEPPED DIRECTLY TOWARD THE OFFICE OF THE archivist for the Holy Roman Church. The cardinal in charge of L'Archivio Segreto Vaticano was not one of his allies, but he hoped the man was perceptive enough not to cross someone who might soon be pope. All appointments ended at a papal death. Continued service was dependent solely on what the next Vicar of Christ decided, and Valendrea well knew that the present archivist wanted to keep his position.

He found the man behind his desk, busy at work. He calmly entered the sprawling office and closed a set of bronze doors behind him.

The cardinal glanced up, but said nothing. The man was nearing seventy and possessed brooding cheeks and a high, sloping forehead. A Spaniard by birth, he'd worked in Rome all his clerical life.

The Sacred College was divided into three categories. Cardinal-bishops who headed the sees of Rome, cardinal-priests who were heads of dioceses outside Rome, and cardinal-deacons who were full-time Curia officials. The archivist was the senior of the cardinal-deacons and, as such, was granted the honor of announcing from the balcony of St. Peter's the name of any newly elected pope. Valendrea was not concerned with that hollow privilege. Instead, what made this old man important was his influence over a handful of cardinal-deacons still wavering in their preconclave support.

He stepped toward the desk and noticed his host did not rise and greet him. "It isn't that bad," he said in response to a look he was receiving.

"I'm not so sure. I assume the pontiff is still in Turin?"

"Why else would I be here?"

The archivist let out an audible sigh.

"I want you to open the Riserva, along with the safe," Valendrea said.

The old man finally stood. "I must refuse."

"That would be unwise." He hoped the man understood the message.

"Your threats cannot countermand a direct papal order. Only the pope can enter the Riserva. No one else. Not even you."

"No one needs to know. I won't be long."

"My oath to this office and the Church means more to me than you seem to assume."

"Listen to me, old man. I'm on a mission of greatest importance to the Church. One that demands extraordinary action." It was a lie, but it sounded good.

"Then you wouldn't mind if the Holy Father granted permission to allow access. I could place a call to Turin."

Time for the moment of truth. "I have a sworn statement from your niece. She was more than happy to provide it. She swears before the Almighty that you forgave her daughter's sin in aborting her baby. How is that possible, Eminence? That's heresy."

"I'm aware of the sworn statements. Your Father Ambrosi was quite persuasive with my sister's family. I absolved the woman because she was dying and fearful of spending an eternity in hell. I comforted her with the grace of God, as a priest should."

"My God—your God—does not condone abortion. That's murder. You had no right to forgive her. A point I'm sure the Holy Father would have no choice but to agree with."

He could see that the old man was fortified in the face of his dilemma, but he also noticed a tremor that shook the left eye— perhaps the precise spot where fear was making its escape.

The cardinal-archivist's bravado did not impress Valendrea. The man's entire life had been spent shoving paper from one file to another, enforcing meaningless rules, throwing roadblocks before anyone bold enough to challenge the Holy See. He followed a long line of *scrittori* who'd made it their life's labor to ensure that the papal archives remained secure. Once they perched themselves on a black throne, their physical presence in the archives served as a warning that permission to enter was not a license to browse. As with an archaeological dig, any revelations from those shelves came only after a meticulous plunge into their depths. And that took time—a commodity the Church had only in the past few decades been willing to grant. The sole task, Valendrea realized, of men like the cardinal-archivist was to protect the mother Church, even from its princes.

"Do as you wish, Alberto. Tell the world what I did. But I'm not allowing you into the Riserva. To get there you will have to be pope. And that is not a given."

Perhaps he'd underestimated this paper pusher. There was more brick to his foundation than the veneer showed. He decided to let the matter rest. At least for now. He might need this man in the coming months.

He turned and stepped toward the double doors. "I'll wait until I'm pope to speak with you again." He stopped and glanced back. "Then we'll see if you're as loyal to me as you are to others."

TWELVE

KATERINA HAD BEEN WAITING IN HER HOTEL ROOM SINCE A little past lunch. Cardinal Valendrea said he would call at two P.M., but he hadn't kept his word. Perhaps he thought ten thousand euros was enough to ensure that she would wait by the phone. Maybe he believed her former relationship with Colin Michener enough incentive to guarantee that she'd do as he asked. Regardless, she didn't like the fact that the cardinal had apparently concluded himself clever in reading her.

True, she was almost out of the money accumulated from freelancing in the United States and tired of sponging off Tom Kealy, who seemed to enjoy that she was dependent on him. He'd done well with his three books, and soon he was going to be doing even better. He liked that he was America's newest religious personality. He was addicted to the attention, which was understandable to a point, but she knew sides of Tom Kealy that his followers never saw. Emotions could not be posted on a website or slipped into a publicity memo. The truly skilled could convey them in words, but Kealy was not a good writer. All three of his books were ghostwritten—one of those *things* only she and his publisher knew, and not something Kealy would want revealed. The man was simply not real. Just an illusion that a few million people—himself among them—had accepted.

So different from Michener.

She hated being bitter yesterday. She'd told herself before arriving in Rome that if their paths crossed, she should watch what she said. After all, a lot of time had passed—they'd both moved on. But when she saw him in the tribunal she realized that he'd left an indelible mark on her emotions, one she was afraid to admit existed, one that churned resentment with the speed of a nuclear reaction.

Last night, while Kealy slept beside her, she'd wondered if her own tortuous path over the past dozen years was nothing but a prelude to this moment. Her career was anything but a success, her personal life dismal, yet here she was waiting for the second most powerful man in the Catholic Church to call and give her a chance to deceive someone she still cared a great deal about.

Earlier, she'd made a few inquiries to contacts in the Italian press and learned that Valendrea was a complex man. He was born to money in one of Italy's oldest patrician families. At least two popes and five cardinals were in his bloodline, and uncles and brothers were involved in either Italian politics or international business. The Valendrea clan was also heavily entrenched in the European arts, and owned palaces and grand estates. They'd been careful with Mussolini and even more so with the revolving-door Italian regimes that followed. Their industry and money had been, and still were, courted, and they were choosy about who and what they supported.

The Vatican's *Annuario Pontifico* noted that Valendrea was sixty years old and held degrees from the University of Florence, the Catholic University of the Sacred Heart, and the Hague Academy of International Law. He was the author of fourteen treatises. His lifestyle required well more than the three thousand euros a month the Church paid its princes. And though the Vatican frowned on cardinals being involved in secular activities, Valendrea was noted as a stockholder in several Italian conglomerates and served on many boards of directors. His relative youth was deemed an asset, as were his innate political abilities and dominating personality. He'd used his post as secretary of state wisely, becoming well known in the Western media. He was a man who recognized the propensities of modern communication and the need to convey a consistent public image. He was also a theological hard-liner who openly opposed Vatican II, a fact made clear during Kealy's tribunal, and was one of the strict traditionalists who felt the Church was best served as it was once served.

Nearly all of the people she'd spoken with concurred that Valendrea was the front-runner to succeed Clement. Not necessarily because he was ideal for the job, but because there was no one strong enough to challenge him. By all accounts he was poised and ready for the next conclave.

But he'd also been a front-runner three years ago and lost.

The phone jarred her from her thoughts.

Her gaze darted to the receiver and she fought the urge to answer, preferring to let Valendrea, if indeed the caller was him, sweat a little.

After the sixth ring she lifted the handset.

"Making me wait?" Valendrea said.

"No more than I've been."

A chuckle came through the earpiece. "I like you, Ms. Lew. You have personality. So tell me, what is your decision?"

"As if you have to ask."

"I thought I'd be courteous."

"You don't impress me as someone who cares about such details."

"You don't have much respect for a cardinal of the Catholic Church."

"You put your clothes on every morning like everybody else."

"I sense you're not a religious woman."

It was her time to laugh. "Don't tell me you actually convert souls in between politicking."

"I really did choose wisely in you. You and I will get along well."

"What makes you think I'm not taping all this?"

"And miss the opportunity of a lifetime? I seriously doubt that. Not to mention a chance to be with the good Father Michener. All at my expense, no less. Who could ask for more?"

His irritating attitude wasn't much different from Tom Kealy's. She wondered what it was about her that attracted such cocksure personalities. "When do I leave?"

"The papal secretary flies out tomorrow morning, arriving in Bucharest by lunch. I thought you might leave this evening and stay ahead of him."

"And where am I to go?"

"Father Michener is going to see a priest named Andrej Tibor. He's retired and works at an orphanage about forty miles to the north of Bucharest, in the village of Zlatna. Perhaps you know the place?"

"I know of it."

"Then you'll have no trouble learning what Michener does and says while there. Also, Michener is carrying some sort of papal letter. Getting a look at its contents would further increase your stock in my eyes."

"You don't want much, do you?"

"You are a resourceful woman. I suggest using those same charms Tom Kealy apparently enjoys. Surely then your mission will be a complete success."

And the line went dead.

THIRTEEN

VALENDREA STOOD AT THE WINDOW IN HIS THIRD-FLOOR office. Outside, the tall cedars, stone pines, and cypresses in the Vatican gardens stubbornly clung to summer. Since the thirteenth century popes had strolled the brick paths lined with laurel and myrtle, finding comfort in the classical sculptures, busts, and bronze reliefs.

He recalled a time when he'd enjoyed the gardens. Fresh from the seminary, posted to the only place in the world where he wanted to serve. Then, the walkways were filled with young priests wondering about their future. He came from an era when Italians dominated the papacy. But Vatican II changed all that, and Clement XV was retreating even farther. Every day another list of orders shuffling priests, bishops, and cardinals filtered down from the fourth floor. More Westerners, Africans, and Asians were being summoned to Rome. He'd tried to delay any implementation, hoping Clement would finally die, but eventually he'd had no choice but comply with every instruction.

The Italians were already outnumbered in the College of Cardinals, Paul VI perhaps the last of their breed. Valendrea had known the cardinal of Milan, fortunate to be in Rome for the last few years of Paul's pontificate. By 1983 Valendrea was an archbishop. John

Paul II finally bestowed him his red biretta, surely a way for the Pole to endear himself with the locals.

But maybe it was something more?

Valendrea's conservative lean was legendary, as was his reputation as a diligent worker. John Paul appointed him prefect over the Congregation for the Evangelization of Peoples. There, he'd coordinated worldwide missionary activities, supervised the building of churches, delineated diocese boundaries, and educated catechists and clergy. The job had involved him in every aspect of the Church and allowed him to quietly build a power base among men who might one day be cardinals. He never forgot what his father had taught him. *A favor offered is a favor returned.*

How true.

Like real soon.

He turned from the window.

Ambrosi had already left for Romania. He missed Paolo when he was gone. He was the only person whom Valendrea felt entirely comfortable with. Ambrosi seemed to understand his nature. And his drive. There was so much to do at just the right time, in just the right proportions, and the chances of failure were far greater than those of success.

There were simply not many opportunities to become pope. He'd participated in one conclave and a second was perhaps not far away. If he failed to achieve election this time, unless a sudden papal death occurred, the next pope could well reign beyond his time. His ability to be a part of the process officially ended at age eighty, a point he still wished Paul hadn't conceded, and no amount of tapes loaded with secrets would change that reality.

He stared across his office at a portrait of Clement XV. Protocol demanded the irritating thing be there, but his choice would have been a photograph of Paul VI. Italian by birth, Roman by nature, Latin in character. Paul had been brilliant, bending only on small points, compromising just enough to satisfy the pundits. That was how he, too, would run the Church. Give a little, keep more. Ever since yesterday, he'd been thinking about Paul. What had Ambrosi said about Father Tibor? *He's the only person left alive, besides Clement, who has actually seen what is contained within the Riserva regarding the Fatima secrets.*

Not true.

His mind drifted back to 1978.

"Come, Alberto. Follow me."

Paul VI rose and tested the pressure on his right knee. The aging pontiff had suffered much over the past few years. He'd endured bronchitis, influenza, bladder problems, kidney failure, and had his prostate removed. Massive doses of antibiotics had warded off infections, but the drugs were weakening his immune system, sapping strength. His arthritis seemed particularly painful and Valendrea felt for the old man. The end was coming, but with an agonizing slowness.

The pope shuffled out of the apartment toward the fourth floor's private eleva-tor. It was late evening, a stormy May night, and the Apostolic Palace was quiet. Paul waved off the security men, saying he and his first assistant secretary would return shortly. His two papal secretaries need not be called.

Sister Giacomina appeared from her room. She was in charge of the domestic retinue and served as Paul's nurse. The Church had long decreed that women who worked in clerical households must be of canonical age. Valendrea thought the rule amusing. In other words, they must be old and ugly.

"Where are you going, Holy Father?" the nun asked, as if he were a child leav-ing his room without permission.

"Do not worry, Sister. I have business to handle."

"You should be resting. You know that."

"I will return shortly. But I feel fine and need to attend to this matter. Father Valendrea will take good care of me."

"No more than half an hour. Clear?"

Paul smiled. "I promise. Half an hour and I'll be off my feet."

The nun retreated to her room and they headed onto the elevator. On the ground floor, Paul inched ahead through a series of corridors to the entrance for the archives.

"I have delayed something for many years, Alberto. I think tonight is the time to remedy that."

Paul continued along with the help of his cane and Valendrea shortened his stride to keep pace. He was saddened by the sight of this once great man. Giovanni Battista Montini was the son of a successful Italian lawyer. He'd worked his way up through the Curia, ultimately serving in the Secretariat of State. After, he became the archbishop of Milan and governed that diocese with an efficient hand, catching the eye of the Italian-dominated Sacred College as the natural choice to succeed the beloved John XXIII. He'd been an excellent pope, serving at a difficult time after Vatican II. The Church would sorely miss him, and so would Valendrea. Of late, he'd been fortunate to spend time with Paul. The old warrior seemed to enjoy his company. There was even talk of a possible elevation to bishop, something he hoped Paul saw the grace to extend before God summoned him.

They entered the archives and the prefect knelt at Paul's appearance. "What brings you, Holy Father?"

"Please open the Riserva."

He liked the way Paul answered a question with a command. The prefect scurried for a set of oversized keys, then led the way into the darkened archives. Paul slowly followed, and they arrived as the prefect completed opening an iron grille and switching on a series of dull incandescent lights. Valendrea knew of the Riserva and of the rule that required papal authority for entry. It was the sacred reserve of the Vicars of Christ. Only Napoleon had violated its sanctity, paying for that insult in the end.

Paul entered the windowless room and pointed to a black safe. "Open that."

The prefect complied, spinning the dials and releasing tumblers. The double doors swung open. Not one sound leaked from the brass hinges.

The pope sat in one of three chairs.

"That will be all," Paul said, and the prefect left.

"My predecessor was the first to read the third secret of Fatima. I am told that afterward he ordered it sealed in this safe. I have resisted the urge to come here for fifteen years."

Valendrea was a little confused. "Did not the Vatican in '67 issue a statement that the secret would remain sealed? That was done without you reading it?"

"There are many things the Curia does in my name of which I have little knowledge. I was told, though, about that one. After."

Valendrea wondered if he might have stumbled with his question. He cautioned himself to watch his words.

STEVE BERRY / 90

"The whole affair amazes me," Paul said. "The mother of God appears to three peasant children—not to a priest, or a bishop, or the pope. She chooses three illiterate children. She seems to always choose the meek. Perhaps heaven is trying to tell us something?"

Valendrea knew all about how Sister Lucia's message from the Virgin had made its way from Portugal to the Vatican.

"I never thought the good sister's words something that commanded my attention," Paul said. "I met Lucia in Fatima, when I went in '67. I was criticized for going. The progressives said I was setting back the progress of Vatican II. Putting too much emphasis on the supernatural. Venerating Mary above Christ and the Lord. But I knew better."

He noticed a fiery light in Paul's eyes. There might still be some fight left in this old warrior.

"I knew young people loved Mary. They felt a pull from the sanctuaries. My going there was important to them. It showed that their pope cared. And I was right, Alberto. Mary is more popular today than ever."

He knew Paul loved the Madonna, making a point throughout his pontificate to venerate her with titles and attention. Perhaps too many, some said.

Paul motioned to the safe. "The fourth drawer on the left, Alberto. Open it and bring me what is inside."

He did as Paul instructed, sliding out a heavy iron drawer. A small wooden box rested inside, a wax seal affixed to the outside bearing the papal crest of John XXIII. On top was a label that read SECRETUM SANCTI OFFICIO, Secret of the Holy Office. He carried the box to Paul, who studied the outside with trembling hands.

"It is said Pius XII placed the label on top and John himself ordered that seal. Now it is my turn to look inside. Could you crack the wax please, Alberto."

He glanced around for a tool. Finding nothing, he wedged one of the corners of the safe's doors into the wax and cracked it away. He handed the box back to Paul.

"Clever," the pope said.

He accepted the compliment with a nod.

Paul balanced the box in his lap and found a set of reading glasses in his cassock. He slipped the stems over his ears, hinged open the lid, and lifted out two packets of paper. He set one aside and unfolded the other. Valendrea saw a newer white sheet encased by a clearly older piece of paper. Both contained writing.

The pontiff studied the older page.

"This is the original note Sister Lucia wrote in Portuguese," Paul said. "Unfortunately, I cannot read that language."

"Neither can I, Holy Father."

Paul handed him the sheet. He saw that the text spanned about twenty or so lines written in black ink that had faded to gray. It was exciting to think that only Sister Lucia, a recognized seer of the Virgin Mary, and Pope John XXIII had touched that paper before him.

Paul motioned with the newer white page. "This is the translation."

"Translation, Holy Father?"

"John could not read Portuguese, either. He had the message translated to Italian."

Valendrea had not known that. So add a third set of fingerprints—some curial official called in to translate, surely sworn to secrecy afterward, probably dead by now.

Paul unfolded the second sheet and started to read. A curious look came to the pope's face. "I was never good at riddles."

The pope reassembled the packet, then reached for the second set. "It appears the message carried to another page." Paul unfolded the sheets. Again, one page newer, the other clearly older. "Portuguese, again." Paul glanced at the newer sheet. "Ah, Italian. Another translation."

He watched as Paul read the words with an expression that shifted from confusion to a look of deep concern. The pope's breaths came shallow, his eyebrows creased together, and the brow furrowed as he again scanned the translation.

The pope said nothing. Neither did Valendrea. He dared not ask to read the words.

The pope read the message a third time.

Paul's tongue wet his cracked lips and he shifted in the chair. A look of astonishment flooded the old man's features. For an instant, Valendrea was frightened. Here was the first pope to travel around the globe. A man who'd stared down an army of Church progressives and tempered their revolution with moderation. He'd stood before the United Nations and pronounced, "Never again war." He'd denounced birth control as a sin and held fast even in a firestorm of protest that shook the Church's very foundation. He'd reaffirmed the tradition of priestly celibacy and *excommunicated dissenters. He'd dodged an assassin in the Philippines, then defied terrorists and presided at the funeral of his friend, the prime minister of Italy. This was a determined vicar, not easily shaken. Yet something in the lines he'd just read affected him.*

Paul reassembled the packet, then dropped both bundles into the wooden box and slammed the lid.

"Put it back," the pope muttered, eyes down at his lap. Bits of the crimson wax dotted the white cassock. Paul brushed them away, as if they were a disease. "This was a mistake. I should not have come." Then the pope seemed to steel himself. Composure returned. "When we return upstairs, compile an order. I want you to personally reseal that box. Then there is to be no further entry on pain of excommunication. No exceptions."

But that order would not apply to the pope, Valendrea thought. Clement XV could come and go in the Riserva as he pleased.

And the German had done just that.

Valendrea had long known of the Italian translation of Sister Lucia's writing, but not until yesterday had he known the name of the translator.

Father Andrej Tibor.

Three questions racked his brain.

What kept summoning Clement XV into the Riserva? Why did the pope want to communicate with Tibor? And, most importantly, what did that translator know?

Right now, he possessed not a single response.

Perhaps, though, over the next few days, among Colin Michener, Katerina Lew, and Ambrosi, he would learn the answers to all three inquiries.

PART TWO

FOURTEEN

MICHENER DESCENDED A SET OF METAL STEPS TO AN OILY TAR-
mac at Otopeni Airport. The British Airways shuttle he'd arrived on
from Rome had been half full, and was one of only four airliners uti-
lizing the terminal.

He'd visited Romania once before, while working in the Secretariat of State under then-Cardinal Volkner, assigned to the section
for Relations with States, that portion of the International direc-
torate charged with diplomatic activities.

The Vatican and Romanian churches had clashed for decades
over a post–World War II transfer of Catholic property to the Orthodox Church, which included monasteries possessed of an
ancient Latin tradition. Religious freedom returned with the fall of
the communists, but the ownership debate lingered and several
times Catholics and Orthodox had violently clashed. John Paul II
started a dialogue with the Romanian government after Ceauşescu
was toppled, and even made an official visit. Progress was slow.
Michener himself was involved in some later negotiations. Recently
there'd been some movement from the centralist government. Close
to two million Catholics compared with twenty-two million Ortho-

dox filled the country, and their voices were beginning to be heard. Clement had made clear that he wanted to visit, but the ownership dispute marred any talk of a papal trip.

The whole affair was just more of the complicated politics that seemed to consume Michener's days. He really wasn't a priest anymore. He was a government minister, diplomat, and personal confidant—all of which would end with Clement's last breath. Maybe then he could go back to being a priest. He'd never really served a congregation. Some missionary work might be a challenge. Cardinal Ngovi had spoken to him about Kenya. Africa could be an excellent refuge for an ex–papal secretary, especially if Clement died before making him a cardinal.

He flushed the uncertainties about his life away as he stepped toward the terminal. He could tell that he'd risen in altitude. The sullen air was cold—in the upper forties, the pilot had explained just before they'd touched down. The sky was smeared with a thick swirl of low-level clouds that denied sunlight any opportunity of finding earth.

He entered the building and headed for passport control. He'd packed light, only a shoulder bag, expecting to be gone no more than a day or two, and had dressed casually in jeans, a sweater, and jacket, honoring Clement's request for discretion.

His Vatican passport gained entrance into the country without the customary visa fee. He then rented a battered Ford Fiesta from the Eurodollar counter just outside customs and learned directions to Zlatna from an attendant. His grasp of the language was good enough that he understood most of what the red-haired man told him.

He wasn't particularly thrilled with the prospect of driving around one of the poorest countries in Europe alone. Research last evening had revealed several official advisories that warned of thieves and urged caution, especially at night and in the countryside. He would have preferred enlisting the help of the papal nuncio in Bucharest. One of the staff could serve as driver and guide, but

Clement had nixed that idea. So he climbed into the rental car and made his way out of the airport, eventually finding the highway and speeding northwest toward Zlatna.

KATERINA STOOD ON THE WEST SIDE OF THE TOWN SQUARE, the cobbles grossly misshapen, many missing, even more crumbling to gravel. People scampered back and forth, their concerns surely more vital—food, heat, water. Dilapidated pavement the least of their everyday worries.

She'd arrived in Zlatna two hours ago and spent an hour gathering what information she could about Father Andrej Tibor. She was careful with her inquiries, since Romanians were intensely curious if nothing else. According to the information Valendrea had provided, Michener's flight touched down a little after eleven A.M. It would take him a good two hours to drive the ninety miles north from Bucharest. Her watch read one twenty P.M. So assuming his flight was on time, he should be arriving shortly.

It felt both strange and comforting to be back home. She was born and raised in Bucharest, but spent a lot of her childhood beyond the Carpathian Mountains, deep in Transylvania. She knew the region not as some novelized haunt of vampires and werewolves, but as Erdély, a place of rich forests, citadel castles, and hearty people. The culture was a mixture of Hungary and Germany, spiced with Gypsy. Her father had been a descendant of the Saxon colonists brought there in the twelfth century to guard the mountain passes from invading Tartars. The descendants of that European stock had withstood a parade of Hungarian despots and Romanian monarchs, only to be slaughtered by the communists after World War II.

Her mother's parents were Ţigani, Gypsy, and the communists were anything but kind to them, orchestrating a collective hatred as

Hitler had done with Jews. Seeing Zlatna, with its wooden houses, carved verandas, and Mughal-style train station, she was reminded of her grandparents' village. Where Zlatna had escaped the region's earthquakes and survived Ceaușescu's systemization, her grand-parent's home had not. Like two-thirds of the country's villages, theirs was ritualistically destroyed, the residents consigned to drab communal apartment buildings. Her mother's parents had even faced the shameful disgrace of having to demolish their own home. *A way to combine peasant experience with Marxist efficiency,* the plan was billed. And, sadly, few Romanians mourned the passing of Gypsy villages. She recalled visiting her grandparents afterward in their soulless apartment, the dingy gray rooms devoid of their ancestors' warming spirits, the essential life drained from their souls. Which was the whole idea. It was later called *ethnic cleansing* in Bosnia. Ceaușescu like to say it was a move toward *progressive living.* She called it madness. And the sights and sounds of Zlatna resurrected all those ugly memories.

From a shopkeeper, she learned that three state orphanages were located nearby. The one where Father Tibor worked was re-garded as the worst. The compound sat west of town and harbored terminally ill children—another of Ceaușescu's insanities.

Boldly, the dictator outlawed contraception and proclaimed that women under the age of forty-five must birth at least five offspring. The result was a nation with more children than their parents could ever feed. The abandoning of infants on the street became com-monplace. AIDS, tuberculosis, hepatitis, and syphilis exacted severe tolls. Eventually orphanages sprang up everywhere, all of them little more than dumping spots, the task of caring for the unwanted left to strangers.

She'd also learned that Tibor was a Bulgarian who was nearing eighty—or maybe older, no one really knew for sure—and he was known as a pious man who'd given up retirement to work with chil-dren who would soon meet their God. She wondered about the courage it took to comfort a dying infant, or tell a ten-year-old he would soon go to a place far better than here. She didn't believe any of that. She was an atheist and always had been. Religion was created by man—as was God himself. Politics, not faith, explained everything for her. How better to regulate the masses than by terrifying them with the wrath of an omnipotent being. Better to trust yourself, believe in your own abilities, make your own luck in the world. Prayer was for the weak and the lazy. Not something she'd ever needed.

She glanced at her watch. A little past one thirty.

Time to make her way to the orphanage.

So she headed off across the plaza. What to do once Michener arrived she'd yet to determine.

But she'd think of something.

MICHENER SLOWED THE CAR AS HE APPROACHED THE ORPHAN-age. Part of the drive from Bucharest had been on the autostrada, the four-laned roadway surprisingly well maintained, but the secondary road he'd taken earlier was vastly different, the shoulder ragged, its surface potholed like a moonscape and dotted with confusing signposts that had twice taken him out of his way. He'd crossed the River Olt a few miles back, traversing a scenic gorge between two forested ranges. As he'd driven north the topography had changed from farmland to foothills to mountains. Along the way, he'd seen black snakes of factory smoke curling up on the horizon.

He'd learned about Father Tibor from a butcher in Zlatna, who told him where the priest could be found. The orphanage occupied a red-tiled, two-story building. The pits and scars in its terra-cotta roof bore witness to the bitter sulfur air that stung Michener's throat. The windows were iron-barred, most of the panes taped their length. Many were whitewashed, and he wondered if it was to prevent people from looking in or looking out.

He motored inside the walled compound and parked.

The hard ground was carpeted with thick weeds. A rusty slide and swing sat to one side. A stream of something black and sludgy bordered the far wall and may have been the source of the foul odor that greeted his nostrils as he stepped from the car. From the building's front door, a nun dressed in a brown ankle-length dress appeared.

"Good day, Sister, I'm Father Colin Michener. I'm here to speak with Father Tibor." He spoke in English, hoping she understood, and added a smile.

The older woman tented her fingers and lightly bowed in a gesture of greeting. "Welcome, Father. I did not realize you were a priest."

"I'm on holiday and decided to leave the cassock at home."

"Are you a friend of Father Tibor's?" Her English was excellent and unaccented.

"Not exactly. Tell him I'm a colleague."

"He's inside. Follow me please." She hesitated. "And, Father, have you ever visited one of these places before?"

He thought the question strange. "No, Sister."

"Please try to be patient with the children."

He nodded his understanding and followed her up five crumbling stone stairs. The smell inside was a horrid combination of urine, feces, and neglect. He fought a rising nausea with shallow breaths and wanted to shield his nose but thought the act would be insulting. Glass chips crunched beneath his soles and he noticed paint peeling from the walls like skin burned by the sun.

Children flooded out from the rooms. About thirty, all male, their ages varying from toddlers to teenagers. They crowded around him, their heads shaven—*to combat lice,* the nun explained. Some walked with a limp, while others seemed to lack muscular control. A lazy eye afflicted many, a speech impediment others. They probed him with chapped hands, clamoring for his attention. Their voices carried a weak rasp and the dialects varied, Russian and Romanian the most common. Several asked who he was and why he was there. He'd learned in town that most of them would be terminally ill or severely handicapped. The scene was made surreal by the dresses the boys wore, some over pants, some bare-legged. Their clothes were apparently whatever could be found that fit their lanky bodies. They seemed all eyes and bones. Few possessed teeth. Open sores spotted their arms, legs, and faces. He tried to be careful there. He'd read last night how HIV was rampant among Romania's forgotten children.

He wanted to tell them God would look out for them, that there was a point to their suffering. But before he could speak a tall man dressed in a black clerical suit, his Roman collar gone, stepped into the corridor. A small boy clung to his neck in a desperate embrace. The old man's hair was cut close to the scalp, and everything about his face, manner, and stride suggested a gentle being. He wore a pair of chrome-rimmed glasses that framed saucer-round, brown eyes beneath a pyramid of bushy white eyebrows. He was wire-thin, but the arms were hard and muscular.

"Father Tibor?" he asked in English.

"I heard you say that you were a colleague." The English carried an Eastern European accent.

"I'm Father Colin Michener."

The older priest set down the child he was carrying. "Dumitru is due for his daily therapy. Tell me why I should delay that to speak with you?"

He wondered about the hostility in the old man's voice. "Your pope needs assistance."

Tibor sucked a deep breath. "Is he finally going to recognize the situation we have here?"

He wanted to speak alone and didn't like the audience surrounding them, especially the nun. The children were still tugging at his clothes. "We need to talk in private."

Father Tibor's face betrayed little emotion as he appraised Michener with an even gaze. He marveled at the physical condition the old man was in and hoped he'd be in half as good a shape when he reached eighty.

"Take the children, Sister. And see to Dumitru's therapy."

The nun scooped the young boy into her arms and herded them down the hall. Father Tibor spit out instructions in Romanian, some of which Michener understood, but he wanted to know, "What kind of therapy does the boy receive?"

"We simply massage his legs and try to get him to walk. It's probably useless, but it's all we have available."

"No doctors?"

"We're lucky if we can feed these children. Medical aid is unheard of."

"Why do you do this?"

"A strange question coming from a priest. These children need us."

The enormity of what he'd just seen refused to leave his mind. "Is it like this throughout the country?"

"This is actually one of the better places. We've worked hard to make it livable. But, as you can see, we have a long way to go."

"No money?"

Tibor shook his head. "Only what the relief organizations throw our way. The government does little, the Church next to nothing."

"You came on your own?"

The older man nodded. "After the revolution, I read about the orphanages and decided this was where I should be. That was ten years ago. I have never left."

There was still an edge to the priest's voice, so he wanted to know, "Why are you so hostile?"

"I'm wondering what the papal secretary wants with an old man."

"You know who I am?"

"I'm not ignorant of the world."

He could see Andrej Tibor was no fool. Perhaps John XXIII had chosen wisely when he asked this man to translate Sister Lucia's note. "I have a letter from the Holy Father."

Tibor gently grasped Michener by the arm. "I was afraid of that. Let us go to the chapel."

They stepped down the hall toward the front of the building. What served as the chapel was a tiny room floored in gritty cardboard. The walls were bare stone, the ceiling crumbling wood. The only semblance of piety came from a solitary stained-glass window where a colored mosaic formed a Madonna, her arms outstretched, seemingly ready to embrace all who sought her comfort.

Tibor motioned to the image. "I found it not far from here, in a church that was about to be razed. One of the summer volunteers installed it for me. The children are all drawn to her."

"You know why I've come, don't you?"

Tibor said nothing.

He reached into his pocket, found the blue envelope, and handed it to Tibor.

The priest accepted the packet and stepped close to the window. Tibor ripped the fold and slipped out Clement's note. He held the paper away from his eyes as he strained to read in the dull light.

"It's been a while since I've read German," Tibor said. "But it's coming back to me." Tibor finished reading. "When I first wrote the pope, I was hoping he would simply do as I asked without more."

Michener wanted to know what the priest had asked, but instead said, "Do you have a response for the Holy Father?"

"I have many responses. Which one am I to give?"

"Only you can make that decision."

"I wish it were that simple." He cocked his head toward the stained glass. "She made it so complicated." Tibor stood for a moment in silence, then turned and faced him. "Are you staying in Bucharest?"

"Do you want me to?"

Tibor handed him the envelope. "There is a restaurant, the Café Krom, near the Piaţa Revoluţiei. It's easy to find. Come at eight. I'll think about this and have your response then."

FIFTEEN

MICHENER DROVE SOUTH TO BUCHAREST, WRESTLING WITH images of the orphanage.

Like many of those children, he'd never known his natural parents. He learned much later in life that his birth mother had lived in Clogheen, a small Irish village north of Dublin. She was unmarried and not yet twenty when she became pregnant. His natural father was unknown—or at least that's what his birth mother had steadfastly maintained. Abortion was unheard of then, and Irish society scorned unwed mothers to the point of brutality.

So the church filled the gap.

Birthing centers was what the archbishop of Dublin labeled them, but they were little more than dumping places, like the one he'd just left. Each was run by nuns—not caring souls like back in Zlatna, but difficult women who treated the expectant mothers in their charge like criminals.

Women were forced to do demeaning labor up to and after giving birth, working in horrid conditions for little or no pay. Some were beaten, others starved, the majority mistreated. To the Church they were sinners, and forced repentance was their only path to salvation. Most, though, were mere peasant girls who could ill afford to raise a child. Some were the other side of illicit relationships that the fathers either did not acknowledge or wished to keep private. Others were wives who had the ill fortune to become pregnant against their husbands' wishes. The common denominator was shame. Not a one of them wanted to bring attention to herself, or to her family, for the sake of an unwanted child.

After birth, the babies would stay at the centers for a year, maybe two, being slowly weaned from their mothers—a little less time together each day. The final notice came only the night before. An American couple would arrive the following morning. Only Catholics were allowed the adoption privilege, and they had to agree to raise the child in the Church and not publicize where he or she came from. A cash donation to the Sacred Heart Adoption Society, the organization created to run the project, was appreciated but not required. The children could be told they were adopted, but the new parents were asked to say that the natural parents had died. Most of the birth mothers wanted it that way—the hope being that the shame of their mistake would pass in time. No one needed to know they'd given a child away.

Michener recalled vividly the day he'd visited the center where he was born. The gray limestone building sat in a wooden glen, a place called Kinnegad, not far from the Irish Sea. He'd walked through the deserted building, imagining an anguished mother sneaking into the nursery the night before her baby would leave forever, trying to muster the courage to say goodbye, wondering why a church and a God would allow such torment. Was her sin that great? If so, why wasn't the father's equal? Why did she bear all the guilt?

And all the pain.

He'd stood before a window on the upper floor and stared down at a mulberry tree. The only breach of the silence had come from a torrid breeze that echoed across the empty rooms like the cries of infants who'd once languished there. He'd felt the gut-wrenching horror as a mother tried to catch a final glimpse of her baby being carried to a car. His birth mother had been one of those women. Who she was, he would never know. Rarely were the children given surnames, so there was no way to match child to mother. He'd only learned the little bit he knew about himself because of a nun's faded memory.

More than two thousand babies left Ireland that way, one of them a tiny infant boy with light brown hair and bright green eyes whose destination was Savannah, Georgia. His adoptive father was a lawyer, his mother devoted to her new son. He grew up on the tidewaters of the Atlantic in an upper-middle-class neighborhood. He'd excelled in school and become a priest and a lawyer, pleasing his adoptive parents enormously. He'd then gone to Europe and found comfort with a lonely bishop who'd loved him like a son. Now he was a servant to that bishop, a man risen to pope, part of the same Church that had failed so miserably in Ireland.

He'd loved his adoptive parents dearly. They fulfilled their end of the bargain by always telling him that his natural parents had been killed. Only on her deathbed had his mother told him the truth—a confession by a sainted woman to her son, the priest, hoping both he and her God would forgive her.

I've seen her in my mind for years, Colin. How she must have felt when we took you away. They tried to tell me it was for the best. I tried to tell myself it was the right thing. But I still see her in my mind.

He hadn't known what to say.

We wanted a baby so bad. And the bishop told us your life would have been hard without us. No one would care for you. But I still see her in my mind. I want to tell her I'm sorry. I want to tell her that I raised you well. I loved you as she would have. Maybe then she could forgive us.

But there was nothing to forgive. Society was to blame. The Church was to blame. Not the daughter of a south Georgia farmer who couldn't have a child of her own. She'd done nothing wrong, and he'd fervently pleaded with God to grant her peace.

He rarely thought about that past anymore, but the orphanage had brought it all back. The smell from its fetid air still lingered, and he tried to rid the stench with the cold wind from a downed window.

Those children would never enjoy a trip to America, never experience the love of parents who wanted them. Their world was limited within a gray retaining wall, within an iron-barred building equipped with no lights and little heat. There they would die, alone and forgotten, loved only by a few nuns and an old priest.

SIXTEEN

MICHENER FOUND A HOTEL AWAY FROM THE PIAŢA REVOLUŢIEI and the busy university district, choosing a modest establishment near a quaint park. The rooms were small and clean, filled with art deco furnishings that looked out of place. His came with a wash-basin that supplied surprisingly warm water, the shower and toilet shared down the hall.

Perched beside the room's only window, he was finishing off a pastry and a Diet Coke he'd bought to tide him over until dinner. A clock in the distance banged out chimes for five P.M.

The envelope Clement had given him lay on the bed. He knew what was expected of him. Now that Father Tibor had read the message, he was to destroy it, without reading its contents. Clement trusted him to do as instructed, and he'd never failed his mentor, though he'd always believed his relationship with Katerina a be-trayal. He'd violated his vows, disobeyed his church, and offended his God. For that, there could be no forgiveness. But Clement had said otherwise.

You think you're the only priest to succumb?
That doesn't make it right.

Colin, forgiveness is the hallmark of our faith. You've sinned and should repent. But that doesn't mean throwing your life away. And was it that wrong, anyway?

He could still recall the curious look he'd given the archbishop of Cologne. What was he saying?

Did it feel wrong, Colin? Did your heart say it was wrong?

The answer to both questions then, and now, was no. He'd loved Katerina. It was a fact he could not deny. She'd come to him at a time, just after his mother's death, when he was tangling with his past. She'd traveled with him to that birthing center in Kinnegad. Afterward, they'd walked the rocky cliffs overlooking the Irish Sea. She'd held his hand and told him that his adoptive parents had loved him and he was lucky to have two people who cared that much. And she was right. But he couldn't rid the thoughts of his birth mother from his mind. How could societal pressure be so great that women willingly sacrificed their babies in order to make a life for themselves?

Why should that ever be necessary?

He drained the rest of the Coke and stared again at the envelope. His oldest and dearest friend, a man who'd been there for him half his life, was in trouble.

He made a decision. Time to do something.

He reached for the envelope and withdrew the blue paper. The words were penned in German, by Clement's own hand.

Father Tibor:

I am aware of the task you performed for the most holy and reverend John XXIII. Your first message to me caused great concern. "Why does the church lie?" was your inquiry. I truly had no idea what you meant. With your second contact, I now realize the dilemma you face. I have looked at the reproduction of the third secret you sent with your first note and read your translation many times. Why have you kept this evidence to yourself? Even after the third secret was revealed by John Paul, only silence from you. If what you sent is true, why did you not speak then? Some would say you are a fraud, a man not to be believed, but I know that to be false. Why? I cannot explain. Just know that I believe you. I have sent my secretary. He is a man to be trusted. You may tell Father Michener what you please. He will deliver your words only to me. If you have no response, tell him so. I can understand if you are disgusted with your Church. I, too, have similar thoughts. But there is much to consider, as you well know. I would ask that you return this note and envelope to Father Michener. I thank you for whatever service you may deem to offer. God go with you, Father.

Clement
P.P. Servus Servorum Dei.

The signature was the pope's official mark. Pastor of Pastors, Servant of the Servants of God. The way Clement signed every official document.

Michener felt bad about violating Clement's confidence. But something was clearly happening here. Father Tibor had apparently made an impression on the pope, enough that the papal secretary was being sent to judge the situation. *Why have you kept this evidence to yourself?*

What evidence?

I have looked at the reproduction of the third secret you sent with your first note and read your translation many times.

Were those two items now in the Riserva? Inside the wooden box Clement kept returning to open?

Impossible to say.

He still knew nothing.

So he replaced the blue sheet into the envelope, walked to the bathroom down the hall, and tore everything into pieces, flushing the scraps away.

KATERINA LISTENED AS COLIN MICHENER CROSSED THE PLANK floor above. Her gaze traced the sound across the ceiling as it faded down the hall.

She'd followed him from Zlatna to Bucharest, deciding it more important to know where he was staying than to try to learn what happened with Father Tibor. She hadn't been surprised when he bypassed central downtown and headed straight for one of the city's lesser hotels. He'd also avoided the papal nuncio's office near Centru Civic—again no surprise, since Valendrea had made clear this was not an official visit.

Driving through downtown she was sad to see that an Orwellian sameness still permeated block after block of yellow-brick apartments, all coming after Ceauşescu bulldozed the city's history to make room for his grandiose developments. Somehow sheer magnitude was supposed to convey magnificence, and it mattered not that the buildings were impractical, expensive, and unwanted. The state decreed the populace would be appreciative—the ungrateful went to prison, the lucky were shot.

She'd left Romania six months after Ceauşescu faced the firing squad, staying only long enough to be part of the first election in the country's history. When no one but former communists won, she realized little would change quickly, and she'd noticed earlier how right that prediction had been. A sadness still filled Romania. She'd felt it in Zlatna, and on the streets in Bucharest. Like a wake after a funeral. And she could sympathize. What had become of her own life? She'd done little the past dozen years. Her father had urged her to stay and work for the new, supposedly free Romanian press, but she'd tired of the commotion. The excitement of revolt stood in stark contrast to the lull of its aftermath. Leave it to others to work a finish into the rough concrete—she preferred to churn the gravel, sand, and mortar. So she left and wandered Europe, found and lost Colin Michener, then made her way to America and Tom Kealy.

Now she was back.

And a man she once loved was walking around, one floor up.

How was she supposed to learn what he was doing? What had Valendrea said? *I suggest using those same charms Tom Kealy apparently enjoys. Surely then your mission will be a complete success.*

Asshole.

But maybe the cardinal had a point. The direct approach seemed best. She certainly knew Michener's weaknesses, and already hated herself for taking advantage of them.

But little choice remained.

She stood and headed for the door.

SEVENTEEN

VALENDREA'S LAST APPOINTMENT CAME EARLY FOR A FRIDAY. Then a dinner scheduled at the French embassy was unexpectedly canceled—some crisis in Paris had detained the ambassador—so he found himself with a rare free night.

He'd spent a torturous hour with Clement just after lunch. The time was supposed to be a foreign affairs briefing, but all they'd done was bicker. Their relationship was rapidly deteriorating, and the risk of a public confrontation was growing by the day. His resignation had yet to be requested, Clement surely hoping he'd cite spiritual concerns and simply quit.

But that was never going to happen.

Part of the agenda for their earlier meeting had entailed a briefing on a visit by the American secretary of state, scheduled in two weeks. Washington was trying to enlist the Holy See's assistance on political initiatives in Brazil and Argentina. The Church was a political force in South America, and Valendrea had signaled a willingness to use Vatican influence on Washington's behalf. But Clement did not want the Church involved. In that respect he was nothing like John Paul II. The Pole had publicly preached the same philosophy, then privately done the opposite. A diversion, Valendrea had often thought, one that rocked Moscow and Warsaw to sleep and eventually brought communism to its knees. He'd seen firsthand what the moral and spiritual leader of a billion faithful could do to, and for, governments. Such a shame to waste that potential, but Clement had ordered that there would be no alliance between the United States and the Holy See. The Argentines and Brazilians would have to solve their own problems.

A knock came on the apartment door.

He was alone, having sent his chamberlain to fetch a carafe of coffee. He crossed his study into an adjacent anteroom and opened the double doors leading out to the hall. Two Swiss guards, their backs against the wall, flanked either side of the doorway. Between them stood Maurice Cardinal Ngovi.

"I was wondering, Eminence, if we might speak a moment. I tried at your office and was told you had retired for the evening."

Ngovi's voice was low and calm. And Valendrea noticed the formal label *Eminence,* surely for the guards' benefit. With Colin Michener plodding his way through Romania, Clement had apparently delegated the task of errand boy to Ngovi.

He invited the cardinal inside and instructed the guards they were not to be disturbed. He then led Ngovi into his study and offered a seat in a gilded settee.

"I would pour coffee, but I sent the steward for some."

Ngovi raised a hand. "No need. I came to talk."

Valendrea sat. "So what does Clement want?"

"It is I who wants something. What was the purpose of your visit to the archives yesterday? Your intimidation of the cardinal-archivist? It was uncalled for."

"I don't recall the archives being under the jurisdiction of the Congregation for Catholic Education."

"Answer the question."

"So Clement does want something, after all."

Ngovi said nothing, an irritating strategy he'd noticed the African often employed—one that sometimes made Valendrea say too much.

"You told the archivist that you were on a mission of the greatest importance to the Church. One that demanded extraordinary action. What were you referring to?"

He wondered how much the weak bastard in the archives had said. Surely he didn't confess his sin in forgiving the abortion. The old fool wasn't that reckless. Or was he? He decided an offensive tack best. "You and I both know Clement is obsessed with the Fatima secret. He's been in the Riserva repeatedly."

"Which is the prerogative of the pope. It is not for us to question."

Valendrea leaned forward in the chair. "Why does our good German pontiff anguish so much over something the world already knows?"

"That is not for you or me to question. John Paul II satisfied my curiosity with his revelation of the third secret."

"You served on the committee, didn't you? The one that reviewed the secret and wrote the interpretation that accompanied its release."

"It was my honor. I had long wondered about the Virgin's final message."

"But it was so anticlimatic. Didn't really say much of anything, beyond the usual call for penance and faith."

"It foretold a papal assassination."

"Which explains why the Church suppressed it all those years. No point in giving some lunatic a divine motive to shoot the pope."

"We believed that was the thinking when John XXIII read the message and ordered it sealed."

"And what the Virgin predicted happened. Somebody tried to shoot Paul VI, then the Turk shot John Paul II. What I want to know, though, is why Clement feels the need to keep reading the original writing?"

"Again, that is not for you or me to question."

"Except when either one of us is pope." He waited to see if his adversary would take the bait.

"But you and I are not pope. What you attempted was a violation of canon law." Ngovi's voice stayed cool, and Valendrea wondered if this sedate man ever lost his temper.

"Plan to charge me?"

Ngovi did not flinch. "If there was any way possible to be successful, I would."

"Then maybe I would have to resign and you could be secretary of state? You'd like that, wouldn't you, Maurice?"

"I would only like to send you back to Florence where you and your Medici ancestors belong."

He cautioned himself. The African was a master of provocation. This would be a good test for the conclave, where surely Ngovi would try every possible way to incite a reaction. "I am not Medici. I am Valendrea. We opposed the Medici."

"Surely only after seeing that family's decline. I imagine your ancestors were opportunists, too."

He realized the confrontation for what it was—the two leading contenders for the papacy, face-to-face. He well knew that Ngovi would be his toughest competition. He'd already listened to taped conversations among cardinals when they thought themselves safe within locked Vatican offices. Ngovi was his most dangerous challenger, made even more formidable by the fact that the archbishop of Nairobi was not actively seeking the papacy. If asked, the wily bastard always stopped any speculation with a wave of his hand and a mention of his respect for Clement XV. None of which fooled Valendrea. An African had not sat on the throne of St. Peter since the first century. What a triumph that would be. Ngovi, if nothing else, was an ardent nationalist, open in his belief that Africa deserved better than it was presently receiving—and what better platform to push for social reform than as head of the Holy See?

"Give it up, Maurice," he said. "Why don't you join the winning team? You won't leave the next conclave as pope. That much I guarantee."

"What bothers me more is *you* becoming pope."

"I know you have the African bloc held tight. But they're only eight votes. Not enough to stop me."

"But enough to become critical in a tight election."

The first mention by Ngovi of the conclave. A message?

"Where is Father Ambrosi?" Ngovi asked.

Now he realized the purpose of the visit. Clement needed information. "Where's Father Michener?"

"I am told he's on holiday."

"So is Paolo. Maybe they went together." He let a chuckle accompany the sarcasm.

"I would hope Colin has better taste in friends."

"As I would for Paolo."

He wondered why the pope was so concerned about Ambrosi. What did it matter? Perhaps he'd underestimated the German. "You know, Maurice, I was being facetious earlier, but you would make an excellent secretary of state. Your support in the conclave could assure that."

Ngovi sat with his hands folded beneath his cassock. "And to how many others have you dangled that cube of sugar?"

"Only those in a position to deliver."

His guest rose from the settee. "I remind you of the Apostolic Constitution, which forbids campaigning for the papacy. We are both bound by that creed."

Ngovi stepped toward the anteroom beyond.

Valendrea never moved from his chair, but called out to the retreating cardinal, "I wouldn't stand on protocol too long, Maurice. We'll all be in the Sistine soon, and your fortunes could drastically change. How, though, is solely up to you."

EIGHTEEN

THE RAP ON THE DOOR STARTLED MICHENER. NOBODY KNEW he was in Romania except Clement and Father Tibor. And absolutely nobody knew he was staying at this hotel.

He stood, crossed the room, and opened the door to see Katerina Lew. "How in the world did you find me?"

She smiled. "You were the one who said the only secrets in the Vatican are the ones a person doesn't know."

He didn't like what he was hearing. The last thing Clement would want was a reporter knowing what he was doing. And who'd betrayed the information that he'd left Rome?

"I felt bad about the other day in the square," she said. "I shouldn't have said what I did."

"So you came to Romania to apologize?"

"We need to talk, Colin."

"This isn't a good time."

"I was told you went on holiday. I thought it the best time."

He invited her inside and closed the door behind her, reminding himself that the globe had shrunk since the last time he was alone with Katerina Lew. Then a troubling thought occurred. If she knew this much about him, imagine how much Valendrea knew. He needed to call Clement and advise him of a leak in the papal household. But he recalled what Clement had said yesterday in Turin about Valendrea—*he knows everything we do, everything we say*—and realized the pope already knew.

"Colin, there's no reason for us to be so hostile. I understand much better what happened all those years ago. I'm even willing to admit I handled things poorly."

"That's a first."

She did not react to his rebuke. "I've missed you. That's really why I came to Rome. To see you."

"What about Tom Kealy?"

"I was involved with Tom." She hesitated. "But he's not you." She stepped closer. "I'm not ashamed of my time with him. Tom's situation is stimulating to a journalist. Lots of opportunities there." Her eyes grabbed his in a way only hers could. "But I need to know. Why were you at the tribunal? Tom told me papal secretaries don't usually bother with such things."

"I knew you'd be there."

"Were you glad to see me?"

He debated his response and settled on, "You didn't look particularly glad to see me."

"I was just trying to gauge your reaction."

"As I recall, there was no reaction from you."

She stepped away, toward the window. "We shared something special, Colin. There's no point denying it."

"No point rehashing it, either."

"That's the last thing I want. We're both older. Hopefully smarter. Can't we be friends?"

He'd come to Romania on a papal errand. Now he was embroiled in an emotional discussion with a woman he once loved. Was the Lord testing him again? He couldn't deny what he felt just being close to her. Like she said, they'd once shared everything. She'd been wonderful as he struggled to learn about his heritage, wondering what happened to his birth mother, curious why his biological father had abandoned him. With her help, he'd arrested many of those demons. But new ones were rising. Perhaps a truce with his conscience might be in order. What could it hurt?

"I'd like that."

She wore a pair of black trousers that clung to her thin legs. A matching herringbone jacket and black leather vest cast a look of the revolutionary he knew her to be. No dreamy lights in her eyes. She was firmly rooted. Perhaps too much so. But down deep there was true emotion, and he'd missed that.

An odd flutter swept across him.

He recalled years ago when he'd retreated to the Alps for time to think and, like today, she'd appeared at his door, confusing him even more.

"What were you doing in Zlatna?" she asked. "I've been told that orphanage is a difficult place, run by an old priest."

"You were there?"

She nodded. "I followed you."

Another disturbing reality, but he let it pass. "I went to talk with that priest."

"Can you tell me about it?"

She sounded interested and he needed to talk about it. Perhaps she could help. But there was another matter to consider.

"Off the record?" he asked.

Her smile brought him comfort. "Of course, Colin. Off the record."

NINETEEN

MICHENER LED KATERINA INTO THE CAFÉ KROM. THEY'D talked in his room for two hours. He'd told her an abridged version of what had happened with Clement XV over the past few months and the reason he'd come to Romania, omitting only that he'd read Clement's note to Tibor. There was no one else, besides Cardinal Ngovi, to whom he would even consider speaking about his concerns. And even with Ngovi he knew discretion was the better tack. Vatican alliances shifted like the tide. A friend today could well be a foe tomorrow. Katerina was not allied to anyone inside the Church, and she was not ignorant of the third secret of Fatima. She told him about an article she'd written for a Danish magazine in 2000 when John Paul II released its text. It dealt with a fringe group who believed the third secret was an apocalyptic vision, the complex metaphors used by the Virgin a clear declaration that the end was in sight. She'd thought them all insane and her article addressed the lunacy such cults extolled. But after seeing Clement's reaction in the Riserva, Michener wasn't so sure about that lunacy anymore. He hoped Father Andrej Tibor could end the confusion.

The priest waited at a table near a plate-glass window. Outside,

STEVE BERRY / 122

an amber glow illuminated people and traffic. A mist clouded the night air. The bistro sat in the heart of the city, near the Piaţa Revoluţiei, and was busy with a Friday-night crowd. Tibor had changed clothes, replacing his black clerical garb with a pair of denim jeans and a turtleneck sweater. He rose as Michener introduced him to Katerina.

"Ms. Lew is with my office. I brought her to take notes as to anything you might want to say." He'd decided earlier that he wanted her to hear what Tibor said, and he thought a lie better than the truth.

"If the papal secretary so desires," Tibor said, "who am I to question?"

The priest's tone was light and Michener hoped the bitterness from earlier had dissipated. Tibor got the waitress's attention and ordered two more beers. The old priest then slid an envelope across the table. "That is my response to Clement's inquiry."

He did not reach for the packet.

"I thought about it all afternoon," Tibor said. "I wanted to be precise, so I wrote it down."

The waitress deposited two steins of dark beer on the table. Michener gulped a short swallow of the frothy brew. So did Katerina. Tibor was already on his second stein, the empty one on the table.

"I haven't thought of Fatima in a long time," Tibor quietly said.

Katerina spoke up. "Did you work at the Vatican long?"

"Eight years, between John XXIII and Paul VI. Then I returned to missionary work."

"Were you actually there when John XXIII read the third secret?" Michener asked, probing gently, trying not to reveal what he knew of Clement's note.

Tibor stared out the window for a long moment. "I was there."

He knew what Clement had asked of Tibor, so he pushed. "Father, the pope is greatly bothered by something. Can you help me understand?"

"I can appreciate his anguish."

He tried to appear nonchalant. "Any insights?"

The old man shook his head. "After four decades I still don't understand myself." He glanced away while he spoke, as if unsure of what he was saying. "Sister Lucia was a saintly woman. The Church treated her badly."

"How do you mean?" Katerina asked.

"Rome made sure she led a cloistered life. Remember, in 1959 only John XXIII and she knew the third secret. Then the Vatican ordered that only her immediate family could visit her, and she was not to discuss the apparitions with anyone."

"But she was part of the revelation when John Paul made the secret public in 2000," Michener said. "She was sitting on the dais when the text was read to the world at Fatima."

"She was over ninety years old. I'm told her hearing and eyesight were failing. And, do not forget, she was forbidden to speak on the subject. There were no comments from her. None whatsoever."

Michener sucked another swallow of beer. "What was the problem with what the Vatican did regarding Sister Lucia? Weren't they just protecting her from every nut in the world who wanted to badger her with questions?"

Tibor crossed his arms before his chest. "I wouldn't expect you to understand. You are a product of the Curia."

He resented the accusation, since he was anything but that. "My pontiff is not the Curia's friend."

"The Vatican demands complete obedience. If not, the Apostolic Penitentiary sends one of their letters commanding you to Rome to account for yourself. We're to do as we're told. Sister Lucia was a loyal servant. She did as she was told. Believe me, the last thing Rome would have wanted was for her to be available to the world press. John ordered her silent because he had no choice, and every pope after continued that order because they had no choice."

"As I recall, Paul VI and John Paul II both visited with her. John Paul even consulted her before the third secret was released. I have spoken to bishops and cardinals who were part of the revelation. She authenticated the writing as hers."

"Which writing?" Tibor asked.

An odd question.

"Are you saying the Church lied about the message?" Katerina asked.

Tibor reached for his drink. "We will never know. The good nun, John XXIII, and John Paul II are no longer with us. All gone, except me."

Michener decided to change the subject. "So tell us what you do know. What happened when John XXIII read the secret?"

Tibor sat back in the rickety oak chair and seemed to consider the question with interest. Finally, the old priest said, "All right. I'll tell you exactly what happened."

"Do you know Portuguese?" Monsignor Capovilla asked.

Tibor glanced up from his seat. Ten months working in the Vatican and this was the first time anyone from the fourth floor of the Apostolic Palace had spoken to him, much less John XXIII's personal secretary.

"Yes, Father."

"The Holy Father needs your assistance. Could you bring a pad and pen and come with me?"

He followed the priest to the elevator and rode in silence to the fourth floor, where he was ushered into the papal apartment. John XXIII sat perched behind a writing desk. A small wooden box with a broken wax seal lay on top. The pope held two pieces of notepaper.

"Father Tibor, can you read these?" John asked.

Tibor accepted the two sheets and scanned the words, not actually registering their meaning, only the fact that he understood. "Yes, Holy Father."

A smile came to the rotund man's face. It was the smile that had galvanized Catholics from around the world. The press had taken to calling him Papa John, a label the pope had embraced. For so long, while Pius XII lay ailing, the papal palace windows had been shrouded in darkness, the curtains drawn in symbolic mourning. Now the shutters were thrown open, the Italian sun pouring through, a signal to all who entered St. Peter's Square that this Venetian cardinal was committed to a revival.

"If you would, sit there by the window and pen an Italian translation," John said. "One page each, separately, as the originals appear."

Tibor spent the better part of an hour making sure his two translations were precise. The original writing was in a distinctly feminine hand, and the Portuguese was of an old style, used more toward the turn of the last century. Languages, like people and cultures, tended to change with time, but his training was extensive and the task relatively simple.

John paid him little attention while he worked, chatting quietly with his secretary. When finished, he handed his effort to the pope. He watched for a reaction while John read the first sheet. Nothing. Then the pope read the second page. A moment of silence passed.

"This does not concern my papacy," John softly said.

Given the words on the page, he thought the comment strange, but said nothing.

John folded each translation with its original, forming two separate packets. The pope sat silent for a few moments, and Tibor did not move. This pope, who'd sat on the throne of St. Peter a mere nine months, had already profoundly changed the Catholic world. One reason Tibor had come to Rome was to be a part of what was happening. The world was ready for something different and God, it seemed, had provided.

John tented his chubby fingers before his mouth and rocked silently in the chair. "Father Tibor, I want your word to your pope and your God that what you just read will never be revealed."

Tibor understood the importance of that pledge. "You have my word, Holy Father."

John stared at him through rheumy eyes with a gaze that pierced his soul. A cold shiver tickled his spine. He fought the urge to shift on his feet.

The pope seemed to read his mind.

"Be assured," John said in barely a whisper, "I will do what I can to honor the Virgin's wishes."

. . .

"I never spoke to John XXIII again," Tibor said.

"And no other pope contacted you?" Katerina asked.

Tibor shook his head. "Not until today. I gave my word to John and kept it. Until three months ago."

"What did you send the pope?"

"You do not know?'

"Not the details."

"Perhaps Clement doesn't want you to know."

"He wouldn't have sent me if he didn't."

Tibor motioned to Katerina. "Would he want her to know, too?"

"I do," Michener said.

Tibor appraised him with a stern look. "I'm afraid not, Father. What I sent is between Clement and myself."

"You said John XXIII never spoke to you again. Did you try to make contact with him?" Michener asked.

Tibor shook his head. "It was only a few days later John called for the Vatican II council. I remember the announcement well. I thought that his response."

"Care to explain?"

The old man shook his head. "Not really."

Michener finished his beer and wanted another, but knew better. He studied some of the faces that surrounded him and wondered if any might be interested in what he was doing, but quickly dismissed the thought. "What about when John Paul II released the third secret?"

Tibor's face tightened. "What of it?"

The man's curtness was wearing on him. "The world now knows the Virgin's words."

"The Church has been known to refashion the truth."

"Are you suggesting the Holy Father deceived the world?" Michener asked.

Tibor did not immediately answer. "I don't know what I'm suggesting. The Virgin has appeared many times on this earth. You'd think we might finally get the message."

"What message? I've spent the past few months studying every apparition back two thousand years. Each one seems a unique experience."

"Then you haven't been studying closely," Tibor said. "I, too, spent years reading about them. In every one there is a declaration from heaven to do as the Lord says. The Virgin is heaven's messenger. She provides guidance and wisdom, and we've foolishly ignored Her. In modern times, that mistake started at La Salette."

Michener knew every detail about the apparition at La Salette, a village high in the French Alps. In 1846 two shepherd children, a boy, Maxim, and a girl, Mélanie, supposedly experienced a vision. The event was similar in many ways to Fatima—a pastoral scene, a light that wound down from the sky, an image of a woman who spoke to them.

"As I recall," Michener said, "the two children were told secrets that were eventually written down, the texts presented to Pius IX. The seers then later published their own versions. Charges of embellishment were leveled. The entire apparition was tainted with scandal."

"Are you saying there's a connection between La Salette and Fatima?" Katerina asked.

A look of annoyance crept onto Tibor's face. "I'm not saying anything. Father Michener here has access to the archives. Has he ascertained any connection?"

"I studied the La Salette visions," Michener said. "Pius IX made no comment after reading each of the secrets, yet he never allowed them to be publicly revealed. And though the original texts are indexed among the papers of Pius IX, the secrets are no longer in the archives."

"I looked in 1960 for the La Salette secrets and also found nothing. But there are clues to their content."

He knew exactly what Tibor meant. "I read the witness accounts of people who watched as Mélanie wrote down the messages. She asked how to spell *infallibly, soiled,* and *anti-Christ,* if I remember correctly."

Tibor nodded.

"Pius IX himself even offered a few clues. After reading Maxim's message he said, 'Here is the candor and simplicity of a child.' But after reading Mélanie's he cried and said, 'I have less to fear from open impiety than from indifference. It is not without reason that the Church is called militant and you see here her captain.'"

"You have a good memory," Tibor said. "Mélanie was not kind when told of the pope's reaction. 'This secret ought to give pleasure to the pope,' she said, 'a pope should love to suffer.'"

Michener recalled Church decrees issued at the time that commanded the faithful to refrain from discussing La Salette in any form on threat of sanctions. "Father Tibor, La Salette was never given the credence of Fatima."

"Because the original texts of the seers' messages are gone. All we have is speculation. There's been no discussion of the subject because the church forbade it. Right after the apparition, Maxim said that the announcement the Virgin told them would be fortunate for some, unfortunate for others. Lucia uttered those same words seventy years later at Fatima. 'Good for some. For others bad.'" The priest drained his mug. He seemed to enjoy alcohol. "Maxim and Lucia were both right. Good for some, bad for others. It is time the Madonna's words not be ignored."

"What are you saying?" Michener asked, frustrated.

"At Fatima heaven's desires were made perfectly clear. I haven't read the La Salette secret, but I can well imagine what it says."

Michener was sick of riddles, but decided to let this old priest have his say. "I'm aware of what the Virgin said at Fatima in the second secret, about the consecration of Russia and what would happen if that wasn't done. I agree, that's a specific instruction—"

"Yet no pope," Tibor said, "ever performed the consecration

until John Paul II. All the bishops of the world, in conjunction with Rome, never consecrated Russia until 1984. And look what happened from 1917 to 1984. Communism flourished. Millions died. Romania was raped and pillaged by monsters. What did the Virgin say? *The good will be martyred, the Holy Father will have much to suffer, various nations will be annihilated.* All because popes chose their own course instead of heaven's." The anger was clear, no attempt being made to conceal it. "Yet within six years of the consecration, communism fell." Tibor massaged his brow. "Never once has Rome formally recognized a Marian apparition. The most it will ever do is deem the occurrence *worthy of assent.* The Church refuses to accept that visionaries have anything important to say."

"But that's only prudent," Michener said.

"How so? The Church acknowledges that the Virgin appeared, encourages the faithful to believe in the event, then discredits whatever the seers say? You don't see a contradiction?"

Michener did not answer.

"Reason it out," Tibor said. "Since 1870 and the Vatican I council, the pope has been deemed infallible when he speaks of doctrine. What do you believe would happen to that concept if the words of a simple peasant child were made more important?"

Michener had never viewed the issue that way before.

"The teaching authority of the Church would end," Tibor said. "The faithful would turn somewhere else for guidance. Rome would cease to be the center. And that could never be allowed to happen. The Curia survives, no matter what. That's always been the case."

"But, Father Tibor," Katerina said, "the secrets from Fatima are precise on places, dates, and times. They talk about Russia and popes by name. They speak of papal assassinations. Isn't the Church just being cautious? These so-called secrets are so different from the gospels that each could be deemed suspicious."

"A good point. We humans have a tendency to ignore that which we do not agree with. But maybe heaven thought more specific instruction was needed. Those *details* you speak about."

Michener could see the agitation on Tibor's face and the nervousness in the hands that wrapped the empty beer stein. A few moments of strained silence passed, then the old man slouched forward and motioned to the envelope.

"Tell the Holy Father to do as the Madonna said. Not to argue or ignore it, just do as she said." The voice was flat and emotionless. "If not, tell him that he and I will soon be in heaven, and I expect him to take all the blame."

TWENTY

MICHENER AND KATERINA STEPPED OFF THE METRO TRAIN AND made their way out of the subway station into a frosty night. The former Romanian royal palace, its battered stone façade awash in a sodium vapor glow, stood before them. The Piaţa Revoluţiei fanned out in all directions, the damp cobbles dotted with people bundled in heavy wool coats. Traffic crawled by on the streets beyond. The cold air stained his throat with a taste of carbon.

He watched Katerina as she studied the plaza. Her eyes settled on the old communist headquarters, a Stalinist monolith, and he saw her focus on the building's balcony.

"That was where Ceauşescu made his speech that night." She pointed off toward the north. "I stood over there. It was something. That pompous ass just stood there in the lights and proclaimed himself loved by all." The building loomed dark, apparently no longer important enough to be illuminated. "Television cameras sent the speech all over the country. He was so proud of himself until we all started chanting, 'Timişoara, Timişoara.'"

He knew about Timişoara, a town in western Romania where a lone priest had finally spoke out against Ceauşescu. When the government-controlled Reformed Orthodox Church removed him, riots broke out across the country. Six days later the square before him erupted in violence.

"You should have seen Ceaușescu's face, Colin. It was his indecision, that moment of shock, that we took as a call to act. We broke through the police lines and . . . there was no turning back." Her voice lowered. "The tanks eventually came, then the fire hoses, then bullets. I lost many friends that night."

He stood with his hands stuffed in his coat pockets and watched his breath evaporate before his eyes, letting her remember, knowing she was proud of what she'd done. He was, too.

"It's good to have you back," he said.

She turned toward him. A few other couples strolled the square arm in arm. "I've missed you, Colin."

He'd read once that in everyone's life there was somebody who touched a spot so deep, so precious, that the mind always retreated, in time of need, to that cherished place, seeking comfort within memories that never seemed to disappoint. Katerina was that for him. And why the Church, or his God, couldn't provide the same satisfaction was troubling.

She inched close. "What Father Tibor said, about doing as the Madonna said. What did he mean?"

"I wish I knew."

"You could learn."

He knew what she meant and withdrew from his pocket the envelope that contained Father Tibor's response. "I can't open it. You know that."

"Why not? We can find another envelope. Clement would never know."

He'd succumbed to enough dishonesty for one day by reading Clement's first note. "I would know." He knew how hollow that denial sounded, but he slipped the envelope back in his pocket.

"Clement created a loyal servant," Katerina said. "I'll give the old bird that."

"He's my pope. I owe him respect."

Her lips and cheeks twisted into a look he'd seen before. "Is your life to be in the service of popes? What of you, Colin Michener?"

He'd wondered the same thing many times over the past few years. What of him? Was a cardinal's hat to be the extent of his life? Doing little more than basking in the prestige of a scarlet robe? Men like Father Tibor were doing what priests were meant to do. He felt again the caress of the children from earlier, and smelled the stench of their despair.

A surge of guilt swept through him.

"I want you to know, Colin, I won't mention a word of this to anyone."

"Including Tom Kealy?" He regretted how the question came out.

"Jealous?"

"Should I be?"

"I seem to have a weakness for priests."

"Careful with Tom Kealy. I get the impression he's the kind who ran from this square when the shooting started." He could see her jaw tighten. "Not like you."

She smiled. "I stood in front of a tank with a hundred others."

"That thought is upsetting. I wouldn't want to see you hurt."

She threw him a curious look. "Any more than I already am?"

KATERINA LEFT MICHENER AT HIS ROOM AND WALKED DOWN the squeaky steps. She told him they would talk in the morning, over breakfast, before he flew back to Rome. He hadn't been surprised to learn she was staying one floor below, and she didn't mention that she, too, would be heading back to Rome, on a later flight, instead telling him that her next destination was up in the air.

She was beginning to regret her involvement with Cardinal Alberto Valendrea. What had started off as a career move had deteriorated into the deception of a man she still loved. It troubled her lying to Michener. Her father, if he knew what she was doing, would be ashamed. And that thought, too, was bothersome, since she'd disappointed her parents enough over the past few years.

At her room, she opened the door and stepped inside.

The first thing she saw was the smiling face of Father Paolo Ambrosi. The sight momentarily startled her, but she quickly caught hold of her emotions, sensing that showing fear to this man would be a mistake. She'd actually been expecting a visit, since Valendrea had said Ambrosi would find her. She closed the door, peeled off her coat, and stepped toward the lamp beside the bed.

"Why don't we let the light remain off," Ambrosi said.

She noticed that Ambrosi was dressed in black trousers and a dark turtleneck. A dark overcoat hung open. None of the garb was religious. She shrugged and tossed her coat on the bed.

"What have you learned?"

She took a moment and told him an abbreviated account of the orphanage and of what Michener had told her about Clement, but she held back a few key facts. She finished by telling him about Father Tibor, again an abridged version, and recounted the old priest's warning concerning the Madonna.

"You must learn what's in Tibor's response," Ambrosi said.

"Colin wouldn't open it."

"Find a way."

"How do you expect me to do that?"

"Go upstairs. Seduce him. Read it while he sleeps afterward."

"Why don't you? I'm sure priests interest you more than they do me."

Ambrosi lunged, wrapping his long thin fingers around her neck and collapsing her down onto the bed. The grip was cold and waxy. He brought his knee onto her chest and pressed her firmly into the mattress folds. He was stronger than she would have thought.

"Unlike Cardinal Valendrea, I have little patience for your smart mouth. I remind you that we are in Romania, not Rome, and people disappear here all the time. I want to know what Father Tibor wrote. Find out, or I might not restrain myself the next time we meet." Ambrosi's knee pressed deeper into her chest. "I'll find you tomorrow, just as I found you this evening."

She wanted to spit in his face, but the ever-tightening fingers around her neck cautioned otherwise.

Ambrosi released his grip and headed for the door.

She clutched her neck and sucked a few breaths, then leaped from the bed.

Ambrosi spun back to face her, a gun in his hand.

She halted her advance. "You . . . fucking . . . mobster."

He shrugged. "History teaches that there truly is an imperceptible line between good and evil. Sleep well."

He opened the door and left.

TWENTY-ONE

VALENDREA CRUSHED OUT HIS CIGARETTE IN AN ASHTRAY AS A knock came on his bedchamber door. He'd been engrossed in a novel for nearly an hour. He so enjoyed American suspense thrillers. They were a welcome escape from his life of careful words and strict protocol. His retreat each night into a world of mystery and intrigue was something he looked forward to, and Ambrosi made sure he always had a new adventure to read.

"Enter," he called out.

The face of his chamberlain appeared. "I received a call a few moments ago, Eminence. The Holy Father is in the Riserva. You wished to be informed if that occurred."

He slipped off his reading glasses and closed the book. "That will be all."

The chamberlain retreated.

He quickly dressed in a knit shirt and trousers, slipped on a pair of running shoes, and left his apartment, heading for the private elevator. At ground level he traversed the empty corridors of the Apostolic Palace. The silence was disturbed only by a soft whine from closed-circuit televison cameras revolving on their lofty perches and the squeak of his rubber soles on the terrazzo. No danger existed of anyone seeing him—the palace was sealed for the night.

He entered the archives and ignored the night prefect, walking through the maze of shelves straight to the iron gate for the Riserva. Clement XV stood inside the lighted space, his back to him, dressed in a white linen cassock.

The doors of the ancient safe hung open. He made no effort to mask his approach. It was time for a confrontation.

"Come in, Alberto," the pope said, the German's back still to him.

"How did you know it was me?"

Clement turned. "Who else would it be?"

He stepped into the light, the first time he'd been inside the Riserva since 1978. Then, only a few incandescent bulbs lit the windowless alcove. Now fluorescent fixtures cast everything in a pearly glow. The same wooden box lay in the same drawer, its lid open. Remnants of the wax seal he'd shattered and replaced adorned the outside.

"I was told about your visit here with Paul," Clement said. The pope gestured to the box. "You were present when he opened that. Tell me, Alberto, was he shocked? Did the old fool wince when he read the Virgin's words?"

He wasn't going to give Clement the satisfaction of knowing the truth. "Paul was more of a pope than you ever could be."

"He was an obstinate, unbending man. He had a chance to do something, but he let his pride and arrogance control him." Clement lifted an unfolded sheet of paper that lay beside the box. "He read this, yet put himself before God."

"He died only three months later. What could he have done?"

"He could have done everything the Virgin asked."

"Do what, Jakob? What is so important? The third secret of Fatima commands nothing beyond faith and penance. What should Paul have done?"

Clement maintained his rigid pose. "You lie so well."

A blind fury built inside him that he quickly repressed. "Are you mad?"

The pope took a step toward him. "I know about your *second* visit to this room."

He said nothing.

"The archivists keep quite detailed records. They have noted for centuries every soul who has ever entered this chamber. On the night of May 19, 1978, you visited with Paul. An hour later, you returned. Alone."

"I was on a mission for the Holy Father. He commanded that I return."

"I'm sure he did, considering what was in the box at that time."

"I was sent to reseal the box and the drawer."

"But before you resealed the box, you read what was inside. And who could blame you? You were a young priest, assigned to the papal household. Your pope, whom you worshiped, had just read the words of a Marian seer and they surely upset him."

"You don't know that."

"If not, then he was more of a fool than I think him to be." Clement's gaze sharpened. "You read the words, then you removed part of them. You see, there once were four sheets of paper in this box. Two written by Sister Lucia when she memorialized the third secret in 1944. Two composed by Father Tibor when he translated in 1960. But after Paul opened the box and you resealed it, no one again opened the box until 1981, when John Paul II read the third secret for the first time. That was done in the presence of several cardinals. Their testimony confirms that Paul's seal was unbroken. All present that day also attested that only two sheets of paper lay inside the box, one written by Sister Lucia, the other Father Tibor's translation. Nineteen years later, in 2000, when John Paul finally released the text of the third secret to the world, there remained only the same two sheets of paper in the box. How do you account for that, Alberto? Where are the other two pages that were there in 1978?"

"You know nothing."

"Unfortunately for both me and you, I do. There was something you never knew. The translator for John XXIII, Father Andrej Tibor, copied the entire two-page third secret onto a pad, then produced a two-page translation. He gave the pope his original work, but later he noticed that upon his pad was left the impression of what he'd written. He, like myself, had the annoying habit of bearing down too hard. He took a pencil, shaded out the words, then traced them onto two sheets. One, the original words of Sister Lucia. The other, his translation." Clement held up the paper in his hand. "One of those facsimiles is this, which Father Tibor recently sent it to me."

Valendrea kept his face frozen. "May I see it?"

Clement smiled. "If you like."

He accepted the page. Waves of apprehension clutched his stomach. The words were the same feminine script he remembered, about ten lines, in Portuguese, which he still could not read.

"Portuguese was Sister Lucia's native tongue," Clement said. "I have compared the style, format, and lettering from Father Tibor's facsimile to the first part of the third secret you so graciously left in the box. They are identical in every way."

"Is there a translation?" he asked, masking all emotion.

"There is, and the good father sent his facsimile along." Clement motioned. "But it is in the box. Where it belongs."

"Photographs of Sister Lucia's original writing were released to the world in 2000. This Father Tibor could have simply copied her style." He gestured with the sheet. "This could be a forgery."

"Why did I know you would say that? It could be, but it's not. And we both know that."

"This is why you have been coming here?" he asked.

"What would you have me do?"

"Ignore these words."

Clement shook his head. "That is the one thing I cannot do. Along with his reproduction, Father Tibor sent me a simple query.

Why does the church lie? You know the answer. No one lied. Because when John Paul II released the text of the third secret to the world, no one knew, besides Father Tibor and yourself, that there was more to the message."

Valendrea stepped back, stuffed a hand into his pocket, and removed a lighter he'd noticed on the walk down. He ignited the paper and dropped the flaming sheet to the floor.

Clement did nothing to stop him.

Valendrea stamped on the blackened ashes as if he'd just done battle with the devil. Then his gaze locked on Clement. "Give me that damn priest's translation."

"No, Alberto. It stays in the box."

His instinct was to shove the old man aside and do what had to be done. But the night prefect appeared at the Riserva's doorway.

"Lock this safe," Clement said to the attendant, and the man rushed forward to do as he was told.

The pope took Valendrea by the arm and led him from the Riserva. He wanted to pull away, but the prefect's presence demanded he show respect. Outside, among the shelves, away from the prefect, he dislodged himself from Clement's grip.

The pope said, "I wanted you to know what awaits you."

But something was bothering him. "Why didn't you stop me from burning that paper?"

"It was perfect, wasn't it, Alberto? Removing those two pages from the Riserva? No one would know. Paul was in his final days, soon to be in the crypt. Sister Lucia was forbidden to speak with anyone, and she eventually died. No one else knew what was in that box, except perhaps an obscure Bulgarian translator. But by 1978 so many years had passed that that translator wasn't a worry in your mind. Only you would know those two pages had ever existed. And even if anyone noticed, things have a tendency to disappear from our archives. If the translator surfaced, without the pages themselves, there was no proof. Only talk. Hearsay."

He was not going to respond to any of what he'd just heard.

Instead, he still wanted to know, "Why didn't you stop me from burning that paper?"

The pope hesitated a moment before saying, "You'll see, Alberto."

Then Clement shuffled away as the prefect slammed shut the Riserva's gate.

TWENTY-TWO

KATERINA HAD SLEPT POORLY. HER NECK WAS SORE FROM AMbrosi's attack, and she was mad as hell with Valendrea. Her first thought was to tell the secretary of state to screw himself and then tell Michener the truth. But she knew that whatever peace they might have forged last evening would be shattered. Michener would never believe that her main reason for allying herself with Valendrea was the chance to again be close to him. All he would see was her betrayal.

Tom Kealy had been right about Valendrea. *That is one ambitious bastard.* More than Kealy ever knew, she thought, staring again at the ceiling of the darkened room and massaging her bruised muscles. Kealy was also right about something else. He once told her there were two kinds of cardinals—those who want to be pope and those who *really* want to be pope. She now added a third kind—those who coveted to be pope.

Like Alberto Valendrea.

She hated herself. There was an innocence about Michener that she'd violated. He couldn't help who he was or what he believed. Maybe that was what actually attracted her to him. Too bad the Church wouldn't allow its clerics to be happy. Too bad the way things had always been controlled what would always be. Damn the Roman Catholic Church. And damn Alberto Valendrea.

She'd slept in her clothes, and for the past two hours she'd patiently waited. Now squeaks in the floorboards above alerted her. Her eyes followed the sound as Colin Michener stepped around his room. She heard water running in the basin and waited for the inevitable. A few moments later footsteps led toward the hall and she heard the door above open and close.

She stood, left the room, and made her way to the stairwell just as the bathroom door in the hall above closed. She crept up the stairs and hesitated at the top, waiting to hear water flowing in the shower. She then hustled down a threadbare runner, over uneven hardwood planks, to Michener's room, hoping he still did not lock anything.

The door opened.

She stepped inside, and her eyes found his travel bag. His clothes from last night and jacket were there, too. She searched the pockets and found the envelope Father Tibor had provided. She recalled Michener's habit of short showers and tore open the envelope:

Holy Father:

I kept the oath that John XXIII imposed upon me because of my love for our Lord. But several months ago an incident caused me to rethink my duty. One of the children at the orphanage died. In the final moments of his life, while he screamed in pain, he asked me about heaven and wanted to know if God would forgive him. I could not imagine what this innocent would need forgiven, but I told him the Lord will forgive anything. He wanted me to explain, but death was impatient and he passed before I could. It was then I realized that I, too, must seek forgiveness. Holy Father, my oath to my pope meant something to me. I kept it for more than forty years, but heaven should not be challenged. It is certainly not for me to tell you, the Vicar of Christ, what needs to be done. That can come only from your own blessed conscience and the guidance of our Lord and Savior. But I must ask, how much intolerance will heaven allow? I mean no disrespect, but it is you who have sought my opinion. So I offer it humbly.

Katerina read the message again. Father Tibor was as cryptic on paper as he had been in person the night before, offering only more riddles.

She refolded the note and slipped the sheet back into a white envelope she'd found among her things. It was a bit larger than the original, but hopefully not different enough to arouse suspicion.

She stuffed the envelope back into the jacket and left the room.

As she passed the bathroom door, the water in the shower stopped. She imagined Michener drying himself, oblivious to her latest betrayal. She hesitated a moment, then descended the stairs, never looking back and feeling even worse about herself.

TWENTY-THREE

VALENDREA PUSHED ASIDE HIS BREAKFAST. HE HAD NO AP-
petite. He'd slept sparingly, the dream so real he still could not rid it
from his mind.

He saw himself at his own coronation, being carried into St.
Peter's Basilica on the regal *sedia gestatoria.* Eight monsignors held
aloft a silk canopy that sheltered the ancient golden chair. The papal
court surrounded him, everyone dressed in sartorial majesty. Os-
trich fans flanked him on three sides and accented his exalted position as Christ's divine representative on earth. A choir sang as a
million people cheered and millions more watched on television.

The strange part was that he was naked.

No robes. No crown. Totally naked and no one seemed to notice, though he was painfully aware. A strange uncomfortableness
passed through him as he kept waving to the crowd. Why did no one
see? He wanted to cover himself, but fear kept him rooted to the
chair. If he stood people might really notice. Would they laugh?
Ridicule him? Then, one face among the millions that engulfed him
stood out.

Jakob Volkner's.

The German was dressed in full papal regalia. He wore the robes, the miter, the pallium—everything Valendrea should be wearing. Above the cheers, the music, and the choir, he heard Volkner's every word, as clear as if they were standing side by side.

I'm glad it's you, Alberto.

What do you mean?

You'll see.

He'd awakened in a clammy sweat and eventually drifted back to sleep, but the dream reoccurred. Finally, he relieved his tension with a scalding shower. He'd nicked himself twice while shaving and nearly slipped on the bathroom floor. Being unnerved was unsettling. He was not accustomed to anxiety.

I wanted you know what awaits you, Alberto.

The damn German had been so smug last night.

And now he understood.

Jakob Volkner knew exactly what happened in 1978.

Valendrea reentered the Riserva. Paul had commanded that he return, so the archivist had been specifically instructed to open the safe and provide him with privacy.

He reached for the drawer and removed the wooden box. He'd brought with him wax, a lighter, and the seal of Paul VI. Just as John XXIII's seal once was stamped on the outside, now Paul's would signify that the box should not be opened, except by papal command.

He hinged open the top and made sure that two packets, four folded sheets of paper, remained inside. He could still see Paul's face as he'd read the top packet. There'd been shock, which was an emotion rarely seen on the face of Paul VI. But there'd been something else, too, only for an instant, but Valendrea had seen it clearly.

Fear.

He stared into the box. The two packets containing the third secret of Fatima were still there. He knew he shouldn't, but no one would ever know. So he lifted out the top packet, the one that had brought such a reaction.

He unfolded and set aside the original Portuguese page, then scanned its Italian translation.

Comprehension took only an instant. He knew what had to be done. Perhaps that was why Paul had sent him? Maybe the old man realized that he would read the words and then do what a pope could not.

He slipped the translation into his cassock, joined a second later by Sister Lucia's original writing. He then unfolded the remaining packet and read.

Nothing of any consequence.

So he reassembled those two pages, dropped them back inside, and sealed the box.

Valendrea stood from the table and locked the doors that led out of his apartment. He then strode into his bedroom and removed a small bronze casket from a cabinet. His father had presented the box to him for his seventeenth birthday. Ever since, he'd kept all his precious things inside, among them photos of his parents, deeds to properties, stock certificates, his first missal, and a rosary from John Paul II.

He reached beneath his vestments and found the key that hung from his neck. He hinged opened the box and shuffled through its contents to the bottom. The two sheets of folded paper, taken from the Riserva that night in 1978, were still there. One penned in Portuguese, the other Italian. Half of the entire third secret of Fatima.

He lifted both pages out.

He could not bring himself to read the words again. Once was more than enough. So he walked into the bathroom, ripped both sheets into tiny pieces, then allowed them to rain into the toilet.

He flushed the basin.

Gone.

Finally.

He needed to return to the Riserva and destroy Tibor's latest facsimile. But any return visit would have to be after Clement's death. He also needed to talk with Father Ambrosi. He'd tried the satellite phone an hour ago without success. Now he grabbed the handset from the bathroom counter and dialed the number again.

Ambrosi answered.

"What happened?" he asked his assistant.

"I spoke with our angel last evening. Little has been learned. She's to do better today."

"Forget that. What we originally planned is immaterial. I need something else."

He had to be careful with his words as there was nothing private about a satellite phone.

"Listen to me," he said.

TWENTY-FOUR

MICHENER FINISHED DRESSING, THEN TOSSED HIS TOILETRIES and dirty clothes into his travel bag. A part of him wanted to drive back to Zlatna and spend more time with those children. Winter was not far away, and Father Tibor had told them last night what a battle it was simply to keep the boilers running. Last year they'd gone two months with frozen pipes, using makeshift stoves to burn whatever wood could be scrounged from the forest. This winter Tibor believed they should be all right, thanks to relief workers who'd spent all summer repairing an aging boiler.

Tibor had said that his fondest wish was that another three months might pass without losing any more children. Three had died last year, buried in a cemetery just outside the wall. Michener wondered what purpose such suffering could serve. He'd been fortunate. The object of the Irish birthing centers had been to find children homes. But the flip side was that mothers were forever separated from their children. He'd imagined many times the Vatican bureaucrat who'd approved such a preposterous plan, never once considering the pain. Such a maddening political machine, the Roman Catholic Church. Its gears had churned undaunted for two thousand years, unfazed by the Protestant Reformation, infidels, a schism that tore it apart, or the plunder of Napoleon. Why then, he mused, would the Church fear what a peasant girl from Fatima might have to say? What would it matter?

Yet apparently it did.

He shouldered his travel bag and walked downstairs to Katerina's room. They'd agreed to have breakfast together before he left for the airport. A note was wedged into the doorframe. He plucked it out.

Colin:

> *I thought it best we not see each other this morning. I wanted us to part with the feeling we shared last night. Two old friends who enjoyed each other's company. I wish you the best in Rome. You deserve success.*

> *Always, Kate*

A part of him was relieved. He'd really not known what to say to her. There was no way they could continue a friendship in Rome. The slightest appearance of impropriety would be enough to ruin his career. He was glad, though, that they were parting on good terms. Perhaps they'd finally made peace. At least he hoped so.

He tore the paper to pieces and stepped down the hall, where he flushed every one of them away. So strange that was necessary. But no remnant of her message could remain. Nothing could exist that might link him and her together. Everything must be sanitized.

Why?

That was clear. Protocol and image.

What wasn't so clear was his growing resentment of both reasons.

Michener opened the door to his apartment on the fourth floor of the Apostolic Palace. His rooms were near the pope's, where papal secretaries had long lived. When he'd first moved in three years ago, he'd foolishly thought the spirits of its former residents might somehow guide him. But he'd since learned that none of those souls was to be found, and any guidance he might need would have to be discovered within himself.

He'd taken a taxi from the Rome airport instead of calling his office for a car, still adhering to Clement's orders that his trip go unnoticed. He'd entered the Vatican through St. Peter's Square, dressed casually, like one of the many thousands of tourists.

Saturday was not a busy day for the Curia. Most employees left and all the offices, save for a few in the Secretariat of State, were closed. He'd stopped by his office and learned that Clement had flown to Castle Gandolfo earlier and was not due back until Monday. The villa lay eighteen miles south of Rome and had served as a papal retreat for four hundred years. Modern pontiffs used its casual atmosphere as a place to avoid Rome's oppressive summers and as a weekend escape, helicopters providing transport back and forth.

Michener knew Clement loved the villa, but what concerned him was that the trip was not on the pope's itinerary. One of his assistants offered no explanation except that the pope had said he'd like a couple of days in the country, so everything was rescheduled. There'd been a few inquiries to the press office on the pontiff's health, not unusual when the schedule was varied, but the standard statement—*the Holy Father enjoys a robust constitution and we wish him a long life*—was promptly issued.

Yet Michener was concerned, so he raised the assistant who had accompanied Clement on the phone.

"What's he doing there?" Michener asked.

"He just wanted to see the lake and walk in the gardens."

"Has he asked about me?"

"Not a word."

"Tell him I'm back."

An hour later the phone rang in Michener's apartment.

"The Holy Father wants to see you. He said a drive south

through the countryside would be lovely. Do you understand what he means?"

He smiled and checked his watch. Three twenty P.M. "Tell him I'll be there by nightfall."

Clement apparently did not want him using the helicopter, even though the Swiss guards preferred air transport. So he rang the car pool and requested that an unmarked vehicle be readied.

The drive to the southeast, through olive orchards, skirted the Alban Hills. The papal complex at Castle Gandolfo consisted of the Villa Barberini, the Cybo Villa, and an exquisite garden, all nestled beside Lake Albano. The sanctuary was devoid of Rome's incessant hum—a spot of solitude in the otherwise endless bustle of Church business.

He found Clement in the solarium. Michener once again looked the role of a papal secretary, wearing his Roman collar and black cassock with purple sash. The pope was perched in a wooden chair engulfed by horticulture. The towering glass panels for the outer walls faced an afternoon sun and the warm air reeked of nectar.

"Colin, pull one of those chairs over here." A smile accompanied the greeting.

He did as he was told. "You look good."

Clement grinned. "I didn't know I ever looked bad."

"You know what I mean."

"Actually, I feel good. And you'll be proud to know I ate breakfast and lunch today. Now, tell me about Romania. Every detail."

He explained what had happened, omitting only his time with Katerina. He then handed Clement the envelope and the pope read Father Tibor's response.

"What precisely did Father Tibor say to you?" Clement asked.

He told him, then said, "He spoke in riddles. Never really saying much, though he was not complimentary to the Church."

"That I understand," Clement muttered.

"He was upset over the Holy See's handling of the third secret. He implied that the Virgin's message was being intentionally ignored. He told me repeatedly for you to do as She said. No argument, no delay, just do it."

The old man's gaze lingered on him. "He told you about John XXIII, didn't he?"

He nodded.

"Tell me."

He did, and Clement seemed fascinated. "Father Tibor is the only person left alive who was there that day," the pope said when he finished. "What did you think of the priest?"

Thoughts of the orphanage flashed through his mind. "He appears sincere. But he was also obstinate." He didn't add what he was thinking—*like you, Holy Father.* "Jakob, can't you now tell me what this is about?"

"There is another trip I need you to take."

"Another?"

Clement nodded. "This time to Medjugorje."

"Bosnia?" he asked in disbelief.

"You must speak with one of the seers."

He was familiar with Medjugorje. On June 24, 1981, two children had reportedly seen a beautiful woman holding a baby atop a mountain in southwestern Yugoslavia. The next evening the children returned with four friends and all six saw a similar vision. Thereafter, the apparitions continued daily for the six children, each one receiving messages. Local communist officials claimed it was some sort of revolutionary plot and tried to stop the spectacle, but people flocked to the area. Within months there were reports of miraculous healing and rosaries turning to gold. Even during the Bosnian civil war the visions continued, and so did the pilgrimages. The children were now grown, the area renamed Bosnia-Herzegovina, and all but one of the six had stopped having visions. As with Fatima, there were secrets. Five of the seers had been entrusted by the Virgin with ten messages. The sixth knew only nine.

Of the nine secrets, all had been made public, but the tenth remained a mystery.

"Holy Father, is such a trip necessary?"

He didn't particularly want to traipse across war-torn Bosnia. American and NATO peacekeeping forces were still there maintaining order.

"I need to know the tenth secret of Medjugorje," Clement said, and his tone signaled that the matter was not open for discussion. "Draft a papal instruction for the seers. He or she is to tell you the message. No one else. Only you."

He wanted to argue, but was too tired from the flight and yesterday's hectic schedule to engage in something he knew would be futile. So he simply asked, "When, Holy Father?"

His old friend seemed to sense his fatigue. "In a few days. That will draw less attention. And again, keep this between us."

TWENTY-FIVE

VALENDREA UNFASTENED HIS SEAT BELT AS THE GULFSTREAM dropped from a cloudy night sky and touched down at Otopeni Airport. The jet was owned by an Italian conglomerate deeply entrenched with the Valendreas of Tuscany, and Valendrea himself regularly made use of the aircraft for quick trips out of Rome.

Father Ambrosi waited on the tarmac dressed in civilian clothes, a charcoal overcoat draping his slim frame.

"Welcome, Eminence," Ambrosi said.

The Romanian night was frigid and Valendrea was glad he'd worn a thick wool coat. Like Ambrosi, he'd dressed in street clothes. This was not an official visit and the last thing he needed was to be recognized. He was taking a risk coming, but he had to gauge the threat for himself.

"What about customs?" he asked.

"Handled. Vatican passports carry weight here."

They climbed into an idling sedan. Ambrosi drove while Valendrea sat alone in the rear. They headed north, away from Bucharest, toward the mountains over a series of rutted roads. This was Valendrea's first visit to Romania. He knew of Clement's desire for an of-

STEVE BERRY / 156

ficial pilgrimage, but any papal missions to this troubled place would have to wait until he was in command.

"He goes there each Saturday evening to pray," Ambrosi was saying from the front seat. "In the cold or heat. Doesn't matter. He's done that for years."

He nodded at the information. Ambrosi had been his usual thorough self.

They drove for nearly an hour in silence. The terrain rose progressively until they were winding up the side of a steep forested incline. Ambrosi slowed near the crest, eased onto a ragged shoulder, and killed the engine.

"It's there, down that path," Ambrosi said, pointing through fogged windows at a darkened lane between the trees.

In the headlights Valendrea noticed another car parked ahead. "Why does he come?"

"From what I was told, he considers the spot holy. In medieval times the old church was used by the local gentry. When Turks conquered the area, they burned all of the villagers alive inside. He seems to draw strength from their martyrdom."

"There is something you must know," he told Ambrosi. His assistant sat in the front seat, his gaze still out the windshield, unmoving. "We are about to cross a line, but it is imperative that we do. There is much at stake. I would not ask this of you if it were not of vital importance to the church."

"There is no need to explain," Ambrosi softly said. "It is enough that you say it is so."

"Your faith is impressive. But you are God's soldier, and a warrior should know what he is fighting for. So let me tell you what I know."

They emerged from the car. Ambrosi led the way beneath a velvet sky bleached by a nearly full moon. Fifty meters into the woods, the darkened shadow of a church appeared. As they approached,

Valendrea noticed the ancient rosettes and the belfry, the stones no longer individual but fused, seemingly without joints. No light shone from inside.

"Father Tibor," Valendrea called out in English.

A black form appeared in the doorway. "Who's there?"

"I am Alberto Cardinal Valendrea. I have come from Rome to speak with you."

Tibor stepped from the church. "First the papal secretary. Now the secretary of state. Such wonders for a humble priest."

He couldn't decide if the tone leaned more toward sarcasm or respect. He extended his hand palm-down, and Tibor knelt before him and kissed the ring he'd worn since the day John Paul II invested him as a cardinal. He was appreciative at the priest's submissiveness.

"Please, Father, stand. We must talk."

Tibor came to his feet. "Has my message already made its way to Clement?"

"It has, and the pope is grateful. But I've been sent to learn more."

"Eminence, I'm afraid that I can say no more than I have. It is bad enough that I have violated the oath of silence I made to John XXIII."

He liked what he was hearing. "So you haven't spoken of this to anyone before? Not even a confessor?"

"That is correct, Eminence. I've told no one what I knew, other than Clement."

"Did not the papal secretary come here yesterday?"

"He did. But I merely hinted at the truth. He knows nothing. I assume you have seen my written response?"

"I have," he lied.

"Then you know I said little there, too."

"What motivated you to craft a reproduction of Sister Lucia's message?"

"Hard to explain. When I returned from my duties to John that day, I noticed the imprints on the pad. I prayed on the matter and something told me to color the page and reveal the words."

"Why keep them all those years?"

"I have asked myself the same question. I do not know why, only that I did."

"And why did you finally decide to make contact with Clement?"

"What has happened with regard to the third secret is not right. The Church has not been honest with its people. Something inside commanded me to speak, an urge I could not ignore."

Valendrea caught Ambrosi's gaze momentarily and noticed a slight tip of his head off to the right. *That way.*

"Let's walk, Father," he said, taking Tibor gently by the arm. "Tell me, why do you come to this spot?"

"I was actually wondering, Eminence, how you found me."

"Your devotion to prayer is well known. My assistant merely asked around and was told of your weekly ritual."

"This is a sacred place. Catholics have worshiped here for five hundred years. I find it comforting." Tibor paused. "It's also because of the Virgin that I come."

They were walking down a narrow path with Ambrosi leading the way. "Explain, Father."

"The Madonna told the children at Fatima that there should be a Communion of Reparation on the first Saturday of each month. I come here every week to offer my personal reparation."

"For what do you pray?"

"That the world will enjoy the peace the Lady predicted."

"I, too, pray for the same thing. As does the Holy Father."

The path ended at the edge of a precipice. Before them spread a panorama of mountains and thick forest, all cast in a pale blue-gray glow. Few lights dotted the landscape, though a couple of fires burned in the distance. A halo sprang from the southern horizon, marking the glow of Bucharest forty miles away.

"Such magnificence," Valendrea said. "A remarkable view."

"I come here many times after praying," Tibor said.

He kept his voice low. "Which must help deal with the agony of the orphanage."

Tibor nodded. "I've received much peace here."

"As you should."

He gestured to Ambrosi, who produced a long blade. Ambrosi's arm swung up from behind and slashed once across Tibor's throat. The priest's eyes bulged as he choked on the first gush of blood. Ambrosi dropped the knife, gripped Tibor from behind, and tossed the old man out over the edge.

The cleric's body dissolved into the blackness.

A second later there was an impact, then another, then silence.

Valendrea stood still with Ambrosi beside him. His gaze remained on the gorge below. "There are rocks?" he calmly asked.

"Many, and a fast-moving stream. The body should take a few days to be found."

"Was it hard to kill him?" He truly wanted to know.

"It had to be done."

He stared at his dear friend through the dark, then reached up and outlined a cross on the forehead, lips, and heart. "I forgive you, in the name of the Father, the Son, and the Holy Spirit."

Ambrosi bowed his head in thanks.

"Every religious movement must have martyrs. And we have just borne witness to the Church's latest." He knelt on the ground. "Come, join me while I pray for Father Tibor's soul."

TWENTY-SIX

CASTLE GANDOLFO
SUNDAY, NOVEMBER 12
12:00 P.M.

MICHENER STOOD BEHIND CLEMENT INSIDE THE POPEMOBILE as the vehicle motored out of the villa grounds toward town. The specially designed car was a modified Mercedes-Benz station wagon that allowed two people to stand, encased within a transparent cocoon of bulletproof shielding. The vehicle was always used when the pope traveled through large crowds.

Clement had agreed to a Sunday visit. Only about three thousand people lived in the village that abutted the papal compound, but they were extraordinarily devoted to the pontiff and such trips were the pope's way of saying thanks.

After their discussion yesterday afternoon, Michener had not seen the pope until this morning. Though he innately loved people and enjoyed good conversation, Clement XV was still Jakob Volkner, a solitary man who treasured his privacy. So it was no surprise that Clement had spent last evening alone, praying and reading, then retiring early.

An hour ago Michener had drafted a papal letter instructing one of the Medjugorje seers to memorialize the so-called tenth secret, and Clement had signed the document. Michener still wasn't looking forward to traveling around Bosnia, and he would just have to hope that the trip was short.

It took only a few minutes to make the drive into town. The village square was packed and the crowd cheered as the papal car inched forward. Clement seemed to come alive at the display and waved back, pointing to faces he recognized, mouthing special greetings.

"It's good they love their pope," Clement said quietly in German, his attention still on the crowd, fingers gripped tight around the stainless-steel hand bar.

"You give them no reason not to," Michener said.

"That should be the goal of all who wear this robe."

The car looped through the square.

"Ask the driver to stop," the pope said.

Michener tapped twice on the window. The wagon halted and Clement unlatched the glass-paneled door. He stepped down to the cobblestones and the four security men who ringed the car instantly came alert.

"Do you think this wise?" Michener asked.

Clement looked up. "It is most wise."

Procedure called for the pope never to leave the vehicle. Though this visit had been arranged only yesterday, with little advance word, enough time had passed for there to be reason for concern.

Clement approached the crowd with outstretched arms. Children accepted his withered hands and he brought them close with a hug. Michener knew one of the great disappointments in Clement's life was not being a father. Children were precious to him.

The security team ringed the pope but the townspeople helped the situation, remaining reverent while Clement moved before them. Many shouted the traditional *Viva, Viva* popes had heard for centuries.

Michener simply watched. Clement XV was doing what popes had done for two millennia. *Thou art Peter and on this rock I will build my Church. And the gates of hell will not stand against it. I will give you the Keys of the*

Kingdom of Heaven: whatever you bind on earth will be bound in heaven; whatever you loose on earth will be loosed in heaven. Two hundred and sixty-seven men had been chosen as links in an unbroken chain, starting with Peter and ending with Clement XV. Before him was a perfect example of the shepherd out among the flock.

Part of the third secret of Fatima flashed through his mind.

The Holy Father passed through a big city half in ruins and half trembling with halting step, afflicted with pain and sorrow. He prayed for the souls of the corpses he met on his way. Having reached the top of the mountain, on his knees at the foot of the big Cross he was killed by a group of soldiers who fired bullets and arrows at him.

Perhaps that declaration of danger explained why John XXIII and his successors chose to quell the message. But a Russian-sponsored assassin ultimately tried to kill John Paul II in 1981. Shortly thereafter, while he recuperated, John Paul first read the third Fatima secret. So why did he wait nineteen years before finally revealing the Virgin's words to the world? A good question. One to be added to a growing list of unanswered inquiries. He decided not to think about any of that. Instead he concentrated on Clement as the pope enjoyed the crowd, and all his fears vanished.

Somehow he knew that no one, on this day, would cause his dear friend harm.

It was two P.M. when they returned to the villa. A light lunch was waiting in the solarium and Clement asked Michener to join him. They ate in silence, enjoying the flowers and a spectacular November afternoon. The compound's swimming pool, just beyond the glass walls, sat empty. It was one of the few luxuries John Paul II had insisted upon, telling the Curia, when it complained about the cost, that it was far cheaper than getting a new pope.

Lunch was a hearty beef soup littered with vegetables, one of Clement's favorites, along with black bread. Michener was partial to the bread. It reminded him of Katerina. They'd often shared some over coffee and dinner. He wondered where she was right now and why she'd felt the need to leave Bucharest without saying goodbye. He hoped that he'd see her again one day, maybe after his time at the Vatican ended, in a place where men like Alberto Valendrea did not exist, where no one cared who he was or what he did. Where maybe he could follow his heart.

"Tell me about her," Clement said.

"How did you know I was thinking about her?"

"It wasn't difficult."

He actually wanted to talk about it. "She's different. Familiar, but hard to define."

Clement sipped wine from his goblet.

"I can't help but think," Michener said, "that I'd be a better priest, a better man, if I didn't have to suppress my feelings."

The pope tabled his glass. "Your confusion is understandable. Celibacy is wrong."

He stopped eating. "I hope you haven't voiced that conclusion to anyone else."

"If I cannot be honest with you, then who?"

"When did you come to this conclusion?"

"The Council of Trent was a long time ago. Yet here we are, in the twenty-first century, clinging to a sixteenth-century doctrine."

"It is the Catholic nature."

"The Council of Trent was convened to deal with the Protestant Reformation. We lost that battle, Colin. The Protestants are here to stay."

He understood what Clement was saying. The Trent Council had affirmed celibacy as necessary for the gospel's sake, but conceded that it was not of divine origin. Which meant it could be changed if the Church desired. The only other councils since Trent, Vatican I and II, had declined to do anything. Now the supreme pontiff, the one man who could do something, was questioning the wisdom of that indifference.

"What are you saying, Jakob?"

"I'm not saying anything. I'm only talking with an old friend.

Why must priests not marry? Why must they remain chaste? If that's acceptable for others, why not the clergy?"

"Personally, I agree with you. But I think the Curia would take a different view."

Clement shifted his weight forward as he pushed his empty soup bowl aside. "And that's the problem. The Curia will always object to anything that threatens its survival. Do you know what one of them said to me a few weeks ago?"

Michener shook his head.

"He said that celibacy must be maintained because the cost of paying priests would skyrocket. We would have to channel tens of millions to payroll for increased salaries because priests would now have wives and children to support. Can you imagine? That is the logic this Church uses."

He agreed, but felt compelled to say, "If you even hinted at a change, you'd be providing Valendrea a ready-made issue to use with the cardinals. You could have open revolt."

"But that's the benefit of being pope. I speak infallibly on matters of doctrine. My word is the last word. I don't need permission, and I can't be voted from office."

"Infallibility was created by the Church, too," he reminded. "It can be changed, along with whatever you do, by the next pope."

The pope was pinching the fleshy part of his hand, a nervous habit Michener had seen before. "I've had a vision, Colin."

The words, barely a whisper, took a moment to sink in. "A what?"

"The Virgin spoke to me."

"When?"

"Many weeks ago, just after Father Tibor's first communication. That is why I went to the Riserva. She told me to go."

First the pope was talking about junking dogma that had stood for five centuries. Now he was proclaiming Marian apparitions. Michener realized this conversation must stay here, only the plants privy, but he heard again what Clement had said in Turin. *Do you think for one moment we enjoy any measure of privacy when at the Vatican?*

"Is it wise to speak of this?" He hoped his tone conveyed a warning. But Clement seemed not to hear.

"Yesterday, She appeared in my chapel. I looked up and She was floating before me, surrounded by a blue and gold light, a halo encircling Her radiance." The pope paused. "She told me that Her heart was encircled with thorns with which men pierce Her by their blasphemies and ingratitude."

"Are you sure of those statements?" he asked.

Clement nodded. "She said them clearly." Clement clinched his fingers together. "I'm not senile, Colin. It was a vision, of that I'm sure." The pope paused. "John Paul II experienced the same."

He knew that, but said nothing.

"We are foolish men," Clement said.

He was becoming agitated with riddles.

"The Virgin said to go to Medjugorje."

"And that's why I'm being sent?"

Clement nodded. "All would be clear then, she said."

A few moments of silence passed. He didn't know what to say. It was hard to argue with heaven.

"I allowed Valendrea to read what is in the Fatima box," Clement whispered.

He was confused. "What's there?"

"Part of what Father Tibor sent me."

"You going to tell me what that is?"

"I can't."

"Why did you allow Valendrea to read it?"

"To see his reaction. He'd even tried to browbeat the archivist to allow a look. Now he knows exactly what I know."

He was about to ask once again what that might be when a light rap on the solarium's door interrupted their conversation. One of the stewards entered, carrying a folded sheet of paper. "This came over the fax machine from Rome a few moments ago, Monsignor Michener. The cover said to give it to you immediately."

He took the sheet and thanked the steward, who promptly left. He unfolded and read the message. He then looked at Clement and said, "A call was received a short while ago from the nuncio in Bucharest. Father Tibor is dead. His body was found this morning, washed ashore from a river north of town. His throat had been cut and he apparently was tossed from one of the cliffs. His car was found near an old church he frequented. The police suspect thieves. That area is riddled with them. I was notified, since one of the nuns at the orphanage told the nuncio about my visit. He's wondering why I was there unannounced."

Color drained from Clement's face. The pope made the sign of the cross and folded his hands in prayer. Michener watched as Clement's eyelids clinched tight and the old man mumbled to himself.

Then tears streaked down the German's face.

TWENTY-SEVEN

4:00 P.M.

MICHENER HAD THOUGHT ABOUT FATHER TIBOR ALL AFTER-noon. He'd walked the villa's gardens and tried to rid from his mind an image of the old Bulgarian's bloodied body being fished from a river. Finally he made his way to the chapel where popes and cardi-nals had for centuries stood before the altar. It had been more than a decade since he'd last said Mass. He'd been far too busy serving the secular needs of others, but now he felt the urge to celebrate a fu-neral Mass in honor of the old priest.

In silence, he donned vestments. He then chose a black stole, draped it around his neck, and walked to the altar. Usually the de-ceased would be laid before the altar, the pews filled with friends and relatives. The point was to stress a union with Christ, a commu-nion with the saints that the departed was now enjoying. Eventually, on Judgment Day, everyone would be reunited and they would all dwell forever in the house of the Lord.

Or so the Church proclaimed.

But as he mouthed the required prayers he couldn't help won-dering if it was all for naught. Was there really some supreme being waiting to offer eternal salvation? And could that reward be earned simply by doing what the Church said? Was a lifetime of misdeeds forgiven by a few moments of repentance? Would not God want more? Would He not want a lifetime of sacrifice? No one was perfect, there'd always be lapses, but the measure of salvation must surely be greater than a few repentant acts.

He wasn't sure when he'd started doubting. Maybe it was all those years ago with Katerina. Perhaps being surrounded by ambitious prelates, who openly proclaimed a love for God but were privately consumed by greed and ambition, had affected him. What was the point of falling to your knees and kissing a papal ring? Christ never sanctioned such displays. So why were His children allowed the privilege?

Could his doubts be simply a sign of the times?

The world was different from a hundred years ago. Everyone seemed linked. Communications were instant. Information had reached a gluttony stage. God just didn't seem to fit. Maybe you were simply born, then you lived, and then you died, your body decomposing back into the earth. *Dust to dust,* as the Bible proclaimed. Nothing more. But if that were true, then what you made of your life could well be all the reward ever received—the memory of your existence your salvation.

He'd studied the Roman Catholic Church enough to understand that the majority of its teachings were directly related to its own interests, rather than those of its members. Time had certainly blurred all lines between practicality and divinity. What were once the creations of man had evolved into the laws of heaven. Priests were celibate because God ordained it. Priests were men because Christ was male. Adam and Eve were a man and woman, so love could only exist between the sexes. Where did these dogmas come from? Why did they persist?

Why was he questioning them?

He tried to switch off his brain and concentrate, but it was impossible. Maybe it was being with Katerina that had started him doubting again. Perhaps it was the senseless death of an old man in

Romania that brought into focus that he was forty-seven years old and had done little with his life beyond riding the coattails of a German bishop to the Apostolic Palace.

He needed to do more. Something productive. Something that helped someone besides himself.

A movement at the door caught his attention. He stared up to see Clement amble into the chapel and kneel in one of the pews.

"Please, finish. I, too, have a need," the pope said as he bowed his head in prayer.

Michener went back to the Mass and prepared the sacrament. He'd only brought one wafer, so he broke the slice of unleavened bread in half.

He stepped to Clement.

The old man looked up from his prayers, his eyes crimson from crying, the features marred by a patina of sadness. He wondered what sorrow had overtaken Jakob Volkner. Father Tibor's death had profoundly affected him. He offered the wafer and the pope opened his mouth.

"The body of Christ," he whispered, and laid communion on Clement's tongue.

Clement crossed himself, then bowed his head in prayer. Michener withdrew to the altar and went about the task of completing the Mass.

But it was hard to finish.

The sobs of Clement XV that echoed through the chapel bit his heart.

TWENTY-EIGHT

KATERINA HATED HERSELF FOR RETURNING TO TOM KEALY, BUT since her arrival in Rome yesterday, Cardinal Valendrea had yet to make contact. She'd been told not to call, which was fine since she had little to report beyond what Ambrosi already knew.

She'd read that the pope had traveled to Castle Gandolfo for the weekend, so she assumed Michener was there, too. Yesterday Kealy had taken a perverse pleasure in taunting her Romanian foray, implying that perhaps a lot more had occurred than she was willing to admit. She'd purposely not told him everything Father Tibor had said. Michener was right about Kealy. He was not to be trusted. So she'd given him an abridged version, enough for her to learn from him what Michener might be involved with.

She and Kealy were sitting in a cozy *osteria*. Kealy was dressed in a light-colored suit and tie, perhaps becoming accustomed to not wearing a collar in public.

"I don't understand all the hype," she said. "Catholics have made Marian secrets an institution. What makes the third secret of Fatima so important?"

Kealy was pouring wine from an expensive bottle. "It was fascinating, even for the Church. Here was a message supposedly direct from heaven, yet a steady stream of popes suppressed it until John Paul II finally told the world in 2000."

She stirred her soup and waited for him to explain.

"The Church officially sanctioned the Fatima apparitions as worthy of assent in the 1930s. That meant it was okay for Catholics to believe in what happened, if they chose to." He flashed a smile. "Typical hypocritical stance. Rome says one thing, does another. They didn't mind people flocking to Fatima and offering millions in donations, but they couldn't bring themselves to say the event actually occurred, and they certainly did not want the faithful to know what the Virgin may have said."

"But why conceal it?"

He sipped the burgundy, then fingered the stem of his glass. "Since when has the Vatican ever been sensible? These guys think they're still in the fifteenth century, when whatever they said was accepted without question. If anybody argued back then, the pope excommunicated them. But it's a new day and that pile just doesn't stink anymore." Kealy caught the waiter's attention and motioned for more bread. "Remember, the pope speaks infallibly when discussing matters of faith and morals. Vatican I pronounced that little jewel in 1870. What if, for one delicious moment, what the Virgin said was contrary to dogma? Now, wouldn't that be something?" Kealy seemed immensely pleased with the thought. "Maybe that's the book we should write? All about the third secret of Fatima. We can expose the hypocrisy, take a close look at the popes and some of the cardinals. Maybe even Valendrea himself."

"What about your situation? Not important anymore?"

"You don't honestly think there's any chance I'll win that tribunal."

"They might be content with a warning. That way they keep you within the fold, under their control, and you can save your collar."

He laughed. "You seem awfully concerned about my collar. Strange coming from an atheist."

"Screw you, Tom." She'd definitely told this man too much about herself.

"So full of spunk. I like that about you, Katerina." He enjoyed another swallow of wine. "CNN called yesterday. They want me for the next conclave."

"I'm glad for you. That's great." She wondered where that left her.

"Don't worry, I still want to do that book. My agent is talking to publishers about that one and a novel. You and I will make a great team."

The conclusion formed in her mind with a suddenness that surprised her. One of those decisions that was instantly clear. There'd be no team. What started out as promising had become tawdry. Luckily, she still had several thousand of Valendrea's euros, enough cash to get her back to France or Germany where she could hire on with a newspaper or magazine. And this time she'd behave herself—play by the rules.

"Katerina, are you there?" Kealy was asking.

Her attention returned to him.

"You looked a million miles away."

"I was. I don't think there's going to be a book, Tom. I'm leaving Rome tomorrow. You'll have to find another ghostwriter."

The waiter deposited a basket of steaming bread on the table.

"It won't be hard," he made clear.

"I didn't think so."

He reached for a piece of the bread. "I'd leave your horse hitched to me, if I were you. This wagon's going places."

She stood from the table. "I can tell you one place it's not going."

"You still have it for him, don't you?"

"I don't have it for anybody. I'm just sick of you. My father once told me that the higher a circus monkey climbed a pole, the more his ass showed. I'd remember that."

And she walked away, feeling her best in weeks.

TWENTY-NINE

MICHENER CAME AWAKE. HE'D NEVER NEEDED AN ALARM clock, his body seemingly blessed with an internal chronometer that always woke him at the precise time he selected before falling asleep. Jakob Volkner, when an archbishop and later a cardinal, had traveled the globe and served on committee after committee, relying always on Michener's ability never to be late, since punctuality was not one of Clement XV's noted traits.

As in Rome, Michener occupied a bedroom on the same floor as Clement's, just down the hall, a direct phone line linking their rooms. They were scheduled to return to the Vatican in two hours by helicopter. That would give the pope enough time for his morning prayers, breakfast, and a quick review of anything that required immediate attention, given there'd been two days with no work. Several memoranda had been faxed last evening, and Michener had them ready for a postbreakfast discussion. He knew the rest of the day would be hectic, as there was a steady stream of papal audiences scheduled for the afternoon and into the evening. Even Cardinal Valendrea had requested a full hour for a foreign affairs briefing later in the morning.

He was still bothered by the funeral Mass. Clement had cried for half an hour before leaving the chapel. They hadn't talked. Whatever was troubling his old friend was not open for discussion. Perhaps later there'd be time. Hopefully, a return to the Vatican and the rigors of work might take the pope's mind off the problem. But it had been disconcerting to watch such an onslaught of emotion.

He took his time showering, then dressed in a fresh black cassock and left his room. He strode down the corridor toward the pope's quarters. A chamberlain was standing outside the door, along with one of the nuns assigned to the household. Michener glanced at his watch. Six forty-five A.M. He pointed to the door. "Not up yet?"

The chamberlain shook his head. "There's been no movement."

He knew the staff waited outside each morning until they heard Clement stirring, usually between six and six thirty. The sound of the pope waking would be followed by a gentle tap on the door and the start of a morning routine that included a shower, shave, and dressing. Clement did not like anyone assisting him with bathing. That was done in private while the chamberlain made the bed and laid out his clothes. The nun's task was to straighten the room and bring breakfast.

"Perhaps he's just sleeping in," Michener said. "Even popes can get a little lazy every once in a while."

His two listeners smiled.

"I'll go back to my room. Come get me when you hear him."

It was thirty minutes later that a knock came to his door. The chamberlain was outside.

"There is still no sound, Monsignor," the man said. Worry clouded his face.

He knew no one, save himself, would enter the papal bedroom without Clement's permission. The area was regarded as the one place where popes could be assured of privacy. But it was approaching seven thirty, and he knew what the chamberlain wanted.

"All right," he said. "I'll go in and see."

He followed the man back to where the nun stood guard. She indicated that there was still silence from inside. He lightly tapped on the door and waited. He tapped again, a little louder. Still nothing. He grasped the knob and turned. It opened. He swung the door inward and stepped inside, closing the door behind him.

The bedchamber was spacious, with towering French doors at one end that opened to a balcony overlooking the gardens. The furnishings were ancient. Unlike the apartments in the Apostolic Palace, which were decorated by each successive pope in a style that made him comfortable, these rooms remained constant, oozing an Old World feel reminiscent of a time when popes were warrior-kings.

No lights were on, but the morning sun poured in through drawn sheers and bathed the room in a muted haze.

Clement lay under the sheets on his side. Michener stepped over and quietly said, "Holy Father."

Clement did not respond.

"Jakob."

Still nothing.

The pope's head faced away, the sheets and blanket pulled halfway over his frail body. He reached down and lightly shook the pope. Immediately he noticed a coldness. He stepped around to the other side of the bed and stared into Clement's face. The skin was loose and ashen, the mouth open, a pool of spittle dried on the sheet beneath. He rolled the pope onto his back and yanked the covers down. Both arms draped lifelessly at Clement's sides, the chest still.

He checked for a pulse.

None.

He thought about calling for help or administering CPR. He'd been trained, as had all the household staff, but he knew it would be useless.

Clement XV was dead.

He closed his eyes and said a prayer, a wave of grief sweeping through him. It was like losing his mother and father all over again.

He prayed for his dear friend's soul, then gathered his emotions. There were things to do. Protocol that must be adhered to. Procedures of long standing, and it was his duty to ensure that they were strictly maintained.

But something caught his attention.

Resting on the nightstand was a small caramel-colored bottle. Several months back, the papal physician had prescribed medication to help Clement rest. Michener himself had ensured that the prescription was filled, and he'd personally placed the bottle in the pope's bathroom. There were thirty of the tablets and, at last count, which Michener had taken only a few days ago, thirty remained. Clement despised drugs. It was a battle to simply get him to take an aspirin, so the vial, here, beside the bed, was surprising.

He peered inside the container.

Empty.

A glass of water resting beside the vial contained only a few drops.

The implications were so profound that he felt a need to cross himself.

He stared at Jakob Volkner and wondered about his dear friend's soul. If there was a place called heaven, with all his fiber he hoped the old German had found his way there. The priest inside him wanted to forgive what had apparently been done, but now only God, if He did exist, could do that.

Popes had been clubbed to death, strangled, poisoned, suffocated, starved, and murdered by outraged husbands.

But never had one taken his own life.

Until now.

PART
THREE

THIRTY

MICHENER WATCHED FROM THE BEDROOM WINDOW AS THE Vatican helicopter touched down. He hadn't left Clement since his discovery, using the phone beside the bed to telephone Cardinal Ngovi in Rome.

The African was the camerlengo, chamberlain of the Holy Roman Church, the first person to be informed of a papal death. Under canon law Ngovi was charged with administering the Church during the *sede vacante,* the Vacant See, which was now the official designation for the Vatican government. There was no supreme pontiff. Instead Ngovi, in conjunction with the Sacred College of Cardinals, would administer a government by committee that would last for the next two weeks, during which time funeral preparations would be made and the coming conclave organized. As camerlengo, Ngovi would not be acting pope, just a caretaker, but his authority was nonetheless clear. Which was fine by Michener. Somebody was going to have to control Alberto Valendrea.

The chopper blades whirled down and the cabin door slid open. Ngovi exited first, followed by Valendrea, both dressed in scarlet regalia. As secretary of state, Valendrea's presence was required. Two more bishops followed Valendrea, along with the papal physician, whom Michener had specifically requested. He'd told Ngovi nothing of the details surrounding the death. Nor had he told the villa staff, merely informing the nun and chamberlain to make sure no one entered the bedroom.

Three minutes passed before the bedchamber door swung open and the two cardinals and physician entered. Ngovi closed the door and secured the latch. The doctor moved toward the bed and examined Clement. Michener had left everything exactly as he found it, including Clement's laptop computer, still on, connected to a phone line, its monitor bright with a screen saver programmed specially for Clement—a tiara crossed by two keys.

"Tell me what happened," Ngovi said, laying a small black satchel on the bed.

Michener explained what he'd found, then motioned to the table. Neither of the cardinals had noticed the pill vial. "It's empty."

"Are you saying the supreme pontiff of the Roman Catholic Church killed himself?" Valendrea asked.

He wasn't in the mood. "I'm not saying anything. Only that there were thirty pills in that container."

Valendrea turned toward the doctor. "What's your assessment, Doctor?"

"He's been dead for some time. Five or six hours, maybe longer. There's no evidence of trauma, nothing to outwardly indicate cardiac arrest. No blood loss or bruising. From a first look, it appears he died in his sleep."

"Could it have been from the pills?" Ngovi asked.

"There's no way to tell, except through an autopsy."

"That's out of the question," Valendrea immediately said.

Michener faced the secretary of state. "We need to know."

"We don't need to know anything." Valendrea's voice rose. "In fact, it's better we know nothing. Destroy that pill vial. Can you imagine the impact on the Church if it became known that the pope took his own life? The mere suggestion could cause irrevocable harm."

Michener had already considered the same thing, but he was determined to handle the situation better than when John Paul I had died suddenly in 1978, only thirty-three days into his pontificate. The subsequent rumors and misleading information—designed simply to shield the fact that a nun had discovered the body instead of a priest—only fueled conspiratorialists with visions of a papal murder.

"I agree," Michener conceded. "A suicide cannot be publicly known. But *we* should know the truth."

"So that we can lie?" Valendrea asked. "This way we know nothing."

Interesting Valendrea was concerned about lying, but Michener kept silent.

Ngovi faced the doctor. "Would a blood sample suffice?"

The physician nodded.

"Take it."

"You have no authority," Valendrea boomed. "That would need a consultation with the Sacred College. You are not pope."

Ngovi's features remained expressionless. "I for one want to know how this man died. His immortal soul is of concern to me." Ngovi faced the doctor. "Run the test yourself, then destroy the sample. Tell the results only to me. Clear?"

The man nodded.

"You're overstepping, Ngovi," Valendrea said.

"Take it up with the Sacred College."

Valendrea's dilemma was amusing. He couldn't overrule Ngovi nor, for obvious reasons, could he take the matter to the cardinals. So the Tuscan wisely kept his mouth shut. Maybe, Michener feared, he was simply giving Ngovi enough rope to hang himself.

Ngovi opened the black case he'd brought with him and removed a silver hammer, then stepped to the head of the bed. Michener realized the ritual about to be performed was required of the camerlengo, no matter how useless the task may be.

Ngovi lightly tapped Clement's forehead with the hammer and

asked the question that had been posed to the corpses of popes for centuries. "Jakob Volkner. Are you dead?"

A full minute of silence passed, then Ngovi asked the question again. After another minute of silence, he asked a third time.

Ngovi then made the required declaration. "The pope is dead."

Ngovi reached down and lifted Clement's right hand. The Fisherman's Ring wrapped the fourth finger.

"Strange," Ngovi said. "Clement did not usually wear this."

Michener knew that to be true. The cumbersome gold ring was more a signet than a piece of jewelry. It depicted St. Peter the fisherman, encircled by Clement's name and date of investiture. It had been placed on Clement's finger after the last conclave by the then-camerlengo and was used to seal papal briefs. Rarely was it worn, and Clement particularly shunned it.

"Maybe he knew we would be looking for it," Valendrea said.

He was right, Michener thought. Apparently, some planning had occurred. Which was so like Jakob Volkner.

Ngovi removed the ring and dropped it into a black velvet bag. Later, before the assembled cardinals, he would use the hammer to shatter both the ring and the pope's lead seal. That way, no one could stamp any document until a new pope was chosen.

"It is done," Ngovi said.

Michener realized the transfer of power was now complete. The thirty-four-month reign of Clement XV, the 267th successor of St. Peter, the first German to hold the throne in nine hundred years, was over. From this moment on he was no longer the papal secretary. He was merely a monsignor in the temporary service of the camerlengo of the Holy Roman Church.

KATERINA RUSHED THROUGH LEONARDO DA VINCI AIRPORT toward the Lufthansa ticket counter. She was booked on a one o'clock flight to Frankfurt. From there she was unsure of her next destination, but she'd worry about that tomorrow or the day after. The main thing was that Tom Kealy and Colin Michener were in the past, and it was time to make something of herself. She felt awful about deceiving Michener, but since she'd never made contact with Valendrea and had told Ambrosi precious little, perhaps the violation could be forgiven.

She was glad to be done with Tom Kealy, though she doubted if he would even give her a second thought. He was on the rise and didn't need a clinging vine, and that was exactly the way she felt. True, he'd need somebody to actually do all the work that he'd eventually take credit for, but she was sure some other woman would come along and take her place.

The terminal was busy, but she began to notice crowds huddled around the televisions that dotted the concourse. She also spotted women crying. Her gaze finally settled on one of the elevated video screens. St. Peter's Square spanned out from an aerial view. Drifting close to the monitor, she heard, "There is a profound sadness here. Clement XV's death is being felt by all who loved this pontiff. He will be missed."

"The pope is dead?" she asked out loud.

A man in a wool overcoat said to her, "He died in his sleep last night at Castle Gandolfo. May God take his soul."

She was taken aback. A man she'd hated for years was gone. She'd never actually met him—Michener had tried once to introduce them, but she'd refused. At the time, Jakob Volkner was the archbishop of Cologne, in whom she saw everything she despised about organized religion—not to mention the other side of a tug-of-war that had yanked at Colin Michener's conscience. She'd lost that battle and had resented Volkner ever since. Not for what he may or may not have done, but for what he symbolized.

Now he was dead. Colin must be devastated.

A part of her said to head for the ticket counter and fly to Germany. Michener would survive. He always did. But there would soon be a new pope. New appointments. A fresh wave of priests, bishops, and cardinals would flood to Rome. She knew enough about Vatican politics to realize that Clement's allies were through. Their careers were over.

None of that was her problem. Yet a part of her said that it was. Maybe old habits truly were hard to break.

She turned, luggage in hand, and headed out of the terminal.

THIRTY-ONE

CASTLE GANDOLFO, 2:30 P.M.

VALENDREA STARED AT THE ASSEMBLED CARDINALS. THE MOOD was tense, many of the men pacing the room in an uncharacteristic show of anxiety. There were fourteen in the villa's salon, mainly cardinals assigned to the Curia or to posts near Rome who'd heeded the call made three hours ago to all 160 members of the Sacred College: CLEMENT XV IS DEAD. COME TO ROME IMMEDIATELY. To those within a hundred-mile radius of the Vatican, an additional message urged that they meet at Castle Gandolfo at two P.M.

The interregnum had begun, that period of time between the death of one pope and the election of another, a lapse of uncertainty when the reins of papal power hung loose. In centuries past this was when cardinals seized control, buying conclave votes with either promises or violence. Valendrea missed those times. The victor should be the strongest. The weak had no place at the apex. But modern papal elections were much more benign. The battles now were fought with television cameras and public opinion polls. Picking a popular pope was deemed far more critical than selecting a competent one. Which, Valendrea had often thought, explained more than anything else the rise of Jakob Volkner.

He was pleased with the turnout. Nearly all of the men who'd come were in his column. By his latest count he was still shy of the two-thirds-plus-one needed for an early ballot victory, but among himself, Ambrosi, and the tape recorders, over the coming two weeks he should secure the needed support.

He was unsure as to what Ngovi was going to say. The two of them had not spoken since earlier in Clement's bedroom. He could only hope the African would use good judgment. Ngovi was standing toward the end of the long room before an elegant white marble fireplace. All the other princes were standing, too.

"Eminences," Ngovi said, "I will have assignments later in the day to enlist your assistance in planning the funeral and conclave. I think it important Clement be given the finest farewell. The people loved him, and they should be given an opportunity to say a proper goodbye. In that regard, we will all accompany the body back to Rome later this evening. There will be a Mass in St. Peter's."

Many of the cardinals nodded.

"Is it clear how the Holy Father died?" one of the cardinals asked.

Ngovi faced the questioner. "That is being ascertained now."

"Is there any problem?" another asked.

Ngovi stood rigid. "He appears to have died peacefully in his sleep. But I am no doctor. His physician will ascertain the cause of death. All of us realized the Holy Father was in declining health, so this is not altogether unexpected."

Valendrea was pleased with Ngovi's comments. Yet another part of him was concerned. Ngovi was in a dominant position and seemed to be enjoying his status. Already, over the past few hours, the African had commanded the papal master of ceremonies and the Apostolic Camera to begin their administration of the Holy See. Traditionally those two departments directed the Curia during the interregnum. He'd also taken possession of Castle Gandolfo by instructing the guards to admit no one, including cardinals, without his express approval, and directed the papal apartments in the Apostolic Palace to be sealed.

He'd further communicated with the Vatican press office, arranged for the release of a prepared statement on Clement's death, and delegated to three cardinals the task of personally communicating with the media. Everyone else had been ordered to decline interviews. The diplomatic corps around the world was similarly warned against press contact, but encouraged to communicate with their respective heads of state. Already tributes had come in from the United States, Britain, France, and Spain.

None of the actions taken so far was outside the camerlengo's duties, so Valendrea could say nothing. But the last thing he needed was for the cardinals to draw strength from Ngovi's fortitude. Only two camerlengos in modern times had been elected pope, so the position was not a stepping-stone to the papacy. Unfortunately, though, neither was secretary of state.

"Will the conclave begin on time?" the cardinal from Venice asked.

"In fifteen days," Ngovi said. "We will be ready."

Valendrea knew, under rules promulgated in John Paul II's Apostolic Constitution, that was the soonest any conclave could begin. The preparation time had been eased by the construction of the Domus Sanctae Marthae, a spacious hotel-like facility normally used by seminarians. No longer was every available alcove converted into makeshift quarters, and Valendrea was glad things had changed. The new facility was at least comfortable. It had been used for the first time during Clement's conclave, and Ngovi had already ordered the building readied for the 113 cardinals below the age of eighty who would be staying there during the voting.

"Cardinal Ngovi," Valendrea said, catching the African's attention, "when will the death certificate be issued?" He hoped only Ngovi understood the true message.

"I have requested the master of papal liturgical celebrations, the cleric prelates, secretary, and chancellor of the Apostolic Camera to be at the Vatican tonight. I've been told the cause of death will be ascertained by then."

"Is an autopsy being performed?" one of the cardinals asked.

Valendrea knew that was a sensitive subject. Only one pope had ever been subjected to an autopsy, and then only to ascertain if Napoleon had poisoned him. There had been talk of a postmortem on John Paul I when he died so unexpectedly, but the cardinals squelched that effort. But this situation was different. One of those pontiffs died suspiciously, the other suddenly. Clement's death was not unexpected. He'd been seventy-four when chosen and, after all, most of the cardinals had elected him simply because he would not live long.

"No autopsy will be performed," Ngovi said flatly.

His tone conveyed that the issue was not open for discussion. Ordinarily, Valendrea would have resented that overstepping, but not this time. He heaved a sigh of relief. Apparently his adversary had decided to play along, and thankfully none of the cardinals challenged the decision. A few glanced in his direction, as if waiting for a response. But his silence served as a signal that the secretary of state was satisfied with the camerlengo's decision.

Beyond the theological implications of a papal suicide, Valendrea could ill afford a wave of sympathy aimed toward Clement. It was little secret that he and the pope did not get along. An inquisitive press might raise questions, and he did not want to be labeled as the man who may have driven a pope to his death. Cardinals terrified for their own careers might elect another man, like Ngovi, who would surely strip Valendrea of all power—tapes or no tapes. He'd learned at the last conclave to never underestimate the power of a coalition. Thankfully, Ngovi had apparently decided the good of the church outweighed this golden opportunity to unseat his chief rival, and Valendrea was glad for the man's weakness. He would not have shown the same deference if the roles were reversed.

"I do have one word of warning," Ngovi said.

Valendrea again could say nothing. And he noticed that the bishop of Nairobi seemed to be enjoying his self-imposed restraint.

"I remind each of you of your oath not to discuss the coming conclave prior to our being locked in the Sistine. There is to be no campaigning, no press interviews, no opinions expressed. Possible selections should not be discussed at all."

"I don't need a lecture," one cardinal made clear.

"Perhaps you don't. But there are some who do."

And with that, Ngovi left the room.

THIRTY-TWO

3:00 P.M.

MICHENER SAT IN A CHAIR BESIDE THE DESK AND WATCHED AS two nuns washed Clement's body. The physician had finished his examination hours ago and returned to Rome with his blood sample. Cardinal Ngovi had already ordered that there would be no autopsy, and since Castle Gandolfo was part of the Vatican state, sovereign territory of an independent nation, no one would question that decision. With precious few exceptions, canon law—not Italian law—governed here.

It was strange staring at the naked corpse of a man he'd known for more than a quarter century. He remembered back to all of the times they'd shared. Clement was the one who'd helped him come to the realization that his natural father simply thought more of himself than of his child, explaining Irish society and the pressures his birth mother surely would have faced as an unmarried mother. *How can you blame her?* Volkner had asked. And he'd agreed. He couldn't. Resentment would only cloud the sacrifices his adoptive parents had made. So he'd finally let go of his anger and forgiven the mother and father he never knew.

Now he was staring at the lifeless body of the man who'd helped make that forgiveness possible. He was here because protocol re-

quired a priest be in attendance. Normally the papal master of ceremonies performed the task, but that monsignor was not available. So
Ngovi had directed that he substitute.

He stood from the chair and paced before the French doors as
the nuns finished their bathing and the funeral technicians entered.
They were part of Rome's largest mortuary and had been embalming popes since Paul VI. They carried five bottles of pink solution
and gently settled each container on the floor.

One of the technicians walked over. "Perhaps, Father, you'd like
to wait outside. This is not a pleasant sight for those unaccustomed
to it."

He headed for the hall, where he found Cardinal Ngovi walking toward the bedroom.

"They're here?" Ngovi asked.

"Italian law requires a twenty-four-hour period before embalming. You know that. This may be Vatican territory, but we've been
through this argument before. The Italians would require us to wait."

Ngovi nodded. "I understand, but the doctor called from Rome.
Jakob's bloodstream was saturated with medication. He killed himself, Colin. No doubt. I can't allow evidence of that to remain. The
doctor has destroyed his sample. He cannot, and will not, reveal anything."

"And the cardinals?"

"They'll be told he died from cardiac arrest. That's what will appear on the death certificate."

He could see the strain on Ngovi's face. Lying did not come easy
to this man.

"We have no choice, Colin. He has to be embalmed. I can't
worry about Italian law."

Michener ran a hand through his hair. This had been a long day,
and it wasn't over yet. "I knew he was bothered by something, but
there was nothing that pointed to him being this troubled. How was
he while I was gone?"

"He went back into the Riserva. I'm told Valendrea was there
with him."

"I know." He told Ngovi what Clement had said. "He showed him what Father Tibor sent. What it was, he wouldn't say." He then told Ngovi more about Tibor and how the pope had reacted on learning of the Bulgarian's death.

Ngovi shook his head. "This is not the way I thought his papacy would end."

"We must ensure his memory is preserved."

"It will be. Even Valendrea will be our ally on that." Ngovi motioned to the door. "I don't think anyone will question our actions in embalming this soon. Only four people know the truth, and shortly no proof will remain if any one of us chooses to speak. But there's little worry that will happen. The doctor is bound by laws of confidentiality, you and I loved the man, and Valendrea has self-interests. This secret is safe."

The door to the bedroom opened and one of the technicians stepped out. "We are nearly finished."

"You will burn the pontiff's fluids?" Ngovi asked.

"That has always been our practice. Our company is proud to be of service to the Holy See. You can depend on us."

Ngovi thanked the man, who returned to the bedroom.

"What now?" Michener asked.

"His pontifical vestments have been brought from Rome. You and I shall dress him for burial."

He saw the significance in that gesture and said, "I think he would have liked that."

The motorcade slowly wound its way through the rain toward the Vatican. It had taken nearly an hour to drive the eighteen miles from Castle Gandolfo, the route lined with thousands of mourners. Michener rode in the third vehicle with Ngovi, the remaining cardinals in an assortment of cars hastily ferried from the Vatican. A hearse led the procession, with Clement's body lying in the rear dressed in robes and miter, illuminated so the faithful could see. Now, inside the city, nearing six P.M., it seemed as if all of Rome filled the sidewalks, the police keeping the way clear so the cars could proceed.

St. Peter's Square was packed, but an alley had been cordoned off among a sea of umbrellas that twisted a path between the colonnades to the basilica. Wails and weeping followed the cars. Many of the mourners tossed flowers on the hoods, so many it was becoming difficult to see out the windshield. One of the security men finally swiped the piles away, but another simply started in its place.

The cars passed through the Arch of the Bells and left the crowds behind. Into the Piazza of the Protomartyrs the procession rounded the sacristy of St. Peter's and headed for a rear entrance into the basilica. Here, safe behind the walls, the airspace above restricted, Clement's body could be readied for three days of public viewing.

A light rain sheathed the gardens in a frothy mist. Walkway lights burned in blurred images like the sun through thick clouds.

Michener tried to imagine what was happening in the buildings around him. In the workshops of the *sampietrini* a triple coffin was being constructed—the inner of bronze, the second of cedar, the outer of cypress. A catafalque had already been assembled and positioned inside St. Peter's, a solitary candle burning nearby, awaiting the corpse it was to support in the days ahead.

Michener had noticed, as they'd inched through the piazza, television crews installing cameras on the balustrades, the choicest spots among the 162 statues surely being claimed fast. The Vatican press office was by now under siege. He'd assisted during the last papal funeral and could envision the thousands of calls that would come in the days ahead. Statesmen from around the world would soon be arriving, and legates would have to be assigned to assist them. The Holy See prided itself on strict adherence to protocol, even in the face of indescribable grief, the task of ensuring success resting with the soft-spoken cardinal sitting beside him.

The cars stopped and cardinals began to congregate near the

hearse. Priests shielded each of the princes with an umbrella. The cardinals wore their black cassocks adorned with a red sash, as required. A Swiss honor guard in ceremonial dress stood at the entrance to the basilica. Clement would not be without them in the days ahead. Four of the guards cradled a bier on their shoulders and paraded toward the hearse. The papal master of ceremonies stood nearby. He was a Dutch priest with a bearded face and a rotund body. He stepped forward and said, "The catafalque is ready."

Ngovi nodded.

The master of ceremonies moved toward the hearse and assisted the technicians with the removal of Clement's body. Once the corpse was centered on the bier and the miter positioned, the Dutchman motioned the technicians away. He then carefully arranged the vestments, slowly creasing each fold. Two priests held umbrellas over the body. Another young priest stepped forward, holding the pallium. The narrow band of white wool marked with six purple crosses signified the plenitude of the pontifical office. The master of ceremonies draped the two-inch band around Clement's neck, then arranged the crosses above the chest, shoulders, and abdomen. He made a few adjustments to the shoulder blocks and finally straightened the head. He then knelt, signaling that he was finished.

A slight nod of Ngovi's head caused the Swiss guard to raise the bier. The priests with umbrellas withdrew. The cardinals fell into line behind.

Michener did not join the procession. He was not a prince of the Church, and what lay ahead was only for them. He would be expected to empty his apartment in the palace by tomorrow. It, too, would be sealed awaiting the conclave. His office must likewise be cleared. His patronage ended with Clement's last breath. Those once in favor departed to make room for those soon-to-be-in-favor.

Ngovi waited until the end to join the line into the basilica. Before he marched off, the cardinal turned and whispered, "I want you to inventory the papal apartment and remove his belongings. Clement would have wanted no other to tend to his possessions. I have left word with the guards that you are to be allowed entrance. Do it now."

The guard opened the papal apartment for Michener. The door closed behind him and he was left alone with an odd feeling. Where once he'd relished his time here, he now felt like an intruder.

The rooms were exactly as Clement had left them Saturday morning. The bed was made, the curtains parted, the pope's spare reading glasses still lying on the nightstand. The leather-bound Bible that usually lay there, too, was at Castle Gandolfo, on the desk beside Clement's laptop, both to be returned to Rome shortly.

A few papers remained on the desk beside the silent desktop computer. He thought it best to start there, so he booted the machine and checked the folders. He knew Clement e-mailed a few distant family members and some cardinals on a regular basis, but he apparently hadn't saved any of those transmissions—there were no files recorded. The address book contained about two dozen names. He scanned all of the folders on the hard drive. Most were reports from curial departments, the written word now replaced by ones and zeros on a video screen. He deleted all the folders, using a special program that removed all traces of the files from the hard drive, then switched off the machine. The terminal would stay and be used by the next pope.

He glanced around. He would have to find boxes for Clement's possessions, but for now he stacked everything in the center of the room. There wasn't much. Clement had led a simple life. A bit of furniture, a few books, and some assorted family items were all that he owned.

The scrape of a key in the lock caught his attention.

The door opened and Paolo Ambrosi entered.

"Wait outside," Ambrosi said to the guard as he came in and closed the door.

Michener faced him. "What are you doing here?"

The thin priest stepped forward. "The same as you, clearing out the apartment."

"Cardinal Ngovi delegated the task to me."

"Cardinal Valendrea said you might need help."

Apparently the secretary of state thought a babysitter in order, but he was not in the mood. "Get out of here."

The priest did not move. Michener was a head taller and fifty pounds heavier, but Ambrosi seemed unintimidated. "Your time has passed, Michener."

"Maybe so. But where I come from there's a saying. *A hen doesn't cackle before she lays the egg.*"

Ambrosi chuckled. "I will miss your American humor."

He noticed Ambrosi's reptilian eyes take in the scene.

"I told you to get out. I may be nothing, but Ngovi is camerlengo. Valendrea can't override him."

"Not yet."

"Leave, or I'll interrupt the Mass for further instructions from Ngovi."

He realized the last thing Valendrea would want was an embarrassing scene before the cardinals. Supporters might wonder why he'd ordered an associate to the papal apartments when that duty clearly fell on the papal secretary.

But Ambrosi did not move.

So he stepped around his visitor and headed for the door. "As you say, Ambrosi, my time's passed. I've got nothing to lose."

He grasped the door handles.

"Stop," Ambrosi said. "I'll leave you to your task." The voice was barely a whisper, the look on Ambrosi's face devoid of feeling. He wondered how such a man could ever have become a priest.

Michener opened the door. The guards were just on the other side and he knew his visitor would say nothing to stimulate their interest. He let a smile form and said, "Have a nice evening, Father."

Ambrosi brushed past and Michener slammed the door, but only after ordering the guards not to admit another soul.

He returned to the desk. He needed to finish what he'd started. His sadness in leaving the Vatican was tempered by a relief in knowing that he would no longer have to deal with the likes of Paolo Ambrosi.

He searched through the desk drawers. Most contained stationery, pens, some books, and a few computer disks. Nothing important until the bottom right drawer, where he found Clement's will. The pope traditionally drafted his will himself, expressing in his own hand his final requests and hopes for the future. Michener unfolded the single sheet and noticed immediately the date, October 10, a little more than thirty days ago:

I, Jakob Volkner, presently possessed of all my faculties and desirous of expressing my last will and testament, do hereby bequeath all that I may possess at the time of my death to Colin Michener. My parents died long ago and my siblings followed in the years after. Colin served me long and well. He is the closest I have left in this world to family. I ask that he do with my belongings as he deems appropriate, using the wisdom and judgment I came to trust during my life. I would request that my funeral be simple and if possible that I be buried in Bamberg, in the cathedral of my youth, though I understand if the church deems otherwise. When I accepted the mantle of St. Peter I likewise accepted the responsibilities, including a duty to rest beneath the basilica with my brethren. I further ask forgiveness from all those I may have offended in words or deeds, and I especially ask forgiveness of our Lord and Savior for the shortcomings I have shown. May He have mercy on my soul.

Tears welled in Michener's eyes. He, too, hoped God would have mercy on his dear friend's soul. Catholic teachings were clear. Human beings were obliged to preserve the honor of life as stewards, not owners, of what the Almighty had entrusted. Suicide was contrary to the love of oneself, and to the love of a living God. It broke the ties of solidarity with family and nation. In short, it was a sin. But the eternal salvation of those who took their own lives was not lost completely. The Church taught that, by ways known only to God, an opportunity for repentance would be provided.

And he hoped that was the case.

If indeed heaven existed, Jakob Volkner deserved admission. Whatever had compelled him to do the unspeakable should not consign his soul to eternal damnation.

He laid the will down and tried not to think about eternity.

He'd found himself of late contemplating his own mortality. He was nearing fifty, not all that old, but life no longer seemed infinite. He could envision a time when his body or mind might not allow him the opportunity to enjoy what he'd come to expect. How much longer would he live? Twenty years? Thirty? Forty? Clement had still been vibrant approaching eighty, working sixteen-hour days with regularity. He could only hope he retained half that stamina. Still, his life would eventually end. And he wondered if the deprivations and sacrifices demanded by his Church, and his God, were worth it. Would there be a reward in the afterlife? Or simply nothing?

Dust to dust.

His mind snapped back to his duty.

The will lying before him would have to be given to the Vatican press office. It was traditional to release the text, but first the camerlengo would have to approve, so he slid the page into his cassock.

He decided to anonymously donate the furniture to a local charity. The books and few personal belongings he'd keep as a remembrance of a man he'd loved. Against the far wall rested the wooden chest Clement had carried with him for years. Michener knew that it had been carved in Oberammergau, a Bavarian town at the base of the Alps famous for its wood craftsmen. It possessed the look and feel of a Riemenschneider, the exterior unstained and adorned with bold portrayals of the apostles, saints, and the Virgin.

In all their years together, he'd never known what Clement kept inside. Now the chest was his. He walked over and tried the lid. Locked. A brass receptacle allowed for a key. He hadn't seen one anywhere in the apartment, and he certainly did not want to inflict any damage prying the box open. So he decided to store the chest and worry about what was inside later.

He stepped back to the desk and finished cleaning out the remaining drawers. In the last one he found a single sheet of trifolded papal stationery. On it was a handwritten note.

I, Clement XV, on this day have elevated to the status of Cardinal Eminence the Reverend Father Colin Michener.

He could hardly believe what he read. Clement had exercised his ability to a appoint a cardinal *in petto*—in secret. Usually cardinals were informed of their elevation through a certificate from the reigning pontiff, openly published, then invested by the pope in an elaborate consistory. But secret appointments became common for cardinals in communist countries, or in places where oppressive regimes might endanger the nominee. The rules for *in petto* appointments made clear that seniority dated from the time of the appointment, not from the time the selection was made public, but there was one other rule that sank his heart. If the pope died before an *in petto* selection was made public, the appointment died, too.

He held the sheet in his hand. It was dated sixty days before.

He'd come so close to a scarlet biretta.

Alberto Valendrea could well be the next occupant of the apartments surrounding him. Little chance existed that an *in petto* appointment of Clement XV's would be affirmed. But a part of him didn't mind. With all that had happened over the past eighteen hours, he hadn't even thought of Father Tibor, but now he considered the old priest. Maybe he'd return to Zlatna and the orphanage and finish what the Bulgarian had started. Something told him that was the thing for him to do. If the Church didn't approve, he'd tell them all to go to hell, beginning with Alberto Valendrea.

You want to be a cardinal? To achieve that, you must grasp the measure of that responsibility. How can you expect me to elevate you when you fail to see what is so clear?

Clement's words from Turin last Thursday. He'd wondered about their harshness. Now knowing that his mentor had already chosen him, he wondered even more. *How can you expect me to elevate you when you fail to see what is so clear?*

See what?

He stuffed the paper into his pocket with the will.

No one would ever know what Clement had done. It didn't matter anymore. All that mattered was that his friend had thought him worthy, and that was enough for him.

THIRTY-THREE

MICHENER FINISHED PACKING EVERYTHING IN THE FIVE BOXES provided by the Swiss guards. The armoire, dresser, and nightstands were now empty. The furniture was being carted out by workmen to be stored in a basement warehouse until he could make arrangements for its donation.

He stood in the corridor as the doors were closed a final time and a lead seal stamped in place. In all likelihood he would never enter the papal apartments again. Few ever made it that far within the Church, and even fewer made a return trip. Ambrosi was right. His time was over. The rooms themselves would not be opened until a new pope stood before the doors and the seals were broken. He shuddered at the thought of Alberto Valendrea being that new occupant.

The cardinals were still assembled in St. Peter's and a requiem funeral Mass was being said before the body of Clement XV, one of many to be offered over the next nine days. While that was happening, there was one task left for him to perform before his official duties ended.

He descended to the third floor.

As with Clement's apartment, there was little in Michener's office that would not stay. All of the furnishings were Vatican requisition. The paintings on the wall, including a portrait of Clement, belonged to the Holy See. Everything he owned would fit into one box, and consisted of a few desk accessories, a Bavarian anniversary clock, and three pictures of his parents. All his postings with Clement had provided whatever tangible things he'd ever needed. Beyond some clothes and a laptop, he owned nothing. He'd managed through the years to save a large portion of his salary and, after taking advantage of some savvy investment tips, a few hundred thousand dollars was on deposit in Geneva—his retirement money—since the Church provided miserably for priests. Reforming the pension fund had been discussed at length, and Clement had been in favor of doing something, but that endeavor would now have to await the next pontificate.

He sat at the desk and switched on his computer for a final time. He needed to check any e-mail messages and prepare instructions for his successor. Over the past week his deputies had handled everything, and he saw that most of his messages could wait until after the conclave. Depending on who was elected pope, he might be needed for a week or so after the conclave to ease the transition. But if Valendrea secured the throne, Paolo Ambrosi would almost certainly be the next papal secretary and Michener's Vatican credentials would be immediately revoked, his services no longer required. Which would be fine by him. He would do nothing to help Ambrosi.

He continued to scroll down the list of e-mails, checking each one, then deleting. A few he saved, tagging a short note for the staff. Three were condolences from bishops who were friends, and he sent back a short reply. Maybe one of them could use an aide? But he dismissed the thought. He wasn't going to do that again. What had Katerina said in Bucharest? *Is your life to be in the service of others?* Perhaps if he devoted himself to something like the cause Father Tibor had deemed important, Clement XV's soul might be granted salvation. His sacrifice could be penance for his friend's shortcoming.

And that thought made him feel better.

The pope's upcoming Christmas schedule appeared on the screen. The itinerary had been transmitted to Castle Gandolfo for review and bore Clement's initials, signifying approval. It called for the pope to celebrate the traditional Christmas Eve Mass in St. Peter's, then deliver his yuletide message the following day from the balcony. Michener noted the time of the return e-mail from Castle Gandolfo. Ten fifteen A.M., Saturday. That was about when he'd arrived back in Rome from Bucharest, long before he and Clement first talked. And even longer before Clement learned of Father Tibor's murder. Strange that a suicidal pontiff had taken the time to review a schedule he had no intention of keeping.

Michener scrolled down to the last e-mail message and noticed no identification tag. Occasionally he received anonymous messages from people who somehow managed to learn his Web address. Most were harmless devotions from folks who wanted their pope to know they cared.

He double-clicked on the entry and saw that the transmission emanated from Castle Gandolfo, dated last evening. Time received, eleven fifty-six P.M.

By now, Colin, you're aware of what I have done. I don't expect you to understand. Just know that the Virgin returned and told me my time had come. Father Tibor was with Her. I waited for Her to take me, but She said I must end my life through my own hand. Father Tibor said it was my duty, the penance for disobedience, and that all would be clear later. I wondered about my soul, but was told the Lord was waiting. I have for too long ignored heaven. I will not this time. You have asked me repeatedly what is wrong. I will tell you. In 1978 Valendrea removed from the Riserva part of the Virgin's third message from Fatima. Only five people know what was originally in that box. Four of them—Sister Lucia, John XXIII, Paul VI, and Father Tibor—are gone. Only Valendrea remains. Of course, he will deny everything and the words you are reading will be deemed the ramblings of a man who took his own life. But know that when John Paul

read the third secret and released it to the world, he was not privy to the en-
tire message. It is for you to set things right. Go to Medjugorje. It is vital.
Not only for me, but for the Church. Consider it a last request from a
friend.

I am sure the Church is preparing for my funeral. Ngovi will do his
duty well. Please, do with my body as you please. Pomp and ceremony do
not make the pious. For me, though, I would prefer the sanctity of Bam-
berg, that lovely city by the river, and the cathedral I so loved. My only re-
gret is that I did not see its beauty one last time. Perhaps, though, my legacy
could still be there. But I shall leave that conclusion to others. God stay
with you, Colin, and know that I loved you dearly, as a father loves his son.

A suicide note, plain and simple, written by a troubled man who
was apparently delusional. The supreme pontiff of the Roman
Catholic Church was saying that the Virgin Mary told him to kill
himself. But the part about Valendrea and the third secret was interesting. Could he give the information credence? He wondered if
Ngovi should be apprised, but concluded that the fewer who knew
about this message, the better. Clement's body was now embalmed,
his fluids consigned to flames, and the cause of death would never
be known. The words glaring back at him from the screen were
nothing but confirmation that perhaps the late pontiff had been
mentally ill.

Not to mention obsessed.

Clement again had urged him to go to Bosnia. He'd not planned
on following through with that request. What was the point? He
still carried the letter signed by Clement addressed to a seer, but the
authority sanctioning that order now emanated from the camerlengo and the Sacred College. There was no way Alberto Valendrea
was going to allow him a jaunt through Bosnia looking for Marian
secrets. That would be an appeasement to a pope he openly despised. Not to mention official permission for any trip would require the cardinals being collectively informed about Father Tibor,
papal apparitions, and Clement's obsession with the third secret of

Fatima. The number of questions generated by those revelations would be staggering. Clement's reputation was too precious to risk. Bad enough four men knew of a papal suicide. He certainly wasn't going to be the one who actually impugned the memory of a great man. Yet Ngovi might still need to read Clement's last words. He recalled what Clement had urged at Turin. *Maurice Ngovi is the closest thing to me you will ever have. Remember that in the days ahead.*

He printed a hard copy.

Then erased the file and switched off the machine.

THIRTY-FOUR

MONDAY, NOVEMBER 27
11:00 A.M.

MICHENER ENTERED THE VATICAN THROUGH ST. PETER'S Square, following a throng of visitors who'd just streamed off buses. He'd vacated his apartment in the Apostolic Palace ten days ago, just before Clement XV's funeral. He was still credentialed with a security pass but, after tending to this last administrative matter, his duties to the Holy See would officially end.

Cardinal Ngovi had asked him to stay in Rome until the conclave convened. He'd even suggested that he join his staff at the Congregation for Catholic Education, but could not promise a position past the conclave. Ngovi's Vatican assignment ended with Clement's death as well, and the camerlengo had already said that if Valendrea achieved the papacy he would return to Africa.

Clement's funeral had been a simple affair, held outdoors in front of the restored exterior of St. Peter's Basilica. A million people had crowded the piazza, the flame of a single candle beside the coffin battered by a steady breeze. Michener had not sat with the princes of the Church, where he might have been if things had developed differently. Instead he took his place among the staff who had served their pope faithfully for thirty-four months. More than a hundred heads of state had attended, the entire ceremony transmitted live by television and radio around the world.

Ngovi did not preside. Instead, he delegated the speaking assignments to other cardinals. A shrewd move, actually, one that would surely endear the chosen men to the camerlengo. Maybe not enough to guarantee a conclave vote, but certainly enough to cultivate a willing listener.

Not surprisingly, none of the assignments went to Valendrea, and justifying that omission was easy. The secretary of state focused on the Holy See's foreign relations during the interregnum. All his attention was on external matters, the task of praising Clement and bidding the pontiff farewell traditionally left to others. Valendrea had taken his duty to heart and been a fixture in the press over the past two weeks, interviewed by every major news organization in the world, the Tuscan's words sparse and carefully chosen.

When the ceremony ended, twelve pallbearers bore the coffin through the Door of Death and down into the grotto. The sarcophagus, hastily readied by stonemasons, bore an image of Clement II, the eleventh-century German pope Jakob Volkner had so admired, along with Clement XV's papal emblem. The grave site was near John XXIII's, something else Clement would have liked. There he was entombed with 148 of his brethren.

"Colin."

His name being called out caught his attention and he stopped. Katerina was making her way across the piazza. He'd not seen her since Bucharest, nearly three weeks ago.

"You're back in Rome?" he asked.

She was dressed in a different style. Chinos, chocolate-brown lamb-suede shirt, and houndstooth jacket. A bit more trendy than he recalled her tastes, but attractive.

"I never left."

"You came here from Bucharest?"

She nodded. Her ebony hair was worked by the wind and she

brushed the strands from her face. "I was on my way to leave when I learned about Clement. So I stayed on."

"What have you been doing?"

"Grabbed a couple of freelance jobs to cover the funeral."

"I saw Kealy on CNN." The priest had been a regular the past week, offering slanted insights into the coming conclave.

"I did, too. But I haven't seen Tom since the day after Clement died. You were right. I can do better."

"You did the right thing. I've been listening to that fool on television. He's got an opinion on everything, and most of them are wrong."

"Maybe CNN should have hired you?"

He chuckled. "Just what I need."

"What are you going to do, Colin?"

"I'm here to tell Cardinal Ngovi that I'm headed back to Romania."

"To see Father Tibor again?"

"You don't know?"

A puzzled look came to her face. He told her about Tibor's murder.

"That poor man. He didn't deserve that. And those children. He was all they had."

"Exactly why I'm going. You were right. It's time I do something."

"You seem happy about the decision."

He glanced around the square at a place he'd once strolled with the impunity of the papal secretary. Now he felt like a stranger. "It's time to move on."

"No more ivory towers?"

"Not in my future. That orphanage in Zlatna is going to be home for a while."

She shifted on her feet. "We've come a long way. No arguments. No anger. Finally, friends."

"Just don't make the same mistakes twice. That's all any of us can hope for." And he saw that she agreed. He was glad they'd run into each other again. But Ngovi was waiting. "Take care, Kate."

"You, too, Colin."

And he walked away, fighting hard the urge to glance back one last time.

He found Ngovi in his office at the Congregation for Catholic Education. The outer warren of rooms bustled with activity. With the conclave starting tomorrow, there seemed a push to get everything finished.

"I actually believe we're ready," Ngovi told him.

The door was closed and the staff had been instructed not to disturb them. Michener was expecting another job pitch, since Ngovi was the one who'd called for the meeting.

"I waited until now to speak with you, Colin. Tomorrow I'll be locked away in the Sistine." Ngovi straightened in the chair. "I want you to go to Bosnia."

The request surprised him. "For what? You and I both agreed the whole thing was ridiculous."

"The matter disturbs me. Clement was intent on something, and I want to carry out his wishes. That's the duty of any camerlengo. He wanted to learn the tenth secret. So do I."

He hadn't mentioned to Ngovi Clement's final e-mail message. So he reached into his pocket and found the copy. "You need to read this."

The cardinal slipped on a pair of spectacles and studied the message.

"He sent that just before midnight on that Sunday. Maurice, he was delusional. If I go traipsing around Bosnia, we're going to do nothing but draw attention. Why don't we let it lie?"

Ngovi removed his glasses. "I want you to go now more than ever."

"You sound like Jakob. What's gotten into you?"

"I don't know. I just know that this was important to him, and we should finish what he wanted. This new information about Valendrea removing part of the third secret makes it vital that we investigate."

He remained unconvinced. "So far, Maurice, there's been no issue raised over Clement's death. You want to take that chance?"

"I've considered that. But I doubt the press will be interested in what you're doing. The conclave will consume their attention. So I want you to go. You still have his letter to the seer?"

He nodded.

"I'll give you one with my signature. That should be enough."

He told Ngovi what he intended to do in Romania. "Can't somebody else handle this?"

Ngovi shook his head. "You know the answer to that."

He could tell that Ngovi was more apprehensive than usual.

"There's something else you need to know, Colin." Ngovi motioned to the e-mail. "It bears on this. You told me that Valendrea went into the Riserva with the pope. I checked. The records confirm their visit on the Friday night before Clement died. What you don't know is that Valendrea left the Vatican Saturday evening. The trip was unscheduled. In fact, he canceled all appointments to make the time. He was gone till early Sunday morning."

He was impressed with Ngovi's information network. "I didn't know you watched so closely."

"The Tuscan is not the only one with spies."

"Any idea where he went?"

"Only that he left the Rome airport in a private jet before dark and returned on the same aircraft early the next morning."

He recalled the uncomfortable feeling in the café while he and Katerina had talked with Tibor. Did Valendrea know about Father Tibor? Had he been followed? "Tibor died Saturday night. What are you saying, Maurice?"

Ngovi held up his hands in a halting gesture. "I'm only reporting facts. In the Riserva, on Friday, Clement showed Valendrea whatever Father Tibor had sent him. Then the priest was killed the next night. Whether Valendrea's sudden trip on Saturday was related to Father Tibor's murder, I do not know. But the priest left this world at quite an odd time, wouldn't you say?"

"And you think there's an answer to all this in Bosnia?"

"Clement believed so."

He now appreciated Ngovi's true motives. But he wanted to know, "What about the cardinals? Would they not have to be informed what I'm doing?"

"You're not on an official mission. This is between you and me. A gesture to our departed friend. Besides, we'll be in conclave by morning. Locked away. Nobody could be informed."

He understood now why Ngovi had waited to speak with him. But he also recalled Clement's warning about Alberto Valendrea and the lack of privacy. He glanced around at walls that had been erected when the American Revolution was being fought. Could someone be listening? He decided it really didn't matter. "All right, Maurice. I'll do it. But only because you asked and Jakob wanted it. After that, I'm out."

And he hoped Valendrea heard.

THIRTY-FIVE

4:30 P.M.

VALENDREA WAS OVERWHELMED BY THE VOLUME OF INFORMAtion the listening devices were uncovering. Ambrosi had worked every night over the past two weeks, sorting through the tapes, weeding out the trivia, preserving the nuggets. The abbreviated versions, provided to him on microcassette, had revealed much about the cardinals' attitudes, and he was pleased to discover that he was becoming quite *papabile* in the eyes of many, even some he'd yet to fully confirm as supporters.

His restrained approach was working. This time, unlike at Clement XV's conclave, he'd shown the reverence expected of a prince of the Catholic Church. And already commentators were including his name on a short list of possible candidates, along with that of Maurice Ngovi and four other cardinals.

An informal head count taken last evening showed there were forty-eight confirmed *yes* votes. He needed seventy-six to win on an early ballot, assuming all 113 eligible cardinals made it to Rome, which, barring serious illness, should happen. Thankfully, John Paul II's reforms allowed for a change in procedure after three days of balloting. If no pope was selected by then, a series of successive votes would occur, followed by a day of prayer and discussion. After twelve full days of conclave, if there was still no pope, a simple majority of cardinals could then elect. Which meant time was on his side, as he clearly possessed a majority, along with more than enough votes to block anyone else's early election. So he could filibuster if need be—provided, of course, he could keep his voting bloc intact over twelve days.

A few cardinals were becoming a problem. They'd apparently told him one thing then, when they'd thought locked doors afforded them privacy, proclaimed another. He'd checked and found that Ambrosi had amassed some interesting information on several of the traitors—more than enough to convince them of the error in their ways—and he planned to dispatch his aide to each of them before morning.

After tomorrow it would be difficult pressuring votes. He could reinforce attitudes but, within the conclave, quarters were simply too confined, privacy too scarce, and something about the Sistine affected cardinals. Some called it a pull from the Holy Spirit. Others ambition. So he knew that the votes would have to be ensured now, the coming assembly only a confirmation that each was willing to uphold his end of the bargain.

Of course, blackmail could muster only so many votes. The majority of his supporters were loyal to him simply because of his standing within the Church and his background, which stamped him the most *papabile* of the favorites. And he was proud of himself for not doing anything over the past few days to alienate those natural allies.

He was still stunned by Clement's suicide. He'd never thought the German would do anything to endanger his soul. But something Clement said to him in the papal apartment nearly three weeks ago swept through his mind. *I actually hope you do inherit this job. You will find it far different than you might imagine. Maybe you should be the one.* And what the pope said that Friday night, after they left the Riserva. *I wanted you to know what awaits you.* And why hadn't Clement stopped him from burning the translation? *You'll see.*

"Damn you, Jakob," he muttered.

A knock came on his office door, then Ambrosi stepped inside and crossed to the desk. He held a pocket tape recorder. "Listen to this. I just dubbed it off the reel-to-reel. Michener and Ngovi about four hours ago in Ngovi's office."

The conversation lasted about ten minutes. Valendrea switched off the machine. "First Romania. Now Bosnia. They will not stop."

"Apparently Clement left a suicide e-mail for Michener."

Ambrosi knew about Clement's suicide. He'd told him that and more in Romania, including what had happened with Clement in the Riserva. "I must read that e-mail."

Ambrosi stood straight before the desk. "I don't see how that's possible."

"We could reenlist Michener's girlfriend."

"That thought occurred to me. But why does it matter anymore? The conclave starts tomorrow. You will be pope by sundown. Surely, by the next day."

Possible, but he could just as easily be locked in a tight election. "What troubles me is that our African friend apparently has his own information network. I didn't realize I was such a high priority with him." It also bothered him that Ngovi had so easily linked his Romanian trip with Tibor's murder. That could become a problem. "I want you to find Katerina Lew."

He'd purposely not talked with her after Romania. No need. Thanks to Clement, he knew everything he needed to know. Yet it galled him that Ngovi was dispatching envoys on private missions. Especially missions that involved him. Still, there was little he could do about it since he couldn't risk involving the Sacred College. There'd be too many questions and he'd have too few answers. It could also provide Ngovi a way to force an inquiry into his own Romanian trip, and he was not about to present the African with that opportunity.

He was the only one left alive who knew what the Virgin had said. Three popes were gone. He'd already destroyed part of Tibor's cursed reproduction, eliminated the priest himself, and flushed Sister Lucia's original writing into the sewers. All that remained was the facsimile translation waiting in the Riserva. No one could be allowed to see those words. But to gain access to that box he needed to be pope.

He stared up at Ambrosi.

"Unfortunately, Paolo, you must stay here over the coming days. I will need you nearby. But we have to know what Michener does in Bosnia, and she is our best conduit. So find Katerina Lew and reenlist her help."

"How do you know she's in Rome?"

"Where else would she be?"

THIRTY-SIX

KATERINA WAS DRAWN TO THE CNN BOOTH, JUST OUTSIDE THE
south colonnade in St. Peter's Square. She'd seen Tom Kealy from
across the cobbled expanse, beneath bright lights and in front of
three cameras. The piazza was dotted with many makeshift television sets. The thousands of chairs and barricades from Clement's
funeral were gone, replaced by souvenir hawkers, protestors, pilgrims, and the journalists who'd flocked to Rome, ready for the conclave that would begin tomorrow morning, camera lenses angled for
the best view of a metal flue high above the Sistine Chapel where
white smoke would signal success.

She drew close to a ring of gawkers huddled around the CNN
dais where Kealy was talking to the cameras. He wore a black wool
cassock and Roman collar, looking very much the priest. For someone with so little regard for his profession, he seemed entirely comfortable with its physical trappings.

"—that's right, in the old days, ballots were simply burned after
each scrutiny with either dry or wet straw to produce black or white
smoke. Now a chemical is added to produce color. There's been a
lot of confusion in recent conclaves about the smoke. Apparently

even the Catholic Church can, at times, let science make matters easier."

"What have you been hearing about tomorrow?" asked the female correspondent sitting beside Kealy.

Kealy turned his attention toward the camera. "My guess is that there are two favorites. Cardinals Ngovi and Valendrea. Ngovi would be the first African pope since the first century and could do a lot for his home continent. Look what John Paul II did for Poland and Eastern Europe. Africa could likewise use a champion."

"But are Catholics ready for a black pope?"

Kealy gave a shrug. "What does it matter anymore? Most of today's Catholics are from Latin and South America and Asia. The European cardinals no longer dominate. All of the popes since John XXIII made sure of that by expanding the Sacred College and packing it with non-Italians. The Church would be better off, in my opinion, with Ngovi than Valendrea."

She smiled. Kealy was apparently having his revenge on the righteous Alberto Valendrea. Interesting how the tide had turned. Nineteen days ago, Kealy was on the receiving end of a Valendrea barrage, on the way to excommunication. But during the interregnum, that tribunal, along with everything else, was suspended. Now here was the accused, on worldwide television, disparaging his chief accuser, a man about to make a serious run for the papacy.

"Why would you say the Church would be better off with Ngovi?" asked the correspondent.

"Valendrea is Italian. The Church has steadily moved away from Italian domination. His choice would be a retreat. He's also too conservative for the twenty-first-century Catholic."

"Some might say a return to traditional roots would be beneficial."

Kealy shook his head. "You spend forty years since Vatican II trying to modernize—do a fairly good job in making your Church a worldwide institution—then toss all that out the door? The pope is no longer merely the bishop of Rome. He's the head of a billion faithful, the vast majority of whom are not Italian, not European, not even Caucasian. It would be suicidal to elect Valendrea. Not when there's somebody like Ngovi, equally as *papabile,* and far more attractive to the world."

A hand on Katerina's shoulder startled her. She whirled around to see the black eyes of Father Paolo Ambrosi. The annoying little priest was only a few inches from her face. A bolt of anger flashed through her, but she kept calm.

"He doesn't seem to like Cardinal Valendrea," the priest whispered.

"Get your hand off my shoulder."

A smile frayed the edges of Ambrosi's mouth and he withdrew his hand. "I thought you might be here." He motioned to Kealy. "With your paramour."

A sick feeling clutched her gut, but she willed herself to show no fear. "What do you want?"

"Surely you don't want to talk here? If your associate were to turn his head, he might wonder why you were conversing with one so close to the cardinal he despises. He might even get jealous and fly into a rage."

"I don't think he's got anything to worry about from you. I piss sitting down, so I doubt I'm your type."

Ambrosi said nothing, but maybe he was right. Whatever he had to say should be said in private. So she led him through the colonnade, past rows of kiosks peddling stamps and coins.

"It's disgusting," Ambrosi said, motioning to the capitalists. "They think this a carnival. Nothing but an opportunity to make money."

"And I'm sure the collection boxes in St. Peter's have been closed since Clement died."

"You have a smart mouth."

"What's wrong? The truth hurt?"

They were beyond the Vatican, on Roman streets, strolling down a *via* lined with a warren of trendy apartments. Her nerves throbbed, keeping her on edge. She stopped. "What do you want?"

"Colin Michener is going to Bosnia. His Eminence wants you to go with him and report what he does."

"You didn't even care about Romania. I haven't heard a word from you till now."

"That became unimportant. This is more so."

"I'm not interested. Besides, Colin is going to Romania."

"Not now. He's going to Bosnia. To the shrine at Medjugorje."

She was confused. Why would Michener feel the need to make such a pilgrimage, especially after his earlier comments?

"His Eminence urged me to make clear that a friend within the Vatican is still available to you. Not to mention the ten thousand euros already paid."

"He said that money was mine. No questions."

"Interesting. Apparently, you're not a cheap whore."

She slapped his face.

Ambrosi showed no surprise. He simply stared back at her through piercing eyes. "You shall not strike me again." There was a bitter edge to his voice, one she did not like.

"I've lost interest in being your spy."

"You are an impertinent bitch. My only hope is that His Eminence tires of you soon. Then, perhaps, I will pay you a return visit."

She stepped back. "Why is Colin going to Bosnia?"

"To find one of the Medjugorje seers."

"What is all this with seers and the Virgin Mary?"

"I assume, then, you are familiar with the Bosnian apparitions."

"They're nonsense. You don't really believe the Virgin Mary appeared to those children every day for all those years, and is still appearing to one of them."

"The Church has yet to validate any of the visions."

"And that seal of approval is going to make it real?"

"Your sarcasm is tiresome."

"So are you."

But a stirring of interest was forming inside her. She didn't want to do anything for Ambrosi or Valendrea, and she'd stayed in Rome only because of Michener. She'd learned that he moved from the

Vatican—Kealy had reported that as part of an analysis on the after-math of a papal death—but she hadn't made any effort to track him down. Actually, after their encounter earlier, she'd toyed with the idea of following him to Romania. But now another possibility had opened. Bosnia.

"When does he leave?" she asked, hating herself for sounding interested.

Ambrosi's eyes flickered in satisfaction. "I don't know." The priest slid a hand under his cassock and came out with a scrap of paper. "That's the address for his apartment. It's not far from here. You could . . . comfort him. His mentor is gone, his life in chaos. An enemy will soon be pope—"

"Valendrea is quite sure of himself."

She ignored his question. "And the problem?"

"You think Colin's vulnerable? That he'll open up to me—even let me go with him?"

"That's the idea."

"He's not that weak."

Ambrosi smiled. "I'm betting that he is."

THIRTY-SEVEN

MICHENER STROLLED DOWN THE VIA GIOTTO TOWARD THE apartment. The quarter surrounding him had evolved into a gathering spot for the theater crowd, its streets lined with lively cafés that had long hosted intellectuals and political radicals. He knew that Mussolini's rise to power had been organized nearby, and thankfully most of the buildings survived Il Duce's architectural cleanup and continued to project a nineteenth-century feel.

He'd become a student of Mussolini, having read a couple of biographies after moving into the Apostolic Palace. Mussolini was an ambitious man who'd dreamed of Italians wearing uniforms and all of Rome's ancient stone buildings, with their terra-cotta rooftops, replaced with gleaming marble façades and obelisks memorializing his great military victories. But Il Duce ended up with a bullet in his head, then was hung by his ankles for all to see. Nothing remained of his grandiose plan. And Michener was worried that the Church might suffer a similar fate with a Valendrea papacy.

Megalomania was a mental disease compounded by arrogance. Valendrea was a clear sufferer. The secretary of state's opposition to Vatican II and all the later Church reforms was no secret. A swift

Valendrea election could be spun into a mandate for radical reversal. The worst part was that the Tuscan could easily rule for twenty or more years. Which meant he would completely reshape the Sacred College of Cardinals, much as John Paul II had managed during his long reign. But John Paul II had been a benign ruler, a man of vision. Valendrea was a demon, and God help his enemies. Which seemed all the more reason for Michener to disappear into the Carpathian Mountains. God or no God, heaven or no heaven, those children needed him.

He found the apartment building and trudged up the stairs to the third floor. One of the bishops attached to the papal household had offered the two-bedroom, furnished apartment rent-free for a couple of weeks, and he appreciated the gesture. He'd disposed of Clement's furniture a few days ago. The five boxes of personal belongings and Clement's wooden chest were stacked in the apartment. Originally he'd planned on leaving Rome by the end of the week. Now he would fly to Bosnia tomorrow on a ticket Ngovi had provided. By next week he would be in Romania, starting a new life.

A part of him resented Clement for what he'd done. History was replete with popes selected simply because they would soon die, and many of them had fooled everyone by lasting a decade or more. Jakob Volkner could have been one of those pontiffs. He was truly making a difference. Yet he ended all hope with a self-induced sleep.

Michener, too, felt like he was asleep. The past couple of weeks, starting with that awful Monday morning, seemed a dream. His life, once resonant with order, now gyrated out of control.

He needed order.

But stopping on the third-floor landing he knew that only more chaos lay ahead. Sitting on the floor, outside his apartment door, was Katerina Lew.

"Why am I not surprised you found me again?" he said. "How did you do it this time?"

"More secrets everybody knows."

She came to her feet and brushed grit from her pants. She was dressed the same as this morning and still looked lovely.

He opened the apartment door.

"Still going to Romania?" she asked.

He tossed the key on a table. "Plan on following?"

"I might."

"I wouldn't book a flight just yet."

He told her about Medjugorje and what Ngovi had asked him to do, but omitted the details of Clement's e-mail. He wasn't looking forward to the trip and told Katerina so.

"The war's over, Colin," she said. "It's been quiet there for years."

"Thanks to American and NATO troops. It's not what I would call a vacation destination."

"Then why go?"

"I owe it to Clement and Ngovi," he said.

"You don't think your debts are paid?"

"I know what you're going to say. But I was considering leaving the priesthood. It doesn't really matter anymore."

Her face registered shock. "Why?"

"I've had enough. It's not about God, or a good life, or eternal happiness. It's about politics, ambition, greed. Every time I think about where I was born, it makes me sick. How could anybody think they were doing something good there? There were better ways to help those mothers, yet nobody even tried. They just shipped us all off." He shifted on his feet and found himself staring down at the floor. "And those kids in Romania? I think even heaven has forgotten them."

"I've never seen you this way."

He stepped toward the window. "Odds are Valendrea will soon be pope. There's going to be a lot of changes. Maybe Tom Kealy had it right after all."

"Don't give that ass credit for anything."

He sensed something in her tone. "All we've talked about is me. What have you been doing since Bucharest?"

"Like I said, writing some pieces on the funeral for a Polish magazine. I've also been doing background work on the conclave. The magazine hired me to do a feature."

"Then how can you go to Romania?"

Her expression softened. "I can't. Wishful thinking. But at least I'll know where to find you."

The thought was comforting. He knew that if he never saw this woman again he would be sad. He recalled the last time, all those years ago, when they'd been alone together. It was in Munich, not long before he was to graduate law school and return to Jakob Volkner's service. She'd looked much the same, her hair a bit longer, her face a moment fresher, her smile equally appealing. Two years he'd spent loving her, knowing the day would come when he would have to choose. Now he realized the mistake he'd made. Something he'd said to her earlier in the square came to mind. *Just don't make the same mistakes twice. That's all any of us can hope for.*

Damn right.

He stepped across the room and took her into his arms.

She did not resist.

Michener opened his eyes and focused on the clock next to the bed. Ten forty-three P.M. Katerina lay beside him. They'd been asleep nearly two hours. He did not feel guilty for what had happened. He loved her, and if God had a problem with that, then so be it. He didn't really care anymore.

"What are you doing awake?" she said through the dark.

He'd thought her sleeping. "I'm not used to waking up with somebody in my bed."

She nuzzled her head against his chest. "Could you get used to it?"

"I was just asking myself the same thing."

"I don't want to leave this time, Colin."

He kissed the top of her head. "Who said you had to?"

"I want to go with you to Bosnia?"

"What about your magazine assignment?"

"I lied. I don't have one. I'm here, in Rome, because of you."

His answer was never in doubt. "Then maybe a Bosnian holiday would do us both some good."

He'd gone from the public world of the Apostolic Palace to a realm where only he existed. Clement XV was ensconced within a triple coffin beneath St. Peter's and he was naked in bed with a woman he loved.

Where it all was going, he could not say.

All he knew was that he finally felt content.

THIRTY-EIGHT

MICHENER STARED OUT THE BUS WINDOW. THE ROCKY COAST whizzed past, the Adriatic Sea choppy thanks to a howling wind. He and Katerina had flown into Split on a short flight from Rome. Tourist buses had lined the airport exits, their drivers clamoring for passengers to Medjugorje. One of the men explained this was the slow time of the year. Pilgrims arrived at the rate of three to five thousand a day in summer, but that number dwindled to several hundred from November through March.

Over the past two hours a guide had explained to the fifty or so making the bus trip that Medjugorje sat in the southern portion of Herzegovina, near the coast, and that a mountainous wall to the north isolated the region both climatically and politically. The guide explained that the name *Medjugorje* meant "land between the hills." Croats dominated the population, and Catholicism flourished. In the early 1990s, when communism fell, the Croats immediately sought independence, but the Serbs—the real power brokers in the former Yugoslavia—invaded, trying to create a Greater Serbia. A bloody civil war raged for years. Two hundred thousand lost their lives until finally the international community stopped the genocide. Another war then flared between Croats and Muslims, but quickly ended when UN peacekeepers arrived.

Medjugorje itself had escaped the terror. Most of the fighting was waged to its north and west. Only about five hundred families actually lived in the area, but the town's mammoth church hosted two thousand, and the guide explained that an infrastructure of hotels, guest houses, food vendors, and souvenir shops was now transforming the place into a religious mecca. Twenty million people from around the world had come. At last count, there'd been some two thousand apparitions, something unprecedented in Marian visions.

"Do you believe any of this?" Katerina whispered to him. "A little far-fetched that the Madonna comes to earth every day to speak with a woman in a Bosnian village."

"The seer believes, and Clement did, too. Keep an open mind, okay?"

"I'm trying. But which seer do we approach?"

He'd been thinking about that. So he asked the guide more about the seers and learned that one of the women, now thirty-five, was married with a son and lived in Italy. Another woman, thirty-six, was married with three children and still lived in Medjugorje, but she was intensely private and saw few pilgrims. One of the males, in his early thirties, tried twice to become a priest but failed and still hoped to one day achieve Holy Orders. He traveled extensively, bringing the Medjugorje message to the world, and would be difficult to find. The remaining male, the youngest of the six, was married with two children and talked little to visitors. Another of the females, almost forty, was married and no longer lived in Bosnia. The remaining woman was the one who continued to experience apparitions. Her name was Jasna, thirty-two years old, and she lived alone in Medjugorje. Her daily visitations were many times witnessed by thousands at St. James Church. The guide explained that Jasna was an introverted woman of few words, but she did take the time to speak with visitors.

He glanced over at Katerina and said, "Looks like our choices are limited. We'll start with her."

"Jasna, though, doesn't know all ten secrets the Madonna has passed to the others," the guide was saying at the front of the bus, and Michener's attention returned to what the woman was explaining.

"All five of the others know the ten secrets. It is said that when all six are told, the visions will end and a visible sign of the Virgin's presence will be left for atheists. *But the faithful must not wait for that sign before they convert. Now is the time of grace. A time for deepening faith. A time for conversion. Because, when the sign comes, it will be too late for many.* Those are the Virgin's words. A prediction for our future."

"What do we do now?" Katrina whispered in his ear.

"I say we still go see her. If for nothing else, I'm curious. She can certainly answer the thousand questions I have."

Outside, the guide motioned to Apparition Hill.

"This is where the first visions occurred to the original two seers in June 1981—a brilliant ball of light in which stood a beautiful woman holding a baby. The next evening, the two children returned with four of their friends and the woman appeared again, this time wearing a crown of twelve stars and a pearl-gray dress. She seemed, according to them, clothed by the sun."

The guide pointed to a steep footpath that led from the village of Podbrdo to a site where a cross stood. Even now, pilgrims were making the climb beneath thick clouds rolling in from the sea.

Cross Mountain appeared a few moments later, rising less than a mile from Medjugorje, its rounded peak standing more than sixteen hundred feet high.

"The cross atop was erected in the 1930s by the local parish and carries no significance to the apparitions, except many pilgrims have reported seeing luminous signs in and around it. Because of that, this spot has become part of the experience. Try to make a trip to the top."

The bus slowed and entered Medjugorje. The village was unlike the multitude of other undeveloped communities they'd passed along the way from Split. Low stone buildings in varied shades of pink, green, and ocher gave way to taller buildings—hotels, the guide explained, recently opened to handle an influx of pilgrims, along with duty-free shops, car rental agencies, and travel bureaus. Shiny Mercedes taxis skirted among transport trucks.

The bus stopped at the twin towered Church of St. James. A placard out front announced that Mass was said throughout the day in a variety of languages. A concrete piazza spanned the front, and the guide explained that the open expanse was a gathering spot at night for the faithful. Michener wondered about tonight, though, since thunder rumbled in the distance.

Soldiers patrolled the square.

"They are part of the Spanish peacekeeping forces assigned to the region and can be helpful," the guide explained.

They gathered their shoulder bags and left the bus. Michener approached the guide. "Excuse me, where could we find Jasna?"

The woman pointed down one of the streets. "She lives in a house about four blocks in that direction. But she comes to the church each day at three, and sometimes in the evening for prayer. She will be here shortly."

"And the apparitions, where do they occur?"

"Most times here in church. That's why she comes. I must tell you, it's unlikely she would see you unannounced."

He got the message. Probably every pilgrim wanted an encounter with one of the seers. The guide motioned toward a visitor center across the street.

"They can arrange for a meeting. Those usually take place later in the afternoon. Talk to them about Jasna. You'll get more of a response. They're sensitive to your needs."

He thanked her, then he and Katerina walked off. "We have to start somewhere, and this Jasna is the closest. I don't particularly want to talk with a group present, and I don't have any needs that require sensitivity. So let's go find this woman ourselves."

THIRTY-NINE

THE PROCESSION OF CARDINALS MADE THEIR WAY OUT OF THE Pauline Chapel, singing refrains from *Veni Creator Spiritus*. Their hands were clasped in prayer, their heads lowered. Valendrea kept pace behind Maurice Ngovi as the camerlengo led the group toward the Sistine Chapel.

All was ready. Valendrea himself had supervised one of the last chores an hour earlier when the House of Gammarelli arrived with five boxes containing white linen cassocks, red silk slippers, rochets, mozzettas, cotton stockings, and skullcaps in varying sizes, all with the backs and hems unsewn, the sleeves unfinished. Any adjustments would be made by Gammarelli himself, just before the cardinal chosen pope first appeared on the balcony of St. Peter's.

On the pretense of inspecting everything, Valendrea had made sure there was a set of vestments—42 to 44 in the chest, 38 in the waist, size 10 slippers—which would require only a few modifications. After, he would have Gammarelli fashion an assortment of traditional white linen outfits, along with a few new designs he'd been mulling over for the past couple of years. He intended to be one of the best-dressed popes in history.

One hundred and thirteen cardinals had made the trip to Rome. Each of the men was attired in a scarlet cassock with a mozzetta encircling his shoulders. They wore red birettas and gold and silver pectoral crosses above their breasts. As they inched forward in a single-file line toward a towering doorway, television cameras captured the scene for billions around the world. Valendrea noticed the grave faces. Perhaps the cardinals were taking heed of Ngovi's sermon at the noon Mass when the camerlengo urged each of them to leave worldly considerations outside the Sistine and, with the help of the Holy Spirit, choose a capable *pastor for the mother Church.*

That word *pastor* was a problem. Rarely had a twentieth-century pope been *pastoral.* Most were career intellectuals or Vatican diplomats. Pastoral experience had been talked about over the past few days in the press as something the Sacred College should look for. Certainly a pastoral cardinal, one who'd spent his career working with the faithful, carried a stronger appeal than a professional bureaucrat. He'd even heard, on the tapes, how many of the cardinals mused that a pope who knew how to run a diocese would be a plus. Unfortunately, he was a product of the Curia, a born administrator, possessed of no pastoral experience—unlike Ngovi, who rose from missionary priest to archbishop to cardinal. He resented the camerlengo's earlier reference and took the comment as a jab at his candidacy—a subtle poke, but more evidence Ngovi could become a formidable opponent in the hours ahead.

The procession stopped outside the Sistine Chapel.

A choir echoed from inside.

Ngovi hesitated at the doors, then started forward.

Photographs portrayed the Sistine as a huge expanse, but it was actually a difficult place in which to accommodate 113 cardinals. It had been built five hundred years ago to be the pope's private chapel, its walls framed in elegant pilasters and covered in narrative frescoes. On the left was the life of Moses, on the right the life of Christ. One set Israel free, the other the entire human race. *The Creation* on the ceiling expressed man's destiny, then foresaw an inevitable fall.

The Last Judgment above the altar was a terrifying vision of divine wrath, one Valendrea had long admired.

Two rows of raised platforms flanked the center aisle. Name cards delineated who sat where, the spots allocated by seniority. Chairs were straight-backed, and Valendrea did not cherish the prospect of sitting in one for long. Before each chair, on a tiny desk, sat a pencil, a pad of paper, and a single ballot.

The men moved to their assigned seats. No one as yet had spoken a word. The choir continued to sing.

Valendrea's gaze fell on the stove. It sat in a far corner, raised off the mosaic floor by a metal scaffolding. A chimney rose, then narrowed into a flue that escaped out one of the windows, where the celebrated smoke would signal success or failure. He hoped there would not be too many fires lit inside. The more scrutinies, the less chance of victory.

Ngovi stood at the front of the chapel, his hands folded before him beneath his cassock. Valendrea took note of the stern look on the African's face and hoped the camerlengo enjoyed his moment.

"Extra omnes," Ngovi said in a loud voice. All out.

The choir, servers, and television crews started leaving. Only the cardinals and thirty-two priests, nuns, and technicians would be allowed to remain.

The room fell under an uneasy quiet as two surveillance technicians made a sweep down the center aisle. They were responsible for ensuring the chapel stayed free of listening devices. At the iron grille the two men stopped and signaled an all-clear.

Valendrea nodded, and they withdrew. That ritual would be repeated before and after each day's voting.

Ngovi left the altar and marched down the aisle between the assembled cardinals. He passed through a marble screen and stopped at the bronze doors the attendants were pulling shut. Total silence draped the room. Where before there'd been music and the shuffle of feet on the mats protecting the mosaic floor, now there was nothing. Beyond the doors, from outside, the sound of a key slipping into place and tumblers engaging echoed.

Ngovi tested the handles.

Locked.

"*Extra omnes,*" he called out.

No one responded. No one was supposed to. The silence was an indication that the conclave had begun. Valendrea knew lead seals were being stamped into place outside to symbolically ensure privacy. There was another way in and out of the Sistine—the route to be taken each day to and from the Domus Sanctae Marthae—but the sealing of the doors was the traditional method of beginning the electoral process.

Ngovi retraced his steps to the altar, faced the cardinals, and said what Valendrea had heard a camerlengo say at that same spot thirty-four months ago.

"May the Lord bless you all. Let us begin."

FORTY

MICHENER STUDIED THE HOUSE, A ONE-STORY BUILT OF STONE, stained the color of moss. Dormant grapevines snaked across an arbor, and the only hint at gaiety sprang from swirling woodwork above the windows. A vegetable patch filled the side yard and seemed eager for the rain that was drawing closer. Mountains loomed in the distance.

They'd found the house only after asking two people for directions. Both had been reluctant to provide help until Michener revealed he was a priest and needed to speak with Jasna.

He led Katerina to the front door and knocked.

A tall woman with an almond-colored complexion and dark hair answered. She was thin as a sapling with a pleasant face and warm hazel eyes. She studied him with a measured mien that he found uncomfortable. She was perhaps thirty, with a rosary draping her neck.

"I'm due at church and really don't have time to speak," she said. "I would be glad to talk with you after the service." Her words came in English.

"We're not here for the reason you think," he said. He told her who he was and why he was there.

She did not react, as if a Vatican envoy contacted her daily. Finally she invited them inside.

The house was sparsely furnished in a mix-and-match decor. Sunlight spilled in from half-open windows, many of the panes cracked their length. A portrait of Mary hung over the fireplace, surrounded by flickering candles. A statue of the Virgin stood in one corner. The carved Madonna wore a gray dress trimmed in light blue. A white veil draped her face and highlighted wavy locks of brown hair. Her blue eyes were expressive and warm. Our Lady of Fatima, if he recalled correctly.

"Why Fatima?" he asked, motioning to the carving.

"It was a gift from a pilgrim. I like it. She seems alive."

He noticed a slight tremor to Jasna's right eye, and her barren expression and bland voice were causing him concern. He wondered if she was on something.

"You don't believe anymore, do you?" she quietly said.

The comment caught him off guard. "Why is that important?"

She shifted her gaze pointedly in Katerina's direction. "She confuses you."

"Why do you say that?"

"Priests rarely come here in the company of women. Especially a priest without his collar."

He had no intention of answering her inquiry. They were still standing, their host yet to offer a seat, and things were starting off badly.

Jasna turned to Katerina. "You don't believe at all. And have not in many years. How your soul must be tormented."

"Are these insights supposed to impress us?" If Jasna's comment bothered Katerina, she apparently was not going to let the woman know.

"To you," Jasna said, "what is real is only what you can touch. But there is so much more. So much you cannot possibly imagine. And though it cannot be touched, it is nonetheless real."

"We are here on a mission for the pope," he said.

"Clement is with the Virgin."

"That is my hope."

"But you do him a disservice by not believing."

"Jasna, I've been sent to learn the tenth secret. Clement and the camerlengo have both provided a written directive for it to be revealed."

She turned back. "I do not know it. And I don't want to. The Virgin will stop coming when that happens. Her messages are important. The world depends on them."

He was familiar with the daily messages from Medjugorje, faxed and e-mailed worldwide. Most were simple pleas for faith and world peace, fasting and prayer urged as a means to accomplish both. Yesterday he'd read some of the more recent in the Vatican library. Websites routinely charged fees for furnishing heaven's mandate, which made him wonder about Jasna's motives. But considering the simplicity of her home and the plain manner of her dress she wasn't reaping any profit. "We realize you don't know the secret, but can you tell us which one of the other seers we could talk with to learn it?"

"All were told to keep the information private, until the Virgin releases their tongues."

"Would not authority from the Holy Father be sufficient?"

"The Holy Father is dead."

He was tiring of her attitude. "Why must you make things so difficult?"

"Heaven has asked the same thing."

It sounded to him an awful lot like Clement's lamentations in the weeks before his death.

"I have prayed for the pope," she said. "His soul needs our prayers."

He was about to ask what she meant, but before he could say a word she crept close to the statue in the corner. Her gaze seemed suddenly distant and transfixed. She knelt on a prie-dieu, saying nothing.

"What's she doing?" Katerina mouthed.

He shrugged.

A bell pealed three times in the distance, and he remembered that the Virgin supposedly appeared to Jasna at three P.M. each day. One of her hands found the rosary that draped her neck. She clutched at the beads and started mumbling words he could not understand. He bent close and followed her gaze upward toward the sculpture, but saw nothing except the stoic wooden face of the Virgin Mary.

He recalled from his research that witnesses at Fatima reported hearing a buzz and feeling a warmth during the apparitions, but he thought that simply part of a mass hysteria that engulfed illiterate souls who desperately wanted to believe. He wondered if he was truly witnessing a Marian apparition or just a woman's delusion.

He moved closer.

Her gaze seemed locked on something beyond the walls. She was unaware of his presence and continued to mumble. For an instant he thought he caught a glimmer of light in her pupils—two quick flashes of a reflected image—a swirl of blue and gold. His head whirled left, searching for the source, but there was nothing. Only the sunlit corner and the silent statue. Whatever was occurring was apparently Jasna's alone.

Finally her head dropped and she said, "The Lady's gone."

She stood and moved toward a table and scribbled on a pad. When she finished, she handed the sheet to Michener.

My children, great is the love of God. Do not close your eyes, do not close your ears. Great is His love. Accept my call and my plea that I am entrusting to you. Consecrate your heart and make a home for the Lord within it. May He dwell within it forever. My eyes and my heart will be here even when I will not be appearing anymore. Conduct yourselves in everything as I'm asking you and leading you to the Lord. Do not reject God's name from yourselves, so that you would not be rejected. Accept my messages so that you would be accepted. It is time for decisions, my children. Be of righteous and innocent heart that I could lead you to your Father. Because this, my being here, is His great love.

"That's what the Virgin told me," Jasna said.

He read the message again. "Is this directed to me?"

"Only you can decide that."

He handed the page to Katerina. "You still haven't answered my question. Who can tell us the tenth secret?"

"No one can."

"The other five seers know the information. One of them can tell us."

"Not unless the Virgin consents, and I'm the only one left who experiences Her visits daily. The others would have to wait to receive permission."

"But you don't know the secret," Katerina said. "So it doesn't matter you're the only one who's not privy. We don't need the Virgin, we need the tenth secret."

"One goes with the other," Jasna said.

He couldn't decide if he was dealing with a religious fanatic or someone truly blessed by heaven. Her impertinent attitude didn't help. In fact, it only made him suspicious. He decided they would stay in town and try, on their own, to speak with the other seers who lived nearby. If nothing was learned, he could return to Italy and track down the one who lived there.

He thanked Jasna and started for the door, Katerina in tow.

Their host stayed rooted in the chair, her expression as blank as when they arrived. "Don't forget Bamberg," Jasna said.

Chilly fingers danced along his spine. He stopped and turned back. Had he heard right? "Why did you say that?"

"I was told to."

"What do you know about Bamberg?"

"Nothing. I don't even know what it is."

"Then why say it?"

"I don't question. I only do as I am told. Perhaps that's why the Virgin speaks to me. There is something to be said for a loyal servant."

FORTY-ONE

VALENDREA WAS GROWING IMPATIENT. HIS CONCERN ABOUT the straight-backed chairs was proving justified, as he'd now spent nearly two agonizing hours sitting upright in the sedate Sistine Chapel. During that time each of the cardinals had walked to the altar and sworn before Ngovi and God that they would not support any interference in the election by secular authorities and, if elected, would be *munus Petrinum*—pastor of the universal church—and defend the spiritual and temporal rights of the Holy See. He, too, had stood before Ngovi, the African's eyes intense while the words were said and repeated.

Another half hour was needed to administer an oath of secrecy to the attendants allowed to remain within the conclave. Then Ngovi ordered everyone but the cardinals from the Sistine and the remaining doors closed. He faced the assembly and said, "Do you wish a vote at this time?"

John Paul II's Apostolic Constitution allowed for a first vote immediately, if the conclave so desired. One of the French cardinals stood and stated that he would. Valendrea was pleased. The Frenchman was one of his.

"If there be any opposition, speak now," Ngovi said.

The chapel stayed in repose. There was a time when, at this moment, election by acclamation could occur, supposedly the result of a direct intervention by the Holy Spirit. A name would be spontaneously proclaimed and all would agree he was to be pope. But John Paul II eliminated that as a means of election.

"Very well," Ngovi said, "we will begin."

The junior cardinal-deacon, a fat, swarthy man from Brazil, waddled forward and chose three names from a silver chalice. Those selected would act as scrutineers, their task to count each ballot and record the votes. If no pope was elected, they would burn the ballots in the stove. Three more names, the revisers, were pulled from the chalice. Their job would be to oversee the scrutineers. Finally, three *infirmarii* were selected to collect ballots from any cardinals who might be taken ill. Of the nine officials, only four could be regarded as solidly Valendrea's. Particularly upsetting was the selection of the cardinal-archivist as a scrutineer. The old bastard might have his revenge after all.

Before each cardinal, beside the pad and pencil, lay a two-inch rectangular card. At the top was printed in black lettering: ELIGO IN SUMMUM PONTIFICEM. I elect as supreme pontiff. The space beneath was blank, ready for a name. Valendrea felt a special attachment to the ballot, as it had been designed by his beloved Paul VI.

At the altar, beneath the agony of Michelangelo's *Last Judgment*, Ngovi emptied the silver chalice of the remaining names. They would be burned with the results of the first balloting. The African then addressed the cardinals, speaking in Latin, reiterating the voting procedures. When he finished, Ngovi left the altar and took a seat among the cardinals. His task as camerlengo was drawing to a close, and less and less would be demanded of him in the hours ahead. The process now would be controlled by the scrutineers until another ballot was required.

One of the scrutineers, a cardinal from Argentina, said, "Please print a name on the card. More than one name will void the ballot and the scrutiny. Once done, fold the ballot and approach the altar."

Valendrea glanced to his left and right. The 113 cardinals were wedged into the chapel elbow-to-elbow. He wanted to win early and be done with the agony, but he knew that rarely had any pope won on a first scrutiny. Usually electors cast their initial ballot for someone special—a favorite cardinal, a close friend, a person from their particular part of the world, even themselves, though none would ever admit that. It was a way for the electors to conceal their true intentions and up the ante for their subsequent support, since nothing made the favorites more generous than an unpredictable future.

Valendrea printed his own name on the ballot, careful to disguise anything that might identify the script as his, then folded the paper twice and awaited his turn to approach the altar.

Depositing ballots was done by seniority. Cardinal-bishops before cardinal-priests, with cardinal-deacons last, each group ranked by date of investiture. He watched as the first senior cardinal-bishop, a silver-haired Italian from Venice, climbed four marble steps to the altar, his folded ballot held high for all to see.

At his turn Valendrea walked to the altar. He knew the other cardinals would be watching so he knelt for a moment of prayer, but said nothing to God. Instead, he waited an appropriate amount of time before rising. He then repeated out loud what every other cardinal was required to say.

"I call as my witness Christ the Lord, who will be my judge, that my vote is given to the one who before God I think should be elected."

He laid his ballot on the paten, lifted the glistening plate, and allowed the card to slide into the chalice. The unorthodox method was a means of ensuring that only one ballot for each cardinal was cast. He gently replaced the paten, folded his hands in prayer, and retreated to this seat.

It took nearly an hour to complete the balloting. After the final vote slid into the chalice, the vessel was carried to another table. There, the contents were shaken, then each vote was counted by the three scrutineers. The revisers watched everything, their eyes never leaving the table. As each ballot was unfolded, the name written upon it was announced. Everyone kept his own tally. The total number of votes cast had to add up to 113 or the ballots would be destroyed and the scrutiny declared invalid.

When the last name was read, Valendrea studied the results. He'd received thirty-two votes. Not bad for a first scrutiny. But Ngovi had amassed twenty-four. The remaining fifty-seven votes were scattered among two dozen candidates.

He stared up at the assembly.

Clearly they were all thinking what he was.

This was going to be a two-horse race.

FORTY-TWO

MICHENER FOUND TWO ROOMS IN ONE OF THE NEWER HOTELS. The rain had started just as they left Jasna's house, and they'd barely made it to the hotel before the sky exploded into a pyrotechnic display. This was the rainy season, an attendant informed them. The deluges came quick, fed by warm air off the Adriatic mixing with frigid northern breezes.

They ate supper at a nearby café crowded with pilgrims. The conversations, mostly in English, French, and German, centered on the shrine. Someone remarked that two of the seers had been in St. James Church earlier. Jasna was supposed to appear, but had failed to show, and one of the pilgrims had noted it was not unusual for her to remain alone during the daily apparition.

"We'll find those two seers tomorrow," he told Katerina, as they ate. "I hope they're easier to get along with."

"Intense, wasn't she?"

"She's either an accomplished fraud or the genuine thing."

"Why did her mention of Bamberg bother you? It's no secret the pope was fond of his hometown. I don't believe she didn't know what the name signified."

He told her what Clement had said in his final e-mail message about Bamberg. *Do with my body as you please. Pomp and ceremony do not make the pious. For me, though, I would prefer the sanctity of Bamberg, that lovely city by the river, and the cathedral I so loved. My only regret is that I did not see its beauty one last time. Perhaps, though, my legacy could still be there.* But he omitted that the message was a last statement from a pope who took his own life. Which brought to mind something else Jasna had said. *I have prayed for the pope. His soul needs our prayers.* It was crazy to think she knew the truth about Clement's death.

"You don't actually believe we witnessed an apparition this afternoon?" Katerina asked. "That woman was strung out."

"I think Jasna's visions are hers alone."

"Is that your way of saying the Madonna wasn't there today?"

"No more than she was at Fatima, or Lourdes, or La Salette."

"She reminds me of Lucia," Katerina said. "When we were with Father Tibor, in Bucharest, I didn't say anything. But from the article I wrote a few years ago, I remember that Lucia was a troubled girl. Her father was an alcoholic. She was raised by her older sisters. Seven kids in the house and she was the youngest. Right before the apparitions started her father lost some of the family land, a couple of sisters married, and the remaining sisters took jobs outside the home. She was left alone with her brother, her mother, and a drunk father."

"Some of that was in the Church's report," he said. "The bishop in charge of the inquiry dismissed most of it as common for the time. What bothered me more were the similarities between Fatima and Lourdes. The parish priest in Fatima even testified that some of the Virgin's words were nearly identical to what was said at Lourdes. The visions at Lourdes were known in Fatima, and Lucia was aware of them." He took a swallow of beer. "I've read all of the accounts from four hundred years of apparitions. There are a lot of matching details. Always shepherd children, particularly young females with little or no education. Visions in the woods. Beautiful ladies. Secrets from heaven. Lots of coincidences."

"Not to mention," Katerina said, "that all of the accounts that exist were written years after the apparition. It would be easy to add details to give greater authenticity. Isn't it strange that none of the visionaries ever revealed their messages right after the appearance? Always decades pass, then little bits and pieces come to light."

He agreed. Sister Lucia had not provided a detailed account of Fatima until 1925, then again in 1944. Many asserted that she embellished her messages with later facts, like mentioning the papacy of Pius XI, World War II, and the rise of Russia, all of which occurred long after 1917. And with Francisco and Jacinta dead, there was no one to contradict her testimony.

And one other fact kept circling through his lawyerly mind.

The Virgin at Fatima, in July 1917, as part of the second secret, talked about the consecration of Russia to her Immaculate Heart. But Russia at that time was a devoutly Christian nation. The communists did not rise to power until months later. So what was the point of any consecration?

"The La Salette seers were a total mess," Katerina was saying. "Maxim—the boy—his mother died when he was an infant and his stepmother beat him. When he was first interviewed after the vision, he interpreted what he saw as a mother complaining about being beaten by her son, not the Virgin Mary."

He nodded. "The published versions of the La Salette secrets are in the Vatican archives. Maxim mentioned a vengeful Virgin who talked of famine and compared sinners to dogs."

"The kind of thing a troubled child might say about an abusive parent. The stepmother used to starve him as punishment."

"He eventually died young, broke and bitter," he said. "One of the original seers here in Bosnia was the same. She lost her mother a couple of months before the first vision. And the others have had problems, too."

"It's all hallucinations, Colin. Disturbed kids who have become troubled adults, convinced of what they imagined. The Church doesn't want anyone to know about the seers' lives. It totally bursts the bubble. Causes doubt."

Rain pounded the café's roof.

"Why did Clement send you here?"

"I wish I knew. He was obsessed with the third secret, and this place had something to do with it."

He decided to tell her about Clement's vision, but he omitted all reference to the Virgin asking the pope to end his life. He kept his voice in a whisper.

"You're here because the Virgin Mary told Clement to send you?" she asked.

He caught the waitress's attention and held up two fingers for a couple more beers.

"Sounds to me like Clement was losing it."

"Exactly why the world will never know what happened."

"Maybe it should."

He didn't like the comment. "I've spoken with you in confidence."

"I know that. I'm just saying, maybe the world should know about this."

He realized there was no way that could ever happen, given how Clement had died. He stared out at the street flooded with rain. There was something he wanted to know. "What about us, Kate?"

"I know where I plan to go."

"What would you do in Romania?"

"Help those kids. I could journal the effort. Write about it for the world. Draw attention."

"Pretty tough life."

"It's my home. You're not telling me anything I don't already know."

"Ex-priests don't make much."

"It doesn't take much to live there."

He nodded and wanted to reach over and take her hand. But that wouldn't be smart. Not here.

She seemed to sense his wish and smiled. "Save it, until we get back to the hotel."

FORTY-THREE

"I CALL FOR A THIRD BALLOT," THE CARDINAL FROM THE Netherlands said. He was the archbishop of Utrecht and one of Valendrea's staunchest supporters. Valendrea had arranged with him yesterday that if no success came on the first two ballots, he was to immediately call for a third.

Valendrea was not happy. Ngovi's twenty-four votes on the first scrutiny had been a surprise. He'd expected him to garner a dozen or so, no more. His own thirty-two were okay, but a long way from the seventy-six needed for election.

The second scrutiny, though, shocked him, and it had taken all his diplomatic reserve to keep his temper in check. Ngovi's support increased to thirty, while his own nudged up to a weak forty-one. The remaining forty-two votes were scattered among three other candidates. Conclave wisdom proclaimed that a front-runner must gain a respectable amount of support with each succeeding scrutiny. A failure to do so was perceived as weakness, and cardinals were notorious for abandoning weak candidates. Dark horses had many times emerged after the second ballot to claim the papacy. John Paul I and II were both elected that way, as was Clement XV. Valendrea did not want a repeat.

He imagined the pundits in the piazza musing over two billows of black smoke. Irritating asses like Tom Kealy would be telling the world the cardinals must surely be divided, no one candidate emerging as front-runner. There'd be more Valendrea-bashing. Kealy had surely taken a perverse pleasure in slandering him for the past two weeks, and quite cleverly he had to admit. Never had Kealy made any personal comments. No reference to his pending excommunication. Instead, the heretic had offered the *Italians-versus-the-world* argument, which apparently played well. He should have pushed the tribunal to defrock Kealy weeks ago. At least then he'd be an ex-priest with suspect credibility. As it stood, the fool was perceived as a maverick challenging the established guard, a David versus Goliath, and no ever rooted for the giant.

He watched as the cardinal-archivist passed out more ballots. The old man made his way down the row in silence and threw Valendrea a quick glare of defiance as he handed him a blank card. Another problem that should have been dealt with long ago.

Pencils once again scraped across paper and the ritual of depositing ballots into the silver chalice was repeated. The scrutineers shuffled the cards and started counting. He heard his name called fifty-nine times. Ngovi's was repeated forty-three. The remaining eleven votes remained scattered.

Those would be critical.

He needed seventeen more to achieve election. Even if he garnered every one of the eleven stragglers, he would still need six of Ngovi's supporters, and the African was gaining strength at an alarming rate. The most frightening prospect was that each one of the eleven scattered votes he failed to sway would have to come from Ngovi's total, and that could begin to prove impossible. Cardinals tended to dig in after the third vote.

He'd had enough. He stood. "I think, Eminences, we have challenged ourselves enough for today. I suggest we eat dinner and rest and resume in the morning."

It wasn't a request. Any participant possessed the right to stop the voting. His gaze strafed the chapel, settling from time to time on men he suspected to be traitors.

He hoped the message was clear.

The black smoke that would soon seep from the Sistine matched his mood.

FORTY-FOUR

MICHENER AWOKE FROM A SOUND SLEEP. KATERINA LAY BESIDE him. An uneasiness flowed through him that seemed unrelated to their lovemaking. He felt no guilt about once more breaching his vow of Holy Orders, but it frightened him that what he'd worked a lifetime to achieve meant so little. Maybe it was simply that the woman lying next to him meant more. He'd spent two decades serving the Church and Jakob Volkner. But his dear friend was dead and a new day was being forged in the Sistine Chapel, one that would not include him. The 268th successor to St. Peter would shortly be elected. And though he'd come close to a red hat, that was simply not to be. His destiny apparently lay elsewhere.

Another strange feeling surged through him—an odd combination of anxiety and stress. Earlier, in his dreams, he kept hearing Jasna. *Don't forget Bamberg . . . I have prayed for the pope. His soul needs our prayers.* Was she trying to tell him something? Or simply convince him.

He climbed from the bed.

Katerina did not stir. She'd enjoyed several beers at dinner and alcohol had always made her sleepy. Outside, the storm was still raging, rain pecking the glass, lightning strobing the room.

He crept to the window and looked out. Water pelted the terra-cotta roofs of the buildings across the street and streamed in rivers from drainpipes. Parked cars lined both sides of the quiet lane.

A lone figure stood in the center of the soaked pavement.

He focused on the face.

Jasna.

Her head was angled up, toward his window. The sight of her startled him and made him want to cover his nakedness, though he quickly realized she could not possibly see him. The curtains were partially drawn, a set of lace sheers between him and the sash, the outer pane smeared with rain. He was standing back, the room dark, outside even darker. But in the wash of the streetlights four stories down, he could see Jasna watching.

Something urged him to reveal his presence.

He parted the sheers.

Her right arm motioned for him to come. He didn't know what to do. She gestured again with a simple wave of her hand. She wore the same clothes and tennis shoes from earlier, the dress pasted to her thin frame. Her long hair was soaked, but she seemed unfazed by the storm.

She beckoned again.

He looked over at Katerina. Should he wake her? Then he stared back out the window. Jasna was shaking her head no, and motioning once more.

Damn. Did she know what he was thinking?

He decided there was no choice and quietly dressed.

He stepped from the hotel's entrance.

Jasna still stood in the street.

Lightning crackled overhead, and a renewed burst of rain poured from the blackened sky. He carried no umbrella.

"What are you doing here?" he asked.

"If you want to know the tenth secret, come with me."

"Where?"

"Must you question everything? Is nothing accepted on faith?"

"We're standing in the middle of a downpour."

"It's a cleanse for the body and soul."

This woman frightened him. Why? He was unsure. Maybe it was his compulsion to do as she asked.

"My car is over there," she said.

A tattered Ford Fiesta coupe was parked down the street. He followed her to it and she drove out of town, stopping at the base of a darkened mound in a parking lot devoid of vehicles. A sign revealed by the headlights read CROSS MOUNTAIN.

"Why here?" he asked.

"I have no idea."

He wanted to ask her who did, but let it go. This was obviously her show, and she intended to play it out her way.

They climbed out into the rain and he followed her toward a footpath. The ground was spongy, the rocks slippery.

"We're going to the top?" he asked.

She turned back. "Where else?"

He tried to recall the details of Cross Mountain the guide had spewed out on the bus trip. More than sixteen hundred feet tall, it held a cross atop that had been erected in the 1930s by the local parish. Though unrelated to the apparitions, a climb to the summit was thought part of "the Medjugorje experience." But no one was partaking tonight. And he wasn't particularly thrilled about being sixteen hundred feet up in the middle of an electrical storm. Yet Jasna seemed unaffected and, strangely, he was drawing strength from her courage.

Was that faith?

The climb was made more difficult by rivulets of water gushing past him. His clothes were soaked, his shoes caked with mud, and only lightning illuminated the way. He opened his mouth and allowed the rain to soak his tongue. Thunder clapped overhead. It was as if the center of the storm had settled directly above them.

The crest appeared after twenty minutes of hard climbing. His thighs ached and the back of his calves throbbed.

Before him rose the darkened outline of a massive white cross, perhaps forty feet tall. At its concrete base, flower bouquets were buffeted by the storm. A few of the arrangements lay strewn about by the wind.

"They come from all over the world," she said, pointing to the blossoms. "They climb and lay offerings and pray to the Virgin. Yet she never once appeared here. But they still come. Their faith is to be admired."

"And mine is not?"

"You have no faith. Your soul is in jeopardy."

The tone was matter-of-fact, like a wife telling a husband to take out the trash. Thunder rumbled past like a bass drum being worked to a beat. He waited for the inevitable flash of lightning and the burst splintered the sky in fractured bolts of blue-white light. He decided to confront this seer. "What's there to have faith in? You know nothing of religion."

"I only know of God. Religion is man's creation. It can be changed, altered, or discarded entirely. Our Lord is another matter."

"But men invoke the power of God to justify their religions."

"It means nothing. Men like you must change that."

"How would I possibly do that?"

"By believing, having faith, loving our Lord, and doing as He asks. Your pope tried to change things. Carry on his efforts."

"I'm no longer in a position to do anything."

"You are in the same position in which Christ found Himself, and He changed everything."

"Why are we here?"

"Tonight will be the final vision of our Lady. She said for me to come, at this hour, and to bring you. She will leave a visible sign of Her presence. She promised that when She first came, and now She will keep that promise. Have faith in this moment—not later, when all will be clear."

"I'm a priest, Jasna. I don't need to be converted."

"You doubt, but do nothing to relieve that doubt. You, more than anyone, need to convert. This is the time of grace. A time for a deepening faith. A time for conversion. That's what the Virgin told me today."

"What did you mean by Bamberg?"

"You know what I meant."

"That's not an answer. Tell me what you meant."

The rain quickened and a fresh burst of wind whipped drops like pinpricks across his face. He closed his eyes. When he opened them, Jasna was on her knees, hands clasped in prayer, the same far-away look from this afternoon in her eyes as she stared up to the black sky.

He knelt beside her.

She seemed so vulnerable, no longer the defiant seer seemingly better than everyone else. He looked skyward and saw nothing but the blackened outline of the cross. A flash of lightning momentarily gave life to the image. Then darkness reenveloped the cross.

"I can remember. I know I can," she said to the night.

Thunder again rolled across the sky.

They needed to leave, but he was hesitant to interrupt. It might not be real to him, but it was to her.

"Dear Lady, I had no idea," she said to the wind.

A bright flash of light found earth and the cross exploded in a burst of heat that engulfed them.

His body rose off the ground and flew backward.

A strange tingling surged through his limbs. His head slammed into something hard. A wave of dizziness swept through him, then sickening nausea claimed his gut. His vision swirled. He tried to concentrate, to force himself to stay awake, but couldn't.

Finally, everything went silent.

FORTY-FIVE

VALENDREA BUTTONED HIS CASSOCK AND LEFT HIS ROOM IN the Domus Sanctae Marthae. As secretary of state he'd been provided one of the larger spaces, normally used by the prelate who managed the dormitory for seminarians. A similar privilege had been extended to the camerlengo and the head of the Sacred College. The accommodations were not what he was accustomed to, but a big improvement from the days when a conclave meant sleeping on a cot and peeing into a bucket.

The route from the dormitory to the Sistine was through a series of secured passages. This was a change from the last conclave when cardinals were bused and escorted when traveling between the dormitory and the chapel. Many had resented having a chaperone, so a sealable route had been created through the Vatican corridors, available only to conclave participants.

He'd quietly made clear during dinner that he wanted to meet with three of the cardinals later, and the three now waited inside the Sistine, at the opposite end from the altar, near the marble gate. Beyond, past the sealed entrance, in the hallway outside, he knew Swiss guards stood ready to throw open the bronze doors once white smoke seeped skyward. No one really expected that to occur after midnight, so the chapel would provide a safe place for a discreet discussion.

He approached the three cardinals and did not give them a chance to speak. "I only have a few things to say." He kept his voice low. "I'm aware of what the three of you have said in previous days. You assured me of support, then privately betrayed me. Why, only you know. What I want is for the fourth ballot to be the last. If not, none of you will be a member of this college by this time next year."

One of the cardinals started to speak and he raised his right hand to silence him.

"I don't want to hear that you voted for me. All three of you have supported Ngovi. But that will change in the morning. In addition, before the first session I want others swayed. I expect a fourth-ballot victory and it's up to you three to make that happen."

"That's unrealistic," one of the cardinals said.

"What's unrealistic is how you escaped Spanish justice for embezzling Church funds. They clearly believed you a thief, they just lacked proof. I have that proof, gladly provided by a young señorita you're quite familiar with. And you other two shouldn't be so smug. I have similar files on each of you, none of the information flattering. You know what I want. Start a movement. Invoke the Holy Spirit. I don't care how it's done, just make it happen. Success will ensure that you stay in Rome."

"What if we don't want to be in Rome?" one of the three asked.

"Would you prefer prison?"

Vatican observers loved to speculate about what happened within a conclave. The archives were replete with journals depicting pious men wrestling with their consciences. He'd watched during the last conclave as cardinals argued that his youth was a disadvantage, since the Church did not fare well with a prolonged papacy. Five to ten years was good. Anything more created problems. And there was truth to that conclusion. Autocracy and infallibility could be a volatile mixture. But they could also be the ingredients of change. The throne of St. Peter was the ultimate pulpit and a strong pope could not be ignored. He intended on being that kind of pope, and he wasn't about to let three petty fools ruin those plans.

"All I want to hear is my name read seventy-six times in the morning. If I have to wait, there will be consequences. My patience was tried today. I would not recommend a repeat. If my smiling face does not appear on the balcony of St. Peter's by tomorrow afternoon, before you make it back to your rooms in the Domus Sanctae Marthae to retrieve your things, your reputations will be gone."

He turned and left, not giving them the chance to utter a word.

FORTY-SIX

MICHENER WATCHED AS THE WORLD SPUN IN A BLURRY HAZE. His head pounded and his stomach flip-flopped. He tried to stand but couldn't. Bile pooled in his throat and his vision winked in and out.

He was still outside, now only a gentle rain soaking his already saturated clothes. Thunder overhead confirmed that the nocturnal storm was still raging. He brought his watch close to his eyes, but multiple images swirled before him and he could not read the luminous dial. He massaged his forehead and felt a knot on the back of his head.

He wondered about Jasna and was just about to call her name when a bright light appeared in the sky. He thought at first it might be another bolt of lightning, like what surely had happened earlier, but this ball was smaller, more controlled. He thought it a helicopter, but no sound preceded the blue-white splotch as it drew closer.

The image floated before him, a few feet above the ground. His head and stomach still would not allow him to stand, so he lay back on the rocky earth and stared up.

The glow intensified.

Warmth radiated outward and comforted him. He raised an arm to shield his eyes and through slits between his fingers saw an image form.

A woman.

She wore a gray dress trimmed in light blue. A white veil draped her face and highlighted long locks of auburn hair. Her eyes were expressive, and the hues of her form fluctuated from white to blue to the palest yellow.

He recognized the face and dress. The statue he'd seen earlier in Jasna's house. Our Lady of Fatima.

The intensity of the glow subsided, and though he still could not focus on anything else beyond a few inches, he could see the woman clearly.

"Stand, Father Michener," she said in a mellow voice.

"I . . . tried . . . I can't," he stammered out.

"Stand."

He pushed himself up to his feet. His head no longer swirled. His stomach was calm. He faced the light. "Who are you?"

"You do not know?"

"The Virgin Mary?"

"You speak the words as if they are a lie."

"I don't mean them to be."

"Your defiance is strong. I see why you were chosen."

"Chosen for what?"

"I told the children long ago that I would leave a sign for all who do not believe."

"So Jasna now knows the tenth secret?" He was angry with himself for even asking the question. Bad enough he was hallucinating, now he was conversing with his own imagination.

"She is a blessed woman. She has done as heaven asked. Other men, who claim to be pious, cannot make that claim."

"Clement XV?"

"Yes, Colin. I am one of those."

The voice had deepened and the image metamorphosized into Jakob Volkner. He stood in full papal regalia—amice, cincture, stole, miter, and pallium—just as he'd appeared at his burial, a shepherd's staff held in his right hand. The sight startled him. What was happening here?

"Jakob?"

"Do not ignore heaven any longer. Do as I asked. Remember, there is much to be said for a loyal servant."

Exactly what Jasna had told him earlier. But why wouldn't his own hallucination include information he already knew? "What is my destiny, Jakob?"

The vision became Father Tibor. The priest appeared exactly as when they'd first met at the orphanage. "To be a sign to the world. A beacon for repentance. The messenger to announce that God is very much alive."

Before he could say anything, the Virgin's image returned.

"Do as your heart commands. There is nothing wrong in that. But do not forsake your faith, for in the end it will be all that remains."

The vision started to rise, becoming a brilliant ball of light that dissolved into the night above. The farther away it receded, the more his head ached. As the light finally vanished, the world around him started to spin and his stomach erupted.

FORTY-SEVEN

BREAKFAST WAS A SOMBER AFFAIR IN THE DINING ROOM OF THE Domus Sanctae Marthae. Nearly half of the cardinals were enjoying eggs, ham, fruit, and bread in silence. Many opted only for coffee or juice, but Valendrea filled a plate from the buffet line. He wanted to show the assembled men that he was unaffected by what had happened yesterday, his legendary appetite still in place.

He sat with a group of cardinals at a window table. They were a diverse lot, from Australia, Venezuela, Slovakia, Lebanon, and Mexico. Two were strong supporters, but the other three, he believed, were among the eleven who'd yet to choose a side. His gaze caught Ngovi entering the dining room. The African was intent in a lively conversation with two cardinals. Perhaps he, too, was trying to project not the slightest hint of concern.

"Alberto," one of the cardinals at the table was saying.

He glanced over at the Australian.

"Keep the faith today. I prayed all evening and feel something will occur this morning."

He maintained a stoic look. "God's will is what drives us forward. My only hope is that the Holy Spirit is with us today."

"You are the logical choice," the Lebanese cardinal said, his voice louder than necessary.

"Yes, he is," a cardinal at another table said.

He looked up from his eggs and saw it was the Spaniard from last night. The stout little man was out of his chair.

"This Church has languished," the Spaniard said. "It's time something be done. I can recall when the pope commanded respect. When governments all the way to Moscow cared what Rome did. Now we are nothing. Our priests are forbidden from political involvement. Our bishops are discouraged from taking a stand. Complacent popes are destroying us."

Another cardinal stood. He was a bearded man from Cameroon. Valendrea hardly knew him and assumed he was Ngovi's. "I didn't consider Clement XV complacent. He was loved throughout the world and did much in his short time."

The Spaniard held up his hands. "I don't mean disrespect. This is not personal. It's about what is best for the Church. Luckily, we have a man among us who carries respect in the world. Cardinal Valendrea would be an exemplary pontiff. Why settle for less?"

Valendrea let his gaze settle on Ngovi. If the camerlengo was offended by the remark, he showed nothing.

This was one of those moments that pundits would later describe. How the Holy Spirit swept down and moved the conclave. Though the Apostolic Constitution banned campaigning prior to convening, there was no such prohibition once locked inside the Sistine. In fact, frank discussion was the entire purpose of the secret gathering. He was impressed with the Spaniard's tactic. He'd not thought the fool capable of such grandstanding.

"I don't consider Cardinal Ngovi a settlement for less," the Cameroon cardinal finally said. "He's a man of God. A man of this Church. Above reproach. He would be an excellent pontiff."

"And Valendrea would not?" the French cardinal blurted out, coming to his feet.

Valendrea marveled at the sight, princes of the Church, adorned in robes, openly debating one another. Any other time they would go out of their way to avoid confrontation.

"Valendrea is young. He is what this Church needs. Ceremony and rhetoric do not make a leader. It's the character of the man that leads the faithful. He's proven his character. He's served many popes—"

"My point exactly," the Cameroon cardinal said. "He's never served a diocese. How many confessions has he heard? How many funerals has he presided over? How many parishioners has he counseled? These pastoral experiences are what the throne of St. Peter demand."

The boldness of the Cameroonian was impressive. Valendrea was unaware that such backbone could still be clothed in scarlet. Quite intuitively, this man had invoked the dreaded *pastoral* qualification. He made a note that this cardinal would be someone to watch in the years ahead.

"What does that matter?" the Frenchman asked. "The pope is no pastor. It's a description scholars like to attach. An excuse we use to vote for one man over the other. It means nothing. The pope is an administrator. He must run this Church, and to do that he must understand the Curia, he must know its workings. Valendrea knows that better than any of us. We've had pastoral popes. Give me a leader."

"Perhaps he knows our workings too well," the cardinal-archivist said.

Valendrea almost winced. Here was the most senior member of the voting college. His opinion would carry much weight with the eleven stragglers.

"Explain yourself," the Spaniard demanded.

The archivist stayed seated. "The Curia already controls too much. We all complain about the bureaucracy, yet we do nothing about it. Why? Because it satisfies our needs. It provides a wall between us and whatever it is we don't want to occur. So easy to blame everything on the Curia. Why would a pope who is ingrained in that institution do anything to threaten it? Yes, there would be changes, all popes tinker, but no one has demolished and rebuilt." The old man's eyes locked on Valendrea. "Especially one who is a product of that system. We must ask ourselves, would Valendrea be so bold?" He paused. "I think not."

Valendrea sipped his coffee. Finally, he tabled the cup and calmly said to the archivist, "Apparently, Eminence, your vote is clear."

"I want my last vote to count."

He tipped his head in a casual gesture. "That is your right, Eminence. And I would not presume to interfere."

Ngovi stepped to the center of the room. "Perhaps there has been enough debate. Why don't we finish our meal and retire to the chapel. There, we can take this up in more detail."

No one disagreed.

Valendrea was thrilled with the whole display.

A little show-and-tell could only be a good thing.

FORTY-EIGHT

KATERINA WAS BEGINNING TO WORRY. AN HOUR HAD PASSED since she'd woken to find Michener gone. The storm had passed, but the morning loomed warm and cloudy. She'd first thought he walked downstairs for coffee, but he was not in the dining room when she checked a few minutes ago. She asked the desk clerk, but the woman knew nothing. Thinking he might have wandered to St. James Church, she walked over. But he was nowhere to be found. It was unlike Colin to leave and not say where he was going, and his travel bag, wallet, and passport were still in the room.

She now stood in the busy square outside the church and debated whether to approach one of the soldiers and enlist their assistance. Buses were already arriving, depositing a new batch of pilgrims. The streets were beginning to clog with traffic as shopkeepers prepared storefronts.

Their evening had been delightful, the talk in the restaurant stimulating, what came afterward even more so. She'd already decided to tell Alberto Valendrea nothing. She'd come to Bosnia to be with Michener, not to act as spy. Let Ambrosi and Valendrea think what they might of her. She was simply glad to be here. She didn't really care about a journalism career any longer. She'd go to Romania and work with the children. Make her parents proud. Make herself proud. For once, do some good.

She'd resented Michener for all those years, but she'd come to realize that fault lay with her, too. Only her shortcomings were worse. Michener loved his God and his Church. She loved only herself. But that was going to change. She'd see to it. During dinner Michener had complained about never once having saved a soul. Maybe he was wrong. Perhaps she was his first.

She crossed the street and checked inside the information office. No one there had seen anyone matching Michener's description. She wandered down the sidewalk, spying into shops on the off chance he was doing a little investigating, trying to learn where the other seers lived. On impulse, she headed in the direction they'd taken yesterday, past the same parade of white-stuccoed dwellings with red-tiled roofs, back toward Jasna's residence.

She found the house and knocked on the door.

No one answered.

She retreated to the street. The shutters were drawn. She waited a few moments for any sign from within, but there was nothing. She noticed that Jasna's car was no longer parked to the side.

She started back toward the hotel.

A woman rushed from the house across the street shouting in Croatian, "It's so awful. So awful. Jesus help us."

Her anguish was alarming.

"What's wrong?" she called out in the best Croatian she could muster.

The older woman stopped. Panic filled her eyes. "It's Jasna. They found her on the mountain, the cross and her hurt by lightning."

"Is she all right?"

"I don't know. They're going after her now."

The woman was distraught to the point of hysteria. Tears flowed from her eyes. She kept crossing herself and clutched a rosary, mumbling a Hail Mary between sobs. "Mother of Jesus, save her. Do not let her die. She is blessed."

"Is it that bad?"

"She was barely breathing when they found her."

A thought occurred to her. "Was she alone?"

The woman seemed not to hear her question and kept muttering prayers, pleading with God to save Jasna.

"Was she alone?" she asked again.

The woman caught herself and seemed to register the question. "No. There was a man there. Bad off. Like her."

FORTY-NINE

VALENDREA MADE HIS WAY UP THE STAIRCASE TOWARD THE SIS-
tine Chapel believing that the papacy was within his grasp. All that
stood in the way was a cardinal from Kenya who was trying to cling
to the failed policies of a pope who'd killed himself. If it were up to
him, and it just might be before the day was through, Clement's
body would be removed from St. Peter's and shipped back to Germany. He might actually be able to accomplish that feat since
Clement's own will—the text of which had been published a week
ago—had proclaimed a sincere desire to be buried in Bamberg. The
gesture could be interpreted as a loving tribute from the Church to
its dead pontiff, one that would surely garner a positive reaction,
and one that would likewise rid hallowed ground of a weak soul.

He was still enjoying the display from breakfast. All of Ambrosi's efforts over the past couple of years were beginning to return
dividends. The listening devices had been Paolo's idea. At first, he'd
been nervous at the possibility of their discovery, but Ambrosi had
been right. He would have to reward Paolo. He regretted not bringing him into the conclave, but Ambrosi had been left outside with
express orders to remove the tape recorders and listening devices

while the election was ongoing. It was the perfect time to accomplish that task since the Vatican was in hibernation, all eyes and ears on the Sistine.

He came to the top of a narrow marble staircase. Ngovi stood on the stoop, apparently waiting.

"Judgment day, Maurice," he said, as he reached the last stair.

"That's one way of looking at it."

The nearest cardinal was fifty feet away and no one else was climbing the steps behind him. Most were already inside. He'd waited until the last moment to enter. "I won't miss your riddles. Yours or Clement's."

"It is the answers to those riddles that interest me."

"I wish you the best in Kenya. Enjoy the heat."

He started to walk away.

"You won't win," Ngovi said.

He turned back. He didn't like the smug look on the African's face, but couldn't help asking, "Why?"

Ngovi did not answer. He simply brushed past and entered the chapel.

The cardinals took their assigned places. Ngovi stood before the altar, appearing almost insignificant before the chaotic vision of color that was Michelangelo's *Last Judgment.*

"Before the voting begins, I have something to say."

All 113 cardinals turned their heads toward Ngovi. Valendrea sucked a deep breath. He could do nothing. The camerlengo was still in charge.

"Some of you seem to think I am the one to succeed our most beloved and departed Holy Father. Though your confidence is flattering, I must decline. If I am chosen, I will not accept. Know that, and govern your vote accordingly."

Ngovi stepped from the altar and took his place among the cardinals.

Valendrea realized that none of the forty-three men supporting Ngovi would stay with him now. They wanted to be part of a winning team. Since their horse had just bolted from the track, their allegiances would shift. With little chance for a third candidate to emerge at this late time, Valendrea quickly clicked off the math. He needed only to keep his present fifty-nine cardinals and add a fraction of Ngovi's headless bloc.

And that could easily be done.

He wanted to ask Ngovi why. The gesture made no sense. Though he denied wanting the papacy, somebody had orchestrated the African's forty-three votes, and he sure as hell didn't believe the Holy Spirit had much to do with it. This was a battle between men, organized by men, and executed by men. One or more of the men surrounding him was clearly an enemy, albeit a covert one. A good candidate for the ringleader was the cardinal-archivist, who possessed both the stature and the knowledge. He hoped Ngovi's strength was not a rejection of him. He would need loyalty and enthusiasm in the years ahead, with dissidents being taught a lesson. That would be Ambrosi's first task. All must understand that there was a price to pay for choosing wrong. But he had to give the African sitting across from him credit. *You won't win.* No. Ngovi was simply handing him the papacy. But who cared.

A win's a win.

The voting took an hour. After Ngovi's surprise announcement, everyone appeared anxious to end the conclave.

Valendrea did not write down the tally, he just mentally added up each repeat of his name. When the seventy-sixth time occurred, he quit listening. Only when the scrutineers pronounced his election with 102 votes did he focus on the altar.

He'd many times wondered what this moment would feel like. Now he alone dictated what a billion Catholics would or would not believe. No longer could any cardinal refuse his command. He would be called *Holy Father,* his every need catered to until the day he died. Cardinals had cried and cowered at this moment. A few had even fled the chapel, screaming their refusal. He realized every eye was about to focus upon him. He was no longer Alberto Cardinal Valendrea, bishop of Florence, secretary of state for the Holy See.

He was pope.

Ngovi approached the altar. Valendrea understood the African was about to perform his final duty as camerlengo. After a moment of prayer, Ngovi walked in silence down the center aisle and stood before him.

"Do you, most reverend Lord Cardinal, accept your election as supreme pontiff, which has been canonically carried out?"

They were words that had been spoken to victors for centuries.

He stared into Ngovi's piercing eyes and tried to sense what the older man was thinking. Why had he refused to be a candidate, knowing a man he despised would almost certainly be selected pontiff? From everything he knew, this African was a devout Catholic. A man who would do whatever was necessary to protect the Church. He was no coward. Yet he'd walked away from a fight he might have won.

He purged those confusing thoughts from his mind and said in a clear voice, "I accept." It was the first time in decades that Italian had been used in response to that question.

The cardinals stood and erupted in applause.

The grief for a dead pope was now replaced by the elation for a new pontiff. Outside the chapel doors Valendrea imagined the scene as observers heard the commotion, the first signal that something might have been decided. He watched as one of the scrutineers carried the ballots toward the stove. In a few moments white smoke would fill the morning sky and the piazza would erupt in cheers.

The ovation subsided. One more question was required.

"By what name will you be known?" Ngovi asked in Latin.

The chapel went silent.

The choosing of a name signaled much of what may be coming. John Paul I proclaimed his legacy by selecting the names of his two immediate predecessors, a message that he hoped to emulate the goodness of John and sternness of Paul. John Paul II conveyed a similar message when he chose his predecessor's dual label. For many years Valendrea had considered what name he would select, debating among the more popular choices—Innocent, Benedict, Gregory, Julius, Sixtus. Jakob Volkner had gravitated to Clement because of his German ancestry. Valendrea, though, wanted his name to send an unambiguous message that the imperial papacy had returned.

"Peter II."

Gasps pierced the chapel. Ngovi's expression never broke. Of the 267 pontiffs, there'd been twenty-three Johns, six Pauls, thirteen Leos, twelve named Pius, eight Alexanders, and a variety of other labels.

But only one Peter.

The first pope.

Thou art Peter and on this rock I will build my Church.

His bones lay only meters away, beneath the largest house of worship in Christendom. He was the first saint of the Catholic Church and the most revered. Over two millennia, no man had chosen his name.

He stood from his chair.

The time for pretense was over. All of the rituals had been dutifully performed. His election was certified, he'd formally accepted, and he'd announced his name. He was now Bishop of Rome, Vicar of Jesus Christ, Prince of the Apostles, *Pontifex Maximus* charged with primacy of jurisdiction over the Universal Church, Archbishop and Metropolitan of the Roman Province, Primate of Italy, Patriarch of the West.

Servant of the Servants of God.

He faced the cardinals and made sure no one misunderstood. "I choose to be known as Peter II," he said in Italian.

No one said a word.

Then one of the three cardinals from last night started to clap.

A few others slowly joined in. Soon the chapel reverberated with thunderous applause. Valendrea savored the absolute joy of victory that no man could take away. Yet his ecstacy was tempered by two things.

A smile that slowly crept onto Maurice Ngovi's lips, and the camerlengo's joining in the applause.

FIFTY

KATERINA SAT BESIDE THE BED AND KEPT WATCH OVER MICHener. The vision of him being carried into the hospital unconscious was still fresh in her mind, and she now knew what the loss of this man would mean.

She hated herself even more for deceiving him. She was going to tell Michener the truth. Hopefully, he'd forgive her. She hated herself for agreeing to Valendrea's requests. But maybe she'd needed prodding since her pride and anger could have otherwise prevented her from ever rediscovering Michener. Their first encounter in the piazza three weeks ago had been a disaster. Valendrea's overtures had clearly made things easier, but it didn't make it right.

Michener's eyes blinked open.

"Colin."

"Kate?" He was trying to focus.

"I'm here."

"I hear you, but I can't see you. It's like looking underwater. What happened?"

"Lightning. It struck the cross on the mountain. You and Jasna were too close."

He reached up and rubbed his brow. His fingers gently probed the scrapes and cuts. "She okay?"

"Seems to be. She was out, like you. What were you doing there?"

"Later."

"Sure. Here, take some water. The doctor said you need to drink." She brought a cup to his lips and he sucked a few sips.

"Where am I?"

"A local infirmary the government operates for the pilgrims."

"They say what's wrong with me?"

"No concussion. Just too close to a lot of voltage. Any closer and you'd both be dead. Nothing's broken, but you've got a nasty lump and a gash on the back of your head."

The door opened and a middle-aged, bearded man entered. "How's the patient doing?" he asked in English. "I'm the doctor who treated you, Father. How do you feel?"

"Like an avalanche rolled over me," Michener said.

"Understandable. But you'll be okay. A small cut, but no skull cracks. I'd recommend a complete exam when you get back home. Actually, considering what happened, you were pretty lucky."

After a quick look and a little more advice the doctor left.

"How'd he know I was a priest?"

"I had to identify you. You scared the hell out of me."

"What about the conclave?" he asked. "Have you heard any-thing?"

"Why am I not surprised that's the first thing on your mind."

"You're not interested?"

Actually she was curious. "There was no news an hour ago."

She reached out and clasped his hand. He turned his head toward her and said, "I wish I could see you."

"I love you, Colin." She felt better having said it.

"And I love you, Kate. I should have told you that years ago."

"Yes, you should."

"I should have done a lot of things differently. I only know that I want my future to include you."

"And what of Rome?"

"I've done all that I said I would. I'm through with that. I want to go to Romania, with you."

Her eyes watered. She was glad he couldn't see her crying. She swiped away the tears. "We'll do good there," she said, trying to keep her voice from quivering.

He tightened his grip on her hand.

And she cherished the feeling.

FIFTY-ONE

VALENDREA ACCEPTED CONGRATULATIONS FROM THE CARDI-
nals, then made his way out of the Sistine to a whitewashed space
known as the Room of Tears. There, the vestments from the House
of Gammarelli hung in neat rows. Gammarelli himself stood at
ready.

"Where is Father Ambrosi?" he asked one of the priests in attendance.

"Here, Holy Father," Ambrosi said, entering the room. He liked
the sound of those words from his acolyte's lips.

The secrecy of the conclave had ended as he left the chapel. The
main doors had been flung open while white smoke spewed from
the rooftop. By now, the name *Peter II* was being repeated throughout the palace. People would be marveling at his choice, and the
pundits would be startled by his audacity. Maybe for once they'd be
speechless.

"You are now my papal secretary," he said, as he lifted his scarlet
robe up over his head. "My first command." A smile came to his lips
as the private promise between them was fulfilled.

Ambrosi bowed his head in acceptance.

He motioned to the vestments he'd spied yesterday. "That set should do fine."

The tailor grabbed the selected garments and presented them saying, *"Santíssimo Padre."*

He accepted the greeting reserved only for a pope and watched as his cardinal robes were folded. He knew they would be cleaned and boxed, custom requiring that they be provided at his death to the then-senior member of the Valendrea clan.

He donned a white linen cassock and fastened the buttons. Gammarelli knelt and began nipping the seam with a threaded needle. The stitching would not be perfect, but adequate enough for the next couple of hours. By then a precise set of vestments, tailored to his measurements, would be ready.

He tested the fit. "A bit tight. Get it right."

Gammarelli ripped the seam and tried again.

"Make sure the thread is secure." The last thing he wanted was for something to fall apart.

When the tailor finished, he sat in a chair. One of the priests knelt before him and began removing his shoes and socks. He already liked the fact that little would ever be done by him anymore. A pair of white stockings and red leather shoes were brought forward. He checked the size. Perfect. He motioned that they should be slipped on his feet.

He stood.

A white *zucchetto* was handed to him. Back during the days when prelates shaved their scalps, the caps protected the bare skin during winter. Now they were an essential part of any high cleric's attire. Ever since the eighteenth century the pope's had been formed from eight triangular-shaped pieces of white silk, joined together. He clasped his hands at the edges and, like an emperor accepting his crown, nestled the cap on his head.

Ambrosi smiled in approval.

Time for the world to meet him.

But first, one last duty.

. . .

He left the dressing room and reentered the Sistine Chapel. The cardinals were standing at their assigned stations. A throne had been placed before the altar. He paraded straight to it and sat, waiting a full ten seconds before saying, "Be seated."

The ritual about to occur was a necessary element of the canonical election process. Each cardinal was expected to come forward, genuflect, and embrace the new pontiff.

He motioned to the senior cardinal-bishop, a supporter, who rose and started the process. John Paul II had broken a long-standing practice of popes sitting before the princes by greeting the college standing, but this was a new day and everyone might as well start adjusting. Actually, they should be glad—in centuries past, kissing the papal shoe had been a part of the ritual.

He stayed seated and offered his ring for a dutiful kiss.

Ngovi approached about halfway through the procession. The African knelt and reached for the offered ring. Valendrea noticed that lips did not actually touch gold. Ngovi then stood and walked away.

"No congratulations?" Valendrea asked.

Ngovi stopped and turned back. "May your reign be all that you deserve."

He wanted to teach the smug son of a bitch a lesson, but this was not the time or place. Maybe that was Ngovi's intent, a provocation to spark an early show of arrogance. So he calmed his emotions and simply said, "I take that to mean good wishes."

"Nothing but."

When the last cardinal departed the altar, he stood. "I thank you all. I will do my best for the mother Church. Now I believe it's time to face the world."

He stomped down the center aisle, through the marble gate, and out the chapel's main entrance. He strode into the basilica and crossed the Regal and Ducal Halls. He liked the chosen route, the massive paintings on the walls making clear the superiority of the papacy over temporal power clear.

He entered the central loggia.

About an hour had passed since his election and the rumors were, by now, at an epidemic stage. Enough conflicting information had surely seeped from the Sistine that no one could, as yet, know anything for sure. And that was the way he was going to keep it. Confusion could be an effective weapon, provided the source of that confusion was him. His choice of name alone should be generating a fair amount of speculation. Not even the great warrior-popes, or the sanctified diplomats who'd managed election over the past hundred years, had dared that move.

He reached the alcove that led out to the balcony. But he would not exit just yet. Instead, the cardinal-archivist, as senior cardinal-deacon, would appear, then the pope, followed by the president of the Sacred College and the camerlengo.

He stepped close to the cardinal-archivist, just inside the doorway, and whispered, "I told you, Eminence, that I would be patient. Now do your last duty."

The old man's eyes betrayed nothing. Surely he already knew his fate.

Without saying a word, the archivist stepped onto the balcony.

Five hundred thousand people roared.

A microphone stood before the balustrade and the archivist stepped to it and said, *"Annuntio vobis gauduium magnum."* Latin was required for this announcement, but Valendrea knew the translation well.

We have a pope.

The crowd exploded in raucous joy. He could not see the people, but their presence could be felt. The cardinal-archivist spoke again into the microphone, *"Cardinalem Sanctae Romanae Ecclesiae . . ."* Valendrea."

The cheers were deafening. An Italian had regained the throne of St. Peter. Shouts of *"Viva, Viva"* grew in intensity.

283 / THE THIRD SECRET

The archivist paused to glance back and Valendrea caught the wintry expression. The old man clearly did not approve of what he was about to say. The cardinal-archivist turned back to the microphone, *"Qui Sibi Imposuit Nomen—"*

The words came back in an echo. The name that has been chosen is—

"Petrus II."

The echo bounced across the massive piazza, as if the statues topping the colonnade were talking to one another, each asking the other in wonderment if they'd heard correctly. The people, for an instant, considered the name, then understood.

The cheers amplified.

Valendrea started for the doorway, but noticed only one cardinal following. He turned. Ngovi had not moved.

"Are you coming?"

"I am not."

"It is your duty as camerlengo."

"It is my shame."

Valendrea took a step back into the alcove. "I let your insolence go in the chapel. Don't try me again."

"What would you do? Have me imprisoned? My possessions seized? My titles stripped? This is not the Middle Ages."

The other cardinal standing nearby seemed clearly embarrassed. The man was a staunch supporter, so some show of power was needed. "I will deal with you later, Ngovi."

"And the Lord will deal with you."

The African turned and walked away.

He wasn't going to let this moment be ruined. He faced the remaining cardinal. "Shall we, Eminence?"

And he stepped out into the sun, his arms extended in a warm embrace to the multitudes who shouted back their approval.

FIFTY-TWO

MICHENER WAS FEELING BETTER. HIS VISION HAD CLEARED and his head and stomach had finally settled down. He could now see that the infirmary room was a cubicle, the cinder-block walls a pale yellow. A window with lace curtains allowed light but no view, the panes coated with a thick layer of paint.

Katerina had gone to check on Jasna. There'd been no word from the doctor and he hoped she was all right.

The door opened.

"She's okay," Katerina said. "Apparently you both were just far enough away. Only a couple of nasty bumps to the head." She stood beside the bed. "And there's more news."

He looked at her, glad to once again see her lovely face.

"Valendrea is pope. I saw it on television. He just finished addressing the crowd in St. Peter's. Made a plea for a return to the Church's roots. And get this, he chose *Peter II* as his name."

"Romania is looking better and better."

She offered a half grin. "So tell me, was the climb to the top worth it?"

"What do you mean?"

"Whatever you and she were doing on that mountain last night."

"Jealous?"

"More curious."

He realized some explanation was owed. "She was supposed to tell me the tenth secret."

"In the middle of a storm?"

"Don't ask me to rationalize it. I woke up and she was outside in the street, waiting for me. It was spooky. But I felt the need to go."

He decided to say nothing about his hallucination, but his memory of the vision remained clear, like a dream that wouldn't let go. The doctor had said he'd been unconscious for several hours. So whatever he saw or heard was only a manifestation of all that he'd learned over the past few months, the messengers two men who weighed heavily on his mind. But what of the Lady? Probably nothing more than the image of what he'd seen at Jasna's house yesterday.

Or was it?

"Look, I don't know what Jasna had in mind. She told me that to learn the secret I needed to come with her. So I went."

"You didn't find the situation a bit strange?"

"This whole thing is strange."

"She's coming here."

"What do you mean?"

"Jasna said she's coming here to see you. They were readying her when I left."

The door opened and a wheelchair guided by an older woman rolled into the cramped room. Jasna looked tired, her forehead and right arm bandaged.

"I wanted to see if you were all right," she said in weak voice.

"I was wondering the same about you."

"I only took you there because the Lady told me to. I meant no harm."

For the first time she sounded human. "I don't blame you for anything. I chose to go."

STEVE BERRY / 286

"I'm told the cross is permanently scarred. A blackened slash down its white length."

"Is that your sign to the atheists?" Katerina asked, a touch of scorn in her inquiry.

"I have no idea," Jasna said.

"Perhaps today's message to the faithful might clear up everything." Katerina apparently wasn't going to cut her any slack.

He wanted to tell her to back off, but he knew she was upset, venting her frustration on the easiest target.

"The Lady has come for the final time."

He studied the features of the woman sitting before him. Her face was sad, the eyes drawn tight, the expression different than yesterday. For twenty-plus years she'd supposedly talked with the mother of God. Real or not, the experience was significant to her. Now all of that was over, and the pain of her loss was evident. He imagined it being akin to the death of a loved one—a voice never to be heard again, counsel and comfort gone forever. As with his parents. And Jakob Volkner.

Her sadness suddenly became his.

"The Virgin revealed to me last night, on the mountaintop, the tenth secret."

He recalled what little he'd heard her say through the storm. *I can remember. I know I can. Dear Lady, I had no idea.*

"I wrote down what she said." She handed him a folded sheet of paper. "The Lady said for me to give it to you."

"Did she say anything else?"

"It was then she vanished." Jasna motioned to the older woman behind the chair. "I'm going back to my room. Get well, Father Michener. I will pray for you."

"And I for you, Jasna," he said, meaning it.

She left.

"Colin, that woman is a fraud. Can't you see it?" Katerina's voice was rising.

"I don't know what she is, Kate. If she's a fraud, she's a good one.

She believes what she's saying. And even if she's a fake, that scam just ended. The visions are over."

She motioned to the paper. "Are you going to read it? There's no papal order this time forbidding it."

That was true. He unfolded the sheet, but focusing on the page made his head ache. He handed the writing to her.

"I can't. Read it to me."

FIFTY-THREE

VALENDREA STOOD IN THE AUDIENCE CHAMBER AND ACCEPTED congratulations from the staff in the Secretariat of State. Ambrosi had already indicated a desire to move many of the priests and most of the secretaries to the papal office. He hadn't argued. If he expected Ambrosi to cater to his every need, the least he could do was allow him to choose his own subordinates.

Ambrosi had left his side only sparingly since the morning, standing dutifully beyond the balcony as he'd addressed the throngs in St. Peter's Square. Ambrosi had then monitored radio and television reports, which he reported were mainly positive, especially at Valendrea's choice of label, the commentators agreeing that this could be a *significant pontificate.* Valendrea imagined even Tom Kealy stuttering a second or so as the words *Peter II* left his mouth. There'd be no more best-selling priests during his reign. Clerics would be doing as they were told. If not, they'd be fired—starting with Kealy. He'd already told Ambrosi to defrock the idiot by the end of the week.

And there would be more changes.

The papal tiara would be resurrected, a coronation scheduled.

Trumpets would sound at his entrance. Fans and drawn sabers would once again accompany him during the liturgy. And the gestatorial chair would be restored. Paul VI had changed most of those—a few momentary lapses in good judgment, or perhaps a reaction to his own times—but Valendrea would rectify all that.

The last of the well-wishers streamed by and he motioned to Ambrosi, who drew close. "There is something I need to do," he whispered. "End this."

Ambrosi turned to the crowd. "Everyone, the Holy Father is hungry. He hasn't eaten since breakfast. And we all know how our pontiff enjoys his meals."

Laughter echoed through the hall.

"For those he has not spoken with, I will make time later in the day."

"May the Lord bless each of you," Valendrea said.

He followed Ambrosi from the hall to his office at the Secretariat of State. The papal apartments had been unsealed half an hour ago, and many of his belongings from his third-floor chambers were now being moved to the fourth floor. In the days ahead he would visit the museums and basement storage facilities. He'd already provided Ambrosi with a list of items he wanted as part of the apartment décor. He was proud of his planning. Most of the decisions made over the last few hours had been contemplated long ago and the effect was of a pope in charge, doing the appropriate thing in the appropriate manner.

In his office, with the door closed, he turned to Ambrosi. "Find the cardinal-archivist. Tell him to be standing before the Riserva in fifteen minutes."

Ambrosi bowed and withdrew.

He stepped into the bathroom adjoining his office. He was still incensed by Ngovi's arrogance. The African was right. There was little he could do to him besides reassignment to a post far from Rome. But that wouldn't be wise. The soon-to-be-ex-camerlengo had amassed a surprising show of support. It would be foolish to pounce this soon. Patience was the call. But that didn't mean he'd forgotten Maurice Ngovi.

He splashed water onto his face and dried off with a towel.

The door to the outer office opened and Ambrosi returned. "The archivist is waiting."

He tossed the towel onto the marble counter. "Good. Let's go."

He stormed from the office and descended to the ground floor. The startled looks on the Swiss guards he passed showed that they were not accustomed to a pope appearing without warning.

He entered the archives.

The reading and collection rooms were empty. No one had been allowed use of the facility since Clement died. He stepped into the main hall and crossed the mosaic floor toward the iron grille. The cardinal-archivist stood outside. No one else was there except Ambrosi.

He approached the old man. "Needless to say, your services will no longer be needed. I would retire, if I were you. Be gone by the weekend."

"My desk is already cleaned out."

"I have not forgotten your comments this morning at breakfast."

"Please don't. When we both stand before the Lord, I want you to repeat them."

He wanted to slap the mouthy Italian. Instead, he simply asked, "Is the safe open?"

The old man nodded.

He turned to Ambrosi. "Wait here."

For so long, others had commanded the Riserva. Paul VI. John Paul II. Clement XV. Even the irritating archivist. No more.

He rushed inside, reached for the drawer, and slid it open. The wooden box came into view. He lifted it out and carried it to the same table Paul VI had sat at all those decades ago.

He hinged open the lid and saw two sheets of paper interfolded. One, clearly older, was the first part of the third secret of Fatima— in Sister Lucia's hand—the back of the sheet still bearing a Vatican mark from when the message was made public in 2000. The other, newer, was Father Tibor's 1960 Italian translation, it, too, marked.

But there should be another sheet.

Father Tibor's recent facsimile, which Clement himself had placed in the box. Where was it? He'd come to finish the job. To protect the Church and preserve his sanity.

Yet the paper was gone.

He rushed from the Riserva and shot straight for the archivist. He grabbed the old man by his robes. A great surge of anger swept through him. The cardinal's face filled with shock.

"Where is it?" he spat out.

"What . . . do . . . you mean?" the old man stammered.

"I'm in no mood. Where is it?"

"I have touched nothing. I swear to you before my God."

He could see the man was being truthful. This was not the source of the problem. He released his grip and the cardinal stepped back, clearly frightened by the assault.

"Get out of here," he told the archivist.

The old man hustled away.

A thought flooded his mind. Clement. That Friday night when the pope allowed him to destroy half of what Tibor had sent.

I wanted you to know what awaits you, Alberto.

Why didn't you stop me from burning the paper?

You'll see.

And when he demanded the remaining portion—Tibor's translation.

No, Alberto. It stays in the box.

He should have shoved the bastard aside and done what had to be done, regardless of whether the night prefect was there.

Now he saw everything clearly.

The translation was never in the box. Did it even exist? Yes, it did. No question. And Clement had wanted him to know.

Now it had to be found.

He turned to Ambrosi. "Go to Bosnia. Bring Colin Michener

back. No excuses, no exceptions. I want him here tomorrow. Tell him if he's not, I'll have a warrant issued for his arrest."

"The charge, Holy Father?" Ambrosi asked, almost matter-of-factly. "So I may say, if he asks."

He thought a moment, then said, "Complicity in the murder of Father Andrej Tibor."

PART
FOUR

FIFTY-FOUR

KATERINA'S STOMACH KNOTTED AS SHE SPOTTED FATHER AM-
brosi entering the hospital. She immediately noticed the addition of
scarlet piping and a red sash to his black wool cassock, signifying an
elevation to monsignor. Apparently Peter II wasted no time handing out the spoils.

Michener was resting in his room. All the tests run on him had
come back negative, and the doctor predicted he should be fine by tomorrow. They planned to leave for Bucharest at lunchtime. The presence of Ambrosi, though, here in Bosnia, meant nothing but trouble.

Ambrosi spotted her and approached. "I'm told Father Michener had a close call with death."

She resented his feigned concern, which was clearly for public
consumption. "Screw you, Ambrosi." She kept her voice low. "This
fountain is dry."

He shook his head in a gesture to convey mock disgust. "Love
truly does conquer all. No matter. We require nothing further from
you."

But she did of him. "I don't want Colin to learn anything about
you and me."

"I'm sure you don't."

"I'll tell him myself. Understand?"

He did not answer.

The tenth secret, written by Jasna, was in her pocket. She almost yanked the slip of paper out and forced the words onto Ambrosi, but what heaven might want was surely of no interest to this arrogant ass. Whether the message was from the mother of God or the lamentations of a woman convinced she was divinely chosen, nobody would ever know. But she wondered how the Church and Alberto Valendrea would explain away the tenth secret, particularly after accepting the previous nine from Medjugorje.

"Where is Michener?" Ambrosi asked, the tone expressionless.

"What do you want with him?"

"I want nothing, but his pope is another matter."

"Leave him alone."

"Oh, my. The lioness bares her claws."

"Get out of here, Ambrosi."

"I'm afraid you don't tell me what to do. The word of the papal secretary, I imagine, would carry much weight here. Surely more than that of an unemployed journalist." He moved around her.

She quickly stepped in his way. "I mean it, Ambrosi. Back off. Tell Valendrea that Colin's through with Rome."

"He's still a priest in the Roman Catholic Church, subject to the authority of the pope. He will do as told, or face the consequences."

"What does Valendrea want?"

"Why don't we go to Michener," Ambrosi said, "and I'll explain. I assure you, it's worth listening to."

She entered the room with Ambrosi following. Michener was sitting up in bed and his face constricted at the site of his visitor.

"I bring you greetings from Peter II," Ambrosi said. "We learned about what happened—"

"And just had to fly over to let me know your deep concern."

Ambrosi kept a stone face. Katerina wondered if he'd been born with the ability or mastered the technique through years of deceit.

"We're aware of why you are in Bosnia," Ambrosi said. "I've been sent to ascertain if you have learned anything from the seers?"

"Not a thing."

She was impressed with Michener's ability to lie, too.

"Must I go and find out if you're being truthful?"

"Do whatever you want."

"The information being circulated around town is that the tenth secret was revealed to the seer, Jasna, last night, and the visions are now over. The priests here are quite upset over that prospect."

"No more tourists? The money flow ended?" She couldn't resist.

Ambrosi faced her. "Perhaps you should wait outside. This is Church business."

"She's not going anywhere," Michener said. "With all you and Valendrea have surely been doing the past two days, you're worried about what's happening here in Bosnia? Why?"

Ambrosi folded both hands behind his back. "I'm the one asking questions."

"Then by all means fire away."

"The Holy Father commands you back to Rome."

"You know what you can tell the Holy Father."

"Such disrespect. At least we openly did not scorn Clement XV."

Michener's face hardened. "That's supposed to impress me? You just did everything possible to thwart what he was trying to do."

"I was hoping you'd be difficult."

The tone of Ambrosi's comment worried her. He seemed immensely pleased.

"I'm to inform you that if you do not come voluntarily, a warrant for your arrest will be issued through the Italian government."

"What are you babbling about?" Michener asked.

"The papal nuncio in Bucharest has informed His Holiness of your meeting with Father Tibor. He's upset he was not part of whatever you and Clement were doing. The Romanian authorities are now interested in talking with you. They, as we, are curious as to what the late pope wanted with that aging priest."

Katerina's throat tightened. This was drifting into dangerous waters. Michener, though, seemed unfazed. "Who said Clement was interested in Father Tibor?"

Ambrosi shrugged. "You? Clement? Who cares? All that matters is you went to see him and the Romanian police want to talk with you. The Holy See can either block that effort, or aid it. Which would you prefer?"

"Don't care."

Ambrosi turned around and faced Katerina. "What about you? Do you care?"

She realized the asshole was playing his trump card. Get Michener back to Rome or he'd learn, right now, how she'd so easily found him in Bucharest and Rome.

"What's she got to do with this?" Michener quickly asked.

Ambrosi hesitated for an agonizing pause. She wanted to slap his face, as she had in Rome, but she did nothing.

Ambrosi turned back to Michener. "I was only wondering what she might think. I understand she's a Romanian by birth, familiar with her country's police. I imagine their interrogation techniques are something one might want to avoid."

"Care to tell me how you know so much about her?"

"Father Tibor spoke with the papal nuncio in Bucharest. He told him about Ms. Lew being present when you talked with him. I simply learned of her background."

She was impressed with Ambrosi's explanation. If not for knowing the truth, she would have believed it herself.

"Leave her out of this," Michener said.

"Will you return to Rome?"

"I'll go back."

The response surprised her.

Ambrosi nodded approval. "I have a plane available in Split. When will you leave this hospital?"

"In the morning."

"Be ready at seven A.M." Ambrosi headed for the door. "And I'll pray this evening—" He paused a moment. "—for your speedy recovery."

Then he left.

"If he's praying for me, I'm in real trouble," Michener said as the door closed.

"Why did you agree to go back? He was bluffing about Romania."

Michener shifted in the bed and she helped him get situated. "I have to talk with Ngovi. He needs to know what Jasna said."

"For what? You can't believe any of what she wrote. That secret is ludicrous."

"Maybe so. But it's the tenth secret of Medjugorje, whether we believe it or not. I need to give it to Ngovi."

She adjusted the pillow. "Ever heard of fax machines?"

"I don't want to argue about this, Kate. Besides, I'm curious what's important enough for Valendrea to send his errand boy. Apparently there's something big involved, and I think I know what it is."

"The third secret of Fatima?"

He nodded. "But it still makes no sense. That secret is known to the world."

She recalled what Father Tibor had said in his messages to Clement. *Do as the Madonna said . . . How much intolerance will heaven allow?*

"This whole thing is beyond logic," Michener said.

She wanted to know, "Have you and Ambrosi always been enemies?"

He nodded. "I wonder how a man like that became a priest. If not for Valendrea, he never would have made it to Rome. They're perfect for one another." He hesitated, as if in thought. "I imagine there's going to be a lot of changes."

"That's not your problem," she said, hoping he wasn't changing his mind about their future.

"Don't worry, I'm not having second thoughts. But I wonder if the Romanian authorities are truly interested in me."

"What do you mean?"

"Could be a smokescreen."

She looked puzzled.

"Clement sent me an e-mail the night he died. In it he told me that Valendrea may have removed part of the original third secret long ago when he worked for Paul VI."

She listened with interest.

"Clement and Valendrea went into the Riserva together the night before Clement died. Valendrea also took an unscheduled trip from Rome the next day."

She instantly saw the significance. "The Saturday Father Tibor was murdered?"

"Connect the dots and a picture starts to form."

The image of Ambrosi, his knee jammed into her chest, his hands wrapped around her throat, flashed through her mind. Had Valendrea and Ambrosi been involved with Tibor's murder? She wanted to tell Michener what she knew, but realized that her explanation would generate far too many questions than she was presently willing to answer. Instead, she asked, "Could Valendrea have been involved with Father Tibor's death?"

"Hard to say. But he's certainly capable. As is Ambrosi. I still think Ambrosi is bluffing, though. The last thing the Vatican wants is attention. I'm betting our new pope will do whatever he can to keep the spotlight off him."

"But Valendrea could direct that spotlight somewhere else."

Michener seemed to understand. "Like onto me."

She nodded. "Nothing better than an ex-employee to blame everything on."

VALENDREA DONNED ONE OF THE WHITE CASSOCKS THE HOUSE of Gammarelli had crafted during the afternoon. He'd been right this morning—his measurements were on file, and it had been easy to fashion the appropriate garments in a short period of time. The seamstresses had done their job well. He admired good work and made a mental note to have Ambrosi forward an official thanks.

He hadn't heard from Ambrosi since Paolo had left for Bosnia. But he had no doubt that his friend would tend to his mission. Ambrosi knew what was at stake. He'd made things clear to him that night in Romania. Colin Michener had to be brought to Rome. Clement XV had cleverly thought ahead—he'd give the German that—and had apparently concluded that Valendrea would succeed him, so he'd purposely removed Tibor's latest translation, knowing there was no way he could start his papacy with that potential disaster looming.

But where was it?

Michener surely knew.

The telephone rang.

He was in his bedroom on the third floor of the palace. The papal apartments were still being prepared.

The phone rang again.

He wondered about the interruption. It was nearly eight P.M. He was trying to dress for his first formal dinner, this one a celebration of thanks with the cardinals, and had left word not to be disturbed.

Another ring.

He lifted the receiver.

"Holy Father, Father Ambrosi is calling and asked that I connect him. He said it was important."

"Do it."

A few clicks and Ambrosi said, "I have done as you asked."

"And the reaction?"

"He will be there tomorrow."

"His health?"

"Nothing severe."

"His traveling companion?"

"Being her usual charming self."

"Let's keep that one happy, for the present." Ambrosi had told him about her assault on him in Rome. At the time she was their best conduit to Michener, but the situation had changed.

"Nothing from me will affect that."

"Till tomorrow then," he said. "Have a safe trip."

FIFTY-FIVE

MICHENER SAT IN THE BACKSEAT OF A VATICAN CAR, KATERINA beside him. Ambrosi was in the front, and on his command they were waved through the Arch of the Bells into the privacy of the St. Damascus courtyard. A warren of ancient buildings surrounded them, blocking the midday sun, casting the pavement in an indigo hue.

For the first time he felt uneasy about being inside the Vatican. The men in charge now were manipulators. Enemies. He needed to be careful, watch his words, and get whatever was about to happen over with as quickly as possible.

The car stopped and they climbed out.

Ambrosi led them into a drawing room encased on three sides with stained glass where popes, for centuries, had greeted guests beneath the impressive murals. They followed Ambrosi through a maze of loggias and galleries littered with candelabra and tapestries surrounded by walls bursting with images of popes receiving homage from emperors and kings.

Michener knew where they were headed, and Ambrosi stopped outside the bronze door leading into the papal library where Gorbachev, Mandela, Carter, Yeltsin, Reagan, Bush, Clinton, Rabin, and Arafat had all visited.

"Ms. Lew will be waiting in the forward loggia when you are through," Ambrosi said. "In the meantime, you will not be disturbed."

Surprisingly Katerina did not object to being excluded and walked off with Ambrosi.

He opened the door and entered.

Three leaded-glass windows bathed the five-hundred-year-old bookshelves with fractured waves of light. Valendrea sat behind a desk, the same one popes had used for half a millennium. A panel depicting the Madonna graced the wall behind him. An upholstered armchair was angled in front of the desk, but Michener knew only heads of state were privileged to sit before the pope.

Valendrea stepped around the desk. The pope held out his hand, palm-down, and Michener knew what was expected of him. He stared deep into the Tuscan's eyes. This was the moment of submission. He debated what to do, but decided discretion was a better tack, at least until he learned what this demon wanted. He knelt and kissed the ring, noticing that the Vatican jewelers had already crafted a new one.

"I am told Clement took pleasure in extracting a similar gesture from His Eminence, Cardinal Bartolo, in Turin. I will pass on to the good cardinal your respect for church protocol."

Michener stood. "What do you want?" He did not add *Holy Father.*

"How are your injuries?"

"Surely you don't care."

"What would make you think otherwise?"

"The respect you've shown me the past three years."

Valendrea stepped back toward the desk. "I assume you're trying to provoke a response. I'll ignore your tone."

He asked again, "What do you want?"

"I want what Clement removed from the Riserva."

"I was unaware anything was gone."

"I am not in the mood. Clement told you everything."

He recalled things Clement had told him. *I allowed Valendrea to read what is in the Fatima box . . . In 1978 he removed from the Riserva part of the Virgin's third message.*

"Seems to me you're the thief."

"Bold words to your pope. Can you back them up?"

He wasn't taking that bait. Let the son of a bitch wonder what he knew.

Valendrea moved toward him. He seemed quite comfortable dressed in white, the skullcap nearly lost in his thick mane. "I'm not asking, Michener. I'm ordering you to tell me where that writing is."

There was a tinge of desperation in the command that made him wonder if Clement's e-mail ramblings were more than those of a depressed soul about to die. "I didn't know anything was gone, until a moment ago."

"And I'm supposed to believe that?"

"Believe what you want."

"I've had the papal apartments and Castle Gandolfo searched. You have Clement's personal belongings. I want them checked."

"What is it you're looking for?"

Valendrea appraised him with a suspicious gaze. "I can't decide if you are being truthful or not."

He shrugged. "Trust me. I am."

"All right. Father Tibor reproduced Sister Lucia's third message of Fatima. He sent his facsimile of both the original the good nun penned and his translation to Clement. The reproduced translation is now gone from the Riserva."

Michener was beginning to understand. "So you did take part of the third secret in 1978."

"I simply want what that priest concocted. Where are Clement's belongings?"

"I gave his furniture to charity. The rest I have."

"Have you been through them?"

He lied. "Of course."

"And you found nothing from Father Tibor?"

"Would you believe me if I answered?"

"Why should I?"

"Because I'm such a nice guy."

Valendrea went silent for a moment. Michener stayed silent, too.

"What did you learn in Bosnia?"

He noticed the shift in subjects. "Not to climb a mountain in a rainstorm."

"I see why Clement treasured you. A quick wit, matched by a sharp intellect." He paused. "Now answer my question."

He reached into his pocket, withdrew Jasna's note, and handed the slip of paper to the pope. "That's the tenth secret of Medjugorje."

Valendrea accepted the offering and read. The Tuscan drew a deep breath and his gaze shifted pointedly from the sheet to Michener's face. A low moan seeped from the pope's mouth and, without warning, Valendrea lunged forward and grabbed two handfuls of Michener's black cassock, the paper still in his hand. Fury filled the eyes that stared upon him. "Where is Tibor's reproduced translation?"

He was shocked by the attack, but kept his composure. "I considered Jasna's words meaningless. Why do they bother you?"

"Her ramblings mean nothing. What I want is Father Tibor's facsimile—"

"If the words are meaningless, why am I being assaulted?"

Valendrea seemed to realize the situation and released his grip. "Tibor's translation is Church property. I want it returned."

"Then you need to dispatch the Swiss guard to locate it."

"You have forty-eight hours to produce it or I'll have a warrant issued for your arrest."

"On what charge?"

"Theft of Vatican property. I'll also turn you over to the Romanian police. They want to know about your visit with Father Tibor." The words crackled with authority.

"I'm sure they'll want to know about your visit with him, too."

"What visit?"

He needed Valendrea to think he knew far more than he did. "You left the Vatican the day Tibor was killed."

"Since you seem to have all the answers, tell me where I went."

"I know enough."

"Do you really believe you can carry that bluff through? You plan to implicate the pope in a murder investigation? That effort would not get far."

He tried another bluff. "You weren't alone."

"Really now? Tell me more."

"I'll wait until my police interrogation. The Romanians will be fascinated. That much I guarantee."

A flushed look invaded Valendrea's face. "You have no idea what's at stake here. This is more important than you could ever realize."

"You sound like Clement."

"On this he was right." Valendrea looked away for a moment, then turned back. "Did Clement tell you that he watched while I burned part of what Tibor sent him? He stood right there in the Riserva and let me destroy it. He also wanted me to know that the rest of what Tibor sent, a facsimile translation of Sister Lucia's complete message, was there, too, in the box. But it is now gone. Clement didn't want anything to happen to it. That much I know. So he gave it to you."

"Why is this translation so important?"

"I don't plan to explain myself. I simply want the document returned."

"How do you know it was even there?"

"I don't. But no one returned to the archives after that Friday night, and Clement was dead two days later."

"Along with Father Tibor."

"What's that supposed to mean?"

"Whatever you want it to mean."

"I'll do whatever I have to do to get that document."

A bitter edge laced to the words. "I believe you would." He needed to leave. "Am I dismissed?"

"Get out. But I'd better hear from you in two days time or you won't like my next messenger."

He wondered what that meant. The police? Somebody else? Hard to say.

"Ever wonder how Ms. Lew found you in Romania?" Valendrea casually asked as he reached the door.

Did he hear right? How did he know anything about Katerina? He stopped and looked back.

"She was there because I paid her to learn what you were doing."

He was stunned, but said nothing.

"Bosnia, too. She went to keep an eye on you. I told her to use her talents to gain your trust, as she apparently did."

He rushed forward, but Valendrea produced a small black controller. "One press and Swiss guards charge into this room. Assaulting the pope is a serious crime."

He halted his advance and repressed a shudder.

"You aren't the first man to be duped by a woman. She's clever. But I'm telling you this as a warning. Careful whom you trust, Michener. There's much at stake. You may not realize it, but I may be the only friend you've got when all this is over."

FIFTY-SIX

MICHENER LEFT THE LIBRARY. AMBROSI WAS WAITING OUTSIDE but did not accompany him to the forward loggia, saying only that the car and driver would take him wherever he wanted to go.

Katerina sat alone on a gilded settee. He was trying to understand what had motivated her to deceive him. He'd wondered about her finding him in Bucharest, then showing up at the apartment in Rome. He wanted to believe everything that had passed between them had been sincere, but he could not help thinking that it was all an act, designed to sway his emotions and lower his defenses. He'd been worried about the household staff or listening devices. Instead the one person he trusted had become his enemy's perfect emissary.

At Turin, Clement had warned him. *You have no idea the depth of a person like Alberto Valendrea. You think you can do battle with Valendrea? No, Colin. You're no match for him. You're too decent. Too trusting.*

His throat tightened as he came close to Katerina. Perhaps his strained expression betrayed his thoughts.

"He told you about me, didn't he?" Her voice was sad.

"You expected that?"

"Ambrosi almost did yesterday. I figured Valendrea certainly would. I'm of no use to them anymore."

Emotions ricocheted through him.

"I told them nothing, Colin. Absolutely nothing. I took Valendrea's money and I went to Romania and Bosnia. That's true. But because I wanted to go, not because *they* wanted me to. I used them, like they used me."

The words sounded good, but were not enough to ease his pain. He calmly asked, "Does the truth mean anything to you?"

She bit her lip and he noticed her right arm trembling. Anger, which was her usual response to a confrontation, had not surfaced. When she did not answer him, he said, "I trusted you, Kate. I told you things I would never tell anyone else."

"And I didn't violate that trust."

"How am I to believe you?" Though he wanted to.

"What did Valendrea say?"

"Enough for us to be having this conversation."

He was rapidly numbing. His parents were gone, as was Jakob Volkner. Now Katerina had betrayed him. For the first time in his life he was alone, and suddenly the weight of being an unwanted baby, born in an institution and stripped from his mother, settled upon him. He was in many ways lost, with nowhere to turn. He'd thought with Clement gone the woman standing before him held the answer to his future. He was even willing to discard a quarter century of his life for the chance to love her and be loved back.

But how could that possibly be now?

A moment of strained silence passed between them. Awkward and embarrassing.

"Okay, Colin," she finally said. "I get the message. I'll go."

She turned to leave.

The heels of her shoes tapped off the marble as she walked away. He wanted to tell her it was okay. *Don't leave. Stop.* But he couldn't bring himself to speak the words.

· · ·

He headed in the opposite direction, down to ground level. He wasn't about to use the car Ambrosi had offered. He wanted nothing more from this place except to be left alone.

He was inside the Vatican without credentials or an escort, but his face was so well known that none of the guards questioned his presence. He came to the end of a long loggia filled with planispheres and globes. Ahead, Maurice Ngovi stood in the opposite doorway.

"I heard you were here," Ngovi said as he approached. "I also know what happened in Bosnia. You okay?"

He nodded. "I was going to call you later."

"We need to talk."

"Where?"

Ngovi seemed to understand and motioned for him to follow. They walked in silence to the archives. The reading rooms were once again full of scholars, historians, and journalists. Ngovi found the cardinal-archivist and the three men headed for one of the reading rooms. Once inside with the door closed, Ngovi said, "I think this place is reasonably private."

Michener turned to the archivist. "I thought you'd be unemployed by now."

"I've been ordered out by the weekend. My replacement arrives the day after tomorrow."

He knew what the job meant to the old man. "I'm sorry. But I think you're better off."

"What did our pontiff want with you?" Ngovi asked.

Michener plopped down in one of the chairs. "He thinks I have a document that was supposedly in the Riserva. Something Father Tibor sent to Clement that concerns the third secret of Fatima. Some facsimile of a translation. I have no idea what he's talking about."

Ngovi gave the archivist a strange look.

"What is it?" Michener asked.

Ngovi told him about Valendrea's visit yesterday to the Riserva.

"He was like a madman," the archivist said. "He kept saying

STEVE BERRY / 312

something was gone from the box. I was truly frightened of him. God help this Church."

"Did Valendrea explain anything?" Ngovi asked him.

He told them both what the pope had said.

"That Friday night," the cardinal-archivist said, "when Clement and Valendrea were in the Riserva together, something was burned. We found ashes on the floor."

"Clement said nothing to you about that?" Michener asked.

The archivist shook his head. "Not a word."

A lot of the pieces were coming together, but there was still a problem. He said, "This whole thing is bizarre. Sister Lucia herself verified in 2000 the authenticity of the third secret before it was released by John Paul."

Ngovi nodded. "I was present. The original writing was taken, in the box, from the Riserva to Portugal, and she confirmed that the document was the same one she penned in 1944. But, Colin, the box contained only two sheets of paper. I myself was there when it was opened. There was an original writing and an Italian translation. Nothing more."

"If the message was incomplete, would she not have said something?" Michener asked.

"She was so old and frail," Ngovi said. "I recall how she merely glanced at the page and nodded. I was told her eyesight was poor, her hearing gone."

"Maurice asked me to check," the archivist said. "Valendrea and Paul VI entered the Riserva on May 18, 1978. Valendrea returned an hour later, on Paul's express order, and stayed there, alone, for fifteen minutes."

Ngovi nodded. "It seems whatever Father Tibor sent to Clement opened a door Valendrea thought long closed."

"And it may have cost Tibor his life." He considered the situation. "Valendrea called whatever is gone a *facsimile translation*. Translation of what?"

"Colin," Ngovi said. "There is apparently more to the third secret of Fatima than we know."

"And Valendrea thinks I have it."

"Do you?" Ngovi asked.

He shook his head. "If I did, I'd give him the damn thing. I'm sick of this and just want out."

"Any thoughts as to what Clement might have done with Tibor's reproduction?"

He hadn't really considered the point. "No idea. Stealing was not like Clement." Neither was committing suicide, but he knew better than to say anything. The archivist had no knowledge of that. But he sensed from Ngovi's expression the Kenyan was thinking the same thing.

"And what of Bosnia?" Ngovi asked.

"Stranger than Romania."

He showed them Jasna's message. He'd given Valendrea a copy, keeping the original.

"We can't put too much credence in this," Ngovi said, motioning with Jasna's words. "Medjugorje seems more a sideshow than a religious experience. This tenth secret could simply be the seer's imagination and, quite frankly, considering its scope, I have to seriously question if that isn't so."

"My thoughts exactly," Michener said. "Jasna has convinced herself it's real and seems caught up in the experience. Yet Valendrea reacted strongly when he read the message." He told them what had just happened.

"That's the way he was in the Riserva," the archivist said. "A madman."

Michener stared hard at Ngovi. "What's going on here, Maurice?"

"I am at a loss. Years back, as a bishop, I and others spent three months studying the third secret at John Paul's request. That message was so different from the first two. They were precise, detailed, but the third secret was more a parable. His Holiness thought guidance from the Church, in its interpretation, was called for. And I agreed. But never did we consider the message incomplete."

Ngovi motioned to a thick, oversized volume lying on the table.

The huge manuscript was ancient, its pages so aged they appeared charred. The cover was scrawled in Latin, surrounded by colorful drawings depicting what appeared to be popes and cardinals. The words LIGNUM VITAE were barely visible in faded crimson ink.

Ngovi sat in one of the chairs and asked Michener, "What do you know of St. Malachy?"

"Enough to question whether the man was genuine."

"I assure you, his prophecies are real. This volume here was published in Venice in 1595 by a Dominican historian, Arnold Wion, as the definitive account of what St. Malachy himself wrote of his visions."

"Maurice, those visions occurred in the middle of the twelfth century. Four hundred years passed before Wion began writing everything down. I've heard all the tales. Who knows what Malachy said, if anything. *His* words have not survived."

"But Malachy's writings were here in 1595," the archivist said. "Our indexes show that. So Wion would have had access to them."

"If Wion's book survived, why didn't Malachy's text?"

Ngovi motioned to the book. "Even if Wion's writing is a forgery, *his* prophecies instead of Malachy's, they, too, are remarkable in their accuracy. Made even more so with what's happened over the past couple of days."

Ngovi offered him three typed sheets. Michener scanned the pages and saw that it was a narrative summary.

Malachy was an Irishman, born in 1094. He became a priest at age twenty-five, a bishop at thirty. In 1139 he left Ireland for Rome, where he delivered an account of his diocese to Pope Innocent II. While there he experienced a strange vision of the future, a long list of men who would one day rule the Church. He committed his vision to parchment and presented Innocent with the manuscript. The pope read the offering, then sealed it in the archives where it remained until 1595, when Arnold Wion again recorded the list of pontiffs Malachy had seen, along with Malachy's prophetical mottoes, starting with Celestine II, in 1143, and ending 111 popes later with the supposed last pontiff.

"There's no evidence that Malachy even experienced visions," Michener said. "As I recall, that was all added to the story in the late nineteenth century from secondhand sources."

"Read some of the mottoes," Ngovi calmly said.

He stared again at the pages in his hand. The eighty-first pope was prophesied to be *The Lily and the Rose.* Urban VIII, who served at that time, came from Florence, which used the red lily as its symbol. He was also bishop of Spoletto, which took the rose for its symbol. The ninety-fourth pope was said to be *A Rose of Umbria.* Clement XIII, before becoming pope, was governor of Umbria. *Apostolic Wanderer* was the predicted motto for the ninety-sixth pope. Pius VI would end his days a wandering prisoner of the French revolutionists. Leo XIII was the 102nd pope. *A Light in the Sky* was his attributed motto. The papal arms of Leo showed a comet. John XXIII was said to be *Shepherd and Sailor.* Apt since he defined his pontificate as that of a shepherd and the badge of Vatican II, which he called into session, displayed a cross and a ship. Also, prior to his election, John was patriarch of Venice, an ancient maritime capital.

Michener looked up. "Interesting, but what does this have to do with anything?"

"Clement was the one hundred and eleventh pope. Malachy labeled him *From the Glory of the Olive.* Do you recall the gospel of Matthew, chapter 24, the signs of the end of the age?"

He did. Jesus left the Temple and was walking away when his disciples complimented the beauty of the building. *I tell you the truth,* He said. *Not one stone here will be left on another; every one will be thrown down.* Then later, on the Mount of Olives, the disciples beseeched Him to say when that would happen and what will be the sign of the end of the age.

"Christ foretold the second coming in that passage. But, Maurice, you can't seriously believe that the end of the age is at hand?"

"Perhaps not something that cataclysmic, but nonetheless a clear ending and a new beginning. Clement was predicted to be the precursor to that event. And there's more. Of Malachy's described popes, starting in 1143, the last of his one hundred and twelve is the current pope. Malachy predicted in 1138 that he would be named *Petrus Romanus.*"

Peter the Roman.

"But that's a fallacy," Michener said. "Some say Malachy never predicted a Peter. Instead, that was added in a nineteenth-century publication of his prophecies."

"I wish that were true," Ngovi said as he slipped on a pair of cotton gloves and gently opened the bulky manuscript. The ancient parchment crackled from the effort. "Read this."

He glanced down at the words, penned in Latin:

In the final persecution of the Holy Roman Church there will reign Peter the Roman who will feed his flock among many tribulations, after which in the seven hilled city the dreadful judge will judge all people.

"Valendrea," Ngovi said, "took the name *Peter* on his own accord. Do you see now why I'm so concerned? Those are Wion's words, supposedly Malachy's as well, written centuries ago. Who are we to question? Maybe Clement was right. We inquire far too much and do what we please, not what we're supposed to do."

"How can you explain," the cardinal-archivist asked, "that this volume is nearly five hundred years old and these mottoes were attributed to these popes long ago? Ten or twenty being correct is coincidence. Ninety percent is something more, and that's what we're talking about. Only around ten percent of the labels seem to have no bearing whatsoever. The vast majority are remarkably accurate. And the final one, Peter, comes exactly at one hundred and twelve. I shuddered when Valendrea took that name."

A lot was coming fast. First the revelation about Katerina. Now the possibility that the end of the world was at hand. *After which in the seven hilled city the dreadful judge will judge all people.* Rome had long been labeled *the seven hilled city.* He looked over at Ngovi. Concern laced the older prelate's face.

"Colin, you must find Tibor's reproduced translation. If Valendrea thinks that document is critical, then so should we. You knew Jakob better than anybody. Locate his hiding place." Ngovi closed the manuscript. "This may be the last day we have access to this archive. A siege mentality is taking hold. Valendrea is purging all dissenters. I wanted you to see this firsthand—to understand the gravity. What the Medjugorje seer wrote is open to debate, but what Sister Lucia penned, and what Father Tibor translated, is quite another."

"I have no idea where that document might be. I can't even conceive of how Jakob removed it from the Vatican."

"I was the only person with the safe's combination," the cardinal-archivist said. "And I opened it only for Clement."

An emptiness swept over him as he thought again of Katerina's betrayal. Concentrating on something else might help, if only for a short while. "I'll see what I can do, Maurice. But I don't even know where to start."

Ngovi's face remained solemn. "Colin, I don't want to dramatize this any more than necessary. But the fate of the Church could well be in your hands."

FIFTY-SEVEN

3:30 P.M.

VALENDREA EXCUSED HIMSELF FROM THE CROWD OF WELL-wishers gathered in the audience hall. The group had traveled from Florence to wish him well, and before leaving he assured them all that his first trip beyond the Vatican would be to Tuscany.

Ambrosi was waiting for him on the fourth floor. His secretary had left the audience chamber half an hour ago and he was curious why.

"Holy Father," Ambrosi said. "Michener met with Ngovi and the cardinal-archivist after he left you."

He now understood the urgency. "What was said?"

"It was behind closed doors in one of the reading rooms. The priest I have in the archives could learn nothing except they had an ancient volume with them, one that ordinarily only the archivist may handle."

"Which one?"

"Lignum Vitae."

"Malachy's prophecies? You've got to be kidding. That's nonsense. Still, it's a shame we don't know what was said."

"I'm in the process of reinstalling the listening devices. But it will take time."

"When is Ngovi scheduled to leave?"

"His office is already cleared. I've been told he departs for Africa in a few days. For now, he's still in his apartment."

And still camerlengo. Valendrea had yet to decide on a replacement, debating among three cardinals who hadn't wavered in their conclave support.

"I've been thinking about Clement's personal effects. Tibor's facsimile has to be among them. Clement could expect no one but Michener to go through his things."

"What are you saying, Holy Father?"

"I don't think Michener will bring us anything. He despises us. No, he'll give it to Ngovi. And I can't let that happen."

He watched Ambrosi for a reaction and his old friend did not disappoint him. "You want to act first?" his secretary asked.

"We need to demonstrate to Michener how serious we are. But not you this time, Paolo. Call our friends and enlist their aid."

MICHENER ENTERED THE APARTMENT HE'D BEEN USING SINCE Clement's death. He'd walked the streets of Rome the past couple of hours. His head started hurting half an hour ago, one of the headaches the Bosnian doctor warned would reoccur, so he went straight to the bathroom and downed two aspirin. The doctor had also told him to have a complete physical once back in Rome, but there was no time for that right now.

He unbuttoned his cassock and tossed it onto the bed. The clock on the nightstand read six thirty P.M. He could still feel Valendrea's hands on him. God help the Catholic Church. A man possessed of no fear was a dangerous thing. Valendrea seemed to dart, unconcerned, from moment to moment, and absolute power vested him with unfettered choices. Then there was what St. Malachy supposedly said. He knew he should ignore the ridiculous, but a dread swelled inside him. Trouble lay ahead. Of that he was sure.

He dressed in a pair of jeans and a buttondown shirt, then trudged into the front room and settled on the sofa. He purposely left all the lights off.

Had Valendrea actually purged something from the Riserva decades ago? Did Clement recently do the same thing? What was happening? It was as if reality had turned itself upside down. Everything and everybody around him seemed tainted. And to cap the whole mess off, an Irish bishop who lived nine hundred years ago may have predicted the end of the world with the coming of a pope named Peter.

He rubbed his temples and tried to dull the pain. Through the windows, scattered rays of weak light found their way inside from the street below. In the shadows beneath the sill lay Jakob Volkner's oak chest. He recalled it being locked the day he moved everything from the Vatican. It certainly seemed like a place where Clement might have secreted something important. No one would have dared to look inside.

He crawled across the rug to the chest.

He reached up, switched on one of the lamps, and studied the lock. He didn't want to damage the chest by breaking it open, so he sat back and thought about the best course.

The cardboard box he'd brought from the papal apartments the day after Clement's death sat a few feet away. Everything of Clement's lay inside. He slid the box toward him and rummaged through the assorted items that had once graced the papal apartments. Most invoked fond memories—a Black Forest clock, some special pens, a framed photograph of Clement's parents.

A gray paper bag contained Clement's personal Bible. It had been sent from Castle Gandolfo the day of the funeral. He hadn't opened the book, merely brought it back to the apartment and placed it in the box.

He now admired the white leather exterior, its gilt edging marred by time. Reverently, he opened the front cover. In German was written, ON THE OCCASION OF YOUR PRIESTHOOD. FROM YOUR PARENTS, WHO LOVE YOU VERY MUCH.

Clement had spoken many times of his parents. The Volkners had been Bavarian aristocracy in the time of Ludwig I, and the family had been anti-Nazi, never supporting Hitler, even in the glory days before the war. They hadn't been foolish, though, and kept their dissension to themselves, doing quietly what they could to help Bamberg's Jews. Volkner's father had harbored the life savings of two local families, safeguarding the funds until after the war. Unfortunately, no one returned to claim the money. Instead, every mark was given to Israel. A gift from the past in the hope of the future.

The vision from last night flashed through his mind.

Jakob Volkner's face.

Do not ignore heaven any longer. Do as I asked. Remember, there is much to be said for a loyal servant.

What is my destiny, Jakob?

But it was Father Tibor's image that answered.

To be a sign to the world. A beacon for repentance. The messenger to announce that God is very much alive.

What did it all mean? Was it real? Or just the delusion of a brain racked by lightning?

He slowly thumbed through the Bible. The pages were like cloth. Some bore underlining. A few had notes scribbled in the margin. He began to notice the marked passages.

Acts 5:29. *Obedience to God carries more authority than obedience to men.*

James 1:27. *Pure unspoiled religion in the eyes of God our Father is this: coming to the help of orphans and widows when they need it and keeping oneself uncontaminated by the world.*

Matthew 15:3–6. *Why do you transgress the commandment of God for the sake of your tradition? In this way you have made God's word null and void by means of tradition.*

Matthew 5:19. *The man who relaxes even one of the least of these commandments and teaches others to act likewise will be considered the very least in the Kingdom of Heaven.*

Daniel 4:23. *Your Kingdom will be preserved for you, but only after you have learned that Heaven rules all.*

John 8:28. *I do nothing on my own authority, but preach only as the father has taught me.*

Interesting choices. More messages from a troubled pope? Or just random selections?

Four strands of colored silk poked from the book's bottom edge, bunched together three-quarters of the way through. He grabbed the strands and folded back to the denoted pages.

Wedged into the binding was a thin silver key.

Had Clement done that on purpose? The Bible had been at Castle Gandolfo on the nightstand beside Clement's bed. The pope could have assumed that no one but Michener would examine the book.

He freed the key and knew what it opened.

He inserted it into the chest's lock. The tumblers gave way and the lid released.

Inside were envelopes. A hundred or more, each addressed to Clement in a feminine hand. The addresses varied. Munich, Cologne, Dublin, Cairo, Cape Town, Warsaw, Rome. All places where Clement had been posted. The return address on every envelope was the same. He knew the sender from a quarter century of handling Volkner's mail. Her name was Irma Rahn, a childhood friend. He'd never asked much about her, Clement only volunteering that they grew up together in Bamberg.

Clement regularly corresponded with a few longtime friends. Yet all of the envelopes in the chest were from Rahn. Why had Clement left such a legacy? Why not simply destroy them? Their implications could easily be misconstrued, especially by enemies like Valendrea. Apparently, though, Clement had decided the risk was worth taking.

Since they were now his property, he opened one of the envelopes, slid out the letter, and started reading.

FIFTY-EIGHT

Jakob:

My heart ached at the news from Warsaw. I saw your name mentioned as being there in the crowds when riots broke out. The communists would like nothing better than for you and the other bishops to fall victim. I was relieved to receive your letter and glad to know you were unharmed. I wish His Holiness would allow a posting to Rome where I know you'll be safe. I know you would never make such a request, but I pray to our Lord that it will happen. I'm hoping you are able to come home for the Christmas season. It would be good to spend a holiday near you. If such is possible, do let me know. As always I await your next letter and know, my dear Jakob, that I love you so.

Jakob:

I visited your parents' grave today. I trimmed the grass and cleaned the stones. I left a bundle of lilies with your name on them. Such a shame they *did not live to see what you have become. An archbishop of the church, perhaps even a cardinal one day. It's a testament to them what you have done. My parents and yours endured so much, too much really. I pray each day for the deliverance of Germany. Perhaps through good men like you our legacy could become something good. I hope your health is good. Mine is fine. I seem blessed with a strong constitution. I might be in Munich over the next three weeks. I will call if I come. My heart longs to see you again. Your precious words in your last letter have warmed me ever since. Take care, dear Jakob. My love, always and forever.*

Jakob:

Cardinal Eminence. A title you so deserve. God bless John Paul for finally elevating you. Thank you again for letting me attend the consistory. Surely no one knew who I was. I sat off to the side and kept my thoughts to myself. Your Colin Michener was there and seemed so proud. He is as you described, a handsome young man. Make him the son we always wanted. Vest in him, as your father vested in you. Leave a legacy, Jakob, through him. There is nothing wrong with that, nothing in your vows to your church or your God forbids that. I still find my eyes watering at the memory of the pope crowning you with a scarlet hat. It was the proudest moment of my life. I love you, Jakob, and only hope that our bond is a source of strength. Take care, my darling, and do write soon.

Jakob:

Karl Haigl died a few days back. At the funeral I was remembering when the three of us were children, playing in the river on a warm summer day. He was such a gentle man and if not for you I may well have loved him. I suspect you know that, though. His wife passed several years ago and he lived alone. His children are an ungrateful and selfish lot. What has happened to our youth? Do they not appreciate from where they came? Many times I would take supper to him and we would sit and talk. He admired you so. Little scrawny Jakob, risen to a cardinal in the Catholic Church. Now it's secretary of state. One step from the papacy. He would have liked to see you again and it's a shame that wasn't possible. Bamberg has not forgotten its bishop and I know its bishop has not forgotten the place of his youth. I have prayed diligently the past few days for you, Jakob. The pope is not well. Soon a new pope will be chosen. I have asked the Lord to watch over you. Maybe he will heed the plea of an old woman who loves both her God and her cardinal deeply. Take care.

Jakob:

I watched on television as you appeared on the balcony of St. Peter's. The pride and love that swelled inside me was too much to describe. My Jakob is now Clement. Such a wise choice in names. At the mention, I recalled the times you and I went to the cathedral and visited the tomb. I remembered how you imagined Clement II. A German risen to pope. Even then there was vision in your eyes. Somehow he was a part of you. Now, as Clement XV, you are pope. Be wise dear Jakob, but be brave. The church is yours to mold or break. Let them remember Clement XV with pride. A pilgrimage back to Bamberg would be so wonderful. Try and arrange that one day. I have not seen you for so long. Just a few moments, even in public, would suffice. In the meantime let what we have warm your heart and mellow your soul. Shepherd the flock with strength and dignity and always know that my heart is with you.

FIFTY-NINE

9:00 P.M.

KATERINA APPROACHED THE BUILDING WHERE MICHENER lived. The darkened street was devoid of people and lined with empty cars. From open windows she heard idle conversation, the squeals of children, and a snatch of music. Traffic rumbled from a boulevard fifty yards behind her.

A light burned in Michener's apartment, and she took refuge in a doorway across the street, safe within the shadows, and stared up three floors.

They needed to talk. He had to understand. She hadn't betrayed him. She'd told Valendrea nothing. Still, she'd violated his confidence. He hadn't been as angry as she expected, more hurt, and that made her feel worse. When would she ever learn? Why did she keep making the same mistakes? Could she not for once do the right thing, for the right reason? She was capable of better, but something seemed perpetually to restrain her.

She stood in the darkness, comforted by her solitude, resolute in knowing what needed to be done. There was no sign of movement in the third-floor window and she wondered if Michener was even there.

She was mustering the courage to cross the street when a car slowly turned off the boulevard and inched its way toward the building. Headlights swept a path ahead and she hugged the wall, sinking into darkness.

The headlights extinguished and the vehicle stopped.

A dark Mercedes coupe.

The rear door opened and a man stepped out. In the glow from the car's cabin light she saw that he was tall, with a thin face split by a long, sharp nose. He wore a loose-fitting gray suit, and she did not like the gleam in his dark eyes. Men like this she'd seen before. Two other men sat in the car, one driving, another in the backseat. Her brain screamed trouble. Ambrosi had surely dispatched them.

The tall man entered Michener's building.

The Mercedes rumbled ahead, farther down the street. The light in Michener's apartment was still on.

No time to call the police.

She emerged from the doorway and hurried across the street.

MICHENER FINISHED THE LAST LETTER AND STARED AT THE ENvelopes scattered around him. Over the past two hours he'd read every word Irma Rahn had written. Certainly the chest did not contain a lifetime of their correspondence. Perhaps Volkner saved only the letters that meant something. The most recent one was dated two months earlier—another touching composition wherein Irma lamented about Clement's health, concerned about what she was seeing on television, urging him to take care of himself.

He thought back through the years and now understood some of the comments Volkner had made, especially when they discussed Katerina.

You think you're the only priest to succumb? And was it that wrong, anyway? Did it feel wrong, Colin? Did your heart say it was wrong?

And just before he died. The curious statement when Clement inquired about Katerina and the tribunal. *It's all right to care, Colin. She's a part of your past. A part you should not forget.*

He'd thought his friend was only offering comfort. Now he realized there was more.

But that doesn't mean you can't be friends. Share your lives in words and feelings. Experience the closeness that someone who genuinely cares can provide. Surely the Church doesn't forbid us that pleasure.

He recalled the questions Clement had posed at Castle Gandolfo, only hours before he died. *Why must priests not marry? Why must they remain chaste? If that's acceptable for others, why not the clergy?*

He couldn't help wondering how far the relationship had progressed. Had the pope violated his own vow of celibacy? Had he done the same thing Thomas Kealy was accused of doing? Nothing from the letters indicated that, which in and of itself meant nothing. After all, who would write such a thing down?

He propped back against the sofa and rubbed his eyes.

Father Tibor's translation was nowhere in the chest. He'd searched every envelope, read every letter, on the chance Clement had secreted the paper inside one of them. In fact, there was no mention of anything even remotely related to Fatima. His effort seemed another dead end. He was right back where he started, except he now knew about Irma Rahn.

Don't forget Bamberg.

That's what Jasna had said to him. And what had Clement written to him in his final message? *I would prefer the sanctity of Bamberg, that lovely city by the river, and the cathedral I so loved. My only regret is that I did not see its beauty one last time. Perhaps, though, my legacy could still be there.*

Then the afternoon in the solarium at Castle Gandolfo, and what Clement whispered.

I allowed Valendrea to read what is in the Fatima box.

What's there?

Part of what Father Tibor sent me.

Part? He hadn't caught the hint until this moment.

The trip to Turin again flashed through his mind, along with Clement's heated remarks about his loyalty and abilities. And the envelope. *Would you mail this for me, please?* It had been addressed to Irma Rahn. He'd thought nothing of it. He'd mailed many letters to her over the years. But the strange request to mail the letter from there, and to do it personally.

Clement had been in the Riserva only the night before. He and Ngovi had waited outside while the pope studied the contents of the box. That would have been a perfect opportunity for any removal. Which meant when Clement and Valendrea were in the Riserva days later, the reproduced translation was already gone. What had he asked Valendrea earlier?

How do you know it was even there?

I don't. But no one returned to the archives after that Friday night, and Clement was dead two days later.

The apartment door burst open.

The room was illuminated only by a single lamp and, within the shadows, a tall, thin man lunged toward him. He was yanked from the floor and a fist rammed into his abdomen.

The breath left his lungs.

His assailant planted another blow into his chest that sent him staggering back toward the bedroom. The shock of the moment paralyzed him. He'd never been in a fight before. Instinct told him to raise his arms for protection, but the man swung again into his stomach, the blow collapsing him onto the bed.

He panted hard and stared up at the blackened form, wondering what was next. Something came from the man's pocket. A black rectangle, about six inches long, with shiny metal prongs protruding from one end like pincers. A flash of light suddenly sparked between the prongs.

A stun gun.

The Swiss guard carried them as a means to protect the pope without bullets. He and Clement had been shown the weapons and told how a nine-volt battery charge could be transformed into two hundred thousand volts that could quickly immobilize. He watched as blue-white current leaped from one electrode to another, cracking the air in between.

A smile came to the thin man's lips. "We have some fun now," he said in Italian.

Michener summoned his strength and pivoted upward, swinging his leg and kicking the man's outstretched arm. The stun gun flew away, toward the open doorway.

The act seemed to genuinely surprise his attacker, but the man recovered and backhanded Michener's face, propelling him flat onto the bed.

The man's hand plunged into another pocket. A click and a knife appeared. With the blade clenched tight in his raised hand, the man lunged forward. Michener braced himself, wondering what it was going to feel like to be stabbed.

But he never felt a thing.

Instead there was a pop of electricity and the man winced. His eyes rolled skyward, his arms went limp, and the body started to convulse in deep spasms. The knife fell away as muscles went limp and he collapsed to the floor.

Michener sat up.

Standing behind his assailant was Katerina. She tossed the stun gun aside and rushed to him. "Are you all right?"

He was holding his stomach, fighting for air.

"Colin, are you okay?"

"Who the hell was . . . that?"

"No time. There's two more downstairs."

"What do you . . . know that I don't?"

"I'll explain later. We need to go."

His mind started working again. "Grab my travel bag. Over . . . there. I haven't emptied it from Bosnia."

"You going somewhere?"

He didn't want to answer her, and she seemed to understand his silence.

"You're not going to tell me," she said.

"Why are you . . . here?"

"I came to talk to you. To try to explain. But this man and two more drove up."

He tried to rise from the bed, but a sharp pain forced him down.

"You're hurt," she said.

He coughed up the air in his lungs. "Did you know that guy was coming here?"

"I can't believe you're asking me that."

"Answer me."

"I came to talk to you and heard the stun gun. I saw you kick it away and then I saw the knife. So I grabbed the thing off the floor and did what I could. I'd think you'd be grateful."

"I am. Tell me what you know."

"Ambrosi attacked me the night we met with Father Tibor in Bucharest. He made it clear that if I didn't cooperate, there'd be hell to pay." She motioned to the form on the floor. "I assume this man is connected to him in some way. But I don't know why he came after you."

"I assume Valendrea was unhappy with our discussion today and decided to force the issue. He told me I wouldn't like the next messenger."

"We need to leave," she said again.

He moved toward the travel bag and slipped on a pair of running shoes. The pain in his gut brought tears to his eyes.

"I love you, Colin. What I did was wrong, but I did it for the right reason." The words came fast. She needed to say them.

He stared at her. "Hard to argue with somebody who just saved my life."

"I don't want to argue."

Neither did he. Maybe he shouldn't be so righteous. He hadn't been totally honest with her, either. He bent down and checked the pulse on his attacker. "Probably going to be pretty ticked off when he wakes up. I don't want to be around."

STEVE BERRY / 332

He headed toward the apartment door and spied the letters and envelopes scattered on the floor. They needed to be destroyed. He moved toward the scattered mess.

He headed toward the apartment door and spied the letters and envelopes scattered on the floor. They needed to be destroyed. He moved toward the scattered mess.

"Colin, we have to get out here before the other two decide to come up."

"I need to take these—" He heard feet pounding the stairs three floors below.

"Colin, we're out of time."

He grabbed a few handfuls of letters and stuffed what he could into the travel bag, but managed to retrieve only about half of what was there. He pulled himself to his feet and they slipped out the door. He pointed up, and they tiptoed toward the next floor as footsteps from below grew louder. The pain in his side made the going difficult, but adrenaline forced him ahead.

"How are we going to get out of here?" she whispered.

"There's another staircase in the rear of the building. It leads to a courtyard. Follow me."

They carefully made their way down the corridor, past closed apartment doors, away from the street side of the building. He found the rear staircase just as two men appeared fifty feet behind them.

He took three steps at a time, electric pain searing his abdomen. The travel bag banging against his rib cage, full of letters, only added to his agony. They turned at the landing, found the ground floor, then darted out of the building.

The courtyard beyond was filled with cars and they zigzagged a path around them. He led the way through an arched entrance to the busy boulevard. Cars whizzed past and people filled the sidewalks. Thank God Romans were late eaters.

He spotted a taxi hugging the curb fifty feet ahead.

He grabbed Katerina and hustled straight for the sooty vehicle. A glance back over his shoulder and he saw two men emerge from the courtyard.

They spotted him and bolted his way.

He made it to the taxi and yanked open the rear door. They jumped inside. "Go, now," he screamed in Italian.

The car lurched forward. Through the rear window he watched the men halt their pursuit.

"Where are we going?" Katerina asked.

"Do you have your passport?"

"In my purse."

"To the airport," he told the driver.

SIXTY

11:40 P.M.

VALENDREA KNELT BEFORE THE ALTAR IN A CHAPEL THAT HIS beloved Paul VI had personally commissioned. Clement had shied away from its use, preferring a smaller room down the hall, but he intended to utilize the richly decorated space for a daily morning Mass, a time when forty or so special guests could share a celebration with their pontiff. Afterward, a few minutes of his time and a photograph would cement their loyalty. Clement had never used the trappings of office—another of his many fallacies—but Valendrea meant to make the most of what popes had slaved for centuries to achieve.

The staff had gone for the night and Ambrosi was tending to Colin Michener. He was grateful for the time alone since he needed to pray to a God he knew was listening.

He wondered if he should offer the traditional Our Father or some other sanctioned plea, but finally decided a frank conversation would be more appropriate. Besides, he was the supreme pontiff of God's apostolic church. If he didn't possess the right to talk openly with the Lord, who did?

He perceived what happened earlier with Michener—his ability to read the tenth secret of Medjugorje—to be a sign from heaven. He'd been allowed to know both the Medjugorje and Fatima messages for a reason. Clearly, Father Tibor's murder had been justified. Though one of the commandments forbade killing, popes had for centuries slaughtered millions in the name of the Lord. And now was no exception. The threat to the Roman Catholic Church was real. Though Clement XV was gone, his protégé lived and Clement's legacy was out there. He could not allow the risks to escalate beyond their already dangerous proportions. The matter required a definitive resolution. Just as with Father Tibor, Colin Michener would have to be dealt with, too.

He clasped his hands and stared up at the tortured face of Christ on the crucifix. He reverently beseeched the son of God for guidance. He'd obviously been chosen pope for a reason. He'd also been motivated to choose the name *Peter.* Before this afternoon he'd thought both just the product of his own ambition. Now he knew better. He was the conduit. Peter II. To him, there was only one course of action, and he thanked the Almighty that he possessed the strength to do what had to be done.

"Holy Father."

He crossed himself and stood from the prie-dieu. Ambrosi filled the doorway at the back of the dimly lit chapel. Concern filled his assistant's face. "What about Michener?"

"Gone. With Ms. Lew. But we found something."

Valendrea scanned the cache of letters and marveled at this latest surprise. Clement XV had possessed a lover. Though nothing admitted to any mortal sin—and for a priest, a violation of Holy Orders would be a grave mortal sin—the meaning was indisputable.

"I continue to be amazed," he said to Ambrosi, glancing up.

They sat in the library. The same room where he'd confronted Michener earlier. He thought back to something Clement had said to him a month ago when the pope learned that Father Kealy had presented the tribunal with few options. *Perhaps we should simply listen to an opposing point of view.* Now he understood why Volkner had been so willing. Celibacy, apparently, was not a concept the German had taken seriously. He stared over at Ambrosi. "This is as far reaching as the suicide. I never realized how complex Clement was."

"And apparently resourceful," Ambrosi said. "He removed Father Tibor's writing from the Riserva, confident in what you would subsequently do."

He didn't particularly care for Ambrosi's reminder of his predictability, but he said nothing. Instead he commanded, "Destroy these letters."

"Should we not hold on to them?"

"We can never use them, as much as I'd like to. Clement's memory must be preserved. Discrediting him would only discredit this office, and that I cannot afford. We'd hurt ourselves, while tarnishing a dead man. Shred them." He asked what he really wanted to know. "Where did Michener and Ms. Lew go?"

"Our friends are checking with the taxi company. We should know soon."

He'd thought earlier that Clement's personal chest may have been his hiding place. But given what he now knew about his former enemy's personality, the German had apparently been far more clever. He lifted one of the envelopes and read the return address. IRMA RAHN, HINTERHOLZ 19, BAMBERG, DEUTSCHLAND.

He heard a soft chime and Ambrosi removed a cellular phone from his cassock. A short conversation and Ambrosi beeped off the receiver.

He continued to stare at the envelope. "Let me guess. They were taken to the airport."

Ambrosi nodded.

He handed the envelope across to his friend. "Find this woman, Paolo, and you'll find what we seek. Michener and Ms. Lew will be there, as well. They're on their way to her now."

"How can you be sure?"

"You can never be sure of anything, but it's a safe assumption. Tend to this task yourself."

"Is that not risky?"

"It is a risk we will have to take. I'm sure you can conceal your presence carefully."

"Of course, Holy Father."

"I want Tibor's translation destroyed the moment you locate it. I don't care how, just do it. Paolo, I'm counting on you to handle this. If anyone, and I mean anyone—this woman of Clement's, Michener, Lew, I don't care who—reads those words or knows of them, kill them. Don't hesitate, just eliminate them."

The muscles in his secretary's face never quivered. The eyes, like those of a bird of prey, stared back with an intense glare. Valendrea knew all about Ambrosi and Michener's dissension—he'd even encouraged it, since nothing ensured loyalty more than a common hatred. So the hours ahead might prove immensely satisfying for his old friend.

"I will not disappoint you, Holy Father," Ambrosi softly said.

"It is not I whom you should worry about disappointing. We are on a mission for the Lord, and there is much at stake. So very much."

SIXTY-ONE

MICHENER STROLLED THE COBBLED STREETS AND QUICKLY came to understand Jakob Volkner's love of Bamberg. He'd never visited the town. Volkner's few trips back home had all been taken alone. They'd planned a papal mission next year as part of a multi-city German pilgrimage. Volkner had told him how he wanted to visit his parents' grave, say Mass in the cathedral, and see old friends. Which made his suicide even more puzzling, since the planning for that joyous journey had been well under way when Clement died.

Bamberg sat where the swift Regnitz and meandering Main River merged. The ecclesiastical half of the city crowned the hills and showcased a royal residence, monastery, and cathedral, the forested crests once the home of prince-bishops. Clinging to the lower slopes, against the banks of the Regnitz, stood the secular portion, where business and commerce had always dominated. The symbolic meeting of the two halves was the river, where clever politicians centuries ago erected a city hall of half-timbered walls tattooed with bright frescoes. The *rathaus* sat on an island, at the center of the two classes, a stone bridge spanning the river, bisecting the building and connecting both worlds.

He and Katerina had flown from Rome to Munich and spent the night near the airport. This morning they'd rented a car and driven north into central Bavaria, through the Franconian hills, for nearly two hours. They now stood in the Maxplatz, where a lively market filled the square. Other entrepreneurs were busy preparing for the start of the Christmas market, which would begin later in the day. The cold air chapped his lips, the sun flashed intermittently, and snow whisked across the pavement. He and Katerina, unprepared for the change in temperature, had stopped in one of the stores and purchased coats, gloves, and leather boots.

To his left, the Church of St. Martin cast a long shadow across the crowded plaza. Michener had thought a talk with the church's priest might prove helpful. Surely he would know of Irma Rahn, and the priest had indeed been accommodating, suggesting she might be at St. Gangolf's, the parish church a few blocks north across a canal.

They found her tending one of the side chapels, beneath a crucified Christ that gazed down in a mournful glare. The air reeked of incense mellowed by the scent of beeswax. She was a tiny woman, her pale skin and crenellated features still suggesting a beauty that had faded little from her youth. If he hadn't known she was nearing eighty, he would have sworn her to be in her sixties.

They watched as she reverently genuflected each time she passed before the crucifix. Michener stepped forward and passed through an open iron gate. A strange feeling swept over him. Was he intruding on something that was none of his business? But he dismissed the thought. After all, Clement himself had led the way.

"Are you Irma Rahn?" he asked in German.

She faced him. Her silver hair fell to her shoulders. The bones in her cheeks and her sallow skin were untouched by makeup. Her wrinkled chin was round and dainty, the eyes soulful and compassionate.

She stepped close and said, "I was wondering how long it would be before you came."

"How do you know who I am? We've never met."

"But I know you."

"You expected me to come?"

"Oh, yes. Jakob said you would. And he was always right . . . especially about you."

Then he realized. "In his letter. The one that came from Turin. He made mention in there?"

She nodded.

"You have what I want, don't you?"

"That depends. Do you come for yourself or someone else?"

A strange question, and he considered his response. "I come for my Church."

She smiled again. "Jakob said you would answer that way. He knew you well."

He motioned for Katerina and introduced them. The old woman flashed a warm smile and the two women shook hands. "It's so nice to meet you. Jakob said you might come, too."

SIXTY-TWO

VALENDREA LEAFED THROUGH *LIGNUM VITAE*. THE ARCHIVIST stood before him. He'd ordered the elderly cardinal to present himself on the fourth floor and bring the volume with him. He wanted to see for himself what had held so much interest for Ngovi and Michener.

He found the section of Malachy's prophecy that dealt with Peter the Roman at the end of Arnold Wion's eighteen-hundred-page account:

> *In the final persecution of the Holy Roman Church there will reign Peter*
> *the Roman who will feed his flock among many tribulations, after which in*
> *the seven hilled city the dreadful judge will judge all people.*

"You actually believe this rubbish?" he asked the archivist.

"You are the one hundred and twelfth pope on Malachy's list. The last one mentioned, and he said you would choose that name."

"So the Church is facing the apocalypse? *From the seven hilled city the dreadful judge will judge all people.* You believe that? You can't be that ignorant."

"Rome is the seven hilled city. That has been its label since ancient times. And I resent your tone."

"I don't care what you resent. I only want to know what you, Ngovi, and Michener discussed."

"I'm not telling you anything."

He motioned to the manuscript. "Then tell me why you believe in this prophecy."

"As if it matters what I think."

He stood from the desk. "It matters a great deal, Eminence. Consider it a final act for the Church. This is your last day, I believe."

The old man's face betrayed nothing of the regret he was surely feeling. This cardinal had served Rome for nearly five decades and had certainly seen his share of joy and pain. But he was the man who'd orchestrated the conclave support for Ngovi—that had become clear yesterday when the cardinals finally began talking—and he'd done a masterful job of collating votes. A shame he hadn't chosen the winning side.

Equally disturbing, though, was a discussion of Malachy prophecies that had arisen in the press over the past two days. He suspected the man standing before him was the source of those stories, though no reporter quoted anyone, only the usual *unnamed Vatican official.* The Malachy predictions were nothing new—conspiratorialists had long warned of them—but journalists were now beginning to make a connection. The 112th pope had indeed taken the name *Peter II.* How could a monk in the eleventh century, or a chronicler in the sixteenth century, possibly have known that was going to happen? Coincidence? Maybe, but it strained the concept to its breaking point.

Valendrea actually wondered the same thing. Some would say he chose the name knowing what was recorded in the Vatican archives. But *Peter* had always been his preference, ever since he decided to achieve the papacy back in the days of John Paul II. He'd never told anyone, not even Ambrosi. And he'd never read Malachy's predictions.

He stared back at the archivist, waiting for an answer to his question. Finally the cardinal said, "I have nothing to say."

"Then perhaps you could speculate where the missing document might be?"

"I know of no missing document. Everything in the inventory is there."

"This document is not on your inventory. Clement added it to the Riserva."

"I have no responsibility for that which is unknown to me."

"Really? Then tell me what you *do* know. What was mentioned when you met with Cardinal Ngovi and Monsignor Michener."

The archivist said nothing.

"From your silence, I must assume that the subject was the missing document and you were involved in its removal."

He realized the jab would tear at the old man's heart. As archivist, his duty was to preserve Church writings. The fact one was missing would forever stain his tenure.

"I did nothing except open the Riserva on order of His Holiness, Clement XV."

"And I believe you, Eminence. I think Clement himself, unbeknownst to anyone, removed the writing. All I want is to find it." He lightened his tone, signaling an acceptance of the explanation.

"I, too, want—" the archivist started, then stopped, as if he might say more than warranted.

"Go on. Tell me, Eminence."

"I'm as shocked as you something may be gone. But I have no idea when that occurred or where it might be." The tone made clear that was his story and he planned to stay with it.

"Where is Michener?" He was already reasonably sure of the answer, but decided verification would ease any concern that Ambrosi might be following the wrong trail.

"I do not know," the archivist said, a slight tremble in the voice.

He now asked what he really wanted to know. "And what of Ngovi? What's his interest?"

The archivist's face registered understanding. "You fear him, don't you?"

He didn't allow the comment to affect him. "I fear no one, Eminence. I'm merely wondering why the camerlengo is so interested in Fatima."

"I never said he was interested."

"But it was discussed during the meeting yesterday, was it not?"

"I didn't say that, either."

He let his gaze drift down to the book, a subtle signal that the old man's obstinance wasn't affecting him. "Eminence, I fired you. I could just as easily rehire you. Would you not like to die here, in the Vatican, as cardinal-archivist of the Catholic Church? Would you not like to see the document now missing returned? Does not your duty mean more to you than any personal feelings about me?"

The old man shifted on his feet, his silence perhaps an indication that he was considering the proposal.

"What is it you want?" the archivist finally asked.

"Tell me where Father Michener has gone."

"I was told this morning he went to Bamberg." The voice was filled with resignation.

"So you lied to me?"

"You asked if I knew where he was. I don't. I only know what I was told."

"And the purpose of the trip?"

"The document you seek may be there."

Now for something new. "And Ngovi?"

"He's waiting for Father Michener's call."

His bare hands tightened on the edge of the book. He hadn't bothered to wear gloves. What did it matter? The manuscript would be ashes by tomorrow. Now for the critical part. "Ngovi is waiting to learn what is in the missing document?"

The old man nodded, as if it pained him to be honest. "They want to know what you seemingly already know."

SIXTY-THREE

MICHENER AND KATERINA FOLLOWED IRMA RAHN THROUGH the Maxplatz, then beyond to the river and a five-story inn. A wrought-iron sign announced the name KÖNIGSHOF, along with the designation 1614—the year, Irma explained, the building was erected.

Her family had owned the property for generations, and she had inherited it from her father after her brother was killed in World War II. Former fishermen's houses surrounded the inn on both sides. Originally the building had served as a mill, the paddle wheel gone for centuries, but the black mansard roof, iron balconies, and baroque detailing were still there. She'd added a tavern and restaurant and now led them inside, where they sat at an empty table beside a twelve-paned window. Outside, clouds dimmed the late-morning sky. More snow seemed on the way. Their host brought them each a stein of beer.

"We're only open for dinner," Irma said. "The tables will be full then. Our cook is quite popular."

Michener wanted to know, "Back in the church, you said Jakob mentioned that Katerina and I would come. Was that really in his last letter?"

She nodded. "He said to expect you and that probably this lovely woman would come with you. My Jakob was intuitive, especially when it came to you, Colin. May I call you that? I feel I know you well enough."

"I wouldn't want you to call me anything else."

"And I'm Katerina."

She threw them both a smile he liked.

"What else did Jakob say?" he asked.

"He told me of your dilemma. Of your crisis in faith. Since you're here, I assume you read my letters."

"I never realized the depth of your relationship."

Beyond the window, a barge chugged by, heading north.

"My Jakob was a loving man. He devoted his entire life to others. Gave himself to God."

"But apparently not completely," Katerina said.

Michener had been waiting for her to make the point. Last night she'd read the letters he'd managed to salvage and was shocked by Volkner's private emotion.

"I resented him," Katerina said in a flat tone. "I envisioned him pressuring Colin into choosing, urging him to put the Church first. But I was wrong. I realize now that he, of all people, would have understood how I felt."

"He did. He talked to me about Colin's pain. He wanted to tell him the truth, show him he wasn't alone, but I said no. The time wasn't right. I didn't want anyone to know of us. That was something intensely private." She faced him. "He wanted you to stay a priest. To change things, he needed your help. I think he knew, even then, that one day you and he would make a difference."

Michener needed to say, "He tried to change things. Not with confrontation, but with reason. He was a man of peace."

"But above all, Colin, he was a man." Her voice trailed off at the end of the statement, as if a memory returned for a moment and she didn't want to ignore it. "Just a man, weak and sinful, like us all."

Katerina reached across the table and cupped the old woman's hand. Both women's eyes glistened.

"When did the relationship start?" Katerina asked.

"When we were children. I knew then that I loved him, and that I always would." She bit her lip. "But I also knew that I would never have him. Not completely. Even then, he wanted to be a priest. Somehow, though, it was always enough that I possessed his heart."

He wanted to know something. Why, he wasn't sure. It was really none of his business. But he sensed that it was all right to ask. "The love was never consummated?"

Her gaze engaged his for several seconds before a slight smile came to her lips. "No, Colin. Your Jakob never violated his oath to his Church. That would have been unthinkable for both him and me." She looked at Katerina. "We must all judge ourselves by the times in which we live. Jakob and I were from another era. Bad enough for us to love one another. It would have been unthinkable to take that farther."

He recalled what Clement had said in Turin. *Restrained love is not a pleasant matter.* "You've lived here, alone, all that time?"

"I have my family, this business, my friends, and my God. I knew the love of a man who shared himself totally with me. Not in the physical sense, but in every other way. Few can make such a claim."

"It was never a problem you weren't together?" Katerina asked. "I don't mean sexually. I mean physically, close to one another. That had to be tough."

"I would have preferred things to be different. But that was beyond my control. Jakob was called to the priesthood early. I knew that, and did nothing to interfere. I loved him enough to share him . . . even with heaven."

A middle-aged woman pushed through a swinging door and spoke a few words to Irma. Something about the market and supplies. Another barge slipped past the window across the gray-brown river. A few flakes of snow tapped the panes.

"Does anybody know about you and Jakob?" he asked after the woman left.

She shook her head. "Neither of us ever spoke of it. Many here in town know that Jakob and I were childhood friends."

"His death must have been awful for you," Katerina said.

She let out a long breath. "You can't imagine. I knew he was looking bad. I saw him on television. I realized it was only a matter of time. We're both getting old. But his time came suddenly. I still expect a letter to arrive in the mail, like it did so many times before." Her voice grew softer, cracking with emotion. "My Jakob is gone, and you are the first people I have spoken to about him. He told me to trust you. That through your visit I could gain peace. And he was right. Simply talking about this has made me feel better."

He wondered what this gentle woman would think if she knew Volkner had taken his own life. Did she have a right to know? She was opening her heart to them, and he was tired of lying. Clement's memory would be safe with her. "He killed himself."

Irma said nothing for the longest time.

He caught Katerina's glare as she said, "The pope took his own life?"

He nodded. "Sleeping pills. He said the Virgin Mary told him that he must end his life through his own hand. The penance for disobedience. He said he'd ignored heaven far too long. But not this time."

Irma still said nothing. She just stared at him with impassioned eyes.

"You knew?" he asked.

She nodded. "He's come to me recently . . . in my dreams. He tells me that it's okay. He's forgiven now. That he would have joined God soon anyway. I didn't understand what he meant."

"Have you experienced any visions while awake?" he asked.

She shook her head. "Just dreams." Her voice was distant. "Soon I'll be with him. That's all that keeps me going. For eternity, Jakob and I will be together. He tells me that in the dream." She looked at Katerina. "You asked me how it was to be apart. Those years of separation are inconsequential compared with forever. If nothing else, I'm a patient woman."

He needed to nudge her toward the point of it all. "Irma, where is what Jakob sent to you?"

She stared down into her beer. "I have an envelope Jakob told me to give to you."

"I need it."

Irma rose from the table. "It's next door in my apartment. I'll be right back."

The old woman lumbered out of the restaurant.

"Why didn't you tell me about Clement?" Katerina asked, as the door closed. The frigid tone matched the temperature outside.

"I would think the answer is obvious."

"Who knows?"

"Only a few."

She stood from the table. "Always the same, isn't it? Lots of secrets in the Vatican." She slipped on her coat and headed for the door. "Something you seem quite comfortable with."

"Just like you." He knew he shouldn't have said it.

She stopped. "I'll give you that one. I deserve it. What's your excuse?"

He said nothing and she turned to leave. "Where are you going?"

"For a walk. I'm sure you and Clement's lover have much more to talk about that doesn't include me, either."

SIXTY-FOUR

KATERINA'S MIND SWIRLED WITH CONFUSION. MICHENER HAD not trusted her with the fact that Clement XV took his own life. Valendrea surely must know—otherwise Ambrosi would have urged her to learn what she could about Clement's death. What in the world was happening? Missing writings. Seers talking to Mary. A pope committing suicide after secretly loving a woman for six decades. Nobody would believe any of it.

She stepped from the inn, buttoned her coat, and decided to head back toward the Maxplatz and walk off her frustration. Bells pealed from all directions signaling noon. She swiped the quickening snow from her hair. The air was cold, parched, and sullen, like her mood.

Irma Rahn had opened her mind. Where years ago she'd forced Michener into a choice, driving him away, hurting them both in the process, Irma had ventured down a less selfish path, one that reflected love, not possession. Maybe the old woman was right. It mattered not about a physical connection. What counted was possessing the heart and mind.

She wondered if she and Michener could have enjoyed a similar relationship. Probably not. Times were different. Yet here she was, back with the same man, seemingly on the same tortuous path of love lost, then found, then tested, then—that was the question. Then, what?

She continued to walk, finding the main plaza, crossing a canal, and spotting the onion-domed twin towers of St. Gangolf's.

Life was so damn complicated.

She could still see the man from last night standing over Michener, knife in hand. She hadn't hesitated in attacking him. After, she'd suggested going to the authorities, but Michener had nixed the idea. Now she knew why. He couldn't risk the exposure of a papal suicide. Jakob Volkner meant so much to him. Maybe too much. And she now understood why he'd journeyed to Bosnia—searching for answers to questions his old friend had left behind. Clearly that chapter in his life could not be closed, because its ending had yet to be written. She wondered if it ever would be.

She kept walking and found herself back at the doors to St. Gangolf's. The warm air seeping from inside beckoned her. She entered and saw the gate for the side chapel, where Irma had been cleaning, remained open. She stepped past and stopped at another of the chapels. A statue of the Virgin Mary, cradling the Christ child in her arms, gazed down with the loving look of a proud mother. Surely a medieval representation—that of an Anglo-Saxon Caucasian—but an image the world had grown accustomed to worshiping. Mary had lived in Israel, a place where the sun burned hot and skin was tanned. Her features would have been Arabic, her hair dark, her body stout. Yet European Catholics would never have accepted that reality. So a familiar feminine vision was fashioned—one the Church had clung to ever since.

And was she a virgin? The Holy Spirit endowing her womb with the son of God? Even if that was true, the decision would have certainly been her choice. She alone would have consented to the pregnancy. Why then was the Church so opposed to abortion and birth control? When did a woman lose the option to decide if she wanted to give birth? Had not Mary established the right? What if she'd refused? Would she still have been required to carry that divine child to term?

She was tired of puzzling dilemmas. There were far too many with no answers. She turned to leave.

Three feet away stood Paolo Ambrosi.

The sight of him startled her.

He lunged forward, spinning her around and hurling her into the chapel with the Virgin. He slammed her into the stone wall, her left arm twisted behind her back. Another hand quickly compressed her neck. Her face was pressed against the prickly stone.

"I was pondering how I might separate you from Michener. But you did it for me."

Ambrosi increased the pressure on her arm. She opened her mouth to cry out.

"Now, now. Let's not do that. Besides, there is no one here to hear you."

She tried to break free, using her legs.

"Stay still. My patience with you is exhausted."

Her response was more struggling.

Ambrosi yanked her away from the wall and wrapped an arm around her neck. Instantly, her windpipe was constricted. She tried to break his hold, digging her fingernails into his skin, but the diminishing oxygen was causing everything before her to wink in and out.

She opened her mouth to scream, but there was no air to form the words.

Her eyes rolled upward.

The last thing she saw, before the world went black, was the mournful glare of the Virgin, which offered no solace for her predicament.

SIXTY-FIVE

MICHENER WATCHED IRMA AS SHE STARED OUT THE WINDOW toward the river. She'd returned shortly after Katerina left, carrying a familiar blue envelope, which now lay on the table.

"My Jakob killed himself," she whispered to herself. "So sad." She faced him. "Yet he was still buried in St. Peter's. In consecrated ground."

"We couldn't tell the world what happened."

"That was his one complaint with the Church. Truth is so rare. Ironic that his legacy is now dependent on a lie."

Which seemed nothing unusual. Like Jakob Volkner, Michener's entire career had been based on a lie. Interesting how alike they'd turned out to be. "Did he always love you?"

"What you mean is, were there others? No, Colin. Only me."

"It would seem, after a while, that you both would have needed to move on. Didn't you wish for a husband, children?"

"Children, yes. That's my one regret in life. But I knew early on that I wanted to be Jakob's and he wished the same from me. I'm sure you realized that you were, in every way, his son."

His eyes moistened at the thought.

"I read that you found his body. That must have been awful."

He didn't want to think about the image of Clement on the bed, the nuns readying him for burial. "He was a remarkable man. Yet I now feel like he was a stranger."

"There's no need to feel that way. There were just parts of him that were his alone. As I'm sure there are parts of you he never knew."

How true.

She motioned to the envelope. "I could not read what he sent me."

"You tried?"

She nodded. "I opened the envelope. I was curious. But only after Jakob died. It's written in another language."

"Italian."

"Tell me what it is."

He did, and she listened in amazement. But he had to tell her that no one left alive, save for Alberto Valendrea, knew what the document in the envelope actually said.

"I knew something was bothering Jakob. His letters the last few months were depressing, even cynical. Not like him at all. And he wouldn't tell me anything."

"I tried, too, but he wouldn't say a word."

"He could be like that."

From the front of the building he heard a door open, then bang shut. Footsteps echoed across a plank floor. The restaurant was to the rear, beyond a small lobby alcove and a staircase leading to the upper floors. He assumed it was Katerina returning.

"May I help you?" Irma said.

He was facing away from the doorway, toward the river, and turned to see Paolo Ambrosi standing a few feet behind him. The Italian was dressed in loose-fitting black jeans and a dark button-down shirt. A gray overcoat fell to his knees and a maroon scarf draped his neck.

Michener stood. "Where's Katerina?"

Ambrosi did not answer. Michener liked nothing about the smug look on the bastard's face. He stood and rushed forward, but Ambrosi calmly withdrew a gun from his coat pocket. He stopped.

"Who is this?" Irma asked.

"Trouble."

"I am Father Paolo Ambrosi. You must be Irma Rahn."

"How do you know my name?"

Michener stayed between them, hoping Ambrosi would not notice the envelope on the table. "He read your letters. I couldn't get them all last night before I left Rome."

She brought a knuckle to her mouth and a gasp seeped out. "The pope knows?"

He motioned to Ambrosi. "If this son of a bitch knows, Valendrea knows."

She crossed herself.

He faced Ambrosi and understood. "Tell me where Katerina is."

The gun stayed on him. "She's safe, for now. But you know what I want."

"And how do you know I have it?"

"Either you do or this woman does."

"I thought Valendrea said it was mine to find." He hoped Irma kept quiet.

"And Cardinal Ngovi would have been the recipient of any delivery you made."

"I don't know what I would have done."

"I assume you do now."

He wanted to pound the arrogance off Ambrosi's face, but there was still the matter of the gun.

"Katerina's in danger?" Irma asked.

"She is fine," Ambrosi made clear.

Michener said, "Frankly, Ambrosi, Katerina is *your* problem. She was your spy. I don't give a damn anymore."

"I'm sure she will be brokenhearted to hear that."

He shrugged. "She got herself into this mess, it's her problem to get herself out." He wondered if he was jeopardizing Katerina's safety, but any show of weakness could be fatal.

"I want Tibor's translation," Ambrosi said.

"I don't have it."

"But Clement did send it here. Correct?"

"I don't know that . . . yet." He needed time. "But I can find out. And there's one other thing." He pointed to Irma. "When I do, I want this lady left out of everything. This doesn't concern her."

"Clement involved her, not me."

"If you want the translation, that's a condition. Otherwise, I'll give it to the press."

There was a momentary flicker in Ambrosi's cold demeanor. He almost smiled. Michener had guessed right. Valendrea had sent his henchman to destroy the information, not retrieve it.

"She's a nonparticipant," Ambrosi said, "provided she hasn't read it."

"She doesn't read Italian."

"But you do. So remember the warning. You will severely limit my options if you choose to ignore what I'm saying."

"How would you know if I read it, Ambrosi?"

"I'm assuming the message is one that's hard to conceal. Popes have shaken before it. So let it be, Michener. This doesn't concern you any longer."

"For something that doesn't concern me, I seem to be right in the middle. Like the visitor you sent calling last night."

"I know nothing about that."

"Same thing I'd say, if I were you."

"What of Clement?" Irma asked, a plea in her voice. She was apparently still thinking of the letters.

Ambrosi shrugged. "His memory is in your hands. I don't want the press involved. But if that occurs, we are prepared to leak certain facts that will be, to say the least, devastating to his memory . . . and yours."

"You will tell the world how he died?" she asked.

Ambrosi glanced over at Michener. "She knows?"

He nodded. "As you do, apparently."

"Good. That makes things easier. Yes, we would tell the world, but not directly. Rumor can do far more harm. People still believe the sainted John Paul I was murdered. Think what they would write about Clement. The few letters we have are damning enough. If you treasure him, as I believe you do, then cooperate in this matter and nothing will ever be known."

Irma said nothing, but tears soaked her cheeks.

"Don't cry," Ambrosi said. "Father Michener will do the right thing. He always does." Ambrosi backed toward the door, then stopped. "I'm told that the famous Bamberg crib circuit begins tonight. All the churches will be displaying nativity scenes. A Mass is said in the cathedral. Quite an audience attends. It starts at eight. Why don't we beat the crowd and exchange what each of us wants at seven."

"I didn't say I wanted anything from you."

Ambrosi flashed an irritating grin. "You do. Tonight. In the cathedral." He motioned to the window and the building crowning a hill on the far side of the river. "Quite public, so we'll all feel better. Or, if you prefer, we can make the exchange now."

"Seven at the cathedral. Now get the hell out of here."

"Remember what I said, Michener. Leave it sealed. Do yourself, Ms. Lew, and Ms. Rahn a favor."

Ambrosi left.

Irma sat silent, sobbing. Finally, she said, "That man's evil."

"Him and our new pope."

"He's connected to Peter?"

"The papal secretary."

"What's happening here, Colin?"

"To know that, I need to read what's in this envelope." But he also needed to safeguard her. "I want you to leave. I don't want you to know anything."

"Why are you going to open it?"

He held up the envelope. "I have to know what's so important."

"That man was quite clear that you were not to do that."

"The hell with Ambrosi." The severity of his tone surprised him.

She seemed to consider his predicament, then said, "I'll make sure you're not disturbed."

She withdrew and closed the door behind her. The hinges

squealed ever so slightly, just like the ones in the archives he recalled from that rainy morning nearly a month ago when somebody was watching.

Surely Paolo Ambrosi.

The muted blare of a horn blew in the distance. From across the river, bells pealed, signaling one P.M.

He sat and opened the envelope.

Inside were two sheets of paper, one blue, one tan. He read the blue sheet first, penned in Clement's hand:

Colin, by now you know that the Virgin left more. Her words are now entrusted to you. Be wise with them.

His hands trembled as he laid the blue sheet aside. Clement had apparently known he would eventually find his way to Bamberg and that he'd read what was inside the envelope.

He unfolded the tan sheet.

The ink was a light blue, the page crisp and new. He scanned the Italian, its translation flashing through his mind. A second pass refined the language. A final read and he now knew what Sister Lucia had written in 1944—the remainder of what the Virgin told her in the third secret—what Father Tibor translated that day in 1960.

Before the Lady left She stated there was one last message which the Lord wished to convey only to Jacinta and me. She told us She was the Mother of God and asked us to make public this message to the entire world at the appropriate time. In so doing we will find strong resistance. Listen well and pay attention was Her command. Men have to correct themselves. They have sinned and trod upon the gift given them. My child, She said, marriage is a sanctified state. Its love knows no boundaries. What the heart feels is genuine, no matter to whom or why, and God has placed no limit on what makes a sound union. Know well that happiness is the only real test of love. Know also that women are as much a part of God's church as men. To be called to the service of the Lord is not a masculine endeavor. Priests of

the Lord should not be forbidden from love and companionship, nor from
the joy of a child. To serve God is not to forgo one's heart. Priests should be
bountiful in every way. Finally, She said, know that your body is yours.
Just as God entrusted me with His son, the Lord entrusts to you and all
women their unborn. It is for you alone to decide what is best. Go my little
ones and proclaim the glory of these words. For that purpose I will always
be at your side.

His hands shook. It wasn't Sister Lucia's words, provocative as
they were. It was something else.

He reached into his pocket and found the message Jasna had
written two days before. The words the Virgin told her on a Bosnian
mountaintop. The tenth secret of Medjugorje. He unfolded and
read the message again:

Do not fear, I am the Mother of God who talks to you and asks you to make
public the present Message for the entire world. In so doing, you will find
strong resistence. Listen well and pay attention to what I tell you. Men
have to correct themselves. With humble petitions they have to ask forgive-
ness for sins committed and those they will commit. Proclaim in my name
a great punishment will fall mankind; not today, not tomorrow, but soon if
my words are not believed. I have already revealed this to the blessed ones
at La Salette and again at Fatima and today I repeat it to you because
mankind has sinned and trod upon the Gift that God has given. The time
of times and the end of all ends will come, if mankind is not converted; and
if all should stay as it is now, or worse, should it worsen even more, the
great and the powerful will perish with the small and the weak.

Heed these words. Why persecute the man or woman who loves differ-
ently from others? Such persecution does not please the Lord. Know that
marriage is to be shared by all without restriction. Anything contrary is the
folly of man, not the word of the Lord. Women stand high in the eyes of
God. Their service has too long been forbidden and that repression dis-
pleases heaven. Christ's priests should be happy and bountiful. The joy of
love and children should never be denied them and the Holy Father would

do well to understand this. My last words are most important. Know that I freely chose to be the mother of God. The choice of a child rests with a woman and man should never interfere with that decision. Go now, tell the world my message, and proclaim the goodness of the Lord, but remember that I shall always be by your side.

He slid out of the chair and fell to his knees. The implications were not in question. Two messages. One written by a Portuguese nun in 1944—a woman with little education and a limited mastery of language—translated by a priest in 1960—the account of what was said on July 13, 1917, when the Virgin Mary supposedly appeared. The other penned by a woman two days ago—a seer who had experienced hundreds of apparitions—the account of what was told to her on a stormy mountain when the Virgin Mary appeared to her for the last time.

Nearly a hundred years separated the two events.

The first message had been sealed in the Vatican, read only by popes and a Bulgarian translator, none of whom ever knew the bearer of the second message. The receiver of the second message likewise would have possessed no way to know the contents of the first. Yet the two messages were identical in content—and the common denominator was the messenger.

Mary, the mother of God.

For two thousand years doubters had wanted proof God existed. Something tangible that demonstrated, without a doubt, He was a living entity, conscious of the world, alive in every sense. Not a parable or a metaphor. Instead, the ruler of heaven, provider to man, overseer of Creation. Michener's own vision of the Virgin flashed through his mind.

What is my destiny, he'd asked.

To be a sign to the world. A beacon for repentance. The messenger to announce that God is very much alive.

He'd thought it all a hallucination. Now he knew it to be real.

He crossed himself and, for the first time, prayed knowing God was listening. He asked forgiveness for the Church and the foolishness of men, especially himself. If Clement was right, and there was now no longer any reason to doubt him, in 1978 Alberto Valendrea removed the part of the third secret he'd just read. He imagined what Valendrea must have been thinking when he saw the words for the first time. Two thousand years of Church teachings rejected by an illiterate Portuguese child. Women can be priests? Priests can marry and have children? Homosexuality is not a sin? Motherhood is the choice of the woman? Then, yesterday, when Valendrea read the Medjugorje message, he'd instantly realized what Michener now knew.

All of that was the Word of God.

The Virgin's words came to him again. *Do not forsake your faith, for in the end it will be all that remains.*

He squeezed his eyes shut. Clement was right. Man was foolish. Heaven had tried to steer humanity on the right course, and foolish people had ignored every effort. He thought about the missing messages from the La Salette seers. Had another pope a century ago accomplished what Valendrea had attempted? That might explain why the Virgin subsequently appeared at Fatima and Medjugorje. To try again. Yet Valendrea had sabotaged any revelation by destroying the evidence. Clement at least tried. *The Virgin returned and told me my time had come. Father Tibor was with Her. I waited for Her to take me, but She said I must end my life through my own hand. Father Tibor said it was my duty, the penance for disobedience, and that all would be clear later. I wondered about my soul, but was told the Lord was waiting. I have for too long ignored heaven. I will not this time.* Those words were not the ramblings of a demented soul, or even a suicide note from an unstable man. He now understood why Valendrea could not allow Father Tibor's reproduced translation to be compared with Jasna's message.

The repercussions were devastating.

To be called to the service of the Lord is not a masculine endeavor. The Church's stand on women as priests had been unbending. Ever since Roman times popes had convened councils to reaffirm that tradition. Christ was a man, so priests would be, too.

Christ's priests should be happy and bountiful. The joy of love and children should never be denied them. Celibacy was a concept conceived by men and enforced by men. Christ was deemed a celibate. So should be His priests.

Why persecute the man or woman who loves differently from others? Genesis described a man and woman coming together as *one body* to transmit life to another, so the Church had long taught that only sin came from a union that could not foster life.

Just as God entrusted me with His son, the Lord entrusts to you and all women their unborn. It is for you alone to decide what is best. The Church had absolutely opposed birth control in any form. Popes had repeatedly decreed that the embryo was ensouled, a human being deserving of life, and that life must be preserved, even at the expense of the mother.

Man's concept of God's Word was apparently far different from the Word itself. Even worse, for centuries, unbending attitudes had proclaimed God's message with a stamp of papal infallibility, which by definition was now proven false since no pope had done what heaven desired. What had Clement said? *We are merely men, Colin. Nothing more. I'm no more infallible than you. Yet we proclaim ourselves princes of the church. Devout clerics concerned only with pleasing God, while we simply please ourselves.*

He was right. May God bless his soul, he was right.

With the reading of a few simple words penned by two blessed women, thousands of years of religious blundering now became clear. He prayed again, this time thanking God for his patience. He asked the Lord to forgive humanity, then asked Clement to watch over him in the hours ahead.

There was no way he could give Father Tibor's translation to Ambrosi. The Virgin had told him that he was a sign to the world. A beacon for repentance. The messenger to announce that God was alive. To do that, he needed the complete third secret of Fatima. Scholars must study the text and eliminate the explainable, leaving only one conclusion.

But to keep Father Tibor's words would jeopardize Katerina.

So he again prayed, this time for guidance.

SIXTY-SIX

KATERINA STRUGGLED TO FREE HER HANDS AND FEET FROM thick tape. Her arms were folded behind her back and she lay sprawled on a stiff mattress draped with a scratchy quilt that smelled of paint. Through a solitary window she could see night approaching. Her mouth was covered with tape, so she forced herself to stay calm and breathe slowly through her nose.

How she'd gotten here was a mystery. She only recalled Ambrosi choking her and the world going black. She'd been awake maybe two hours, and had yet to hear anything besides an occasional voice from the street. It appeared she was on an upper story, perhaps in one of the baroque buildings that lined Bamberg's ancient streets, near St. Gangolf's since Ambrosi couldn't have carried her far. The cold air was drying her nostrils and she was glad he hadn't removed her coat.

For an instant in the church she'd thought her life was over. Apparently she was deemed more valuable alive—surely the bargaining chip Ambrosi would use to coerce what he wanted from Michener.

Tom Kealy had been right about Valendrea, but he was wrong

about her being able to hold her own. The passions of these men were way beyond anything she'd ever known. Valendrea had told Kealy at the tribunal that he was clearly with the devil. If that were true, then Kealy and Valendrea kept the same company.

She heard a door open, then close. Footsteps approached. The door to the room opened and Ambrosi stepped inside, yanking off a pair of gloves. "Comfortable?" he asked.

Her eyes followed his movements. Ambrosi tossed his coat across a chair, then sat on the bed. "I would imagine you thought yourself dead in the church. Life is such a great gift, is it not? Of course you can't answer, but that's okay. I like answering my own questions."

He seemed pleased with himself.

"Life is indeed a gift, and I bestowed that gift on you. I could have killed you and been done with the problem you pose."

She lay perfectly still. His gaze raked her body.

"Michener has enjoyed you, hasn't he? Such a pleasure, I'm sure. What was it you told me in Rome. You pee sitting down, so I would not be interested. You think I don't lust for a woman? You think I wouldn't know what to do? Because I'm a priest? Or because I am queer?"

She wondered if this show was for her benefit or his.

"Your lover said he couldn't care less what happens to you." Amusement laced his words. "He called you my spy. Said you were my problem, not his. Perhaps he's right. After all, I recruited you."

She tried to keep her eyes calm.

"You think His Holiness enlisted your aid? No, I'm the one who learned about you and Michener. I'm the one who considered the possibility. Peter would know nothing, but for me."

He suddenly wrenched her up and yanked the tape from her mouth. Before she could utter a sound he pulled her toward him and locked his lips on hers. The thrust of his tongue was revolting and she tried to recoil, but he maintained the embrace. He bent her head sideways and gripped her hair, sucking the breath from her lungs. His mouth tasted of beer. Finally, she clamped her teeth on his tongue. He pulled back and she lunged forward, snapping at his lower lip and drawing blood.

"You fucking bitch," he cried as he slammed her to the bed.

She spat his saliva from her mouth, as if exorcising evil. He leaped forward and swiped the back of his hand across her face. The blow stung and she tasted blood. He lashed out one more time, the force driving her head into the wall at the edge of the bed.

The room started to spin.

"I should kill you," he muttered.

"Fuck you," she managed to say as she rolled onto her back, but the dizziness was still there.

He dabbed his bleeding lip with his shirtsleeve.

A trickle of blood seeped from the side of her mouth. She bobbed her face on the quilt. Red splotches stained the cloth. "You better kill me. Because if you don't, given the chance I will kill you."

"You'll never have the chance."

She realized she was safe until he got what he wanted. Colin had done the right thing making the idiot think she was unimportant.

He came back close to the bed and dabbed his lip. "I only hope your lover ignores what I told him. I'm going to enjoy watching you both die."

"Big words, little man."

He lunged forward, rolled her flat, and straddled her. She knew he would not kill her. Not yet, anyway.

"What's the matter, Ambrosi, don't know what to do next?"

He quivered with anger. She was pushing him, but what the hell.

"I told Peter, after Romania, to leave you alone."

"So that's why I'm being beaten by his lapdog."

"You're lucky that's all I'm doing to you."

"Maybe Valendrea would be jealous. Perhaps we ought to keep this between us?"

The taunt brought pressure to her throat. Not enough to block her breathing, but enough to let her know to shut up.

"You're a tough man to a woman with her hands and feet bound. Untie me and let's see how brave you are."

Ambrosi rolled off her. "You're not worth the effort. We only have a couple of hours left. I'm going to get some dinner before I finish this." His gaze bore into her. "For good."

SIXTY-SEVEN

VALENDREA STROLLED THROUGH THE GARDENS AND ENJOYED an unusually mild December evening. This first Saturday of his papacy had been busy. He'd celebrated Mass in the morning, then met with a procession of people who'd traveled to Rome to offer him their best wishes. The afternoon had started with a gathering of cardinals. About eighty were lingering in town, and he'd met with them for three hours to outline some of what he intended. There'd been the usual questions, only this time he'd taken the opportunity to announce that all appointments of Clement XV would remain in place until the following week. The only exception was the cardinal-archivist, who, he'd said, had tendered his resignation for health reasons. The new archivist would be a Belgian cardinal who'd already returned home, but was on his way back to Rome. Beyond that, he'd made no decisions and would not until after the weekend. He'd noticed the look on many in the chamber, waiting for him to make good on preconclave assurances, but no one questioned his declarations. And he liked that.

Ahead of him stood Cardinal Bartolo, waiting where they'd arranged earlier after the cardinals' gathering. The prefect from

Turin had been insistent they talk today. He knew Bartolo had been promised the position as secretary of state and now, apparently, the cardinal wanted that promise kept. Ambrosi was the one who'd made the promise, but Paolo also had advised him to delay that particular selection for as long as possible. After all, Bartolo had not been the only man assured the job. For the losers, excuses would have to be found to eliminate them as contenders—sufficient reasons to quell bitterness and prevent retaliation. Certainly alternative posts could be offered to some, but he well knew that secretary of state was something more than one senior cardinal coveted.

Bartolo stood near the Pasetto di Borgo. The medieval passageway extended through the Vatican wall into the nearby Castel Sant'Angelo, a fortification that had once protected popes from invaders.

"Eminence," Valendrea greeted as he approached.

Bartolo bowed his bearded face. "Holy Father." The older man smiled. "You like the sound of that, don't you, Alberto?"

"It does have a resonance."

"You've been avoiding me."

He waved off the observation. "Never."

"I know you too well. I'm not the only one the secretary of state position has been offered to."

"Votes are hard to come by. We must do what we must." He was trying to keep the tone light, but realized Bartolo was not naïve.

"I was directly responsible for at least a dozen of your votes."

"Which turned out not to be needed."

The muscles in Bartolo's face tightened. "Only because Ngovi withdrew. I imagine those twelve votes would have been critical if the fight had continued."

The rising pitch of the old man's voice seemed to sap the strength from the words, gestating them into a plea. Valendrea decided to get to the point. "Gustavo, you are too old to be secretary. It is a demanding post. Much travel is required."

Bartolo glared at him. This man was going to be a difficult ally to

369 / THE THIRD SECRET

placate. The cardinal had indeed delivered a number of votes, confirmed by the listening devices, and had been his champion from the beginning. But Bartolo's reputation was one of a slacker with a mediocre education and no diplomatic experience. His selection for any post would not be popular, especially one as critical as secretary of state. There were three other cardinals who'd worked equally hard, with exemplary backgrounds and greater standing within the Sacred College. Still, Bartolo offered one thing they did not. Unremitting obedience. And there was something to be said for that.

"Gustavo, if I considered appointing you, there would be conditions." He was testing the waters, seeing how inviting they might be.

"I'm listening."

"I intend to personally direct foreign policy. Any decisions will be mine, not yours. You would have to do exactly as I say."

"You are pope."

The response came quick, signaling desire.

"I would not tolerate dissension or maverick actions."

"Alberto, I have been a priest nearly fifty years and have always done as popes said. I even knelt and kissed the ring of Jakob Volkner, a man I despised. I cannot see how you would question my loyalty."

He allowed his face to melt into a grin. "I'm not questioning anything. I just want you to know the rules."

He eased a bit down the path and Bartolo followed. He motioned upward and said, "Popes once fled the Vatican through that passageway. Hiding like children, afraid of the dark. The thought makes me sick."

"Armies no longer invade the Vatican."

"Not troops, but armies do still invade. Today's infidels come in the form of reporters and writers. They bring their cameras and notebooks and try to destroy the Church's foundation, aided by liberals and dissidents. Sometimes, Gustavo, even the pope himself is their ally, as with Clement."

"It was a blessing he died."

He liked what he was hearing, and he knew it wasn't platitudes. "I intend to restore glory to the papacy. The pope commands a million or more when he appears anywhere in the world. Governments should fear that potential. I intend to be the most traveled pope in history."

"And you would need the constant assistance of the secretary of state to achieve all that."

They walked a bit farther. "My thoughts exactly, Gustavo."

Valendrea glanced again at the brick passageway and imagined the last pope who'd fled the Vatican as German mercenaries stormed through Rome. He knew the exact date—May 6, 1527. One hundred and forty-seven Swiss guards died that day defending their pontiff. The pope barely escaped through the brick-enclosed corridor rising above him, tossing off his white garments so no one would recognize him.

"I will never flee the Vatican," he made clear to not only Bartolo, but also the walls themselves. He was suddenly overcome with the moment and decided to disregard what Ambrosi had counseled. "All right, Gustavo, I'll make the announcement Monday. You will be my secretary of state. Serve me well."

The old man's face beamed. "In me you will have total dedication."

Which made him think of his most loyal ally.

Ambrosi had phoned two hours ago and told him that Father Tibor's reproduced translation should be his at seven P.M. So far, there was no indication that anyone had read it, and that report pleased him.

He glanced at his watch. Six fifty P.M.

"Must you be somewhere, Holy Father?"

"No, Eminence, I was only considering another matter that is, at this moment, being resolved."

SIXTY-EIGHT

MICHENER CLIMBED A STEEP PATH TOWARD THE CATHEDRAL OF
St. Peter and St. George and entered a sloping, oblong piazza. Below,
a landscape of terra-cotta roofs and stone towers rose from the
town proper, illuminated by pools of light that dotted the city. The
dark sky yielded a steady fall of spiraling snow, but did not deter
the crowds already making their way toward the church, its four
spires splashed in a blue-white glow.

The churches and squares of Bamberg had celebrated Advent
for more than four hundred years by displaying decorative nativity
scenes. He'd learned from Irma Rahn that the circuit always started
in the cathedral and, after the bishop's blessing, everyone would fan
out through the city to view the year's offerings. Many came from all
over Bavaria to take part, and Irma had warned that the streets
would be crowded and noisy.

He glanced at his watch. Not quite seven.

He glanced around him and studied the families parading
toward the cathedral's entrance, many of the children chatting in-
cessantly about snow, Christmas, and St. Nicholas. Off to the right,
a group was huddled around a woman wrapped in a heavy wool coat.

She was perched on a knee-high wall, talking about the cathedral and Bamberg. Some kind of tour.

He wondered what people would think if they knew what he now knew. That man had not created God. Instead, just as theologians and holy men had counseled since the beginning of time, God was there, watching, many times surely pleased, other times frustrated, sometimes angry. The best advice seemed the oldest advice. Serve Him well and faithfully.

He was still fearful of the atonement that would be required for his own sins. Maybe this task was part of his penance. But he was relieved to know that his love for Katerina had never, at least in heaven's view, been a sin. How many priests had left the Church after similar failures? How many good men died thinking they'd fallen?

He was about to edge past the tour group when something the woman said caught his attention.

"—the seven hilled city."

He froze.

"That's what the ancients called Bamberg. It refers to the seven mounds that surround the river. Hard to see now, but there are seven distinct hills, each one in centuries past occupied by a prince or a bishop or a church. In the time of Henry II, when this was the capital of the Holy Roman Empire, the analogy brought this political center closer to the religious center of Rome, which was another city referred to as *seven hilled.*"

In the final persecution of the Holy Roman Church there will reign Peter the Roman who will feed his flock among many tribulations, after which in the seven hilled city the dreadful judge will judge all people. That's what St. Malachy had supposedly predicted in the eleventh century. Michener had thought *the seven hilled city* was a reference to Rome. He'd never known of a similar label for Bamberg.

He closed his eyes and prayed again. Was this another insight? Something vital to what was about to happen?

He glanced up at the funnel-shaped entrance to the cathedral.

The tympanum, bathed in light, depicted Christ at the Last Judgment. Mary and John, at his feet, were pleading for souls arising from their coffins, the blessed pushing forward behind Mary toward heaven, the damned being dragged to hell by a grinning devil. Had two thousand years of Christian arrogance come down to this night—to a place where nearly a thousand years ago a sainted Irish priest had predicted humanity would come?

He sucked in a breath of frigid air, steeled himself, then elbowed his way into the nave. Inside, the sandstone walls were bathed in a soft hue. He took in the details of the heavily ribbed vaulting, stout piers, statuary, and tall windows. A choir perch soared on one end. The altar filled the other. Beyond the altar was the tomb of Clement II, the only pope ever buried in German soil, and Jakob Volkner's namesake.

He stopped at a marble font and dabbed his finger into the holy water. He crossed himself and said another prayer for what he was about to do. An organ poured out a soft melody.

He glanced around at the crowd filling the long pews. Robed acolytes busily prepared the sanctuary. High to his left, standing before a thick stone balustrade, was Katerina. Beside her stood Ambrosi, wearing the same dark coat and scarf from earlier. Twin staircases rose on the left and right of the railing, the steps filled with people. Between the staircases sat the imperial tomb. Clement had also spoken of it—a Riemenschneider, rich in elaborate carvings depicting Henry II and his queen, in which their bodies had rested for half a millennium.

He realized a gun was near Katerina, but he didn't believe Ambrosi would risk anything here. He wondered if reinforcements might be concealed among the crowd. He stood rigid as people filed past him.

Ambrosi gestured for him to ascend the left staircase.

He did not move.

Ambrosi gestured again.

He shook his head.

Ambrosi's gaze tightened.

He withdrew the envelope from his pocket and displayed it for his nemesis to see. The look on the papal secretary's face showed recognition of the same envelope from earlier in the restaurant, lying innocently on the table.

He shook his head again.

Then he remembered what Katerina had told him of how Ambrosi had read her lips when she cursed him in St. Peter's Square.

Screw you, Ambrosi, he mouthed.

He saw the priest understood.

He pocketed the envelope and headed for the exit, hoping he would not regret what was going to happen next.

KATERINA WATCHED MICHENER MOUTH SOMETHING THEN turn to leave. She'd offered no resistance on the walk to the cathedral because Ambrosi had told her he was not alone, and if they did not appear there at seven Michener would be killed. She was doubtful there were others, but her best bet was to get to the church and wait for an opportunity. So in the instant Ambrosi took to register Michener's betrayal, she ignored the gun barrel boring into her back and ground her left heel onto Ambrosi's foot. She then shoved the priest away and yanked the gun from his grip, the weapon clattering across the tile floor.

She sprang for the gun as a woman beside her screamed. She used the confusion to grab the pistol and bolt for the staircase, catching a glimpse of Ambrosi rising to his feet.

The steps were crowded, and she plowed her way down before deciding to vault over the railing onto the imperial crypt. She landed on the stone effigy of a woman lying next to a robed man, then leaped to the floor. The gun was still in her hand. Voices rose. A panic swept the church. She pushed her way through a knot of people at the door and emerged into the frigid night.

Pocketing the gun, her eyes searched for Michener, and she saw him at the path that led down to the town center. A commotion behind her warned that Ambrosi was trying to make an exit, too.

So she ran.

MICHENER THOUGHT HE SAW KATERINA AS HE STARTED DOWN the winding path. But he couldn't stop. He had to keep going. If it was Kate she'd follow and Ambrosi would pursue, so he loped down the narrow stone path, brushing past more people on their way up.

He made it to the bottom and hurried toward the town hall bridge. He crossed the river through a gateway that bisected the rickety timbered building and entered the busy Maxplatz.

He slowed and risked a quick glance behind.

Katerina was fifty yards back, heading his way.

KATERINA WANTED TO CRY OUT AND TELL MICHENER TO WAIT, but he was moving at a determined gait, heading into Bamberg toward the bustling Christmas market. The gun was still in her pocket, and behind her Ambrosi was rapidly advancing. She'd been on the lookout for a policeman, anyone in authority, but this night of merriment seemed a government holiday. No uniforms were in sight.

She had to trust Michener knew what he was doing. He'd deliberately flaunted Ambrosi, apparently gambling that her assailant would not harm her in public. Whatever was contained in Father Tibor's translation must be important enough that Michener did not want Ambrosi, or Valendrea, to have it. But she wondered if it was important enough to risk what he'd apparently decided to ante in this seemingly high-stakes game.

Up ahead, Michener dissolved into the crowds surveying booths filled with Christmas wares. Bright lights illuminated the outdoor market in a daylight glow. The air reeked of grilled sausages and beer.

She slowed, too, as people enveloped her.

MICHENER HUSTLED THROUGH THE REVELERS, BUT NOT FAST enough to draw attention. The market spanned about a hundred yards down the winding cobblestoned path. Half-timbered buildings lined its perimeter, wedging people and booths into a congested column.

He came to the last of the booths and the crowd thinned.

He regained a running pace, rubber soles slapping the cobbles as he left the noisy market and headed for the canal, crossing a stone bridge and entering a quiet part of town.

Behind him, more soles to stone could be heard. Up ahead, he spotted St. Gangolf's. All of the revelry was centralized back in the Maxplaz, or across the river in the cathedral district, and he was counting on some privacy for at least the next few minutes.

He only hoped he wasn't tempting fate.

KATERINA WATCHED MICHENER ENTER ST. GANGOLF'S. WHAT was he doing there? This was stupid. Ambrosi was still behind her, yet Colin had deliberately come straight to the church. He must know she was following, and that her assailant would, too.

She glanced at the buildings around her. Few lights burned in the windows and the street ahead was empty. She raced to the church doors, yanked them open, and bolted inside. Her breaths were coming fast.

"Colin."

No answer.

She called his name again. Still no answer.

She trotted down the center aisle toward the altar, passing empty pews that sliced thin shadows in the blackness. Only a handful of lamps illuminated the nave. The church was apparently not a part of this year's celebration.

"Colin."

Desperation now laced her voice. Where was he? Why wouldn't he answer? Had he left through another door? Was she trapped here alone?

The doors behind her opened.

She dove into a row of pews and clawed the floor, trying to slip across the gritty stone to the far side.

Footsteps stopped her advance.

MICHENER SAW A MAN ENTER THE CHURCH. A SHAFT OF LIGHT revealed the face of Paolo Ambrosi. A few moments earlier, Katerina had entered and called out his name, but he'd intentionally not answered. She was now huddled on the floor between the pews.

"You move fast, Ambrosi," he called out.

His voice bounced off the walls, the echo making it difficult to pinpoint his location. He watched as Ambrosi moved right, toward the confessionals, his head sweeping back and forth so his ears could judge the sound. He hoped Katerina did not betray her presence.

"Why make this hard, Michener?" Ambrosi said. "You know what I want."

"You told me earlier things would be different if I read the words. For once you were right."

"You never could obey."

"How about Father Tibor? Did he obey?"

Ambrosi was approaching the altar. The priest moved with cautious steps, still searching the darkness for Michener's location.

"I never spoke with Tibor," Ambrosi said.

"Sure you did."

Michener stared down from the raised pulpit, eight feet above Ambrosi.

"Just come on out, Michener. Let's resolve this."

As Ambrosi turned, his back momentarily to him, Michener leaped down. Together they pounded the floor and rolled.

Ambrosi pushed himself away and sprang to his feet.

Michener started to rise, too.

Movement to his right caught his attention. He saw Katerina rushing toward them, a gun in hand. Ambrosi pivoted off a row of pews and vaulted toward her, thrusting his feet into her chest, sending her to the floor. Michener heard a thud as skull found stone. Ambrosi disappeared over the pews and came back into view with the gun in his grip, yanking a limp Katerina to her feet and ramming the gun barrel into her neck. "Okay, Michener. Enough."

He stood still.

"Give me Tibor's translation."

Michener took a few steps toward them and withdrew the envelope from his pocket. "This what you want?"

"Drop it on the floor and back away." The hammer on the gun clicked into place. "Don't push me, Michener. I possess the courage to do what needs to be done because the Lord gives me the strength."

"Perhaps He's testing to see what you will do?"

"Shut up. I don't need a theology lesson."

"I might be the best person on earth for that at the moment."

"Is it the words?" The tone was quizzical, like a schoolboy inquiring of his teacher. "They give you courage?"

He sensed something. "What is it, Ambrosi? Valendrea didn't tell you everything? Too bad. He held back the best part."

Ambrosi tightened his grip on Katerina. "Just drop the envelope and back away."

The desperate look in Ambrosi's eyes signaled that he might well make good on the threat. So he tossed the envelope to the floor.

Ambrosi released his hold on Katerina and shoved her toward Michener. He caught her and saw she was dazed from the head blow.

"You okay?" he asked.

Her eyes were glassy, but she nodded.

Ambrosi was examining the envelope's contents.

"How do you know that's what Valendrea wants?" he asked.

"I don't. But my instructions were clear. Get what I can and eliminate the witnesses."

"What if I made a copy?"

Ambrosi shrugged. "A chance we take. But, fortunately for us, you will not be here to offer any testimony." The gun came level, pointed straight at them. "This is the part I will truly enjoy."

A form emerged from the shadows and slowly inched close to Ambrosi from behind. Not a sound came from the approaching steps. The man was clad in black trousers and a loose-fitting black jacket. The outline of a gun appeared in one hand, and it was slowly raised to Ambrosi's right temple.

"I assure you, Father," Cardinal Ngovi said. "I, too, will enjoy this part."

"What are you doing here?" Ambrosi asked, surprise in his voice.

"I came to speak with you. So lower the weapon and answer some questions. Then you're free to go."

"You want Valendrea, don't you?"

"Why else do you think you're still breathing."

Michener held his breath as Ambrosi weighed his options. When he'd telephoned Ngovi earlier, he was banking on Ambrosi's survival instincts. He assumed that though Ambrosi might profess great loyalty, when it came to a choice between himself or his pope, there really was no choice at all. "It's over, Ambrosi." He pointed to the envelope. "I read it. Cardinal Ngovi read it. Too many know now. You can't win this one."

"And what was worth all this?" Ambrosi asked, the tone signaling that he was considering their proposal.

"Lower the gun and find out."

Another long moment of silence passed. Finally, Ambrosi's hand came down. Ngovi grabbed the weapon and stood back, his gun still trained on the priest.

Ambrosi faced Michener. "You were bait? The idea was to get me to follow?"

"Something like that."

Ngovi stepped forward. "We have some questions. Cooperate and there will be no police, no arrest. Just disappear. A good deal, considering."

"Considering what?"

"Father Tibor's murder."

Ambrosi chuckled. "That's a bluff and you know it. This is about you two bringing down Peter II."

Michener stood. "No. It's about you bringing Valendrea down. Which shouldn't matter at all. He'd do the same to you if the roles were reversed."

Without question the man standing before him had been involved in Father Tibor's death, most likely the actual murderer. But Ambrosi was surely smart enough to realize that the game had changed.

"Okay," Ambrosi said. "Ask away."

The cardinal reached into his jacket pocket.

A tape recorder came into view.

MICHENER HELPED KATERINA INTO THE KÖNIGSHOF. IRMA Rahn met them at the front door.

"Did it go all right?" the older woman asked Michener. "I've been frantic for the last hour."

"It went well."

"Praise God. I was so worried."

Katerina was still woozy, but feeling better.

"I'm going to take her upstairs," he said.

He helped her to the second floor. Once inside the room she immediately asked, "What in God's name was Ngovi doing there?"

"I called this afternoon and told him what I'd learned. He flew to Munich and arrived here right before I headed to the cathedral. It was my job to lure Ambrosi to St. Gangolf's. We needed a place away from the festivities. Irma told me the church wasn't displaying a crib scene this year. I had Ngovi talk with the parish priest. He doesn't know anything, only that Vatican officials needed his church for a little while." He knew what she was thinking. "Look, Kate, Ambrosi wouldn't hurt anyone until he had Tibor's translation. He could never be sure of anything until then. We had to play it out."

"So I was bait?"

"You and me. Defying him was the only way to make sure he'd turn on Valendrea."

"Ngovi's a tough one."

"He was raised a street kid in Nairobi. He knows how to handle himself."

They'd spent the past half hour with Ambrosi, recording what would be needed tomorrow. She'd listened and now knew everything, except the entire third secret of Fatima. He removed an envelope from his pocket. "Here's what Father Tibor sent to Clement. It's the copy I offered Ambrosi. Ngovi has the original."

She read the words, then commented, "That's similar to what Jasna wrote. You were just going to give Ambrosi the Medjugorje message?"

He shook his head. "Those are not Jasna's words. Those are the Virgin's, from Fatima, written by Lucia dos Santos in 1944, and translated by Father Tibor in 1960."

"You can't be serious. Do you realize what that would mean if the two messages were essentially the same?"

"I've realized that since this afternoon." His voice was low and calm and he waited while she considered the implications. They'd talked many times about her lack of her faith. But he'd never been one to judge, considering his own lapses. *After which in the seven hilled city the dreadful judge will judge all people.* Maybe Katerina was the first of many to judge themselves.

"The Lord seems to have made a comeback," he said.

"It's unbelievable. Yet what else could it be? How could those messages be the same?"

"It's impossible, considering what you and I know. But doubters will say we fashioned Father Tibor's translation to match Jasna's message. They'll say it's all a fraud. The originals are gone and the drafters are all dead. We're the only ones who know the truth."

"So it's still a matter of faith. You and I know what happened. But everybody else would have to simply take our word." She shook her head. "Seems God is destined to always be a mystery."

He'd already considered the possibilities. The Virgin told him in Bosnia that he was to be *a sign to the world. A beacon for repentance. The messenger to announce that God is very much alive.* But something else the Virgin said was equally important. *Do not forsake your faith, for in the end it will be all that remains.*

"There is a consolation," he said. "I berated myself badly years ago for violating Holy Orders. I loved you, but believed that what I felt, what I did, was a sin. I know now that it wasn't. Not in God's eyes."

He heard John XXIII's urging to the Vatican II council again in his mind. His pleading with traditionalists and progressives to work in unison so *the earthly city may be brought to the resemblance of that heavenly city where truth reigns.* Only now did he fully understand what that pope meant.

"Clement tried to do what he could," she said. "I'm so sorry for the way I thought of him."

"I think he understands."

She threw him a smile. "What now?"

"Back to Rome. Ngovi and I have a meeting tomorrow."

"Then what?"

He knew what she meant. "To Romania. Those kids are waiting on us."

"I thought maybe you were having second thoughts."

He pointed skyward. "I think we owe it to Him. Don't you?"

SIXTY-NINE

MICHENER AND NGOVI WALKED DOWN THE LOGGIA TOWARD the papal library. Bright sunshine swept in through towering windows on both sides of the wide corridor. They were dressed in clerical robes, Ngovi in scarlet, Michener in black.

The papal office had been contacted earlier, and Ambrosi's assistant had been enlisted to speak directly with Valendrea. Ngovi wanted a papal audience. No subject matter was provided, but Michener was banking on the fact that Valendrea would understand the significance that he and Ngovi needed to talk with him, and Paolo Ambrosi was nowhere to be found. The tactic apparently worked. The pope himself granted permission for them to enter the palace, allocating fifteen minutes for the audience.

"Can you accomplish your business in that time?" Ambrosi's assistant had asked.

"I believe so," Ngovi answered.

Valendrea had kept them waiting nearly half an hour. Now they approached the library and entered, closing the doors behind them. Valendrea stood before leaded-glass windows, his stout form, dressed in white, flooded in sunshine.

"I have to say, my curiosity was piqued when you requested an audience. You two would be the last people I'd expect to be here on a Saturday morning. I thought you, Maurice, were in Africa. And you, Michener, in Germany."

"Half right," Ngovi said. "We were both in Germany."

A curious expression came to Valendrea's face.

Michener decided to get to the point. "You won't be hearing from Ambrosi."

"What do you mean?"

Ngovi removed the recorder from his cassock and flipped on the machine. Ambrosi's voice filled the library as he explained about Father Tibor's murder, the listening devices, the files on cardinals, and the blackmail used to secure conclave votes. Valendrea listened impassively as his sins were revealed. Ngovi switched off the machine. "Clear enough?"

The pope said nothing.

"We have the complete third secret of Fatima and the tenth secret of Medjugorje," Michener said.

"I was under the impression I possessed the Medjugorje secret."

"A copy. I know now why you reacted so strongly when you read Jasna's message."

Valendrea seemed jittery. For once, this obstinate man was not in control.

Michener stepped closer. "You needed to suppress those words."

"Even your Clement tried," Valendrea said in defiance.

Michener shook his head. "He knew what you'd do and had the foresight to get Tibor's translation away from here. He did more than anybody. He gave his life. He's better than any of us. He believed in the Lord . . . without proof." His pulse pounded with excitement. "Did you know Bamberg was called *the seven hilled city*? Remember Malachy's prediction? *After which in the seven hilled city the dreadful judge will judge all people.*" He pointed to the tape. "For you, truth is the dreadful judge."

"That tape is merely the ramblings of a man caught," Valendrea said. "It's not proof of anything."

Michener wasn't impressed. "Ambrosi told us about your trip to

Romania, and supplied more than enough details to mount a prosecution and obtain a conviction, especially in a former communist-bloc nation where the burden of proof is, shall we say, loose."

"You're bluffing."

Ngovi removed another microcassette from his pocket. "We showed him the Fatima message and the one from Medjugorje. We did not have to explain their significance. Even an amoral man like Ambrosi saw the majesty of what awaits him. After that, his answers came freely. He begged me to hear his confession." He motioned with the cassette. "But not before he spoke for the record."

"He makes a good witness," Michener said. "You see, there actually is an authority higher than you."

Valendrea paced across the room, toward the bookshelves, looking like an animal examining his cage. "Popes have been ignoring God for a long time. The La Salette message has been missing from the archives for a century. I'd wager the Virgin told those seers the same thing."

"Those men," Ngovi said, "can be forgiven. They considered the messages the seer's, not the Virgin's. They rationalized their defiance with caution. They lacked the proof you possessed. You knew the words to be divine and still would have killed Michener and Katerina Lew to suppress them."

Valendrea's eyes flashed hot. "You sanctimonious ass. What was I to do? Let the Church crumble? Don't you realize what this revelation will do? Two thousand years of dogma has been rendered false."

"It is not for us to manipulate the Church's fate," Ngovi said. "God's Word is His alone, and apparently His patience has run out."

Valendrea shook his head. "It is for us to preserve the Church. What Catholic on this earth would listen to Rome if he knew we lied? And we're not talking about minor points. Celibacy? Women priests? Abortion? Homosexuality? Even the essence of papal infallibility."

Ngovi seemed unaffected by the plea. "I'm more concerned how I would explain to my Lord why I ignored His command."

Michener faced Valendrea. "When you went back into the Riserva in 1978, there was no tenth Medjugorje secret. Yet you removed part of the message. How did you know Sister Lucia's words were genuine?"

"I saw fear in Paul's eyes when he read them. If *that* man was scared, then there was something to it. That Friday night, in the Riserva, when Clement told me of Tibor's latest translation, then showed part of the original message to me, it was as if a devil had returned."

"In a sense, that's exactly what happened," Michener said.

Valendrea stared at him.

"If God exists, then so does the devil."

"So which one caused the death of Father Tibor?" Valendrea asked, defiance in his voice. "Was it the Lord, so that the truth would be revealed? Or the devil, so that the truth would be revealed? Both would have been motivated toward the same goal, would they not?"

"That's why you killed Father Tibor? To prevent that?" Michener asked.

"In every religious movement there have been martyrs." Not a speck of remorse laced the words.

Ngovi stepped forward. "That's true. And we intend one more."

"I already assumed what you had in mind. You're going to have me prosecuted?"

"Not at all," Ngovi said.

Michener offered Valendrea a small caramel-colored vial. "We expect you to join that list of martyrs."

Valendrea's brow creased in amazement.

Michener said, "This is the same sleeping medication Clement took. More than enough to kill. If in the morning your body is found, then you'll have a papal funeral and be entombed in St. Peter's with all ceremony. Your reign will be short, but you will be remembered in much the same way as John Paul I. On the other hand, if tomorrow you're alive, the Sacred College will be informed of everything we know. Your memory then will be of the first pope in history to stand trial."

Valendrea did not accept the vial. "You want me to kill myself?"

Michener never blinked. "You can die as a glorious pope, or be disgraced as a criminal. Personally, I prefer the latter, so I'm hoping you don't have the guts to do what Clement did."

"I can fight you."

"You'll lose. With what we know, I'd wager there are many in the Sacred College simply waiting for the opportunity to take you down. The evidence is irrefutable. Your co-conspirator will be your chief accuser. There's no way you can win."

Valendrea still would not take the vial. So Michener poured its contents out on the desk, then glared at him. "The choice is yours. If you love your Church as much as you profess, then sacrifice your life so it may live. You were quick to end Father Tibor's life. Let's see if you're as liberal with your own. The dreadful judge has judged and the sentence is death."

"You're asking me to do the unthinkable," Valendrea said.

"I'm asking you to save this institution the humiliation of forcibly removing you."

"I am pope. No one can remove me."

"Except the Lord. And in a manner of speaking, that's exactly who's doing this."

Valendrea turned to Ngovi. "You'll be the next pope, won't you?"

"Almost certainly."

"You could have won election in conclave, couldn't you?"

"There was a reasonable chance."

"So why drop out?"

"Because Clement told me to."

Valendrea looked perplexed. "When?"

"A week before he died. He told me you and I would eventually be locked in that battle. But he said that you should win."

"Why on earth would you have listened to him?"

Ngovi's face hardened. "He was my pope."

Valendrea shook his head in disbelief.

"And he was right."

"Do you plan to do as the Virgin said too?"

"I will abolish all dogma contrary to Her message."

"You'll have revolt."

Ngovi shrugged. "Those who disagree are free to leave and form their own religion. Such is their choice. They will receive no opposition from me. This Church, though, will do as told."

Valendrea's face became incredulous. "You think it's going to be that easy? The cardinals will never allow it."

Michener said, "This isn't a democracy."

"So no one will know the actual messages?"

Ngovi shook his head. "That isn't necessary. Skeptics would claim Father Tibor's translation was simply conformed to the Medjugorje message. The sheer magnitude of the message would do nothing but ignite criticism. Sister Lucia and Father Tibor are gone. Neither can verify anything. It is not necessary the world know what happened. The three of us know and that is what matters. I shall heed the words. This will be *my* act and *mine* alone. I will take the praise and the criticism."

"The next pope will simply reverse you," Valendrea muttered.

Ngovi shook his head. "You have so little faith." The African turned and headed for the door. "We will await the news in the morning. Depending on what that is, we may or may not see you tomorrow."

Michener hesitated before following. "The devil himself will find it difficult dealing with you."

Not waiting for a response, he left.

SEVENTY

11:30 P.M.

VALENDREA STARED AT THE PILLS LYING ON THE DESK. FOR decades he'd dreamed of the papacy, and he'd devoted his entire adult life to achieving that goal. Now he was pope. He should have reigned twenty or more years, becoming the hope of the future by reclaiming the past. Only yesterday he'd spent an hour going over the details of his coronation, the ceremony a scant two weeks away. He'd toured the Vatican museum, personally inspected adornments his predecessors had relegated to exhibits, and ordered their preparation for the event. He wanted the moment the spiritual leader of a billion people assumed the reins of power to be a spectacle every Catholic could watch with pride.

He'd already thought about his homily. It would have been a call for tradition. A rejection of innovation—a retreat to a sacred past. The Church could and would be a weapon for change. No more impotent denunciations that world leaders ignored. Instead religious fervor would have been used to forge a new international policy. One emanating from him as *the* Vicar of Christ. *The* pope.

He slowly counted the capsules on the desk.

Twenty-eight.

If he swallowed them, he'd be remembered as the pope who reigned for four days. He'd be regarded as a fallen leader, taken by the Lord far too quickly. There was something to be said for dying suddenly. John Paul I had been an insignificant cardinal. Now he was venerated simply because he died thirty-three days after the conclave. A handful had reigned shorter, many more longer, but none had ever been forced into the position in which he now found himself.

He thought about Ambrosi's betrayal. He wouldn't have thought Paolo so disloyal. They'd been together many years. Maybe Ngovi and Michener had underestimated his old friend. Perhaps Ambrosi would be his legacy, the man who would ensure that the world never forgot Peter II. He hoped he was right in believing Ngovi might one day regret letting Paolo Ambrosi roam free.

He eyes returned to the pills. At least there'd be no pain. And Ngovi would make sure there was no autopsy. The African was still camerlengo. He could envision the bastard standing over him, gently tapping his forehead with a silver hammer and asking three times if he was dead.

He believed that if he was alive tomorrow, Ngovi would bring charges. Though there was no precedent for removing a pope, once he was implicated in murder he would never be allowed to remain in office.

Which raised his greatest concern.

Doing what Ngovi and Michener asked would mean he'd be soon answering for his sins. What would he say?

Proof that God existed meant there was also an immeasurable force of evil that misled the human spirit. Life seemed a perpetual tug between those two extremes. How would he explain his sins? Would there be forgiveness or only punishment? He still believed, even in the face of all he knew, that priests should be men. God's Church was started by men and, over two millennia, male blood had been spilled to preserve that institution. The interjection of women into something so decidedly male seemed sacrilegious. Spouses and children were nothing but distractions. And to slaughter an unborn child seemed unthinkable. A woman's duty was to bring forth life, no matter how it was conceived, whether wanted or unwanted. How could God have gotten everything so wrong?

He shifted the pills on the desk.

The Church was going to change. Nothing would ever be the same. Ngovi would make sure extremism prevailed. And that thought turned his stomach.

He knew what awaited him. There'd be an accounting, but he was not going to shrink from the challenge. He'd face the Lord and tell Him that he'd done what he believed was right. If he be damned to hell, then there would be some pretty austere company. He was not the first pope to defy heaven.

He reached out and arranged the capsules in groups of seven. He scooped up one set and balanced them in the palm of his hand.

A certain perspective truly did come in the final moments of life.

His legacy among men was safe. He was Peter II, pope of the Roman Catholic Church, and no one could ever take that from him. Even Ngovi and Michener would have to publicly venerate his memory.

And that prospect gave him solace.

Along with a burst of courage.

He tossed the pills into his mouth and reached for the tumbler of water. He grabbed up another seven and swallowed them. While his fortitude was there, he gathered the remaining pills and let the remaining water send them to his stomach.

I'm hoping you don't have the guts to do what Clement did.

Screw you, Michener.

He stepped across the room to a gilded prie-dieu facing a portrait of Christ. He knelt, crossed himself, and asked the Lord to forgive him. He stayed on his knees for ten minutes, until his head started spinning. It should add to his legacy that he was called to God during prayer.

The drowsiness became seductive and for a while he fought the urge to surrender. A part of him was relieved he would not be associated with a Church that was contrary to everything he believed. Perhaps it was better to rest beneath the basilica as the last pope of the way things used to be. He imagined Romans flooding into the piazza tomorrow, distraught over the loss of the their beloved *Santíssimo Padre*. Millions would watch his funeral and the world press would write about him with respect. Eventually books about him would appear. He hoped traditionalists used him as a rallying point for their opposition to Ngovi. And there was always Ambrosi. Dear, sweet Paolo. He was still out there. And that thought pleased him.

His muscles craved sleep and he could no longer fight the urge, so he surrendered to the inevitable and collapsed to the floor.

He stared at the ceiling and finally let the pills take hold. The room winked in and out. He no longer fought the descent.

Instead he allowed his mind to drift away, hoping that God was indeed merciful.

SEVENTY-ONE

MICHENER AND KATERINA FOLLOWED THE CROWD INTO ST. Peter's Square. Around them, men and women openly wept. Many clutched rosaries. The basilica's bells tolled solemnly.

The announcement had come two hours ago, a curt statement in the usual Vatican rhetoric that the Holy Father had passed during the night. The camerlengo, Maurice Cardinal Ngovi, had been summoned and the papal physician had confirmed that a massive coronary claimed the life of Alberto Valendrea. The appropriate ceremony with the silver hammer occurred, and the Holy See was declared vacant. Cardinals were once again being summoned to Rome.

Michener had not told Katerina about yesterday. It was better that way. In a sense he was a murderer, though he did not feel like one. Instead he felt a great sense of retribution. Especially for Father Tibor. One wrong had been righted by another in a perverted sense of balance that only the odd circumstances of the past few weeks could have created.

In fifteen days another conclave would convene and another pope would be elected. The 269th since Peter and one beyond the list of St. Malachy. The dreadful judge had judged. The sinners had been punished. Now it would be up to Maurice Ngovi to see heaven's will be done. Little doubt existed he would be the next pope. Yesterday, as they left the palace, Ngovi had asked him to stay on in Rome and be a part of what was coming. But he'd declined. He was going to Romania with Katerina. He wanted to share his life with her and Ngovi understood, wishing him well and telling him Vatican doors would always be open.

People continued to surge forward, filling the piazza between Bernini's colonnades. He wasn't sure why he'd come, but something seemed to summon him, and he sensed a peace within himself that he hadn't felt in a long time.

"These people have no idea about Valendrea," Katerina whispered.

"To them, he was their pope. An Italian. And we could never convince them otherwise. His memory will have to stand as it is."

"You're never going to tell me what happened yesterday, are you?"

He'd caught her studying him last evening. She realized something significant had occurred with Valendrea, but he hadn't allowed the subject to be explored and she did not press.

Before he could answer her, an older woman, near one of the fountains, collapsed in a fit of grief. Several people came to her aid as she lamented that God had taken so good a pope. Michener watched as the woman sobbed uncontrollably and two men helped her toward the shade.

News crews were fanning across the square interviewing people. Soon the world press would return to ponder what the Sacred College might do within the Sistine Chapel.

"I guess Tom Kealy will be back," he said.

"I was thinking the same thing. The man with all the answers." She threw him a smile he understood.

They approached the basilica and stopped with the rest of the mourners before the barricades. The church was closed, its interior, he knew, being readied for another funeral. The balcony was draped in black. Michener glanced to his right. The shutters of the papal bedroom were closed. Behind them, a few hours ago, the body of Alberto Valendrea had been found. According to the press he'd been praying when his heart gave out, the corpse discovered on the floor beneath a portrait of Christ. He smiled at Valendrea's last audacity.

Somebody grabbed his arm.

He turned.

The man standing before him was bearded with a crooked nose and bushy reddish hair. "Tell me, Padre, what are we to do? Why has the Lord taken our Holy Father? What is the meaning of this?"

Michener assumed his black cassock had drawn the inquiry and the answer formed quickly in his mind. "Why must there always be meaning? Can you not accept what the Lord has done without question?"

"Peter was to be a great pope. An Italian finally back on the throne. We had such hopes."

"There are many in the Church who can be great popes. And they need not be Italian." His listener gave him a strange look. "What matters is their devotion to the Lord."

He knew that of the thousands gathered around him, only he and Katerina truly understood. God was alive. He was there. Listening.

His gaze drifted from the man standing before him to the basilica's magnificent façade. For all its majesty, it was still nothing more than mortar and stone. Time and weather would eventually destroy it. But what it symbolized, what it meant, would last forever. *Thou art Peter and on this rock I will build my Church. And the gates of hell will not stand against it. I will give you the Keys of the Kingdom of Heaven; whatever you bind on earth will be bound in heaven; whatever you loose on earth will be loosed in heaven.*

He turned back to the man, who was saying something.

"It's finished, Father. The pope is dead. Everything is finished before it even started."

He wasn't going to accept that and he wasn't going to let this stranger accept defeatism, either. "You're wrong. It's not over." He threw the man a reassuring smile. "In fact, it's only just beginning."

WRITER'S NOTE

In researching this novel, I traveled to Italy and Germany. But this book grew out of my early Catholic education and a lifelong fascination with Fatima. Over the past two thousand years, the phenomena of Marian visions have occurred with surprising regularity. In modern times, the visions at La Salette, Lourdes, Fatima, and Medjugorje are most notable, though there are countless other lesser-known experiences. As with my first two novels, I wanted the information included in the story to both educate and entertain. Even more so than with the first two books, this one contains a wealth of reality.

The scene at Fatima, depicted in the prologue, is based on eyewitness accounts, most notably Lucia herself, who published her version of what happened in the early part of the twentieth century. The Virgin's words are Hers, as are most of Lucia's. The three secrets, as quoted in chapter 7, are verbatim from the actual text. Only my modification detailed in chapter 65 is fictional.

What happened to Francisco and Jacinta, along with the third secret's curious history—how it stayed sealed in the Vatican until May 2000, read only by popes (chapter 7)—is all true, along with the Church's refusal to allow Sister Lucia to speak publicly about Fatima. Sadly, Sister Lucia died shortly before this book was published, in February 2005, at the age of ninety-seven.

The La Salette visions from 1846, as mentioned in chapters 19 and 42, are accurately related—as is the history of those two seers, their biting public comments, and Pope Pius IX's poignant observations. That particular Marian vision is one of the strangest on record and was mired by scandal and doubt. Secrets were part of the apparition and the original texts are indeed missing from the Vatican record, which further clouds what may have happened in that French Alpine village.

Medjugorje is similar, though it stands alone among Marian visions. Not a single event, or even several visions spread over a few months' time, Medjugorje involves thousands of apparitions over more than two decades. The Church has yet to formally acknowledge anything relative to what may have happened, though that Bosnian village has become a popular pilgrimage site. As noted in chapter 38, there are ten secrets associated with Medjugorje. Including this scenario within the plot seemed hard to resist, and what happens in chapter 65, linking the tenth secret of Medjugorje and the third secret of Fatima, evolved into the perfect way to finally prove that God exists. Yet, as Michener notes in chapter 69, even with this proof, the ultimate belief still comes down to faith.

The predictions attributed to St. Malachy, as detailed in chapter 56, are all true. The accuracy of the labels associated with the predicted popes is uncanny. His final prophecy concerning the 112th pope, one to be named Peter II, along with his statement that "in the seven hilled city the dreadful judge will judge all people," are likewise accurate. Currently John Paul II is the 110th pope on St. Malachy's list. Two more to go to see if St. Malachy's prophecy will be fulfilled. Similar to Rome, Bamberg, Germany, was once labeled *the seven hilled city.* I learned that fact while there and, after visiting, knew that this enchanting locale had to be included.

Sadly, the Irish birthing centers depicted in chapter 15 were real, as was all the pain they caused. Thousands of babies were taken from their mothers and adopted away. Little or nothing is known of their individual heritage and many of those children, now adults, have wrestled, as Colin Michener did, with the uncertainty of their existence. Thankfully, those centers no longer exist.

Equally sad is the plight of the Romanian orphans depicted in chapter 14. The tragedy befalling these children is ongoing. Disease, poverty, and desperation—not to mention exploitation by the world's pedophiles—continue to ravage the ranks of these innocent souls.

All of the Church's procedures and ceremonies are accurately reported, save for the ancient silver hammer being tapped on the dead pope's forehead in chapters 30 and 71. That procedure is no longer used, but its former drama was hard to ignore.

The divisions within the Church between conservative and liberal, Italian and non-Italian, European and rest-of-the-world are real. The Church currently struggles with this divergence, and the conflict seemed a natural backdrop for the individual dilemmas faced by Clement XV and Alberto Valendrea.

The Bible verses noted in chapter 57 are, of course, accurate and are interesting when read in context with the novel's plot. Likewise the words of John XXIII in chapters 7 and 68 when, in 1962, he addressed the opening session of the Vatican II council. His hope for reform—so *the earthly city may be brought to the resemblance of that heavenly city where truth reigns*—is fascinating considering he was the first pope to ever actually read the third secret of Fatima.

The third secret itself was released to the world in May 2000. As Cardinals Ngovi and Valendrea discussed in chapter 17, references to a possible papal assassination could explain the Church's reluctance to publicize the message sooner. But overall, the riddles and parables contained within the third message are far more cryptic than threatening, which caused many observers to wonder if there might be more to the third secret.

The Catholic Church is unique among man's institutions. It has not only survived for more than two millennia, but continues to grow and prosper. Yet many wonder what will be its fate in the coming century. Some, like Clement XV, want to fundamentally change the Church. Others, like Alberto Valendrea, want a return to its traditional roots. But perhaps Leo XIII, in 1881, said it best.

The Church needs nothing but the truth.

ABOUT THE AUTHOR

STEVE BERRY is the author of *The Amber Room* and *The Romanov Prophecy.* He is a trial lawyer with more than twenty years of courtroom experience who has traveled extensively throughout the Caribbean, Mexico, Europe, and Russia. He lives with his wife and daughter in Camden County, Georgia, and is currently at work on his next novel. Visit the author's website at www.steveberry.org.

ABOUT THE TYPE

This book was set in Requiem, a typeface designed by the Hoefler Type Foundry. It is a modern typeface inspired by inscriptional capitals in Ludovico Vicentino degli Arrighi's 1523 writing manual, *Il modo de temperare le penne*. An original lowercase, a set of figures, and an italic in the "chancery" style that Arrighi helped popularize were created to make this adaptation of a classical design into a complete font family.